Blood Tears

Michael J Malone

Five Leaves Publications
www.fiveleaves.co.uk

Blood Tears

by Michael J Malone

Published in 2012
by Five Leaves Publications
PO Box 8786, Nottingham NG1 9AW
www.fiveleaves.co.uk

ISBN 978 1 907869 34 1

Five Leaves acknowledges support
from Arts Council England

Five Leaves is represented to the trade by Turnaround
and distributed by Central Books

Typeset by Five Leaves
Cover design by Four Sheets Design and Print

Printed in the UK by Russell Press, Nottingham

Prologue

He closed the door, his hand trembling. Walking across the floor towards the desk, he removed all his clothes. He bent to retrieve the black costume from the floor, draped it on a perfumed hanger and hung it neatly in its place. His shoes were last. Ladies size 7. Black leather with a sensible heel, they were tucked under the chair. He massaged his toes, which had been stuffed into the neat fit. Blood stained one toe where the nail from the neighbouring pinkie had torn flesh.

Apart from the desk and chair, the room was empty. The floor was paved in stone tiles and the windows covered with dark, patternless drapes. The walls, if the light had been strong enough, would have shown a similar lack of effort on the decorator's part. They were painted cream, and bare, save for the mirror above the desk. Above that hung a crucifix, Christ's face distorted with pain and anguish for man's sin.

He sat before the mirror and, filling his lungs, flicked a switch. Lights framing the mirror blazed unkindly on to his face. He breathed again and closed his eyes. And again, he breathed, revelling in the speed of his pulse. So this is what it means to be alive, he thought. Every nerve in his body thrummed with electricity. This is what it means to belong.

Muscles along his shoulders and down through his arms and legs relaxed as if bathed in liquid and heat. Had his eyes been open, he would have seen the slow spread of a smile stretch his lips.

It had begun.

An eye for an eye, the Bible said. A life for a life. But how many lives were enough, he considered, to replace the one lost? As many as it takes.

Breathe slowly, he told himself. In for a count of nine. And out for a count of nine. The old man had fought well, for his age.

Who would have thought? Realisation that his life was about to end would have lent him strength. But he had been no real contest. A quick blow to the solar plexus, tighten the garrotte and it was all but over.

Stopping at the right time was crucial. Keeping him alive long enough; easing pressure on the stranglehold before he passed from unconsciousness into death was key.

The old man barely stirred as the hoop of barbed wire was squeezed on to his head. The metal thorns slid into the pale flesh of his forehead as easily as communion wine slips down the throat.

Reliving the moment when the man stirred and their eyes met forced a flood of blood into his groin. The sweet ache that encapsulated sin. But the ache was even more pronounced in his heightened state. And all the more difficult to ignore.

Questions forced their way through the old man's clenched teeth. His need to know who and why was such that it acted as an anaesthetic.

'Who... are you?' He groaned. 'Why are you... doing this to me? Please... please... please don't hurt... me... any more.' *Sweat diluted the colour of the blood on his forehead.*

'Hurt? You don't know the meaning of the word. Yet.'

Terror bloomed in the old man's pupils, the iris all but swallowed in black, 'Please... let me go... I can give you... money.'

'Money? I don't want your money. I want your pain. I want your repentance.'

'For what?' *he used all his remaining energy to ask.* 'Who are you?'

'I am the avenging angel. I am he who will deliver you.' *He stifled a giggle. He'd rehearsed that part. It sounded even better out loud.*

Again the old man asked, 'Who are you?'

'You have no idea, do you?'

The old man coughed. Blood frothed from his mouth, 'Whoever you are... I'm sorry... whatever I did... I'm sorry.' *Anguish coated every word.*

'Before you die, you at least deserve to know why.' *In truth, he wanted to delay the moment of completion.*

He bent forward and whispered in the man's ear.

He slid open the long, middle drawer under the desktop and pulled out two items, a white, featureless mask and a scalpel. He placed the mask over his face and regarded the eyes that looked back. They were brown and framed in long, black lashes that were the envy of any woman who saw them.

But within them lay layers he could only guess at. The mask brought into play a distance between him and his actions. The mask could feel, while he could not. The mask could reason, while he dare not. The mask could mourn, while he should not.

The eyes within the mask flared as he remembered the moment before the nails went in.

'You... are... practising on me?' the old man asked.

'Yes... and you're the most... deserving candidate.'

Then came the score of a knife. Four six inch nails. A twist of the garrotte.

And a last, withered exhalation.

'Don't worry,' he whispered into the dead man's ear, 'there will be more.'

Long fingers picked up the scalpel and aimed the point towards the mask. While one hand held the mask carefully in place, the other pressed finely honed steel against the lower, right eyelid, until blood welled on to the blade. Then, after placing the knife on the desktop, his right hand pressed the cheek of the mask so that blood slid on to its surface.

As a single drop of blood glided down the white cheek of the mask, he considered the long dead, the newly deceased and those yet to die, and he enjoyed the tear.

Chapter 1

'Right, guys, the drinks are on me,' I say as we pile into the bar at the end of the shift.

'Woohoo!' Ten voices: nine male, one female, chime in unison.

'Colour me purple and roger me rotten,' shouts Dave Harkness. 'Put a note in your diary, guys 'n' gal. DI Ray McBain is splashing the cash.'

Hoots of laughter and various ribald comments follow.

'Enjoy it while it lasts, DS Harkness,' I say and punch him on the arm. Then I lower my voice to a stage whisper. 'Meet me out the back later. I'll bring the purple paint.'

Everybody laughs. Laughter that's out of scale with the humour of the joke but laden with pleasure and relief that another case has been successfully closed.

'You wish,' Harkness grins. 'Mine's a pint of 80 Shilling.' He pats me on the shoulder and moves towards a collection of seats along the window. Several other orders are shouted at me as the rest of the crew joins Dave.

I face the barman and allow the spread of a smile to heat my face. We had a good result this week. Some solid police work, and the bad guy is minus tie and shoelaces while he waits to go to court in the morning.

'Give you a hand, sir?'

DC Allessandra Rossi is standing beside me. Although she is tall for a woman the top of her head only reaches my chin. She's slim in a black, tailored suit, her long brown hair pulled back into a ponytail. She's got that Italian thing going, which works well among all of us pale Celts. Her brown eyes spark with intelligence, her lips are plump with promise... for the right man. I don't do romance on the job. It complicates.

'Thanks, Allessandra,' I smile. 'Seems like the men have forgotten their manners. Thank God you're in the team. Bring a touch of class to the environment.' And I've no idea how I'm going to remember what they all ordered.

'What can I say?' She digs her hands in her pockets. 'A woman's touch and all that.' She grins and then looks away, but not before I catch a slight colouring to her cheeks. Then she looks me straight in the eye and says. 'And it was 80 Shillings for everyone apart from Daryl. He wants a bottle of Budweiser.' She offers a smile. 'I'll have a pint of Stella.'

'Good memory, Rossi,' I say. '... and a suggestion of more class with an order of Stella Artois.'

She pushes a strand of hair behind an ear and picks up a couple of pints, raises her eyebrows. 'Cheers,' she offers.

At the table with the team, drinks placed in front of everyone, I pretend to drink. My trick is to place my tongue over the mouth of the bottle so that little spills into my mouth. Some form of professional distance is to be maintained. It wouldn't do for the boss to get pissed and make an arse of himself. I have one drink to their three. No-one notices, as long as I laugh at their jokes.

My cheeks are aching from it.

Maybe if I joined them on Planet Booze I would find them funny, but I have another form of celebration in mind tonight and too much alcohol will put a stop to anything happening there.

I look around the characters placed at the table. Boss or not, these guys are the closest I have to friends. How sad is that? Need to get your life together, McBain. Don't work so hard. Get somebody else's life. Aye, right!

Still, I've not done too badly. Cracked a couple of big profile cases, got pushed up the ladder. My work methods were questioned by some, but too bad. Results are all that matters. Get the bad guys and lock them up for a very long time.

'What you smilin' at, Ray?' asked Daryl Drain. The last joke had evidently been so bad that nobody laughed.

'Just thinkin' what a bunch of tossers you lot are.'

'Even me, sir?' asks Allessandra. This brings a chorus of highly pitched 'Oooo's from the table's other inhabitants.

'Eh, apart from you, Allessandra. But only because I don't know the female equivalent.'

'I think the term applies equally to both genders, sir.' Allessandra has trouble with my request that when the team is on their own they call me by my first name.

'Okay, Tosser Rossi,' I grin, 'I stand corrected.'

She grins back, prompting a memory of her first day with the team. The case, my first case as the boss, demanded more men. For once, we got somewhere. Asked for three. Got one. Allessandra Rossi. Newly out of uniform. Her face was scrubbed of artifice, her long, dark hair pulled back. A flash of red lipstick her one claim to femininity on the job.

I introduced her to the team, explained who she was and partnered her with Dave Harkness, an experienced cop, but one who'd never gone far because of his habit of acting like the team comedian.

'Any questions, Dave?' I was prompted to ask by the thoughtful expression on his face. I should have known better.

'Just one, sir.'

'Yes...'

'Can I ask Detective Constable Rossi if she is vaginally or clitorally stimulated?' Laughter bounced around the room. I was surprised that the guys knew what a clitoris was and as much as I like a wee bit of smut, Harkness' joke was not in keeping with the force's determination to make life more comfortable for our female colleagues.

'Quieten down, guys. That's enough. Harkness, any more of that and you're on report.' I quelled the laughter. Looking at Allessandra I was surprised to see her expression calm, her colouring normal.

Just as the laughter died down and before anyone else could speak, 'If I could answer Dave's query, sir?' she managed to place lots of emphasis on the word 'query'. I nodded, wondering what she was about to do. She then took a step forward and looked pointedly at his groin.

'Whatever it takes, Dave, a penis is required.' A smile of commiseration. 'Sorry, wee man.' The laughter was even louder this time.

Harkness laughed as loudly as anyone in the room. Since then the two of them have been the best of buddies.

'Hey, big guy, fancy another beer?' Daryl addresses me.

'Aye.' I hold up my bottle and grin. Then I look along the table at the team. I see Jim Peters hunched in his seat. Peters is renowned for being first out of the taxi and last into the pub.

He positions himself last in the 'whose round is it' queue, hoping that by the time his turn comes back round everyone is too pissed to notice. He's not getting away with it tonight.

'Is it no' about time that Jim bought a drink?' I look along the table.

With a glare in my direction Jim stands up. He shrugs, attempting to appear good-natured.

'Somebody follow him and make sure the fucker actually spends some money,' I say. Raucous laughter along the table.

Peters gives me a look from the bar. I wink and raise my bottle to him. Memo to me. Watch out for DS Peters. Ten years older than me and nursing an unhealthy dose of professional jealousy, I'm sure. Passed over for promotion several times, his file told me.

Resents me, his body language shouts.

I'm bored now. I could go to Theresa's early. Though I'd better think of an excuse. Shouldn't need one, I'm the boss. Besides, my presence after a certain point in the proceedings will only put a dampener on things.

By this time Peters has carried over his round.

Harkness smiles, 'The bastard's just spent twenty quid.' A cheer goes round the table. Jim shrugs his shoulders, attempting to enter into the spirit of it. But anybody with a sober eye on them can see he's gutted. Excellent. But, unfortunately it's a lesson I doubt he'll learn.

I stand up, 'Listen guys, sorry to break up the party, but some of us need our beauty sleep.'

'Two years should be enough to do something about your cross-eyes then, Ray,' Dave Harkness pipes up from the end of the table.

I clamber across a row of limbs, 'Very funny.'

'Who is it tonight then, Ray?' asks Daryl Drain. He and I have come up through the ranks together. I would trust him with my life. But not my wife, if I had one. 'Would her name be Susan, Marie or Rosa?'

'Or Roger?' asked Peters, just loud enough for everyone to hear. I am aware of the gossip. People love to speculate, don't they? If you're not married and don't have a live-in partner by a certain age, then your sexual orientation is up for discussion. I'm in my early thirties, well past the stage when I should have an indentation on my ring finger. Well past the stage when questions would be asked. And well past giving a fuck.

I turn to Peters and pout, 'Would it make a difference, Jim?' I ruffle his hair. Everyone laughs at his obvious discomfort.

'That's sexual harassment, you know,' he complains.

'You wish,' I answer and push the back of his head. He says nothing, merely raises his eyebrows as if he's keen to stay in the humour of the moment, but he can't quite get there.

Chapter 2

At least the owners are making an effort with the female toilets, thinks Allessandra as she fingers the small bowl of pink and purple pot pourri. Shame it doesn't distract the eye from the cracked mirror and the rust-stained sink.

After all this is a 'polis' pub, the landlord tells her. Handy for regional headquarters, and there are more and more lovely young ladies like her joining up all the time, he says, his jaw hanging open in a smile like the drawer from an open till. Maybe if he wanted to increase future profits, he should get in one of those kari-coki machines. And she could be his star turn.

Aye, Allessandra had laughed, and said that'll be the day his profits fall lower than a tart's knickers.

He had begun to smile at what he thought was going to be a funny comment from a welcome punter. It froze half-formed on his face when the young lady in front of him didn't match up to his internal picture of ladylike.

While washing her hands Allessandra considers her face, slightly bent out of shape and given a sepia tint by the ancient mirror. She'd never be a contestant on *Britain's Next Top Model*. Not that she wanted to be; she'd rather sit through one of her mother's coffee mornings at St John's Roman Catholic Church. She shudders at the thought. All those cupcakes and good intentions.

The boys used to call her *kipper lips* because of the naturally bee-stung look she had. As a teenager she spent too many evenings in front of a mirror, practising how to speak while trying to pull her lips in. It didn't work. Just made her look slightly demented. She was also too tall for the boys in her class, ten pounds too heavy and way too much was going on behind those eyes. Her dad told her that from the moment she pushed her way out of her mother's womb there was a knowing look in her eyes.

A look that often unnerved people. A look that Allessandra used to good effect. And boy, had she found the right job to do that.

What a world of difference this was from being in uniform. No more standing on point. No more splitting up domestics. No more searching female shoplifters. If she had thought she would have become that intimate with the female half of the criminal world she would have taken a quick course in gynaecology.

Her mother reacted to the news of her joining up as if Allessandra had spat in her Earl Grey. It was bad enough that she had squandered her university education in a series of meaningless, minimum-wage jobs, but to then choose to come into daily contact with some of the planet's most undesirable people was more than her mother could stand. She had set off round the west of Scotland's scone country, with the other, very nice, daughter, Sheila, in search of calm. And found nothing but a burgeoning ulcer and a particularly nice carrot cake at a bookshop/café up by Loch Lomond.

Approval had been gained when Allesandra married Roberto. He was from a good Scots-Italian family and he was something in banking. Approval was then lost when after five years of marriage there was no offspring.

A round of laughter barrels in the door. Allessandra is instantly reminded of her father. If he was here he would have been the cause of it. A man who had to stoop at every doorway, he was equally large in character. His quick wit always provided him with a humorous retort and his meaty hand was always ready to heat someone's shoulder with comfort.

Strange to think he had died more than half of her life ago, just before her sixteenth birthday. A hit and run, they were told. The driver and the car were never found.

How Allessandra misses him. Even now she hears his profound bass in the warning bark of a dog, glimpses his face in a crowd and at odd moments smells the cheap Avon aftershave she and Sheila gave him each Christmas.

'My favourite,' he would boom and scoop both giggling girls up in the air on one arm.

The police did everything they could to find the driver. Well, they would, for one of their own. Every man at the funeral swore to Allessandra's mother that they would find the bastard who did this, even if it took until they retired.

Her mother only nodded her head and offered a weak smile to every threat of retribution. She had known this would happen. She expected the knock at the door every night of her eighteen-year marriage and when it finally came it was almost a relief. Now, she could relax.

Dad used to tease her mother into smiling; each curve of her lips his trophy in a hard-fought campaign. He used to say she worried too much because she loved too much. Allessandra worked it out at age thirteen: her mother just didn't know how to be happy.

He is the reason Allessandra is here and she will do everything she can to make him proud of her. It had been a secret source of worry as she grew up that she knew her future was in the police force, but she knew Mother would go book herself into the nearest sanatorium at the mere mention of it.

Finally she found the courage. She wasted enough time behind the counter at Frasers, building up the strength to defy her mother. Now that she is in the job, she plans to prove her wrong and work her way up the career ladder. It doesn't matter that she is a woman in what is still mostly a man's world; she is going places. She simply won't allow the glass ceiling or the innuendo to hold her back.

Allessandra dares to dry her hands on the nearly white and blue towel hanging from the plastic box on the wall and considers her workmates. By and large they are a good crew. There are a couple she could learn a lot from, Daryl Drain and Jim Peters maybe. DI McBain, certainly, but she will have to keep a distance from him.

The resemblance wasn't immediately apparent. It was only after watching him talk for an hour at her first briefing session that the height, the girth and the voice wove their spell. It was like looking at her father.

Chapter 3

Theresa's house is on the other side of Glasgow, in Newton Mearns. The house is in darkness when I get there. It's only just gone eleven o'clock. Fuck it. I'll take the risk. I give the taxi driver the amount that bleeds into the cabin from his meter. And a little extra for keeping his mouth shut, following my blunt request. Sometimes I can keep up with the most verbose taxi driver. Tonight I just want to sit in silence and savour the flavour of another successful case.

Some sicko murdered a prostitute, but not before he had smashed her face so badly even her own mother wouldn't have recognised her.

The killer was a respectable pillar of the community. A city councillor, no less. We were ordered by the brass to get the job done. But do it quietly. The City Fathers didn't want a scandal in the papers.

The problem was the wife gave him an alibi. Presumably she didn't want to lose out on the comfortable lifestyle. Apart from his position on the Council, he was a senior lecturer at Glasgow University, a sizeable income to be lost there then.

But then a suspect from another case fingered him. A suspect I knew would come up with the goods. A suspect I leaned on until...

Then we accidentally let the wife see a photograph of the murdered prostitute and she quietly and calmly rescinded her alibi. Said she must have been mistaken. She was at a friend's that night, had too much to drink and slept in the spare room.

For as long as I work in this job I don't think I'll ever get used to human nature and the way we respond to things. We had just proved to her that her husband was a vicious killer. She didn't shout. She didn't cry. She simply changed her mind; a knot of muscle working away in her jaw the only outward sign

16

of emotion. As we led him away in the squad car she stared impassively from the large bay window of their Victorian townhouse. One arm tight round her waist like a belt, the other seesawing a cigarette back and forth to her mouth.

I throw a stone at Theresa's bedroom window. Moments later, her head pops out. Her voice a harsh whisper.

'McBain! You trying to get me a divorce? I'll be right down. Don't make a sound.'

I hear the sound of bare feet pad down the stairs. The door opens.

'In.'

'I have often walked down this street before,' I sing, willing my voice to sound like Nat King Cole. I step in the doorway.

'Ray, shut up.'

'But the pavement always stayed beneath my feet before.' I can barely sing for laughing. So much for Mr Cole.

'Ray!'

'All at once am I twenty storeys high, 'cos I'm here on the street where you live.'

She closes the door behind me and stops me the way she knows will be most effective. Her lips are hard on my mouth, her tongue a slow slip against mine. She pulls away.

'Needed that,' she grins, looking beautiful in that tousled, just awake way.

'Billy will be gone for some time, I take it?'

'What day's this... Wednesday?' She lifts some hair back from her face and smiles. 'He'll be back Friday.' Her smile promises and I feel my heartbeat quicken.

I take her hand and move towards the stairs, 'Excellent!'

In the bedroom, I make to throw off my clothes.

'Shoes only, for now,' orders Theresa.

'Huh?'

'You know what we do first.'

'Right,' I spot the incense already burning on the bedside cabinet. Theresa converted me to the art of meditation, by the simple expedient of proving that sex was outstanding afterwards.

Mr Pecker at attention, I sit cross-legged, leaning against the headboard. I've been practising this on my own, so my body recognizes the position and relaxes almost immediately. Well, apart from a certain part of my anatomy. It takes a little longer to curl back into its wiry nest.

After what feels like moments, but will have been at least fifteen minutes, Theresa's hand touches mine and I hear her voice sing my name.

But just before this, a fragment of a recurring dream blooms in my mind. All I can see is a white feather. All I can hear is my panicked breath. Then it begins to snow feathers. My excitement dims. Then it's rekindled by Theresa's voice.

'Okay, convent boy, let's be having you.' Theresa is one of the few people who know about my childhood. She loves to bring up my former status as she takes me to bed. From the grin on her face as she says it, she enjoys a slightly perverse thrill at the idea of sleeping with someone whose formative years were spent under the watchful eye of a group of nuns.

Afterwards, I'm lying in post-coital bliss. If someone were to hold a gun to my head, I doubt if I could move.

'Hey, mister,' says Theresa, 'don't even think about falling asleep. You're out of here before the neighbours start to stir.'

'But, Theresa...'

'Don't "But Theresa" me, sunshine. I don't want Billy to get even a whisper of what's going on.'

'So why let me in, in the first place?'

'You know why.' She pokes me in the belly for emphasis. 'I can't resist your masculine charms, you sexy big hunk of blubber.'

'Gee, ta.' The thought of Billy finding out fills me with dread too. Not because I'm afraid of the guy. I'm more afraid of this relationship having a clearer definition. An illicit affair suits me quite nicely, thank you. For now.

'So, you got your guy,' Theresa slides her hand across my chest and squeezes, 'Well done, big man,' moving the subject on to safer ground.

'Yeah... pleased to get that sick fucker.' This is an understatement. 'How's your life?'

'Oh you know... great, wonderful and amazing,' a deep sigh, 'if you want to live in Groundhog Central.' When Billy proposed to Theresa, he promised to set her up in a beautiful house in a posh part of the city. He also promised that she'd never work again. Theresa loved the idea of being a kept woman. Doing lunch and shopping were her ideal. The reality turned out not to be so enjoyable.

'So get a job.' I suggest.

'Billy won't hear of it. He says no woman of his should go out to work.'

'How delightfully unreconstructed of him.'

'And meantime, he's working all the hours to keep me in the style he's accustomed to... and I'm miserable. Bored out of my tits.'

'And lovely tits they are too,' I give one a squeeze.

'But what can I do? All I'm trained for is teaching... no way I'm going back to that.'

'Why not? You were a good teacher.' That was the impression she gave anyway.

'Why not? The wee shites made my life a misery. That's why not.'

'So what're you going to do?' I ask, not really looking for an answer. I just want to sleep.

'Don't know.'

'So think of something.'

'Like what?'

'I don't know, you're the one who's bored.'

'Yeah and I'm bored with this conversation.' Her hand slides down my chest and rests a millimetre from my groin. Heat jumps into my penis. I'm awake again.

'Right, sleepy,' an elbow in my ribs, 'Time you made a decent woman of me.'

'Mmmm.'

'Ray McBain, will you move it!'

'Oh Tess, can I not have another five minutes?' I mumble into the pillow. I save this moniker for special occasions. Like this one, when I want to melt her heart, so she'll let me sleep.

'Another five minutes and my foot will have to be surgically removed from your arse.'

My phone rings. Shrill and insistent. Saves me from an embarrassing medical procedure.

'Uh?' I manage.

'McBain.' The voice on the other end of the phone is a bucket of ice down my shorts.

I wake up instantly.

'Yessir?' It's the high heidyin. My boss, David Campbell.

'We've a dead body for you. See if you can leave your lovely ladyboy and get your backside over here pronto.'

19

Chapter 4

The body is safely in its bag by the time I arrive. Briefly sanitized, before the next part of the detection process can begin. There's enough blood in the vicinity to hint that the deceased did not die of natural causes. We are in a small ex-local authority house. The attention lavished on this house and its neighbours hint at a pleasant, quiet place to live. A place where the inhabitants take pride in their ability to own their own home and make the best use of the excess funds they manage to borrow from their bank. I walk past the constable on point duty and through the front door.

Jim Peters is here and talking to the boss. And he looks as if he's slept like the proverbial log. Bastard doesn't even have the decency to suffer a hangover.

'Right, Jim. What have we got so far?' I give him a brief smile of acknowledgement. He looks at his watch before answering; a non-verbal comment on my apparent tardiness. I don't say anything; I match his stare until his eyes drop from mine and I log it away for future reference. Don't you just love office politics?

'Elderly male, sir. Caucasian. Name of Patrick Connelly. Victim appears to have sustained multiple wounds. Wrists and feet pierced with sharp object. Stab wound on the right side of deceased's chest. Ligature marks on his neck...'

'And strange scratch marks around his forehead.' I speak without realizing.

'How the fuck did you know that?'

'It's the stigmata. You mentioned the wrists, feet and wound on the side. The next item on the list was the wounds on the forehead.'

'Looks like we've a religious nutter on our hands,' says the boss. 'Let's find this guy before he goes for a full crucifixion.'

A moan sounds from behind us. I turn and see a head of white hair just before I hear feet drum up the stairs.

I leave the room and follow the woman I expect to be the deceased's wife. The stairs end at what appears to be the bathroom, judging by the tasteful sign on the door. Then a passage stretches along to my left, with another two doors off it. Loud sobbing allows me to open the correct door.

'Sorry, sir.' A young WPC is sitting on the edge of the bed, one arm around a small woman.

'Mrs Connelly, I'm sorry you had to hear that.' I glare at the WPC. She shouldn't have let the woman come down the stairs.

'It's not Mrs, it's Miss,' comes from the small frame.

'Miss Connelly is the deceased's sister, sir,' offers the WPC.

'I can speak for myself, hen.' She forces herself to sit up and visibly steels herself against any further displays of emotion.

'Can we get you a cup of tea?' I motion with my head for the constable to leave the tiny room. With three of us in it, I'm starting to feel claustrophobic.

'If anybody else asks me that, I think I'll scream.' Her hair is pulled tight across her head and tied at the back. This has the effect of sharpening a nose that already looks as if it could be used to crochet. Her lips are almost non-existent, but what is there is painted bright red. Lipstick leaks from the straight line of her lips into the cracks radiating around her mouth, like rust. A bit early to be putting the war paint on, I think. She's cradling a brown pipe in her hand. I don't think it's hers.

'DI McBain. Mind if I sit down?' I ask, aware that my size might intimidate her.

'It's a free country,' is the sharp reply. So much for intimidation. I sit as far away from her on the bed as I can.

'I won't bite, you know.' Tears are no longer in evidence. Miss Connelly has made a remarkable recovery.

'How old was Patrick?'

'Seventy-two. I was his big sister, by two years.' She is staunchly in the camp of being proud of her age then.

'Do you know of anyone who might want to kill your brother, Miss Connelly?'

'Kill Paddy? I don't know who would do such a thing. He might have been a miserable old bugger, but I didn't think anyone would be driven to that extreme. Unless modelling yourself on Victor Meldrew has become a capital offence.' I think again of how composed the woman before me has become. Then I notice the small hanky poking out from a tight fist. Blue veins and brown liver spots stand out in stark contrast to the tight, white knuckles. She is mourning, just in her own particular fashion.

I spot the crucifix above the bed and the statue of Our Lady, arms outstretched, on the dressing table.

'You a Catholic, son?'

'Once upon a time,' I answered.

'Once a Catholic, always a Catholic.'

'Was Paddy a regular church-goer?' I ignore her pointed comment.

'Never missed it.'

'Did he have many friends?'

'Are your ears painted on? He was the spit of Victor Meldrew. People avoided the daft sod. He had... acquaintances.'

'Acquaintances?'

'Your ears are painted on, son. Acquaintances as in folk he bumped into now and again. Folk would normally speak to him only when cornered. They ran a mile when they saw him coming.'

'Do you know of anyone who would want to do your brother harm?'

'Jim Phillips at number 23. Our Patrick had his garden fork for well over a year. That's about the only person I can think of that might be annoyed with him.'

'A garden fork?' People say some weird things when they are trying to find a frame of reference in their mind for an event as vast as this.

'Aye, but you don't know Jim Phillips. Treats that garden like it was his bairn.' She paused and looked out of the small window. The view was a sky of concrete grey. Defiance, or whatever was keeping her in the conversation, fell away and before me I saw a small, frightened woman.

'Miss Connelly, do you have somewhere you can go?'

'They're no' putting me out of my home, son.' Steel returned to her spine, but fear and fatigue pulled at the muscles of her face.

'I'm not suggesting that it's permanent, just until you can get someone in to clean the place. It'll be some while until we're finished examining your home. You don't want to have to face that every day and it would help us find the killer faster if we have a free rein in the house.' I don't have to ask, but it feels like the right thing to do.

'Aye, you're right, son. I wasn't thinking. Our Agnes has a house down in Ayr. I'll give her a phone and ask if I can sleep in her spare room for a wee while.'

22

'Be sure to give the female constable a note of where Agnes stays, so we can keep in touch with you.'

'Aye.' She looked deep into my eyes. 'You'll find him, son. Won't you? Patrick was a miserable old git, but he didn't deserve this. You'll get him won't you?' Her hand gripped at my sleeve.

Back at the station, the shift has gathered to hear the news. I'm standing waiting for the din to die down. Everyone's talking about last night. A good time was had by all, if the noise of the chatter is anything to go by.

There's a box of cakes on the table in front of me. Must be somebody's birthday.

'Okay, folks. Rein it in. Time to review what's happened this morning. Peters was first on the scene.' Against my better judgement, I give him his place. 'Tell everyone what we know.'

As Peters reviews the facts we'd determined so far, my mind chases ahead of him. Had Connelly been killed where his body had been found, or was the kill zone elsewhere? The spray of blood should indicate the murder was committed in the victim's home... and the amount of blood indicates the wounds were inflicted before death.

The sick bastard wanted the old man to suffer.

He must have made some noise as those wounds were inflicted. Surely his sister would have heard and come to investigate? Unless they'd been carried out post-mortem... which I'm sure wasn't how it happened. She must have cuddled up in bed with a tub of Temazepam. If he wasn't killed there, then where? And how did the killer get him back inside his home without waking up Miss Connelly? Unless she was the killer. Nah. No way. She appeared way too frail to be able to carry out a crime like that.

'Stigmata?' I hear someone ask.

Peters looks at me. 'You're the expert, sir.'

'For those of you who didn't see the film of the same name... it's a religious... thing. It refers to the wounds that Christ received on the cross.'

'Did the killer not get it wrong then, sir?' asks Daryl Drain, chewing a pen. 'The wounds were on the wrists, not the deceased's hands.'

'No, in fact the scholars would say he got it dead right. Religious artefacts usually depict the wounds on the palms of Christ's hands. But there is an argument that if he was hung from a cross by nails piercing the palms of his hands, his weight would have pulled him off the wood. Nails through the wrists, however, would have better supported his weight on the cross. Stronger formation of bones.'

'Where did you pick up that little titbit of information, sir?' asks Harkness.

'Let's just say I had a misspent youth,' I answer. In the convent orphanage. A child of nine or ten, I read of the saints who displayed these marks and was deeply impressed. I wanted them too and went as far as drawing them on with a red pen.

Sister Mary dumped me in a bath straight away, after boxing my ears. As she scrubbed my flesh with a nailbrush to get rid of the marks, she called me a thousand different kinds of heathen, each one punctuated by another knock on the head. She was disgusted that I would mock the saints in such a way. But my ambitions were far higher than mere mockery. I wanted to become one. In the world of black and white that is a child's, I couldn't hear enough stories of these men and women who were good enough to receive the ultimate sign of their piety. We were fed religious dogma with our porridge. In that environment, what impressionable child wouldn't want to earn their place in heaven, while wearing the marks that proved their eligibility?

'Okay guys, let's do some digging.' I shout over the suggestions as to exactly how I'd misspent my youth, 'A man has just been horribly killed. Drain, you look into Mr Connelly's past. I want a complete biography. Rossi and Harkness, door to door around the neighbourhood. Find out if anyone saw something on the night of the murder. Peters, see if you can piece together a timetable of Mr Connelly's movements for the few hours preceding his death.'

'One last thing, people,' I kept my expression grim, and then looked down at the cakes, 'I'm on the Empire Biscuit.' It won't kill me. I'll start the diet for real on Monday.

Chapter 5

The lock eventually gives. Allessandra kicks the door open and bends to pick up her food shopping bought at TV dinner heaven. She'd received a text from Roberto earlier in the day:

Working late, babes. Don't stay up. xxx.

She shrugged and thought; what's new?

Belly full, a cool-ish glass of Sauvignon Blanc in her hand and legs tucked under her on the sofa, she allows her body to relax. A smile of satisfaction forms on her face. Excellent. She's involved in another murder case. If she does a good job here, who knows where it could lead?

She enjoyed the door to door exercise. It felt like she was doing real police work. Although Harky had a face on him. A face that suggested he'd been stung on his wee man by a wasp. Mind you, none of the neighbours were very helpful. The deceased was a quiet old chap. Never as much as bothered a fly. Kept mostly to himself. And no, they didn't hear a noise the night he died.

Allessandra didn't do much talking, she simply observed Dave Harkness at work. He had been in the job for twenty years; surely there was something she could learn from him. Not that there was much on show; a house to house investigation in a self-respecting working class neighbourhood wasn't going to show up much of the city's underclass.

At least they got a laugh when Mrs Jamieson at number 42 came to the door minus her false teeth. Throughout the interview, her husband hissed at her to go and put her teeth in, but she was so excited to have such an event on her doorstep she ignored him. When it became clear to them that the couple knew nothing, they made to leave.

'So whit happened, hen?' Mrs Jamieson mashed each word out of her gummy mouth. 'How did the old bugger die?'

'We can't be certain of that yet, madam,' answered Harky with a warning look to Rossi. 'We have still to perform an autopsy.'

'Oh. Just like they do on the telly.' She hugged herself with a rubber-necker's glee. 'Just like that *CSI*?' she sprayed over Harky's face.

'Strange isn't it,' Harky said as we passed over her doorstep. 'Just like *CSI*. Real life comes to your living room.'

'Aye,' she answered oblivious to his sarcasm. 'It's just as good as the telly. You fine people investigating a murder right on our doorstep.'

The bottle finished, Allessandra picks up her mobile and examines the screen. Nothing. She checks the time. 8:30pm. She knows how pissed off Roberto gets if she pesters him to find out when he will be back home so she resists the impulse to send him a text. She reconsiders and sends one anyway:

... when you coming home? xxx

She waits a few minutes. No reply. Then, feeling a twist of loneliness, she scrolls down her contact list. Drinking too much wine is not a good idea when you're on your own, she tells herself. Makes you needy. The high she'd been on after her day's work had completely dissipated. Mum's number comes up first and she thinks, God no. Sheila's next and is also dismissed as she'll be watching her soaps. Then she scrolls through her other contacts and dismisses them one by one. They are all women she's worked with in the past, but what do you talk about to people who don't understand what you go through on a day-to-day basis? She faces sex crimes, violence and murder; the most important decision they've made that day is what to have for lunch or whether to end a letter with "faithfully" or "sincerely".

At the end of her contact list she comes across the numbers of Ray and Daryl. They are the only two worth talking to. And she's just going to come across as Ali Nae Pals if she phones either of them. With a sigh she closes down her phone and makes her way to her kitchen. She opens the fridge door and peers in. It's empty apart from a clove of garlic and some goat's milk.

She closes it and opens what Roberto calls with a hint of irony and a touch of dashed expectations, the food cupboard. Apart from a tin of alphabet spaghetti — Roberto's — and a jar of honey — hers — it's also empty. Note to self, thinks Allessandra; do a proper food shop. Just as soon as you can be arsed.

With a sigh, she walks down the long hallway to her bedroom, taking her clothes off and dropping them on the floor as she walks. That'll really piss Roberto off. He has a typical Italian view of how houseproud a woman should be and she delights in proving him wrong at every opportunity.

In her bedroom she closes the thick, red velvet drapes — being married to a high-achiever has its perks — and puts on her pyjamas. The ones that tell Roberto he needs to keep his hands to himself.

She flicks off the switch on the lamp, curls into the foetal position under the quilt and sends a silent prayer that sleep comes quickly.

Chapter 6

The door had to be here. Somewhere along this length of wall. A thick coat of ivy hampered his progress. An ivy he'd never seen before. Green with yellow braid. A gust of wind. Leaves lifted along the wall. Giving the impression that the wall lives, moves with each inhalation.

He fought for breath. The air that reached his lungs is sweetened with incense. He pushed a hand through the leaves, hoping for the wood of a door. He looked down at the other hand. It held a small rusted key. Rust leaked on to his skin. He felt it stain the three deep lines; love, life and heart.

His pulse jumped in his throat. Shoulders rose and fell as he worked air into his body, energy into his limbs. Fingers raced along stone, their sensitive pads replacing eyes. Where's the gate?

He punched a toe on the root of a tree. The pain was sharp, almost pleasurable. He leaned forward to nurse his foot. It was bare. Where were his shoes? Where were his clothes? He was naked and unaccountably hard. Shame at his arousal turned his head. He looked in every direction. What if anyone saw him like this?

There was a building behind him. A memorial to the lost lives of a thousand boys. Its shadow reached almost to his feet and he felt the touch of countless eyes from behind sightless windows. His scrotum shrunk. Sweat broke out down the cold length of his spine. Someone was watching him. Laughing at his nakedness, his pathetic nakedness. And laughing at his fear.

I'm in front of a mirror. A stage mirror. The table top is covered with a veil of tiny, white feathers. People are dancing behind me. In the corner a nun sits in a bath, fully clothed. Her face is arctic white, her lips blue.

Now I'm being chased through unfamiliar streets. I run in one door and come out the back door of another house. My limbs are heavy, my feet sticking on the ground, but I need to get away. I've never known fear like it. Every hair on my body is erect.

I'm running down a dead-end. I have a small blade of some sort in my hand. It glints in the moonlight. Before me is a white wall. It has two windows halfway up, shaped like a semicircle. Like a pair of eyes. Red liquid wells up on the sill of one and begins its slow slide down the wall. I know with the certainty of the devout, if the blood reaches the floor, I die.

'Ray, Ray, wake up,'

'Wha...' I sit up. I remember instantly. I had come to Theresa's straight from work. After a hard day I needed her particular brand of attention. I feel wet hair line my forehead.

'Will you sleep somewhere else if you're going to have nightmares? Man, that was scary.'

'Nightmares,' I say unconvincingly, 'I don't have nightmares.' The dream fades, leaving an aftertaste. I can hear my pulse thump in my ears. 'What are you on about?' I reach over and switch on a bedside lamp.

'Ray, that was scary.' Theresa is sitting up, her knees pulled up to her chest.

'Hey. It was only a dream.'

'A bloody scary one. Your voice. It was weird. Didn't sound like you.'

'Who did it sound like then?'

'A wee boy.'

'Eh? You sure you're no' the one that was having the bad dream?'

'Christ, how could anyone sleep through that? No, you were having the dream. I was sitting here terrified to leave you. Terrified to stay.' She ran a hand through her hair. Fighting back tears. 'And you wouldn't wake up.'

'Oh, sweetheart,' I slide across the bed and put an arm over her shoulder, 'It was only a dream.'

'If that was only a dream, I'm never going to sleep again.' She pushes me away.

'What was so scary then?'

'You... your voice, what you were saying.'

'What was my voice like? What was I saying?'

'It was like a wee boy. I told you that.'

'What was I saying?'

'Nothing.'

'But…'

'Nothing, all right? Just my vivid imagination.' She moved as if she was leaving the bed. 'I'm going for a cuppa. You want one?'

'Theresa, tell me. Why won't you tell me?'

She turned her face to mine, her lips tight, and her pupils large. Whatever she heard really freaked her out. She took a steadying breath, 'Okay, here's what you said…' she shook her head, 'what the boy said. It was only a short phrase, but you… he, I refuse to believe that was coming out of your mouth. He… it was like a mantra, over and over and over again.'

'Theresa, for fuckssake will you tell me what I said.'

'But it was said with such… relish. Over, and over and over again.'

'THERESA!'

'Jesus doesn't save, you said. He kills.'

Chapter 7

I'm at a gym. One of these big fancy new ones that's been springing up around the city. Glasgow has another class division: the fat and the fit. The place is a triumph of chrome and mirrors. Everything looks brand new. I'm here for an assessment, to see how unhealthy I am.

The sight accosting me in the mirror has become too much to bear. Need to do something about it. Needed to do something about it a long time ago.

The place is quiet. Mind you, it would be quiet at ten o'clock at night. But it's the only time I can get here. Only a few people are sweating at the variety of machines that populate the floor. Gratifying to see that they are almost as out of shape as I am.

While I wait for the instructor to put me through my paces, I review the day's information. A bottle of sleeping pills was found in the bathroom cabinet. Prescribed to Miss Connelly, and apparently of a strength to knock out a rhinoceros. The amount of planning it would have taken to inflict those wounds on the deceased suggests that the killer would have left nothing to chance, and might have known of Miss Connelly's sleeping habits. Someone close to the family, perhaps? I suppress a shudder; whoever it was, we have a determined man here. A man with a plan. A man on a mission. The clichés are pouring into my mind, but they appear apt.

'Mr McBain?' A smiling child who looks as if she's been scrubbed with a wire brush dipped in Dettol stands before me. 'I'm Yvonne and I'm your instructor. Would you come with me?' The smile doesn't dim in wattage. Used to be that folk would say, you know you're getting old when the police are looking younger than you. Let's change that profession to Gym Instructor. I feel I should ask if her parents know where she is.

Yvonne takes a few measurements with a variety of instruments that look vaguely medical. Yvonne talks and I listen. My seat is uncomfortable. I'm squirming, getting red in the face. Perhaps it's not the chair that's the problem.

'You're edging into the medical category of obese, Mr McBain,' she says cheerfully. I want to pencil in some of her teeth. No, make it indelible black ink. 'But with a programme of regular exercise and calorie reduction, we'll get you back into shape.'

She must have read the look of disbelief on my face, 'You've taken the hardest step, Mr McBain. To realise there's a problem and to do something about it. Lots of people don't get that far. So well done you.'

My hand grips the arm of the chair: by now I want to chip away at her smile with a toffee hammer.

On the way home, I stop off for pie and chips. Well, I've had nothing to eat all day, there must be some calories in the bank. Besides, my body can only take so much of a shock at the one time.

I'm sitting on my couch in front of the telly. The news is on. I hold the first chip in front of my mouth, let the saliva start to flow, smell the vinegar and fat. Yes. Life doesn't get much better than this. The diet can start tomorrow.

Mouth full, I look around the flat. Not bad for a solitary male. All creams and browns, leather and wood. Very Scandinavian. Might even lend credence to the rumours of my homosexuality, if it weren't so masculine. Or is that what gays go for?

Ignoring the TV, I look out of the large window over the park, towards the steeple that's scratching at the sky. For someone who's sworn off religion, I've chosen to live in an area of the city that's plagued with them. What would a psychologist say about that?

I break a piece of crust off the pie. This is part of the ceremony. Eat the circular crust first and then the meat. Chewing, I take a pad from my pocket and read.

Connelly was indeed Victor Meldrew made flesh, it would seem. Nobody had a good word to say about the man. They didn't have a bad word to say either, but the protestations of sorrow at the news had no basis in honest emotion. The most honest person was the barmaid at the bowling club.

'Horrible to get murdered, right enough,' she shuddered. 'But maybe noo that he's deid, he'll be happy,' she said.

The team's digging around did throw up a couple of interesting facts though. The deceased was seen with a woman on the eve of the murder. This was sufficiently odd to cause a few comments. I'm going to interview the barman at that particular establishment tomorrow. This has already been done, but there are some things I like to do myself.

The most interesting fact, though, came from the deceased's employment history. He'd been a caretaker at quite a few children's homes over the years. Seemed to stay at one place for only a few years at a time. Did he get bored? Or was he forced to move on each time?

The bar is one of those wee rooms that proliferate in Glasgow. Short on aesthetics, big on good-sized measures. A quarter-gill, no less. By the look on the face of the barman, he's not too pleased by our entry. Might frighten the punters to have cops in their midst. Tough.

The barman has a body that's been well lived in and a strawberry-shaped nose that hints at what he might do with his profits. He pulls up his waistband with hands that could hold three full pint glasses at a time, 'What can I do for youse?' His tone is at odds with his words.

'I'm DI McBain and this is DS Drain. We're here to ask you about Paddy Connelly.'

'Your guys were here yesterday. I told them all I know, mate.'

'We'd like to hear it again, mate.' I smile, 'If you don't mind.' I try the good cop approach.

'Can I get youse something to drink?' He puts his hand on the till to let us know the house won't be paying.

'No thanks.' I see a couple of guys drain their pints. They suddenly have an appointment elsewhere. I fix their faces in my mind. Keep them in my scrapbook. Scanning the room, I spot a familiar face. One that looks as out of place as a blue sock in a barrel of green ones, despite the fact that he's trying to dumb down his appearance. A blue skip hat, with the skip pulled forward to hide part of his face, covers his normally perfectly blond hair and his trademark camel coat is nowhere to be seen. Instead he's wearing a dark blue Harrington jacket over a dark blue turtle-neck sweater. I pretend I don't see him. If he's here incognito, I don't want to spoil it for him. He may be a criminal and a highly successful one at that, but he doesn't

33

murder anyone, at least not to my knowledge, and that means I leave him alone. Besides, outside of work, he's the closest thing I have in this world to a friend. I swing my line of vision back to the barman.

'Do you know anyone that might want to kill Mr Connelly?' I ask.

'Only if being a miserable bastard has become a capital offence, mate.'

'Not as far as I'm aware,' still smiling. 'Who did he drink with?'

'Look around you, officer.' I do. 'Guys don't come here for the chat.' He's right. The room is dotted with men and a couple of women all staring purposefully at their drinks.

Wondering if he serves razors with his drinks I ask, 'So what about this woman he was with on the night of his death?'

'Hey, that caused a stir around here. Paddy with a wummin.' He puts a flabby palm up to his mouth and looks quickly around, 'Any of these sad bastards with a wummin is front page news.'

'Can you describe her?'

'Again? I went through all this the other day. This is harassment, mate.'

'Listen, mate.' I load the word with sarcasm, 'A patrol car parked at your door every day might be construed as harassment.' I pause to let this sink in. The flab on his face sags even more at the thought of what this might do to his trade.

'But I'm sure we could persuade the courts otherwise.'

'She was... five-eight, say. Well-built. Not fat, mind. Almost muscly. Brown hair to her shoulders, quite plain. Tiny tits.'

'Age?'

'Looked around thirty... forty?' Well that's pinned her age down then.

'Was there anything remarkable about her?'

His lips bunch below his nose, as he thinks, 'Na. Except... she paid for all their drinks. That's what made me think she couldn't be a prossie. That and the well-hidden female charms... she looked more like a nun on her day off. Shy as well.'

'How so?'

'Kept hiding behind her hair.'

'How did she pay?' Fingers crossed there would be a cheque, or a credit card slip.

'Cash. No credit here, mate.' We must be back on friendly terms again.

'Did you manage to overhear any of their conversation? Pick up a name, perhaps?'

'Na.'

'What did she drink?' Daryl Drain asks.

'Budweiser. Bottle.'

'Did that not strike you as odd,' I ask, 'a woman drinking from a bottle of beer?'

He smiles, pleased to have found a weakness. 'Quite acceptable for women to drink beer nowadays. You don't get out much, mate, do you?'

'Na, mate,' my face devoid of humour, 'Too many arseholes needing locked up.'

He wasn't listening. Judging by his vacant stare, his memory was replaying the events of that evening.

'Her hands. They were strange. I was just thinking about her with a bottle of beer in her hands, when it came to me.'

'What about her hands?'

'The colour. If Dulux were to put them on one o' them paint charts they'd call it "Scrubbed Pink".'

Back in the car.

'Do you want me to order a patrol car to park here for a few days, give the bastard a shock?' Daryl asks as he clicks his seatbelt in place.

'Don't tempt me.'

'Do you think the woman's our man, so to speak?'

'Mmmm.' I was thinking about her hands.

'What do you think that stuff about the hands means?'

'A woman whose hands are scrubbed pink? Someone who works as a cleaner?'

'She should wear gloves,' Daryl grins. 'I mean, look at mine.' He holds his hands out for my perusal. I laugh. The back of every finger sports a tuft of dark hair and each one of his fingers is as thick as my thumb. 'Never do the dishes without me Marigolds.'

I haven't been down to Ayrshire for years. Tend to avoid it. Stopped by memories of summer holidays where it was either raining or about to. The nuns subscribed wholeheartedly to the view that you had to visit the coast during the summer months. You had to swim in the sea regardless of the temperature. A summer thunderstorm was good reason not to swim in the sea. A summer hailstorm was not. And when it was sunny, you had to strip to your swimming costume all day and not cry in the evening when they burst the sunburn blisters on your shoulders. There was no factor-30 sun protection in those days. The adults used cooking oil and iodine. We kids had to rely on our own meagre natural defences.

Grey skies, grey seas and green plastic shoes make up most of my childhood summer memories. The shoes had a grid on the front of them that over the summer left a nice chessboard effect on your feet. Weather-beaten and white. That, and calluses on your heels.

'A penny for your thoughts, Ray,' says Allessandra Rossi.

'Take more than a penny, nosy.' Didn't take long for her to come out of her shell.

She grins and then her expression grows serious, 'What do you make of Connelly's sister?'

'She's a cold fish. But what do you expect; having to live with Old Meldrew can't have been a picnic. Some of that misery was bound to rub off. But I don't think she had a part to play in the murder if that's why you are asking.'

'Just wondered what kind of approach you're going to take.'

Mental note to me: although Allessandra is sharp as a blade she is relatively new to the job.

'What kind of approach would you take, if I wasn't there?'

'Display empathy and understanding,' she answered without pausing to think, '...and then we grill her till her teeth rattle in her gums.'

'You had me there,' I smile, 'Right up to the rattle.' I turn my head to the right and watch the Fenwick Hotel slide past. 'Good answer though. Empathy, not sympathy. We have a case to solve. The outcome of which may depend on the information in that head of hers.

'Too nicey-nicey and all we'll get out of her will be tears and snot.'

We're now approaching the town centre of Ayr. Lots of cars about. We'd be quicker walking. A huge poster catches my eye. A carnival mask with only one eye socket filled. We're past before I can read the slogan. Traffic lights. Traffic lights. More traffic lights, then I follow the one-way system down towards the beach-front. To the right of the County Buildings, I was told. They loom before me. Imposing. The sheriff court is sited here, the building designed to serve as a reminder to those on trial that the weight of society is against them, if they are guilty. There is a disabled ramp at the side of the main entrance. If the building represents society, what does the ramp represent?

Our goal is the imaginatively titled guest-house, *Seaview*. We pass it twice before we find a parking space. "Our Agnes' house in Ayr" is a fairly substantial Bed & Breakfast. A white face appears from behind a net curtain, then at the door.

'You'd better come in. Before you frighten the neighbours,' Irene Connelly says.

'Good afternoon, Miss Connelly.' I go for the charm offensive.

'It was until you guys turned up.' Maybe I'll let Allessandra lead on this one. Miss Connelly is looking at me like I have some dreaded contagious disease. I stand aside and let Allessandra enter the house first. As she passes I give her a look and nod at the object of our visit. She inclines her head slightly; she knows I want her to do most of the talking. I'm impressed. This girl is a quick study. Her old man had an excellent reputation. Some of it must have rubbed off.

We're shown into what the wooden door plaque tells us is *The Lounge*. A bookcase filled with Wilbur Smith and Danielle Steel books blocks one corner, a TV and DVD player the other. Two sofas and two armchairs are arranged around the room. Large bay windows look out on to the houses opposite. Absently, I wonder where the sea view is.

Allessandra is talking. Sounds like she's been doing this for years, instead of months.

'How are you keeping, Miss Connelly? Getting over the shock?'

She is twisting a white handkerchief in her hands, 'I'll never get over that shock till the day I die, dear.'

'Is your cousin Agnes taking good care of you?'

'Aye, dear. She's a good soul that one.'

At this the door opens and a short, slim woman with long black hair enters the room.

'Can I get you officers a tea or a coffee?' She smiles and loses about five years of my initial estimate of her age. I'd put her at 45-ish. Her hair hangs below ample breasts that push at a rose-patterned fabric. Her trousers are black and expensive. Our Agnes is doing well for herself. A smile hangs on her face like a garland, like she still believes in the tooth fairy. I warm to her immediately. Steady on, McBain, I tell myself. You don't hit on a relation to a major witness to a murder. Or to put it the way my old sergeant, Bill Thomson used to, you don't piss in your own tent.

Allessandra and I give her our drink orders. Irene Connelly scowls at her cousin, as if annoyed that this might postpone our departure. The drinks arrive within seconds. They'd obviously been part prepared before the question was asked. Was this Agnes' way of being included in the conversation? What would she have to offer by way of evidence?

As she hands out the drinks, a steady flow of conversation passes her well-sculpted lips. Conversation of inconsequence that her B&B punters would lap up, would feel at home with.

'Have you ever spent much time in Ayr?' She is speaking to me.

'Oh, eh, yes.' The top button is loose on her blouse. 'Sorry, no...' but I can't see anything, 'I used to come down to Ayrshire for holidays when I was wee. Doon the watter and all that.' I grin and adopt a broad Glasgow accent, 'Doon to Err fur the ferr.'

She laughs, 'People that come down to Ayr for the Fair fortnight are my bread and butter. God bless them.'

Allessandra looks at me. Get your brain out of your pants, is what she's saying. 'What can you tell us about Paddy, Miss Connelly?' she asks.

'I already told your man there everything,' she nods over at me.

'You have no idea who might want to kill Paddy?'

'Do you people not talk to one another?' She manages to catch us both in her glare. 'I've nothing more to tell you. He was a miserable so-and-so, but he didn't deserve that.' Miss Connelly is sitting forward in her chair, legs crossed, arms crossed, with a bony forearm resting on her knee.

Allessandra clasps her hands in front of her and leans forward. 'It was a truly terrible thing that happened to your brother.'

'Aye.'

'And for you to be the one to find him like that...'

'Aye,' Miss Connelly and Allessandra are nodding in time with one another.

The older woman's eyes glaze with fatigue. A liver-spotted hand moves towards her face, and with her thumb and forefinger she pinches the corners of her eyes.

'He wasn't the most sociable kind of guy, you know? He liked to be left to himself. A read of the papers in the morning, the afternoon in the bookie's and a couple of pints in Harry's Bar in the evening. Every other day he went to the bowling club. For a wee change.' She sips at her cup, as if her mouth is too dry. 'That was his sorry existence, in just a few lines. Sad isn't it? Nothing that qualifies for the sort of attention he received.'

'He worked hard over the years didn't he?' Allessandra's voice is soft. Irene nods in agreement. Pleased to acknowledge something worthy of note in the man she called 'brother'.

'What was he? A caretaker? Janitor kind of guy?'

'Aye.' She softens in her chair.

'In children's homes?'

'What are you insinuating?' She is wound tight again. Eyes like pebbles. Why did she react so quickly to what was phrased like an innocuous question? Allessandra has struck a seam of oil. Time for me to get involved.

'Allessandra isn't insinuating anything. Merely asking a question. According to our research your brother moved about job-wise. We would like to know why.'

A shadow moves across her eyes. Her throat dilates as if holding back the words she really wants to use.

'What can I say? He was easily bored.'

'Or, he had an even more compelling reason to move on,' I ask.

Agnes, eyebrows raised in warning asks, 'Can I pour you more tea?'

'Sorry, eh, no thanks,' I wonder at Agnes' reaction, mentally review my question and realise the tone may have been a bit strong.

Just then, we hear the front door slam and the quick footsteps of children, before the lounge door is flung open and a family walks in. Two small boys dive towards the TV, while Mum and Dad notice the four of us in the room.

'Sorry, we...' the woman begins to speak.

'It's okay, love,' Agnes stands up and smiles. Then she turns to us. 'Why don't we all go through to the kitchen? There's plenty of room there.'

As we walk through, I hear Agnes ask the couple if she can get them anything.

They politely decline and apologise for interrupting. The boys have a more honest reaction to the mores of society and the music of a Disney movie follows us out into the hall.

The kitchen is huge. A black range hugs the far wall and a long, wooden table takes pride of place in the middle of the floor. I would take bets that a lot of family crises have been sorted across the scrubbed varnish of that table.

I walk over to the shelf at shoulder-height above the range. A pipe I'm sure I've seen before rests on it. I pick it up.

'That's Patrick's,' says Miss Connelly. 'Found that in my pocket when I arrived here. Don't know how it got there.' I remember the bedroom and her holding it in her hands. I run my fingers along its stem and feel the weight of the bowl at the end. This belonged to a man who has just suffered a horrible death. I looked at it resting in my hand as if it might provide some answers.

'He loved that pipe,' Miss Connelly whispers. 'It was like his best pal. Never answered back. Didn't let him down. All it needed was a wee bit of tobacco and the heat of a flame. Better than a marriage.' She reached up and wiped a tear off her cheek with the back of her hand as if it was a bug.

Chapter 8

The late autumn air has bite in it. Allessandra crosses her arms and holds her jacket against her chest, searching for some warmth. She and I lean against the bonnet of my car. I am still eating a bag of chips. Allessandra sent her scrunched up newspaper sailing into the big black bin provided by the local council for the chip-munchers who come from all around to eat deep-fried potato slices by the sea.

'I like a woman that enjoys her chuck. Can't be arsed with people going on diets all the time,' I say.

There is clearly nothing that Allessandra can think of as a retort, so she remains silent. I finish off my chips with a smack of my lips and move towards the bin. As I near it I pause and look at a white seagull feather at my feet. I shudder and kick it.

Allessandra looks at me with a quizzical expression.

'Seagulls.' I shudder again, searching for an explanation of my behaviour. Bird feathers have always bothered me and I've never been able to understand why. 'Horrible creatures. White rats with wings.'

We are facing a sea wall and a line of sand that stretches either side of us for what seems at least a mile in either direction. More than a few people are dotted about on its length, throwing sticks to a breeder's catalogue of dogs.

The sky is a cloudless palette of silver. The sea sliding lazily on to the beach. The Isle of Arran lines the horizon looking close enough to reach with a bracing swim.

'This is the life, eh, boss?' It had been Allessandra's idea to get a bag of chips and eat them by the sea. Can't come down to Ayr and not eat chips by the sea, was her argument.

'Aye, some poor bastard gets cut up and we get a wee trip down to the seaside.'

'Sorry sir, I'm just...'

'Just trying to remind me that life is not all corpses and grieving relatives.' I throw the car keys to Allessandra. 'You drive, will you? I've got some thinking to do.'

As Allessandra aims the car in the direction of Glasgow and as the miles flick past I replay the interview over and over in my head. Hadn't Allessandra done well? Asked some strong questions. Listened to the answers carefully. Not bad for a newbie. One thing was clear however, the meeting was effectively over as soon as they entered that kitchen. Whatever momentum they had built up was dissipated by the physical act of changing rooms.

Irene Connelly refused to say any more. Too tired, she said. I slipped a business card towards her across the table and asked her to call anytime, day or night.

'The old dear was close to cracking.' Now they were outside the urban sprawl of Glasgow, Allessandra obviously felt it was safe enough to begin a conversation again.

'Mmm.'

'She was hiding something. Something important.'

'I'll have to go back down and see Cousin Agnes some time.' I think out loud.

'You think she'll talk?'

'Did you see the way she kept looking at Irene? Like she was urging her to.'

Allessandra nodded in agreement.

A mobile sets off. Farmyard noises. I shrug and smile in a *what can you do* kind of way before speaking.

'DI McBain here.'

'It's Agnes from the Seaview here, Inspector.'

'Hello, Agnes.' I look over at Allessandra and raise my eyebrows. 'What can I do for you?'

At the next morning's briefing I tell the team everything that Agnes Cowan told me on the phone. The table in front of me is groaning with cakes again.

'Who's bloody birthday is it now?' I mumble through a mouthful of sugar-coated doughnut. The diet *definitely* starts tomorrow.

'Bloody mine, sir,' grins Dave Harkness.

'You guys please stop buying cakes. I've got a date with a heart surgeon if I don't stop eating them.' I take another huge bite for comedic effect. This earns some pale laughter.

'Right, Allessandra. Recap for those who couldn't hear me for the flies buzzing around in the cavity of their skull.'

'The deceased, sir, was a paedophile with a long career behind him. He worked at a variety of orphanages, most of them run by the Catholic Church. He worked as a handyman, janitor guy. Never stayed at any one home for more than five years. Was found out several times, but with the Church's past Ostrich Syndrome when dealing with abuse cases, he was given no more than a slap on the wrist and a reference for his next job. Where more little girls were subjected to his particular brand of caring.'

When Allessandra stops speaking, the room is silent for once. Most of the guys here have children of their own and by the looks on their faces, they are thinking about what they would do with a sick man like Connelly. Call me stupid, but I would guess sympathy for the deceased is no longer on the agenda.

'So what light does that shed on the crime?'

'Gives us motive, sir.'

'You bet your life it does. Some equally sick bastard got his revenge. More legwork, guys, to find out whom. I've written the names of the homes where Connelly worked on the board.' I nod at Allessandra, 'Pair off and go through them. Get dates for when he worked there and lists of the kids staying there at the time who might have been abused by him. Was it just the girls? Or did he go for the boys as well?'

'All of the homes, sir?' asks Jim Peters, with a sullen look on his face.

'All of them.'

'But the murderer's MO suggests a religious nutter, sir. Shouldn't we concentrate solely on the Catholic homes?'

'No. I want them all checked out.'

'But with all due respect,' the tone of his voice suggests that respect is the last thing on his mind, 'we could be talking about hundreds of children here. This is a highly stylised crime with strong religious overtones. It's got Catholicism written all over it.'

'We are investigating a murder, DS Peters. That means we are single-minded. We have a single-mindedness matched only by a jealous lover. We look at every possibility. Every possibility.' I pause and look round the room making sure every pair of eyes is on me. This case is becoming important to me. I can't begin to explain why, but I need to transmit that sense of urgency to everyone in the room. 'We've got to know everything. Details that Connelly himself would have forgotten will provide the key to this case. We want to know what he ate, what he wore, what he read. What he thought. Details, guys. Details.'

Work is doled out for the day. I tell Allessandra Rossi she's with me. I'm going to one of the first orphanages on the list. The trail will be colder here, but I believe in rolling my sleeves up along with the guys. I don't ask them to do anything I wouldn't. Besides, I have another reason.

'So what's this home called again, sir?'

'Bethlehem House,' I answer. 'It's a convent. Between Glasgow and Kilmarnock.' What I don't tell her, but may become apparent, is that I spent my formative years there. I'm about to exorcise a few ghosts and I can't say I'm looking forward to it.

Chapter 9

The building is just as I remember. An impassive row of windows stretches from one side to the other. There are four rows altogether, held together by red sandstone and a grey slate roof. The convent doubled as an orphanage and an old folks' home: the first floor was for the old people, the second floor was for the children, and apart from the chapel on the third floor I never got to find out what was on the other two floors.

The drive up to the main entrance circles round a statue of Christ, before stopping below a flight of stairs. Thirteen of them. I counted them as a child. Thirteen to represent Jesus and his twelve disciples, Sister Anna's voice whispers through the years. She was the nice nun. Everyone liked her. We were always happy when Sister Mary was sick and Sister Anna had to look after us.

To the right of the building, a path is lined with trees. This was the path we walked every Sunday morning, in pairs, like a line of ducklings, to church. It was on that path, on the way to Sunday Mass, that Margaret Sheridan told me about sex, our hot little heads pressed close together so that no-one would hear what we were saying. If they had heard us we would have earned a fist on the side of the head. Margaret told me that the boy put his thing in the girl's thing and wiggled it about and then a baby was born. I can still hear my indignant reply.

'You're soft in the head. You made that up.' She swore it was true. I was having none of it and didn't talk to her all the rest of the way to Mass.

'What's the joke, sir?' asks Allessandra. She's looking at me with a quizzical expression.

'Oh, nothing, Allessandra.' I smile. 'A goose just walked over my grave.'

'Looks like it gave you a wee tickle while it was at it, sir.' Allessandra looks around her.

'Some place. You sure we should park here? Looks like nobody uses this drive.'

She is right. The red chips on the drive look as if they've not moved in thirty years. That's because the correct entrance is around the back. I am being indulgent. I always wanted to come in this way when I was a boy, but that was never allowed. Only visiting dignitaries were allowed in this way. Minimum qualification: Bishop.

I sit in the car while Allessandra gets out. I take a deep breath. It's been a long time. While I was here it felt like a lifetime. Ten years. I lock up murderers for less now. All I did was have a father on the juice and a mother in the loony bin.

I try to remember what the boy looked like all those years ago. But I fail. It's like trying to eat soup with a fork. I have no photographs of that stage of my life. Just a bunch of fractured memories. I was a skinny boy with white-blond hair and scarred knees.

The nuns dressed the boys in short trousers. I fell a lot. Consequently, picking scabs off my knees became a hobby. I got it down to a fine art. Pick it off too soon and it would only bleed again, but choose the right moment, just when it began to itch and you would find brand-new perfect, pink skin underneath. I grew my thumbnail especially. I would hook it under one edge and peel with care. Then pocket the scab.

I try to remember Connelly. Was he here at the same time that I was? There was a handyman/gardener type of character, but I can't remember anything about him other than a vague male shape hunched over a flower bed.

Allessandra is looking at me strangely again, like I've sprouted horns and a tail. We climb up the stairs and crunch across the gravel moat that surrounds the building. More stairs and we enter the recess that feeds the main door. I can barely bring myself to press the buzzer. What if someone recognises me? Perhaps I want them to. Look at me, Sister Mary, haven't I done well? The boy you said would amount to nothing. I wasn't the only recipient of that fine piece of character building. It was one of her mantras. She had all manner of insults. Her stubby fingers warmed them up as she fingered her rosary beads.

Mind you, she must be dead by now. She was ancient then.

The door is answered quickly. A middle-aged face shrouded in the familiar uniform looks at us.

'Yes? Can I help?' Her face has the colour and texture of putty. I wonder if I push my finger into her cheek, would it leave an indent?

'DI McBain. This is DC Rossi. I believe you are expecting us, Sister.' The honorific escapes before I realise it. Bloody hell, don't habits die hard. I haven't spoke to a nun for more than twenty years and out it slips, like phlegm from a consumptive lung.

'Ah, yes. You're here to ask about an old groundsman, Patrick Connelly. I'm Sister Margaret. Follow me.' Her smile is large with welcome and her soft Irish tones caress my ears. She opens the door wide and beckons us in. She leads us to a small room to the right of the door. I was in here once. I remember the location of the room, because it was so unusual that one of the kids would be allowed in. But I had an audience with the Bishop, I remember bragging. I wanted to become a priest and the Bishop came to see me. And tried to talk me out of it. 'To leave one religious institution,' he said — his face fascinated me, it seemed twice the size of mine — 'and join another, without seeing a little more of life on the outside, would be unwise.'

Excellent advice. Except I didn't want to hear it. I wanted to escape. But I had nowhere else to go. My father hadn't dried up, my mother hadn't dealt with her problems.

Neither of them ever would.

A table and four hard chairs sit in the middle of the small floor. The walls are bare apart from a crucifix and a picture of Our Lady. We sit down. I try to centre myself and ignore the memories that crowd for recognition. You're here to do a job, McBain. Remember that.

'As I'm sure you'll have heard. Mr Connelly is... no longer with us.'

'Yes, I heard,' Sister Margaret says, her hand hovering over her heart. 'It shocked us all.'

'Were you resident at this home while Mr Connelly was working here?' I ask.

'No, I was in our Aberdeen home at that point. Just a novice.' She smiles. 'Were you?'

I hear a barely suppressed gasp from Allessandra. My pulse booms in my ear. 'I can't remember, Sister. I think he was before my time.' Somebody must have remembered my name.

'When were you here?' She's all smiles. 'Sure, it's great to see one of our old boys has done so well for himself. You a big policeman and all.'

47

'Thank you, Sister.' I feel my face heat. 'Can we get back to Mr Connelly? Is there anyone still here that can remember him?'

'Of course there is.' Her expression is kindly, almost apologetic for triggering my blush. 'It caused an awful shock around the building when we saw the news on the telly. Holy Mary mother of Jesus, what's the world coming to when an old man gets murdered in his own home?'

'Are any of the Sisters available to speak to us?'

'Certainly. Mother will be with you in a moment. She remembers him.' She laughs, 'And she's wanting to speak to you. Soon as she heard your name she was all a twitter. "Why, that's one of mine," she said.'

'But Mother Superior must be at least a hundred.' If the nuns appeared elderly to us children, Mother Superior looked as if she was old when Jesus was a boy.

'No, silly.' More laughter. 'We have a new Mother Superior... well, must be a couple since you were here. You'll remember her better as Sister Mary.'

Fuck. 'Ah. Sister Mary,' I try to smile, but succeed only in baring my teeth. 'I remember her.'

'Not easy to forget.' Sister Margaret whispers out of the side of her mouth. 'Sure you're all grown up now.' Her voice is louder now, '...and none the worse for wear.' So the nuns must have known what she was like. If that's the case, how in God's name did she get to become Mother Superior?

Just then the door is pushed open and the object of our conversation brushes in.

'Ray McBain. Stand up and let me look at you,' she booms and manages to dismiss Sister Margaret at the same time. I do as I am told. Too quickly. But note with some satisfaction that I tower over her.

'Jesus, Mary and Joseph, would you look at you? My, you've turned into a handsome man. A bit on the beefy side, mind,' she approximates a smile. 'And you're a big policeman, we hear. I always said you'd amount to something, Ray me lad.'

'I wanted to ask you...' It takes me a moment to remember the Ray McBain I'd become. The boy is cramming my psyche. I feel myself begin to shrink. An old fear of this woman saps at my confidence. It's like I never left the place. I cough, 'I wanted to ask you about Mr Connelly.' I review her face as I wait for her reply. It has barely changed. A few more lines, but it's essentially

48

the same face that controlled a generation of children. And the voice has lost none of its power.

'Ah, poor Paddy. Who on God's earth would want to do a thing like that?'

'That's why we're here.' The word "Mother" hovers on my tongue. I can't quite bring myself to use it.

'Surely, you're not thinking someone here's responsible?'

'Not exactly "here", but perhaps someone who was here while Mr Connelly was.'

'But why? He was a lovely man. You children loved him. He was always singing his songs around the place as he did his work. I can't imagine in a month of Sundays why anyone would take such an offence to the poor man.'

'So you would say he was well-loved?' I'm enjoying this now. She's lying through her tea-stained dentures. Trying to protect the Church, no doubt. 'Did you spend much time with the man yourself?' I ask, as if I'm at a wake and celebrating the life of an old friend.

'Not that much. He did all of the handyman stuff. But I worked with him in the garden now and again. A garden is such a gift from God, don't you think?' She aims this last comment at Allessandra, whom she has barely acknowledged until now. 'That was my way of relaxing after spending the day with you young scallywags.' That was an adjective she would rarely have used in her day. *Heathens, wastrels, demon spawn*, would have spun off her tongue like bullets from a Gatling gun.

'So, no-one would have had even as much as a run in with Mr Connelly?' I ask.

'Rare is the person who could claim that sort of record, Ray. But he did get on well with most of us most of the time.' She crossed her arms. I remember those arms, with the sleeves rolled up, washing me in a cold bath.

I shiver.

Then another memory of this woman asserts itself in my mind. The day I left here to go to the seminary. She held out a small brown, paper bag with a sandwich inside it. She fumbled with it, making sure it was closed.

'Here.' She all but shoved the bag into my hand. 'Can't have you going away hungry.' She turned, but not before I saw a solitary tear glide down her cheek.

I remember standing watching her walk away. Her small black shape receding into the distance of the corridor as I tried to assess what had just happened. The sandwich. The tear. Good grief, I remember thinking Sister Mary must have actually liked me. Someone had to prod me with their finger to remind me that the bus driver was waiting.

I cough.

'Mr Connelly was a convicted... paedophile.' I suddenly feel out of sorts. As if my memory isn't to be trusted. 'Two girls from this convent testified against him fifteen years ago. It was probably a huge media event at the time. Surely you couldn't have missed it?' I realise my tone is a bit too strong. I enjoy it, but need to calm down a little.

'We are closeted here from the world,' she sits as if her back was lined with the wall. '... we rely on good men like yourself to keep us all safe.' Her expression and her voice are polite, so why do I feel she's taking the piss?

'Mother Superior,' I don my professional mask as easily as a frog would swallow a python. 'I expect you want to catch this murderer as much as we do. We really need your help with our investigation. I apologise...' although it's costing me five years of my life. '... for my tone. There is an evil man out there and we need to find him in case anyone else is in danger.'

She sits down, her hand to her throat. I'd said the magic word... *Evil*.

'Do you think he'll come after anyone else?' Her face is as pale as bleached linen.

'We can't be sure, but from what we can guess of his motivation, we suspect this is a one-off. A revenge killing for some poor child's lost childhood.' My pulse is just getting back to normal.

'Frightful, just frightful. May the good Lord bless his soul.' She looks into my eyes, her own devoid of emotion. We stare at each other, neither wishing to speak first. I can hear a little boy scream, look away, look away, look away. He is sweating and his legs have lost all strength.

I steel myself against her gaze, determined I will not move my eyes away first. My mouth is dry. It's like looking into the eyes of a photograph. I'm getting nothing back.

'Do you have a list of children who were here around the same time as Patrick Connelly?' asks Allessandra.

'Of course we do, my dear.' Mother moves her eyes to her. Then straight back to me.

She smiles, letting me know she could have held my gaze for just as long as it took.

'Sister Margaret,' she booms. Sister Margaret walks into the room carrying a large ledger. She drops it on the table with relief.

'We thought you might like to look at this,' she says.

The book is large. About eighteen inches tall, twelve wide and ten deep. It is bound in black cracked leather and the front is gilded with a Celtic border. Someone has stuck a piece of lined paper on the front and written on it '1965 to 1975'. The pages are thick and rustle like a distant thunderclap as I open them.

A list of names appears before me. Children who spent their formative years here as I had done. What scars do they bear, I wonder? How many have been assimilated successfully into society? How many occupy our jails and mental homes?

I took my relative success in life for granted until a social worker helping me with a case found out I was brought up in an orphanage. Of the children who are reared in that environment, he informed me, seventy-five percent do not make a positive contribution to society. By that he meant they were junkies, thieves or worse. It shocked me. It's not usually cruelty that causes it, he told me. It's the absence of love.

'It will take a while to go through this, Mother. Can we take it away? Or do you have a photocopier?'

'I'm afraid the answer to your questions is, regrettably, no, Ray.' A small, triumphant smile. 'This is a document that is precious to the Order. We can't let it out of our possession, without a judge intervening.'

'That can be arranged.'

Mother slams the cover down. I manage to get my fingers out in time. 'In the meantime,' she warns, '... if that's the path you decide to take, the killer's trail will be colder than the good Lord's tomb.'

Lifting the cover up again, I reply, 'We'll just take some notes for now. If we need to produce anything at a trial... I assume a court order will be obeyed?'

'We follow a higher court, Ray, as you may have forgotten.' Her hackles are still at attention, 'But we will do what is necessary to help give this killer his earthly justice.'

She stands up. 'Sister Margaret will attend to you now. The good Lord saw fit to grant me a wonderful burden. But this place doesn't run itself.' She looks at Allessandra.

'Miss Rossi, you have my sympathy. He was a difficult child. From what I can see, little has changed.'

The small room seems huge now that she has left.

Allessandra pulls out a notepad, her face as unreadable as a blank piece of paper.

'Why don't you read them out, sir, and I'll write them down.' My thoughts are too busy for me to be concerned about what Allessandra is thinking right now. I'll worry about her later.

I thumb through the pages until I find the years in question. I don't want to be here doing this, where people can see me. I want to be in a quiet room, on my own.

Up until now, if I'd discussed my childhood with anyone, I would have expressed the view that I had adjusted well to my less than conventional past. The emotions that pull at the corners of my mouth and threaten to spill from my eyes take me completely by surprise. I hold my hands under the table, to hide their tremble and take a deep, slow breath. I exhale through pursed lips.

'Sir?'

'I'll... Give me a second... right, found the place.' I read the first name, my voice just audible. 'Carol Connor. Date of birth: seventh of October nineteen fifty-eight.' As I read, I'm surprised at how few names I can put a face to. Most of the names ring with faint familiarity, but few faces appear in my mind's eye.

Ah, there's one... and another. Who could forget the twins; John and Jim Leonard. Your archetypal, inseparable twins. The fact that they had no living relatives other than each other doubtless cemented the bond provided to them by nature. They were so alike the nuns put a sticking plaster on the back of their necks with their names inked on them. I prided myself on being one of the first to be able to name them on sight. There was no one thing I could pinpoint as the recognisable feature. I just knew which was which.

The children had a pecking order. You could always back up your stance, provided you were right, with the phrase, 'I've been here longer than you.' This was always sufficient to make the other child back down, regardless of the argument. John and Jim had no need of this. They had each other. Their combined weight was enough to do the job. That is, until John died.

Chapter 10

'Sir...' Allessandra is looking at me again. My gaze is fixed on the book, but I've stopped reading. I can only see the past.

'Right... where was I?' I pull myself into the present. You have a job to do, McBain. Then a name jumps out at me, before I put voice to the words. Shit. I was here at the same time as Connelly. This could complicate matters. I quickly read the next name on the list. Not quickly enough.

'That was your name there, was it not, sir?'

'There's no pulling the wool over your eyes, Allessandra, is there?' I say.

She examines her notebook.

'I don't think we need to concern ourselves with that, now do we? I'm hardly likely to be a suspect.' As a potential suspect, albeit one that could quickly be wiped from the list, I would be withdrawn from the case. There's no way that's happening. Even temporarily. I'm just moving to a position that I would be in eventually anyway. I'm just... circumventing the correct procedure. I carry on reading. A few other names snap open memories from my past. But none as memorably as the twins.

Of the two I knew John a little better. We were comrades in punishment for a couple of years. The crime: wetting our beds. The punishment: a cold bath.

Each morning at five-thirty, the sheets would be pulled back from our beds to examine their state. If they were dry, we would be left to go back to sleep for another half an hour before rising for morning Mass. If they were wet, we were marched by the earlobe into the bathroom. As the cold water rose in the bath, we were left to stand naked, while we contemplated the sin we had just committed. A sin that would see us in Hell. A sin we could still feel burning our groins and thighs.

Sister Mary kept a special treatment for either of us who managed to sin for more than three days in a row. She would wrap us in our urine-sodden bed sheet. We would only be allowed to bathe once the other children had attended Mass, eaten breakfast and were on their way to school. This had the added dimension of making us late for school.

Our shame didn't end there. Public humiliation was a strong weapon in Sister Mary's arsenal. At her earliest convenience the subject of bed-wetting would come up.

'What else can we expect from a boy who wets the bed?' She would address everyone in the vicinity. Then she would laugh, throwing her head back like a pantomime villain.

All those present would be expected to join in. Ears burning, staring at the floor, you could do nothing but wait until something or someone else attracted her attention.

Children are wonderful mimics. And in Sister Mary they had a wonderfully persistent teacher. As a result, taunting the bed-wetter became a ritual, like going to Mass or saying the Rosary. At least when other children began to taunt you out of earshot and sight of the nuns, a well-placed knee or elbow would quickly persuade your tormentor to choose someone else.

Fortunately for me, I outgrew my sinful bladder before John did his. His shame continued for some time. Until the morning he didn't turn up at school.

I passed his bed that last morning, just as Sister Mary left the room. On hearing a cough that made me think someone had sneaked a dog into the room I had one last chant at him before I went off to Mass.

'Hey, wet-the-bed,' I hoped that it was loud enough for the nun to hear, 'you're going to Hell.'

John was propped up on a pillow, wrapped in his foul-smelling sheets. His small frame shook with the force of his coughing as he tried to answer me back, his expression hot with anger. My face burned with shame when I gauged his reaction. I didn't like it when people did it to me. Why was it right to do it someone else?

'Shut... it.' he managed a syllable before another cough wracked his body, almost lifting him off the bed with its force. 'Tell Jim... I'll be... down... later.' Leaning forward I looked at his face. Coughs and colds were a normal occurrence in the Home, but I'd never seen such a white face before.

When I turned to leave Jim was right behind me. So close behind me that I walked into him as I turned. His expression was one of naked hate. At the time I remembered wondering who he was angry at. Me or John? It must have been me. Why would he hate his brother? Jim's eyes burned through me as I moved away from the bed and towards the door. I stuck my tongue out at him and walked from the room, knowing as I walked that it was important that I didn't show any fear. But not knowing why.

We were never told how John died, although the play-field at the back of the convent was buzzing with guesses. As one of the last people to see him alive I was granted some status in the debate. The cough I heard was altered till it resembled a wolf howling at the moon. The colour of his face I described as a plate of ice cream, minus the jelly.

We were simply told that he had been taken to hospital. A week later we were told he was dead. His brother Jim withdrew from life at the Convent.

Always the quieter of the two, he became as insubstantial as a shadow and was often seen talking to the empty space to his side. The nuns couldn't tolerate this behaviour for long and he too disappeared. We were told that Jim wasn't well and that he had been taken to a place where he could be looked after properly. In no time at all he would be better and would rejoin us. We never saw him again.

'Thank you, Sister.' I stand up and leave. We have taken down all the names of the children who stayed here while Connelly was sowing his evil oats. With one notable exception. I would have to have a word with Allessandra, make sure she understood.

'If we can be any more help,' Sister Margaret has one hand on the door, preparing to close it. 'Please come back and see us.'

'We will, Sister. Thank you,' says Allessandra.

At the car, I throw her my keys. I need to think. Theresa would describe it as brooding.

'You drive.'

We circle the statue of Jesus and, at the gates, as we prepare to join the stream of traffic on the main road, I look over my shoulder. Christ is standing on his plinth, wearing a smile, his arms spread wide to embrace the world, his terrible wounds on display.

We're having a briefing in the incident room the same day. My mind has its ball bearings back in its runners. Just as well, or Rossi would be reporting me to the boss and I would be withdrawn from the case. I look around the room. Just about every face is sporting a five o'clock shadow, wearing it like an announcement of a hard day out of the office. Ties and top buttons are loose. Uniform posture of the hour is The Slouch.

'Right, people. What've we got?'

'We got something interesting, Ray,' Peters sits up. Keen to speak. 'Let's just say, the Papes don't have a monopoly on being fucked up.'

A few catcalls from the Catholics around the room at Peters' use of the derogatory term.

'Of the kids who were there at that time... we have two or three who've been done for burglary... stealing to feed their habit... another two or three been up for Serious Assault...'

'Is it two *or* three, Peters?'

'Eh...' he looks at his notes. I see his neck stain red. '... two, Ray.'

'So stop fucking exaggerating.' To hide my abrupt manner, I add, '... I've told you nine hundred and ninety-nine times.'

Under my smiling response to the laughter, I question my irritation. What was that all about?

'There's more.' The flush on Peters' face reduces. He thinks he's got something here. 'An old worker at the place was there at the same time as Connelly, remembers the cases against him. Says there was a younger brother of a rape victim. Threatened to kill Connelly when he grew up.' There's a career ambition, I thought. What do you want to be when you grow up, son? I want to kill the fucker who raped my sister. And so it feeds on itself. Revenge spoils the innocent. Makes them no better than the person responsible. The victim becomes a perpetrator.

'Have we located the victim or her brother?'

'Yes.' Peters can barely contain his excitement. 'The brother's been in and out of jail for violent crimes. His sister killed herself just after the trial.' The last comment a tragic footnote that's tacked on at the end without a thought. Mind you it's best not to think. Too much.

'What kind of violent crimes?'

'Mostly slashings. One with a pickaxe. Gang stuff.'

'Was he in or out of the nick at the time of the murder?'

'Out.'

'Have you located this paragon of aggression then?'

'Yeah. Lives here in Glasgow. We'll bring him in, in the morning.'

'Good.' That's as much as I can offer by way of apology for my terse manner. 'Anything else?' I address the room.

'Just a list of names as yet, Ray.' answers Gary Wilson. His eyes are just about aligned with his nostrils, he's that tired. He was up at Aberdeen first thing this morning. No wonder he's knackered, driving all that way and back in the one day.

'What about you and Allessandra, Ray?' asks Harkness. 'How did you guys get on?' I look at Allessandra and nod for her to speak. We'd gone for a bite to eat before we got here. Had a little talk.

From the road, the little restaurant looks okay. *The Trattoria*, the legend reads over the window. The closest it comes to Italy, however, is the plastic grapes going to dust on every available shelf and posters of Florence on every wall. Facing you as you come in is a framed print of The Last Supper. Only three tables are in use. Allessandra says later that we should have taken note of all that and ran out screaming, but I was a little distracted.

A quick look at the menu on the wall and we order our meal at the till. As we sit down, I take the opportunity to speak.

'So what did we learn today, Allessandra?'

She is facing me, rubbing at a stain on the table-cover with a napkin. Then she meets my eyes. I present a calm, but expectant demeanour. I am telling her I expect her cooperation and I will brook no arguments.

'Not much, as yet, sir. A few names to look into.'

'Anyone we know of?'

She shakes her head in response. Her eyes back on the stain.

'Was it that bad, sir?' Allessandra asks, then makes a face as if she regrets the words as soon as they spill from her mouth.

'It was a fucking picnic.' I pause on the edge of a threat and force some calm into my mind. I'm making life difficult enough for her. She doesn't deserve what I was about to say.

'Sorry,' I offer. 'Could've been worse.'

Allessandra's mouth opens as if she is about to speak. Then she thinks better of it. Her eyes narrow. Her mouth opens again.

'With all due respect, sir,' she begins, her face red and her hands under the table. 'We'll play it your way for now. But if this knowledge compromises the case, I'm going straight to the Super.'

'Allessandra. Do you really think I'm a suspect?' My arms are wide, my expression full of apology.

'No.'

'No harm done then. Eh?' Our food arrives. Fish and chips for Allessandra and a ham and pineapple salad for me. Allessandra looks at my plate with a grimace.

'Starving yourself then?'

It is an insult to call what is on my plate a salad. Two baby tomatoes, a large lettuce leaf, browning around the edges like a warning of autumn, a strip of celery and four slices of ham so thin you can see the plate's pattern through them.

'Waiter,' I say and look around. Other diners study their plates.

'Ray, you have mine.' Allessandra pushes her plate towards me.

'No thanks, Allessandra. Waiter.' Even louder. The kitchen door opens and a young man walks towards us. A resigned expression on his face. He stands at the table, holding his hands in front of his swollen belly.

'Is there something wrong?' His face is a curious mix of masculine and feminine. Cropped hair, finely arched eyebrows, long lashes, a nose that looks as if it has taken a punch or two and lips straining not to explode. His voice is also ambiguous. The sound is deep bass, but the rise in tone at the end of the question purely female. I wonder if he is a transvestite out of hours. It must take dedication to get eyebrows as neatly curved as that.

'What the hell do you call this?' I ask.

'It's a ham and pineapple salad. Just as you ordered.' The waiter's expression doesn't register the use of language or the aggressive tone. I could be commenting on the state of the traffic for all the reaction he allows.

'Where's the pineapple, then?'

'It's heavily disguised. As a stick of celery.' A half-smile. He is so outrageous, I can't help but laugh, the raw edge of my anger burned off by the waiter's complete lack of response.

He nods at the kitchen and lowers his voice. 'The chef's on the sick. Chronic depression. We got a wee lassie in off the brew. *Chef sans papiers*, you might say. Doesn't know her tits fae her elbows. Still, we've kept her off the streets for a few hours.' He smiles, showing a set of fabulously white teeth. 'Can we tempt you with something else? *Amuse bouche*? *Coq au vin*? *Steak au poivre*? Egg and chips?'

'What the hell. I've had a long day. I deserve it.' I join in with his attempt at levity and shrug at Allessandra in a *sometimes it's better to just laugh it off* kind of way. 'Egg and chips.'

'How would Sir like his eggs?' he bows.

'Medium-rare. Hold the sauce.' A McBain smile.

The waiter retreats. We sit in silence, both lost in our own thoughts until...

'Ray?'

'What?'

'What do you make of Peters?' She pushes a couple of chips around on her plate, hitting them against some peas.

'Em... all right, if you like that sort of thing. How do you mean?'

'Well. As a policeman. I mean. I don't fancy him or anything. Just, you know... I want to be a good cop, Ray. And sometimes the best way to learn is to copy someone who's been there.' She stops playing with the cutlery, her eyes fixed on mine.

'As a policeman...' I speak slowly, carefully considering my response. 'He's an OK cop. Does an OK job.'

The waiter appears and slides a plate before me.

'*Plat du Jour*.' Grin.

More silence.

'You sleeping ok, boss?' Allessandra asks and again looks as if she regrets issuing the words.

'What makes you ask that?' I ask, surprised.

'You just look a wee bit tired, that's all.'

'It's nothing to worry about,' I answer through a mouthful of food. 'Just a few sleepless nights. Nothing some greasy food can't cure.' Even I can feel my smile is too large and completely without humour.

'Boss?'

'What?'

'I've just had a thought.'

'Yes?'

'The murder happened the night we were all at the pub together. So you couldn't be a suspect anyway.'

'Correct.' My smile is real this time.

Chapter 11

He doesn't know what the feeling is; only that he doesn't like it. He compares it to walking around with a space beside him, a tear in the fabric of the energy field we are all part of. In any case, recognising it for what it is may well be beyond him. That would require some emotion, an ability to tap into the experience the rest of humankind shares. He recognises that it needs to be filled, but how? There are few things that satisfy him. He watches others watching children and is amazed at the energy they receive from what are simply human beings with smaller legs. So why are other men and woman so easily affected by them? They smile and laugh and cry while watching their behaviour, while he looks on with numb curiosity. Perhaps if he were to have one of his own, it might fill the space, he might learn the emotional reaction that brings the physical reaction of a smile?

Could he learn it? Might it be the saving of him? He is undoubtedly intelligent, but it is an intelligence bereft of the experience of warmth. It functions best in the dark and looks for darkness to keep it company. Occasionally he touches it with his mind, sends out the probe of a thought, pushes against the membrane and then recoils as if burned. Heat and black nothingness is the only way he can describe it.

He managed to touch it and enjoy the burn, the day he killed the old man. Then the heat welcomed him, sent energy coursing through him. The heat he now knows, from watching others, is emotion. Emotion is feeling.

But the feeling is fading. He needs to get it back. He needs to chase away the darkness with more dark. With another death.

Soon.

Not yet, but soon.

Then he might enjoy again the heat of a smile.

I'm sitting up in bed in complete darkness, the quilt tangled around my feet. Every cell in my body is sparking with adrenalin. What the fuck was that? I've been dreaming again. Someone was walking towards me. Streetlights were shining off the puddles, but they weren't strong enough to highlight his face. All I could see were two pale stripes on his jumper. His movements were quick and assured. Feral. I was his target. Frozen words formed a lump in my throat. I wanted to shout a warning at this man. Fuck off. You don't know who you are messing with. I needed a weapon.

I needed to move. Sheer terror held me tighter than rigor mortis. As he passed, his face turned to me. His features were encased in shadow, but I could sense his smile.

Then it began to snow. White flakes floating down to coat the earth in a chilled cushion. Except they weren't cold. They didn't melt when they landed on my skin. I looked up into the sky and watched them fall. Something tickled my nose. This wasn't snow. It was feathers. Small and white and unmistakeably feathers. They are falling, falling, falling. I looked at my feet and kick through the mound of feathers I see there. Something catches. It's a man. He's old. His eyes are accusing. Staring in death at his killer.

Me.

I forced my eyes away from his silent accusation. Guilt and shame pulled me to my knees. What had I done? I screamed at the sky. My mouth filled with feathers. One caught in my throat. I choked. Coughed. Need to breathe. Need to breathe. Need to...

I wake up. Chest heaving. Christ that was vivid. The old man. His eyes. The guilt. I could feel each feather in my mouth. They were clogging my airwaves. I was choking. It went on and on. I couldn't move my jaws to spit out the feathers. I couldn't breathe.

The alarm clock burns green into the dark. Five-thirty. God, that was scary. I am still breathless and my skin prickles with an adrenalin after-burn. I need to get up and shake off the dream. I throw my legs to the side of the bed and stand up and almost fall back on to it. My legs are drained of energy. The dream must've taken a lot more out of me than I thought.

At the kitchen table, a mug of coffee in my hands, my arms are resting on the table. My hands are shaking too much to allow me to hold it without spilling the stuff over my arms. McBain, what the fuck is going on?

On the way into work, an hour early, with an empty stomach and frazzled with caffeine, I review the dream again. The details remain clear, particularly those dead eyes and the choking sensation of the feathers.

There was blood. Christ, I've just remembered, there was lots of blood. Feathers were in red and white clumps at his wrists. His ribs. I could see his ribs through an open wound.

I want to gag.

And hide in the dark soothing of an empty confessional box.

I've never been convinced about the importance of dreams. Symbols and portents my arse. The subconscious just likes to play tricks on us. But I've never had a dream so vivid. I've been in a lot of dangerous situations and I've never felt terror like that in my life. My limbs were solid with fear, my hair was on end and my heart... it still hasn't slowed down. Need to get a grip, McBain. There's work to do. A real killer to catch.

In the office, Peters has been busy. The brother of a victim we discussed yesterday has been brought in for questioning and Peters finds it difficult to hide his disappointment that I'm here.

'You want to sit in, Ray?' he asks. His expression reads he'd rather I go and lie in front of a combine harvester.

'That would be nice,' I exaggerate a smile. 'Give me some detail on the guy.'

'Paul Crichton. Age 25. Unemployed. Lives with his girlfriend. She's pregnant with their second child. The first one is ten months old.'

Peters' words set up a picture that is fulfilled when I see the man in question.

He in turn eyes me up and down as I enter the room. Something flits across his eyes. Could it have been recognition? He looks vaguely familiar to me. Wonder if I've arrested him before.

'So it's the heavy mob, is it?' He looks at my gut and smirks. What a piece of work, only twenty-five and looking like he belongs in this room. Occupational hazard, don't you know. His head has a ten o'clock shadow, obviously needs another shave. His body is medium height and thin like a railway sleeper, his cheeks are hollow and his eyes haunt his face. Pockmarks on his cheeks tell of teenage years ruined with explosive acne. Surprisingly, he is expensively and fashionably dressed, *a la* Matrix, complete with long black leather coat. A packet of cigarettes lies unopened on the Formica tabletop. In deference to the public smoking policy? I would think not. Looks like the kind who wouldn't give two fucks about someone else's discomfort. Besides, if we want information from someone, this is one regulation we are happy to play with.

'I want a lawyer.'

'Why? Something to hide, Paul?' asks Peters.

'I'm saying nothing without a lawyer.'

Peters sits on a chair facing Crichton. 'Been watching *The Bill*, big man?'

I sit beside Peters and decide I'll let him do most of the talking.

'Don't patronise me, you prick. I know my rights.' Obviously, he's happy to help us with our enquiries. This will be interesting. I peel the clear plastic film off the tapes and insert one in the recorder's drawer.

'Don't worry, Paul. You can see a lawyer. You are entitled to free and independent legal advice.' Now that the tape is running Peters issues the caution quickly, anxious to get to the interesting bit.

'You are not under arrest. You are free to leave, Paul. We just want to ask you some questions.'

'Is that right? I'm free to leave?' He speaks the last sentence in a high camp voice, as if he is mimicking Peters. Trying to piss him off.

'What do you know about Patrick Connelly?' Peters is unmoved.

Crichton leans back on his chair and folds his arms, 'He's dead. Seen it in the papers. Can't say I'm chief mourner. Know what I mean?'

'Did you want him dead?'

'Every fucking day of my life, mate.' He sits forward, his eyes bright. 'He was worse than scum.' He picks up the cigarettes, unwraps them and pulls one out. He waves the cigarette at both of us in turn, his way of asking for a light. 'Is that what this is all about? You think I did it?' Pleasure dances the length of his smile. 'Believe me, I would love to have done it. But hey, you know how it is with your goals,' he shrugs, 'life gets in the way sometimes.' He sticks his cigarette in the flame of a match held out by Peters and breathes in deep. Deep with hunger. He closes his eyes and takes the nicotine hit. 'Fuckin' magic.' He regards us both, his gaze frank and fearless.

'Didnae do it, guys. Wish I did. But ah didnae.' He leans back in his seat as if he's in his favourite pub. Usually I can ignore this, but today, for some reason it really pisses me off. Keep a lid on it, McBain, this is Peters' interview. I take a deep breath, force my shoulders down and sit back in my chair.

'Where were you on the night of September 23rd?'asks Peters.

'Damn, would you look at that?' He sits up and pats down his pockets. 'I've left my diary in the house.'

'Keep your cheap sarcasm for your mates, son. Just answer the question.'

'I was in the house,' he fidgets with the cigarette packet, like something just occurred to him, 'with the wife and wean.'

'How long you been married?'

'A few months.' He takes a deep drag, his eyes squinted against the smoke. Or was it something else?

'Did you guys have a long engagement?'

'What the fuck is this? An interview for daytime TV? Am I going to be on *Jeremy Kyle* or something? We shagged, she got pregnant. I wanted to do the right thing by her. Didn't want a wean of mine being brought up a bastard.'

'Was your wife grateful?'

'What the fu...'

'I'd bet most of the lassies on the scheme, when they got caught, would be left on their own. They'd be left to carry the baby.'

'Well, I said,' he preens a little, '...that I would stand by her.'

'So she's grateful?'

'Leave my wife out of this.'

'Grateful enough to lie for you?'

'You calling my wife a liar?'

'You religious, Paul?' I ask. Time to change the pattern of the interview. Keep him on the hop.

He snorts. 'No thanks. The opiate of the masses? I prefer my drugs to be more... literal. If you get my drift.'

He's got a brain then, I think. 'You don't believe in Jesus?'

'Listen mate, I was brought up in a home where he was used as a role-model, 'cept them that taught it, forgot it. Do as I say, and all that shite. Most o' they bastards wouldn't know a Christian thought if it came up and fucked them.'

Inwardly, I nod. This is a sentiment I share.

'Nice clothes, Paul.' I say. Time for another change of direction.

Smiling, he looks down at himself and gives each lapel of leather a quick tug. 'Not too shabby, eh? Got this down the market.'

'You do know that reset is a crime, don't you?' I don't give him enough time to answer. 'That means buying stolen goods. You've been in trouble before, haven't you, Paul? It wouldn't do to get another crime on your sheet, would it?'

'Piss off and prove it, tosser.' He crosses his arms.

'Previous. You've got previous. Got a bit angry, didn't you, Paul?'

'Aye. So? Bastards deserved...'

'Quite a brutal crime, eh?'

'Like I said the...'

'A lot of hate bottled up there, Paul?'

'Ah didn't dae Connelly.' He unbuttons his leather jacket.

'A lot of anger. Mr Connelly died violently, Paul. He died screaming. Did you enjoy it?'

'What is this?' He sat upright. 'Fucking bad cop, bad cop?' His eyes. There's something about his eyes. Where have I seen him before? Then he stands up. 'I've seen the papers. I know what you guys do. Can't find the killer, so you'll stitch somebody else up. You said I was free to go. I'm leaving.'

As he turns towards the door, his jacket swings open, revealing a sweatshirt with two white stripes across the middle.

'No you're not.' I stand up. I'm aware of Peters' questioning stare — *whose interview is this* — but there's something about this guy.

'Going to stop me, big man?' He throws his shoulders back and chest forward in the classic pose of the ned. 'I know my rights.'

I lean over to the tape recorder and switch it off. 'You know fuck all, pal.' I want to punch his smug smile through to the other side of his head. I want to jump on his head until it is pulp. I am so fucking angry and I don't know why.

'Ray,' Peters warns.

'Come ahead.' says Crichton.

'Sit.' I bark. He obeys me, with a look that says, *for now, asshole.* I sit down and stare him out.

As I look into his eyes the world shifts. I'm back in the dream. This time the fear won't beat me. This time I will act. The room is suddenly colder and darker.

I can see the outline of a cross in shadow on the far wall. I hear the discordant note of chair legs, as they are forced across the tiled floor. Crichton and Peters are staring at me from their seats, so it's me who stood up. I'm having difficulty reading

65

their expressions. It's like I'm looking at them through a gauze curtain.

'*Not yet, but soon.*'

'What did you say?'

Crichton stubs out a cigarette. Is that a smile?

'*I know where you live.*' Who said that?

My hands are round Crichton's neck and my breath is scouring his face. 'Nobody threatens a police officer,' I hear my voice from the far end of a tunnel. There's fear and anger in it and an absence of light.

Peters is trying to pull me off. If he doesn't stop, he'll be next.

The dream. But it's not a dream. It's much more: the sense of danger, the fear that had me gagging on the words I was trying to speak. My hands are shaking, their grip tightening. What the fuck is going on? All I know is that I need to get out of this room. Pronto.

Somebody is tugging at my sleeve, Crichton's face is purple as he struggles for air. I can see the pink of the roof of his mouth and a row of black fillings. This strikes me as a strange observation to make when I'm so deep into my fury.

But then, why am I so angry?

'Ray.' A voice penetrates into my brain.

'Wha...' Hands pull mine away from Crichton's neck. I slump to my seat. What the hell is happening to me?

Crichton's shoulders are moving up and down as he works air back into his lungs. 'You... are... a psycho... mate. You should be locked up.' His face is turning a healthier colour. 'I'm going to sue your arse for every last penny, you sick fuck.'

'Shut up, Crichton, before I really hurt you.' I smile. 'Besides, nothing happened, did it?' I face Peters. He's wearing an expression of outrage. In fact he's so angry, he can barely talk. Sanctimonious prick. He meets my gaze. Looks to the floor. I can almost see the thoughts tick across his head. If he grasses me up, he knows I can make life miserable for him. Besides, no matter how right they are, whistleblowers are never really trusted again by their fellow officers. But I must have looked really fucked up there for a minute. What was that all about?

'Nothing happened. Did it, DS Peters?' I ask with a calm I don't feel and don a mask of normality. I'm aware of the picture I now present to Peters; the professional, competent, and superior police-man is back in situ. I changed so quickly, the raving lunatic has been consigned to some false memory.

'Aye.' He looks at the tape recorder, which missed all of this. 'Aye.' He is trying to convince himself. 'Nothing happened.'

Peters calls a halt to the interview and I leave the room like my shirt's on fire. On the way to the toilet I ignore a couple of greetings. Once inside I feel a huge surge of gratitude that it is empty and lock myself in a cubicle. I sit on the seat with my elbows on my thighs and look at my shaking hands.

I sit up, straighten my back and try to force my shoulders to relax. A few slow deep breaths and I don't feel any better. With the cold porcelain of the toilet's water tank against my back I try to force some semblance of calm into my mind.

It's at times like these that my meditation practice should come in useful, but the fear is visceral and it feels like my life is in danger. The bogeyman of my childhood has come to life and he is stalking me.

It's just a dream, I tell myself. A dream. Nothing more. You've had dreams before, Ray. Feathers have featured. But I can't remember much in the way of blood, or dead bodies. Christ. The look on that man's face. He was staring right at me with a word imprinted on his stare: murderer.

'It's only a dream, you daftie. Get back to work.'

Once back at my desk I lose myself in the minutiae of a detective's day. I really should speak to Peters about Crichton. Ask for his thoughts on the guy's culpability, but I think he needs some space before I talk to him again. Perhaps he can tell himself it was only a dream as well.

As soon as I have done a decent amount of hours I clear my desk and go home. It is only as I open my car door that I realise that no-one approached me all day for any guidance or with any information. Word must've gotten round that I had lost it.

Peters wouldn't waste much time in spreading the muck around.

Just as I park in front of my house, my mobile rings. I really must change the ringtone. Farmyard sounds seemed amusing six months ago.

'I'm bored, big guy.' It's Theresa.

'What do you want me to do about that?' I mean to be flirtatious but my tone sounds wrong even to my ears. More mad guy with pickaxe than smooth guy with hard-on.

'You crabbit?' She sounds hurt.

'Sorry, sweetheart. This case I'm working on...'

'No wonder you're still single, McBain. Who would put up with your shit? Between the job and your winning personality...'

'Who fuckin' phoned who?'

Silence. Then the phone dies. I wonder if I should call her back. Nah, can't be arsed. I mentally review the contents of my fridge and my cupboards. Nothing there that's making me salivate. The lights from the chip shop are winking at me. Deep-fried pizza. Now you're talking. Should really eat a light snack before going to the gym. But I'd rather pierce my scrotum with a fishhook. I mentally flip a double-headed coin. Heads it is. Chip shop here I come.

It's only later, when my dinner is nothing more than a straining belly and a faint scent of vinegar wafting from the kitchen bucket that I regret my tone with Theresa. The feeling I've had all day hasn't faded and I really could do with some company to take me out of myself. I suddenly seem to be surrounded with too much space. The telly is on, beaming utter crap into my living room. Some celebrity tosser is trying to be something he hasn't the training or the talent for and the camera is following his every move. But if I switch it off, there'll be just me... and the dream. And the pictures. And the thoughts.

A body lying in a pool of blood and feathers. I remember more. His wrists were slashed. But it's not Connelly. This guy's older. If I think harder I can hear voices. Screams. And the laughter of children.

Whoa. Enough. There's only one likely outcome to stepping further into that movie. Being driven mental.

I screw my eyes tight against the images. 'Go away. I'm not mad. I'm perfectly sane.' Perhaps a spot of meditation could clear my head.

Making myself comfortable, I prepare my body. I tell each part to sleep and within seconds my limbs are heavy as though encased in concrete. In the spot where my third eye resides I hang a crystal and enjoy the rays of light it sheds. And so I try to lose myself...

A memory squeezes past the spinning crystal.

Sister Mary towers over me. 'What are you doing, boy?'

Instantly, I recoil. I must be about five. Although I've only been in the orphanage a matter of weeks I am already sensitive to the anger that emanates from the lady in the strange clothes in front of me. I liken it to the statue of Our Lady with the beams of light exploding out from around her head, except with Sister Mary the colour is black.

'Nothing,' I whisper. Everything that had been going on in my life in the previous ten minutes has been wiped from my memory with the force of her anger. All I could think of was that my hands had been in my pockets. What was so wrong with that?

Sister stares at me, her eyes as black as her habit. Each word is clipped and edged in fury.

'What you have just done is evil of the purest kind. Just look at you. You're covered in sin, boy. ' I don't see her fist move. Next thing I know the side of my head is exploding with pain and I'm on all fours. 'If I ever see anything like that again, you will be sent before Mother Superior.'

The other side of my head attracted her fist.

'May God have mercy on your immortal soul.'

What have I done that is so evil? If the lady says I'm covered in sin, then there's no hope for me. The pain this induces is worse than that pulsing on each side of my head. That is already beginning to fade and I know it will show no scars.

I'm lying on my side on the bed. Nerves on the sides of my head throb with the memory. My cheeks are wet with tears. I'm pulling my knees up to my chest. Loud sobs fill the room. It's like I'm two people: the man in pain on the bed, each spasm causing him to raise his legs in towards his chest, and the other man, watching and wondering with detached calm. Was that really me all those years ago? Why did that memory surface now?

Chapter 12

After this morning's shower, I catch myself avoiding my naked reflection in the full-length mirror. What's that all about? I make myself go back and stand in front of it. Time for honesty. Look at that belly. And the tits. I cup one in each hand. If they weren't so hairy, this could be quite pleasing. I grin. Nah. Maybe not.

Still. Theresa likes it. I mentally shrug. That's got to be worth something.

I move my hands down to my belly and pinch about six inches either side. You're a heart attack in waiting, McBain. Time to get your act together. Somebody at work mentioned a soup diet the other day. I'll ask around and see if I can get a copy. Seems you can lose half a stone in a week.

I'm in a good mood, if I had any more dreams last night they have stayed in the dreamzone. I feel good. Rested and optimistic. I grab my belly and give it another forceful wobble. You are gone, fatboy. The diet is back on and under here is a six-pack in waiting.

'Whose fucking birthday is it now?' I'm at this morning's briefing and there's another box of cakes on the table, strawberry tarts. The jelly on them quivers with the promise of tongue-coating, tooth-decaying sweetness.

'The boss handed them in, sir. He didn't say anything, just flung them on the table,' answers Drain. 'Probably doesn't want us to know his age.'

'What do you reckon?' asks Gary Wilson. His right hand is pulling at his left ear, his arm almost hidden behind his head. Looks like a contortionist. 'Late fifties?'

'Is that sore?' asks Peters.

'What? This?' He lifts his arm up and waves his hand about. 'I dislocated my arm at school. Can nearly pull it out the socket.

Want to see?'

'For fuck's sake, Wilson. Are you going to get your dick out next?' I wonder if some men ever grow up. 'Right, listen up people. We need to talk about our suspects so far. What have we got?'

Peters describes the young man he and I spoke to the previous day. 'There's something about this guy. He has the motive. And a flimsy alibi.' He avoids my gaze. Obviously still unsure about what to do. The fact that I am standing in front of him at the moment, I take as a good sign. Means he has kept his own counsel for the moment. And if Crichton had complained, things would also be vastly different.

'Why flimsy?' I ask suddenly feeling the need to argue with somebody.

'Says he was with his wife and weans. His wife's a junkie. Could easily be discredited in court.'

'That doesn't make him a murderer though, does it? Gary, did you pick up anything interesting in Aberdeen?' I ignore the shadow that falls over Peters' face.

'One possible so far. Another avenging relative.'

'Name?'

'Ally Irving. But he's Mr Respectable. Nice wife. 2.2 children in the nice house. Beamer in the drive. But the kids aren't his. It's her second marriage. Her first husband died three years ago in a car crash.'

'From your tone I detect you don't approve of Mr Irving?'

'Can't put my finger on it, sir. Just spoke to him on the phone. Seemed a right smarmy bastard.'

'What does he do for a living?'

'He's in computer sales.'

'Well that explains the smarm. Doesn't make him a murderer or you lot would be away for twelve to fifteen.'

'It's not that,' he continues, unruffled by my comments. It takes more than sarcasm from yours truly to wind up Gary Wilson. 'I can't put my finger on it.'

'Right. We'll go and see him.'

'What, all the way up to Aberdeen?'

'You got anything better to do? A booking to get your back waxed at the Rainbow Room perhaps?'

He smiles, 'People in glass houses...'

'Shut it.' I turn. 'Allessandra...' I trust her, but there is always room for doubt. And I have to ask her. It would look odd if I didn't. 'Have you done any digging on our people from Bethle-hem House?'

'Nothing concrete as yet, sir.' She can't quite meet my eyes either. 'I've managed to get current addresses for most of them. Just one missing,' she flicks the pages of her notebook with an index finger, and reads. 'A chap called Leonard. Can't find where he's got to.'

'Right. Good work. Keep digging. Aberdeen here I come.'

All heads in the room turn as the door squeaks open.

'Ray. Can I see you in my room?'

I follow Detective Superintendent Campbell into his office. I can feel sweat lining my palms. Did someone talk? I'd bet my next month's wage it was Peters.

Campbell sits down behind his desk, motions for me to take a seat and sits with his elbows on the desktop, his hands in a prayer pose before his mouth. He looks about to say something but he examines my face and says something else.

'You okay, Ray?'

'Fine, Tom. Thanks for asking.' What is this about?

'You're not... sick or anything?'

'No. I'm not sick or anything. Why do you ask?'

'It's just... you look like shit.'

'Oh. Right. Thanks.'

'So. Any good leads yet?' he asks, his two seconds in the act of caring senior officer obviously over for now. He sits back in his chair and fixes the cuffs on his shirt. Ensures the creases are just so and the cufflinks are square to the end of the sleeves.

'A couple, Tom. But nothing concrete as yet.' I force calm into my mind and my pulse to settle. No-one had talked. Yet.

'Give me a time-frame.'

I lift my hand in the air before us and pretend to pluck something from it. I look down at my hand, 'Three months.'

A fucking time frame he wants.

'Don't be a smart arse, McBain.'

'Well, with all due...'

'All due... kiss my arse. We need answers. Now. You know as well as I do that the trail runs cold the longer the killer goes undetected.' One thing we both know, most killers are known to their victim. Recent stats quote ninety per cent. When there is a connection between the two a conviction usually follows. No quickly discernible connection, no quick conviction. No nasty killer locked up behind bars.

'We're doing our best, sir.' Sometimes it works well to play to his ego. Remind him who's the boss and then go and do what the fuck I like.

We stop in a wee roadside café a few miles north of Perth on the Aberdeen road. A sign ahead points the way to Kinnaird. The café has a large car park in front, polka-dotted with puddles.

There's a large wooden wheel at either side of the door, as if someone had the idea of going for a Western theme. Nothing else in the location hints at this, apart from the chequered curtains. Maybe that was the extent of their imagination.

'You sure you want to go in here?' I ask Gary Wilson. I have a recent bad track record when picking places to eat. The early signs are not good.

'Aye. I'm starving. I could eat a bullock between two bread vans. I could eat a scabby-headed two-year-old. I could eat...'

'Shut the fuck up, will you? If you mention anything else you could eat, I'll no' be able to eat anything.'

The sign inside the door reads *Self Service*. There's a chrome guardrail defending the food counter from the hungry hordes, who have obviously decided to eat elsewhere. Wilson and I follow the path dictated by the rail and peruse the choice, which is not too bad. Lentil soup heads the menu. I love lentil soup. The Soup Diet flashes through my brain. This could be a start, I think.

'Yes?' A young girl leans against the till, prepared to take my order. She has black hair that looks as if it's been dyed blacker. Her eyelids have been shaded by what I could guess at as being coal. The only colour on her face is a spot on the left of her chin that could fill custard pies in its spare time. From the expression on her face she would rather dip her no doubt black-varnished toes into a pool of toxic waste than serve us. I stretch my face into as wide a smile as I can.

'Hello, gorgeous,' I say.

'Can I help you?' She raises one eyebrow. 'Sir.' This she adds as an afterthought. In case the boss is listening.

'Having a busy day?'

'Aye,' she looks over my shoulder pointedly at the empty room, opens her mouth as if to say something else. Then closes it as if I'm not worthy of her witty riposte. She stares at her pad, pen poised.

'A plate of your finest lentil soup.'

"Zat all?'

I see a basket of homemade muffins. Toffee and banana or apple and cinnamon. They look huge. And gorgeous.

'A muffin, please. Toffee.' I hand over the required amount and I'm served with my soup straight away.

Gary joins me at the table. 'Nice tits on the waitress.'

'Hadn't noticed. I was waiting for the zit to explode and fill my soup plate.' The soup is delicious. The spoon catches a sliver of ham. Just the way I like it.

'So what else do we know about this guy?'

'Just what I told you, so far. He appears to have everything that we would all want. The family, the house, the business. But as my old ma used to say, if it looks too good to be true, it probably is.'

Briefly, I considered that curiously British trait of bringing down the successful. He's done well for himself, so we'll be pleased at first. And then we'll think he must be a rank, rotten bastard to have gotten that far. And then we'll look for evidence to prove it.

'Let's just wait and see what he's like when we meet him.' I look at my muffin, feeling strangely full. 'You want this?'

'Aye, magic.' He grabs it from my hand.

We are shown into his office. Everything looks and smells brand new. It is all red cedar lined with chrome. There is no clutter, everything is designed to give the illusion of space. It makes me think of the mask we wear to hide our true selves from each other. This man even extends his mask to his surroundings. There is nothing here to indicate the type of individual seated behind the desk.

He doesn't look away from his seventeen-inch flat computer screen. With a hand that wields a silver pen, he simply motions for us to sit down. I take the opportunity to get a better look around the office. No, nothing of the man himself in here. Except... I notice a photograph by the door. A woman in her late twenties and a girl of nine or ten, I would guess. The staging of the subjects is bland. They are both wearing shirts of exactly the same colour of purple. I wonder what arse thought of that. I wonder what happened to the son. According to Gary he's a little older. Perhaps he doesn't like the new man of the house. Perhaps the new man of the house doesn't want him around his new women-folk.

It is clearly not the best place to view the photograph, if you were looking at it from the desk. The potted plant obscures it. But as people left the room they would get a good view, and be reminded that the office's occupant was a good guy: a family man.

'Eileen. Where's that report?' he shouts over the screen. The door behind us opens enough to see a head of brown, permed hair.

'It's just about ready, Mr Irving.' She sounds as if she is about to burst into tears.

'I want it five minutes ago. Please?' He glares at the door. Only then does he move his eyes to address us. He smiles, as if he'd learned it from a book. Placing his pen on the desk, he smooths down his fringe between his index finger and his middle finger.

'You can't get the staff,' he laughs. And then has the decency to look discomfited when we don't join in. Women would be attracted to this man, I thought. Despite themselves. He is a cliché of good looks; blond hair and blue eyes. Except the blond hair is receding and the eyes warn of remoteness.

He leans forward on his elbows, 'How can I help you?' We introduce ourselves. The smile recedes from his face as if it would never return when he realises that we are not prospective customers.

'We're here to investigate the murder of Patrick Connelly,' I reply. He leans back on his high-backed leather chair and looks up at the ceiling as if flipping through a mental index of acquaintances.

'Sorry,' he purses his lips after a pause long enough to indicate he'd given this his full consideration. 'That's not a name I'm familiar with. Was he a client of mine?'

'He was a caretaker cum odd-job man at Bethlehem House, here in Aberdeen, while you were staying there.'

His eyebrows all but meet on the bridge of his nose as he continues the charade of reviewing the name. 'But that was years ago. How am I supposed to remember that? I was only a bairn.'

'He abused your twin sister, Mr Irving. Perhaps that will clear the cobwebs from your memory,' I say.

'Right,' he picks up his pen and retracts the nib with a loud click. 'I... of course I remember that. But I didn't remember the evil bastard's name.' Click. 'So how can I help you?' Thoughts fly across his face. Like an actor reviewing his performance, he quickly dons a variety of expressions and then just as quickly throws them off. Puzzlement, denial, anger. And several others I have trouble naming. Click. 'You don't think it was me, do you?'

'We just want to ask you a few questions. So we can eliminate you from our enquiries,' I say. He obviously then decides to adopt his "I want to, but can't really help you" expression. I ask him where he was on the night of the murder. He slides his mouse over his desk and examines his computer screen.

'Just looking at my diary... I saw the Hendersons that morning. Got a great sale. Celebrated with a glass of wine or two at home that evening.'

'Can anyone corroborate your whereabouts that night?'

'My wife and the kids, that's them in the photograph by the door... they were at her mother's that week. She has a home in Spain. My wife likes her own space.'

He offers us a let's commiserate together, man-to-man expression. He gets no takers.

'Would anyone else be able to prove you were where you say you were?'

'No,' he shrugs. In my experience, innocent people who've had little contact with the police become a little bit uncomfortable around now. I call it The Customs Moment. Like when you're walking through the Nothing to Declare section. You have nothing illegal about your person, but still you feel the eyes of everyone in the room drilling into your luggage. It's a behavioural double negative.

He doesn't have an alibi for the evening in question and it either doesn't cause him a moment's concern or he is a consummate actor. Whatever it is, there is something not quite right here. Perhaps I can shake him out of his tree.

'So. You have no alibi for the evening a man was murdered? A man we know raped your sister. A man we know you threatened to kill.' The last statement is thrown in for effect. But who wouldn't make threats in such circumstances.

'People say things like that when they are distraught. I made that threat when I was only a boy.'

'Boyhood promises can take on the aura of quests.'

'Quests?' he snorts a laugh. 'You've been watching *The Lord of the Rings*?'

'It's not looking good for you. No alibi, a threat in front of witnesses and a strong motive.'

'I believe the burden of proof is yours. Now if you'll excuse me, I'm busy.' He stands up. Gary stands up as well. I remain in my seat. A question leaps from my mouth, without conscious thought.

'How do you get on with your stepdaughter?' I stand up now.

'My stepdaughter? Fine... why do you ask?' He puts one hand in his trouser pocket, the other reaches across the desk for the pen. I grab it first.

'Nice pen.' A Mont Blanc.

'Thanks. I won it. Top salesman.'

'Top salesman. Nice. So it really is possible to fool most of the people most of the time.' I click his pen. Petty, I know, but hey we can't all be perfect.

As we pass the reception desk, Eileen is busy pretending to be busy. After years of observing people from the point of view of suspicion you can generally tell when someone is distracted.

Eileen has a perm out of the seventies, shoulder pads from the eighties and looks so mousy it's a wonder there isn't a gang of cats ready to pounce.

'Enjoy your job, Eileen?' I ask.

She nods, meets my gaze for a second and squeaks, 'Yes.'

'Is Mr Irving a good boss?'

'The pay's no' too bad.' Her fingers move over the keyboard and she checks their progress. Not a good sign for a secretary.

'You worked here long, Eileen?'

Her curls bob as she nods. This is an easier question to answer. The keyboard goes unchecked. 'Ten years.'

'That was a lovely photograph of Mrs Irving I saw as I left the office.'

'Aye, the bairns are lovely. I've known them since they were just wee tots.' Eileen's shoulders drop a little and her fingers hover. She smiles wistfully. Probably single, with no kids and no prospect of them either. The mousy secretary in front of me fits the stereotype rather well.

'Bairns?' I ask. 'There's only one in the photograph.'

Worry creases Eileen's brow. 'Kenny didn't take too well to the new man in the house. You'd have thought he would love to have a father figure around the place. But no. As soon as Mr Irving moved in with his mother that wee boy changed. It's a sad, sad story.'

The slow relaxation of Eileen freezes as I sense a presence at my back.

'Eileen, could you hurry up with those invoices?' Irving retreats back into his office and mumbles, 'You just can't get the staff.'

Chapter 13

I'm in the Gents. Locked in a cubicle at the station. I had the dream last night again. That's five nights in a row. Five nights when I've woken up shaking like an epileptic. Five days when I've gone through the motions, dreading the moment when my head falls on to the pillow. It's always the same dream with the dead guy and the feathers. It stays with me all day like my own personal haunting. I can't take much more if this.

Drink. I could go and get pissed.

Except I don't really drink. Fair enough, I'll have the odd one when I'm out with the team, but I've never been one for boozing. Everyone else can make an arse of themselves, I'll just watch, thanks.

Not long after leaving the seminary I can remember listening to a group of my peers in a toilet. We were in a disco, as we called them in those days.

'I'm going to get blootered the night,' one ambitious youth said.

'Aye. Me too,' said another.

'Aye. Ken what? If you get a half o' cider, half o' lager, mix it with a vodka and coke, before you know it you'll be rat-arsed.' They all laughed and roared, 'Yes!' And then charged out of the toilet towards the bar. I felt like I was on a different planet. Why get so drunk you don't know what you're doing? Is it that much fun to throw fluid down your throat all night, lose track of your mental faculties and wake up feeling like you've got the flu?

Actually, when you put it like that, Ray me lad, it could prove useful. My watch tells me I've half an hour before finishing for the day. Half an hour before I can go and carry out a little experiment. Maybe if I get wasted on drink I will get some sleep.

Feeling that I am asserting some control over the situation, I review my day. And what a boring day it's been. Nobody to speak to other than the team. Nothing to do but go through lists of names, checking them against the system.

Hollywood movies give a false impression of detective work. It's fewer thrilling car chases and more sanity-threatening drudgery. Mind you, seeing Keanu Reeves mulling over a computer print-out for five hours at a stretch is hardly likely to pull in the crowds.

I'm in a bar on St Vincent Street. I asked one of the young guys where I should go for a drink that I didn't have to walk too far to. He directed me here. And it's not bad. Brown leather and wood. Contrasting textures. Very trendy, but the place is so quiet I expect to see tumbleweed roll past. It's Tuesday, so I expect that's why it's not busy. Or perhaps I've just come to the least trendy bar in the city. The barman looks like he's just out of school. He's all teeth and vitality. His eyes shine like a beacon of health. I order a pint of lager with a whisky chaser. He places them before me on the counter.

'Get your laughing gear round that, mate.'

'G'day.' I offer a reply he's bound to hear a thousand times a day. Serves him right for being Australian. And for being so fucking healthy.

Looking around me I see a few more people have come in. They're all wearing suits. Must be in from the office. Smiles are the order of the day. I wonder what they've got to be so happy about.

'Same again, Bruce.' I risk offending the bar man. Original thought is not my forte tonight. He just smiles in reply. A smile that says I've heard it all before and you're a tosser.

The second round doesn't taste any better than the first. I loosen my tie and mentally observe my reactions to the alcohol. My face feels warmer and I'm pleasantly dizzy. If my stomach is full, my bladder is dangerously so. I'm not any happier. In fact I feel miserable. The group in the corner is getting on my tits. Judging by the noise they're making, they must be on laughing gas.

'What are they drinking?' I ask Bruce. My head has stopped showing me pictures. Instead, my vision is slightly blurred. This drinking malarkey is working.

'Cocktails. It's happy hour.'

'Ah. The very thing.' I motion with my hands that I would like to try one.

He slaps a cocktail menu on the bar in front of me. Reading through it, I'm forced to smile. Some of these titles are quite funny, in a crass sort of way. The ones that intrigue me most are the "Rusty Nail" and a "Bruised Nipple".

Feeling a tad self-conscious I order the Bruised Nipple and while my new best friend Bruce pours it out I go and relieve my beleaguered bladder.

I make it to the toilet and back without too much trouble. The stairs are a wee bit tricky on the way down and too much hard work on the way back up. This makes me think cocktails might suit me better than pints. Less fluid, more alcohol. I can get pissed without going back to the toilet too much.

My drink is waiting for me when I get back to the bar. It is elaborately staged with a paper umbrella, a straw and a brightly coloured plastic mixer stick that is shaped like a naked woman. I bend forward to take a sip, miss, and nearly poke my eye out with the mixer stick.

'Fuck!' I give it a rub. Bruce grins.

'Sorry mate. Shoulda warned you about the dangers of cocktail drinking.'

I take a sip. Not bad. Syrupy sweetness almost completely disguises the taste of alcohol.

'This is okay, my man.' I grin. It probably looks more like a grimace. 'Just give me another one of these.'

Bruce leans over the bar towards me. He's trying to be discreet. 'Don't you think you've had enough for now, mate?'

'Thanks for your... concern,' I lean in to him. He moves back, out of breathing range. 'If it's good enough for the old man, it's good enough for me.'

He shrugs. 'It's your liver, mate.' He turns to one of the guys from the corner group who has come over to the bar to order a round of drinks. A piece of paper is slipped across the polished wood. Bruce reads it and then turns to his array of drinks to start mixing the various orders.

'Evening,' the guy at the bar says when he notices me looking at him.

'Evening,' I reply. He's friendly enough. Some nose on him though.

'What's the occasion tonight then?' I ask. Did I just call him Big Nose?

'What?' He can't quite tie up the insult and the smiling face in front of him. Decides he misheard, 'Oh, nothing in particular. Cheap booze on a Tuesday. We come in once a month. Have a laugh.'

'Wish I knew what was so fucking funny.' Did I just say it again?

'Sorry?' he faces me. His eyebrows are raised and his head leans in towards me. I aim a smile at him. Belligerence is just too much effort tonight.

'Nothing.' The urge to be sociable has passed as quickly as it came upon me. I hope Big Nose fucks off pretty soon. We settle in to a moment of quiet. Both of us leaning on the bar, staring at the gantry in the manner of strangers at a urinal. His drinks are squeezed on to a tray. Notes are handed over and Big Nose turns away with an expression designed to tell me how lucky I am. 'Cheers,' I offer. I'm glad he's away. The conversation was getting too much for me.

A strange sensation fills my abdomen. It takes a moment before it registers. I'm starving. 'Do you do food here?' I ask Bruce.

'Not tonight, mate. Chef's night off.'

'Any crisps?' It occurs to me that food will only soak up the alcohol. That would defeat the purpose of the whole exercise. 'Nah, sorry mate.' Bruce picks up a cloth and starts to dry off some glasses. This simple action absorbs my attention. It's like the whole world has reduced to me at a bar and some guy drying the glasses. His movements are practiced and efficient. Soon there is nothing left to clean. Oops, and my glass is empty. I find this hilarious and start to giggle.

'What's so funny?' he asks.

'Fucked if I know,' I answer. 'Here's another glass to wash.' I realise I'm exaggerating my pronunciation. Each word is coming out as if it's in slow motion. 'One for the road, Bruce.'

'You sure?'

'Yeah. The road is particularly thirsty tonight.' See. Give me a few drinks and my patter is just dazzling,

The movie in my head has stopped. Besides, my stomach is protesting too much. Hunger is something I've always had trouble ignoring. The drink arrives and I throw it down my throat. Now I know what they mean when they say "never even touched the sides". I hand Bruce a note. Not sure what denomination. 'Keep the change.'

'Cheers, mate.' He grins. I walk towards the door. Each step carefully measured. The world and its axis are on a different setting from mine. Wouldn't do to stumble and make an arse of myself.

As I near the door it opens and a couple walks in. He holds the door open for her to enter first. Just as a man of his age should. He's a good bit older than she is. Then I realise I know him. It's Peters. I look at the girl with renewed interest. There's a surprise. It's Allessandra Rossi. They've spotted me. A look of pleasure spreads across Peter's face, while Allessandra finds the floor suddenly fascinating.

'All right, guys?' I arrange my features into what I hope is a sober expression. Peters looks as if he's just won the Lottery. Did I just sway there, I wonder? Allessandra's eyes meet mine.

'We just thought we'd have a wee drink after a hard day, Ray.'

'Aye,' says Peters. 'Just two colleagues sharing a drink.' He looks really pleased with himself. He's out for a drink with an attractive younger woman. Bet that hasn't happened to him for a while. 'Not a problem, is it Ray?'

I shrug in slow motion and re-arrange my face into a *here's twenty pence, phone somebody that gives a fuck* expression.

'Starvin',' I say. 'Got to go.' One part of me couldn't care less, the other part is furious I've been caught like this. Before you know it, the whole shift will be saying I've got a problem. Drink as much as you like while you are part of a crowd and you're a good guy. Drink gallons then and no-one will bat an eyelid. Do it on your own and you're branded a problem drinker. Whoa. You're getting away ahead of yourself, Ray me lad. No-one has said a thing. They probably don't even notice that I'm drunk.

I'm in the taxi when it dawns on me. Just two colleagues sharing a drink, Peters said. If that's the case why didn't they ask me to join them?

Chapter 14

Looking over her shoulder, Allessandra watches DI McBain through the glass door as he hails a taxi. He *is* drunk, isn't he? She isn't just imagining things?

'Well, well, well,' says Peters. 'The great Ray McBain on the piss.'

Allessandra detects more than a note of pleasure in his voice and for the twentieth time within the last twenty minutes wonders at herself for accepting "a wee drink" from Peters at the end of the shift. The offer had been aimed at the whole office, but she had been the first to say yes and then had to listen while everyone else refused. It left her feeling a tad awkward. How could she get out of it without offending the man? As a precaution, she popped into the toilet before leaving, to freshen up her lipstick, but had actually sent a text to her sister, Sheila, and asked her to reply in an hour's time. This meant if she was having a really bad time, she could concoct some story of a family crisis and leave.

She prays that McBain doesn't put two and two together and come up with legs eleven. She wanted to ask him to join them but quickly realised from how long it took him to focus on her face just how deep he was in his cups.

'Maybe he's had some really bad news,' she says to Peters.

'McBain a secret drinker? Probably can't handle the job.' He looks like he's just won the office sweep. He rubs his hands together. 'You get us a drink and I'll get us a table. Mine's a Stella Artois.'

'Such a gentleman,' Allessandra forces a smile. 'Mine's a Stella as well and we can drink just as fine at the bar.' They are not in the office now and different rules apply. Without waiting for a response she walks towards the bar and leans against a stool.

While Peters orders from the barman Allessandra strikes a pose that says, I'm friendly but unavailable. She crosses her feet and her arms and faces the door. If anyone sees them together like this they can't possibly imagine there is anything going on.

Every place she's ever worked in has been the same. Constant speculation about who is sleeping with whom, and the polis isn't any different and she's not about to give the gossips any fodder.

She stretches round and picks up her glass, 'Cheers.'

'Fancy that,' Peters begins to crow again. 'I thought he'd been looking a bit rough round the edges recently. That wee show as we came in explains everything.'

Allessandra sends a thought to her sister, text me now, don't wait for an hour.

'You think he'll be alright?' she asks after five minutes of silence.

'You worried about him?' Peters turns to face her.

'It's just not like him.'

'How long have you been in the job?'

'Long enough to know when someone's hurting.' She mentally finishes off her sentence with the words, 'you patronising prick.'

'Don't kid yourself, Allessandra. Ray McBain has the hide of a rhino. He doesn't hurt.' As Peters speaks he places his right foot on the ankle-high brass pole running the length of the bar. Allessandra doesn't bother responding. She doesn't feel much like listening to someone bitch about her boss.

'Not you as well,' Peters judges her expression and slams his pint so hard on the bar some beer splashes over on to his wrist. 'Makes me sick that no-one else can see through him. The man's a danger to us all and tonight proves it.'

'All it proves is that he can't hold much booze.'

'Exactly. Who manages to get as pissed as that within an hour of leaving the office?'

'Something must be up.' Allessandra feels compelled to stick up for him.

'I'm sorry, Allessandra,' Peters slumps against the bar. 'I don't mean to sound like the office bitch. And I'm sorry you ended up coming out with me on your own. You look like you'd rather be forced to dig your teeth out with a spoon than sit here any longer with me.' He sips at his beer. 'If you want to go home, I won't mind.'

Allessandra looks sideways at him, fights her blushed reaction at the accuracy of his assessment and smiles. Maybe he isn't too bad after all.

'How about we start again?' She swivels in her chair till she is fully facing him. 'Looks like it's cocktail night. And oops, I've got a tenner in my hand. What are you having?'

'The closest I come to drinking cocktails is adding lemonade to my lager,' Peters says with a grin. 'But you have one.'

Allessandra searches the menu and asks for the cocktail with the most accessories. An hour and two repeats later and Allessandra is feeling much more disposed to the man in front of her. He isn't quite so bad when he loosens his top button and his M&S blue-checked silk tie.

'What's Roberto up to these days?' Peters asks.

'His knees. In rich clients.'

'My wife is bored with me,' Peters ignores the umbrella that Allessandra threw into his drink. 'Says I am so dependable Switzerland could run its trains by my internal clock.'

'Dependable must be an asset in this job,' says Allessandra hoping that this isn't a precursor to a lame chat-up line.

'Mmm. But there's more to life than this job, Allessandra. And don't you let anyone tell you differently. Just look at McBain.'

'Och, he's just going through a bad patch.'

'A bad patch? Is that what you call throwing yourself at suspects and half-throttling them?'

'He did what? When?'

'Just the other day. The Connelly case. A young guy, Crichton. McBain went mental. I had to pull him off the lad.'

'Je-sus.' Allessandra considers her recent experiences with the man. His recent drunkenness, the scene at the convent with the Mother Superior, telling her to keep her mouth shut in the café. And that thing with the feathers. What was that?

Peters reads her discomfort. 'Everything okay, Allessandra?'

'Aye...' Something niggles about that visit Allessandra has yet to articulate. Peters senses her slight withdrawal from the conversation.

'Listen,' he says, 'If you don't want to say anything, I'll understand. Ray McBain can be quite an impressive man.'

Allessandra bristles. 'There's nothing like that...'

'Sorry, that's not what I meant...'

'There's... no... that interview at the convent went okay.' Actually it didn't, and it just occurs to Allessandra why. McBain is a big man. In fact he dwarfed the tiny nun, yet he appeared frightened of her. Just what was going on in that man's head?

Chapter 15

Fragments of the night before pierce the pain in my head. I'm at the kitchen table, wearing a dressing gown and clutching a cup of coffee like it's a wonder of modern medicine. My legs are aching. It feels as if somebody gave me a kicking last night. But hey. Result. No dreams.

I can remember the taxi. The driver's face is a blur. The crumpled up newspaper on the kitchen floor testifies to the supper I had. The swamp of regurgitated food on the carpet at the foot of the bed tells me what happened to it.

I must have fallen asleep as soon as my head sunk into the pillow. Then I woke up, God knows when. Two things struck me at the same time. I was going to be sick and I was completely disorientated. Where the fuck had the door gone? I groped my way along the wall. Too late.

The smell was horrific. I would have to get a new carpet. That would never come out. I should have cleaned it up at the time. But I just lay back down on the bed, curled up and fell fast asleep again.

Shit. And I brought a woman home. She'd been waiting for a taxi. We shared. She fell for my version of charm. The rest, as they say, is my sordid history. Mind you she didn't stay long. Just long enough to put me to bed. I can't remember what she looked like, can't remember her name. Can't remember a thing about her.

My head is so sore, I can barely move it. Instead I put my hands on either side of my face and move them. Doesn't make it any better really, but I'll pretend it helps.

Oh no. Rossi and Peters. I met them last night. Shit. It will be all around the cop shop. Unless they don't want to attract attention to themselves. Although Peters is a more senior officer, he's not her boss, so it shouldn't have any ramifications.

And I have a horrible feeling I phoned Theresa last night. That would mean I'd broken the golden rule. She'd made me promise from the very beginning that I don't phone her. She would phone me if and when she wanted to see me. It suited me just fine. Until now.

As the alcohol kept out what the nuns might have called "dark thoughts", it replaced them with thoughts of Theresa.

I can't remember what I said, or who I spoke to. Shit.

And Allessandra Rossi. What was all that about? What does she see in Peters? She doesn't strike me as the type to go for the older man. He'd be delighted if everyone knew about it. Recently divorced, an attractive young woman interested in him. The fucker will be really pleased with himself. We can only hope she's just using him.

The boss calls me into his office. I fall into a chair. He looks like he's ready for a police promotional photo-shoot: like he's already been airbrushed for the occasion.

'You look like shit, Ray.' One trimmed eyebrow is higher than the other.

'Yeah. Couldn't sleep last night,' I mumble. He leans towards me, grimaces and sits back in his chair.

'And you stink of booze.'

Memo to me. Don't drink when you're working the next day. Nausea swirls in my stomach and flows up my throat. Another memo to me. Don't fucking drink ever again.

'Sorry, sir. Won't happen again.'

'So. What developments have we got then?' he asks. I want to laugh at his use of the royal "we", but my head is too sore.

'It's a struggle to find a strong enough connection with the deceased and any of the suspects.'

'What about this chap in Aberdeen?'

'Yes.' I pretend to think, it hurts my head too much to actually do it. 'He's a possibility. There's definitely something wrong there.'

'Ray!' he claps his hands. 'Get with it. We've a murderer to catch. You can suffer a hangover in your own time. Don't bring it into work with you.'

Bastard.

I walk along the corridor towards my office. Is it just my imagination or are people staring at me? They'll be delighted.

Ray McBain, wonder-boy, has slipped from his pedestal. Why were you so stupid? I berate myself. Fuckwit.

'Sir.' It's Allessandra Rossi. She's actually pulling at my sleeve. I stop and turn to her. Slowly.

'Yes, Allessandra.' I half-expect Peters to be with her, but he's nowhere to be seen.

'There's a name on the Bethlehem House list.' She steps back from me. Presumably the smell of booze and vomit is too much for her of a morning. 'I think it might be quite interesting. Carole Devlin.'

A face flips forward from my memory-bank. Black NHS spectacles and brown, stringy hair. She was a good bit older than me and a Donny Osmond freak. Used to scream, actually scream, when he was on the TV. On one occasion she pretended to faint.

Allessandra is still talking. 'We've been going on the assumption that it's a man. What if the "woman" seen with the deceased actually was a woman?'

'Then she'd need to be built like the proverbial brick shit-house to subdue and kill our guy.'

'S'possible.' She inclines her head to the side.

'True. We should never discount anything.' Right, McBain. Police work. But my head is so sore. 'What's come up on the system?'

'Serious Assault, sir. And get this. The victim was a man.'

'Was it a domestic?'

'Well... yes. They weren't married. Just living together. She claimed it was self-defence.'

'Anything else on her record.'

'No...' she pauses in thought. Her head to the side again. 'DD was the arresting officer. We can ask him if he remembers her.'

On cue, Daryl Drain stalks across the corridor to the toilets. He turns and faces us. Senses our attention.

'What?' he asks.

'Carole Devlin?' says Allessandra.

'Who?'

'Carole Devlin.'

'Assault?' asks Drain.

'Yes.'

'What can you tell us about her?' I join in the less than elaborate discourse.

'Nutter... Look guys, can I go for a piss first?'

'What do you mean "nutter"?' I ask. I realise through the fog of exhaustion and pain that I could have some fun here.

'Just that. Something not quite right.'

'What do you remember about the case?'

He's all but holding his groin in his need to go to the toilet. 'I... can this wait for two seconds?'

'Was it a domestic?' asks Allessandra realising where I'm going with this.

'Read the report, for chrissake.'

'Was it a domestic, Daryl?' I ask.

His body is facing the toilet door, straining towards the urinals. Only his face is pointed in our direction. 'Yes.'

'Were they married?' We edge closer to him.

'No... look... give us a...' He looks like he's going to start hopping from one leg to the other.

'They were living together then?'

'Aye.' The fingers of his left hand are wrapped round the door handle, those of his right are travelling towards his zipper.

'What damage was done to the victim?' I ask.

'He was in a bad way... look can this not wait for two minutes?' His eyes are watering.

'How bad was he?' Allessandra asks. I'm struggling to keep my face straight. Allessandra on the other hand looks like she would be a great poker player.

'She battered him with a...' he stops. 'You bastards.' Ignoring our laughter, he pulls open the door and all but runs towards the urinals.

'That was funny.' I chuckle. And groan. Laughter makes the pain in my head throb at an even greater intensity. Allessandra is leaning one hand against the wall.

'Did you see the look in his...' fresh laughter peals from her lips. 'That was brilliant.'

Heads pop out of various rooms along the corridor as people wonder at the hilarity. Seeing only Allessandra and me, they all close their doors.

By the time we recover Drain is back.

'Very funny.'

'Prostate problems?' asks Allessandra.

'I'm not that old.' He looks at me as if for the first time. 'Jesus, Ray. You look like shit. If I didn't know you better I'd think you were on the sauce last night.' He leans towards me and sniffs. His eyebrows jump three inches higher. 'You were...'

'Can we get back to work now?' I've had enough camaraderie for the moment.

What can I say? Touchy subject. I walk into the office, followed by the two of them. I fill a glass with water from the cooler.

'Devlin?' I face Drain.

'Yeah. I remember it quite well. Any women I've come across in that situation have tended to act in the heat of the moment. But she waited until the poor bastard was relaxing in the bath before she went at him with one of his steel, toe-capped boots.'

The classic equalizer. Wait until the larger individual was in a more vulnerable position and then strike.

Chapter 16

To be on the safe side, Rossi is driving. I'm probably still well over the alcohol limit. She takes a corner too neatly. My brain swims within my skull. Much more of this and I'll be sick.

'What's the fucking rush?' I ask.

She shoots a glance at me, 'Sorry, sir. I forgot you were feeling... fragile this morning.'

'Touch of the flu.' I examine the other cars in the traffic as the obvious lie stumbles from my mouth.

'Right.' In a disbelieving tone.

We're on the M8 headed towards the east of the city. Impressive buildings line our route. Here and there cranes stretch their frames into the sky. Glasgow is a "happening" city, I read daily in the papers. One of the top shopping destinations in the UK. Oh happy day. Used to be the Second City of the British Empire. Examine how our priorities have changed.

I look beyond the buildings towards the sky. Nature is reminding us that whatever we come up with, she can trump it with a simple light show. The sky is a bright, light blue. For once the clouds are sparse. Those that do appear in the sky are in the formation of a shoal of fish. Their underbellies are aflame from the rays of the sun, as it begins its journey for the day.

I think about Theresa. She hasn't called for a few days. I surprise myself, find that I miss her. I think about her smiling. One eyebrow is raised. Her lips are plump. Ripe. Opened in laughter. Her issues are so... normal. Whether or not to go out and work? Whether to wait for the sales or buy that coat now. Whether to cheat on her husband that night?

Her arm is across my shoulders. I can feel her lips pressed against my cheeks, her breath damp on my skin, like a prelude to the connection. But there's a shadow behind her. The shape shifts in a slight breeze. Reforms and shifts again. I can see the outline of a head and shoulders. Wide shoulders. The arms that hang off them taper down to the full stop of clenched fists.

'Do you want to go for a bottle of Irn Bru?' asks Rossi.

'What for?' I'm dazed by the dream. And a little disturbed. Was it a warning about Theresa's husband, or am I just seriously fucked up? 'Irn Bru?' I try to enter the conversation with Allessandra.

'Best flu cure known to man.' She examines me. 'You all right?'

'How does it work for a hangover?' I ignore her question. She's a bright girl; I better get my act together. Don't want her asking too many questions.

Teeth coated in sugar, stomach filled with gas, I knock on Carole Devlin's door.

The neighbourhood looks like it's never seen any good days. The only cars on the street look like they are held together with rust. Some of the windows are boarded up. A couple of residents have defied the collective state of mind and worked on their gardens. Everywhere else grass and weeds flourish.

If the path to her door had any more cracks on it, it could be described as crazy paving. The door opens. A round face appears. Her cheeks are pockmarked. I pulled a dead body from the Clyde once. Its face had more colour than hers. Carole's hair is brown and lifeless, hanging round her ears like a proclamation of her lack of care. She is wearing a baggy black T-shirt and a pair of black leggings. We introduce ourselves. She turns and walks into her house without a word.

Her living room comes as a surprise. The furniture looks fairly new and the table pushed against the wall reflects enough to base a close shave on. A door at the end of the room leads into a kitchen. It is open, I can see a half-built cupboard. Arranged on the floor is an array of tools.

She reaches a leg behind her on to an armchair and drops on top of it. Once seated she pulls her T-shirt over her outstretched knee with strangely pink hands and looks at us. Challenges us.

'What do you want?'

I had taken a calculated gamble coming here. If memory serves me well, Carole is at least five years older than me. Chances are I hadn't even registered on her childhood radar. Her eyes skim past my face and move to Allessandra. Good, she doesn't know me. But I remember her well.

The attraction was purely linguistic. She could speak French. I wanted to learn. A Spanish boy and his pretty sister were attending our school temporarily. They were exotic to a ten-year-old and French was close enough. The nuns were horrified. Carole Devlin was a bad influence on a young boy like me, they said. She'll lead you right to the gates of Hell, they said. I ignored what they said in the interests of international relations.

'DI McBain and DC Rossi. We just want to ask you a few questions about Paddy Connelly,' I say.

'Who?' Her eyes flicker behind the lens of her thick glasses.

'He was a caretaker at Bethlehem House.'

'Never heard of him.' She frees her foot from her perch, then crosses her legs and her arms.

'He was murdered a few weeks ago.'

'Shame.' She would have shown more emotion if I told her the dry weather wasn't going to last.

I turn my head to the kitchen. 'Doing a wee bit of DIY?'

'Who needs a man when you know the business end of a screwdriver?' She aims her humourless smile at Allessandra.

'You're better than me.' I go for the nice cop routine. 'I'd rather get someone in to do it for me. I'm hopeless.'

She just looks at me. Like I'm completely without worth. I feel uncomfortable under her gaze and I'm lost for an explanation. Usually an interviewee displays some kind of emotion. It can range across the spectrum from admiration to hate, mild irritation to fury. But her eyes reveal nothing. Only her movements prove a person inhabits the shell.

'So you have no recollection of Paddy Connelly?' I fill in the silence.

'No.'

'How was your time at Bethlehem House?' asks Rossi.

'Oh you know. Great. All that was missing was the balloons.'

'Eh?'

'It was like living in a 24-hour party. Just fucking lovely. A pile of balloons would have just made it perfect.'

'There's no need for sarcasm,' says Rossi.

Devlin squeezes up the sides of her mouth in a formation loosely based on a smile. Her expression reads more eloquently than the spoken word would have. Ask a stupid question.

'So, it wasn't very nice, I guess,' I say.

'No.'

'Paddy Connelly was a caretaker in the home while you were there. You say you can't remember him.'

'You callin' me a liar?'

Allessandra butts in, 'Do you live here on your own?'

'Mostly.'

'Who stays with you?'

'Why you askin' that?'

'Answer the question, please.'

'Go look it up in the voters' roll.' She looks around herself at the photos that sit on every available surface. A boy in various stages of his life smiles out at us. There are two women in some of the photos, Carole and another woman. She is thinner than Carole. Her cheeks are sunken almost to the extent of being able to count teeth through the impressions they make on her paper-thin skin. Her eyes are dark and anxious and at odds with the beginning of the curl of a smile below them. It looks like clever camera work, putting the mouth and eyes of two different people together. She appears in most of the boy's younger photos.

'Good looking lad,' I say.

'Yes.' Usually when you compliment the offspring of even the most taciturn individuals they respond. Not Carole. Not even a flicker.

'What age is your son?' There's a photo I take to be quite recent. He looks in his late teens. I consider the street outside and the type of individual who makes it his hunting ground. I don't know if I'd like a son of mine growing up in an area like this.

'He's no' mine.' Was that regret that flitted across her face?

'Sorry.'

She shrugs. 'It's no' your fault.' Normal service is resumed.

'Does he still live with you?' Rossi looks at me. She's wondering where this line of questioning is going. The boy is important here. I know it. I just don't know why.

'No. The ungrateful bastard left me to go and study in England.'

'What happened to his mother?'

'Life,' is the cryptic answer. From her tone, I assume she's dead. And the reason is one of the myriad of ways men and women make their existence miserable.

'Is he your nephew then?'

'No.' She gathers her eyebrows together in irritation. 'What is this? You fancy him or something?' Then she looks to the side as she processes other possibilities for my line of questioning.

'You don't think he did it. Do you?' Her tone is one of complete amazement.

I smile. 'This is an early stage of our investigation. We are not discounting any possibilities.' There is something I'm missing here. Why would this woman take on another woman's child? She hardly evidences the milk of human kindness.

'Christ. You're a smug bastard.'

'That's as may be.' I smile again. Hold it in silence for a second. 'Can you tell me where the boy was on the night of the murder?' I give her the date.

'That's easy,' she twists her face, in an attempt to match what she sees as my smugness. 'He's studying Media down in Manchester. He's no' been back since term began. See what I mean about abandoning me?'

'You keep the place nice and clean,' I say. I'm trying to unsettle her. See what rises to the surface once the cold irritation has been stirred.

'And what the fuck is that supposed to mean?' she glares.

'Nothing.'

'Just because I stay in a rundown street, doesn't mean I have to live like a pig does it?' A row of white knuckles sticks out from the scrubbed pink of her flesh.

'Not at all.' I decide to be a little more direct. My head is still beating its hangover drum. 'Where were you on the night of the murder?'

'Why would I want to crucify a man I'd never met?' The word hangs in the air between us.

'I don't think I ever mentioned that the deceased was crucified. Did you, Allessandra?'

'No.'

'So someone knows more that they're telling.'

'I must have read it in the papers.'

'And the fact that you didn't know the man made it all the more memorable?'

'I didn't know him,' she assures me.

'C'mon Carole. You expect me to believe that? You stayed in the convent. You were there the same time as a serial child rapist and he somehow escaped your attention. It's not as if you've the excuse of being too young. You would have been what, a teenager while Connelly was at it?'

'I don't remember him.'

'What are you hiding from us, Carole?'

She sits back in her chair and crosses her arms, 'Nothing.'

'Do you like a drink, Carole?' I remember the beer Connelly's companion drank on the night preceding the murder.

'What's wrong,' she leers. 'Can't get a girlfriend, Ray?' Then in a quieter tone, 'or are boys more your type?'

'They might be if you were the only other option.' My head is not feeling any better and I'm getting tired of this verbal tennis. Rossi gives me a look that says, "Way to go, McBain. Why don't you just really piss her off?"

Carole Devlin stands up. 'Next time you want to ask me some questions, make it formal down the station.'

Allessandra and I are in the car. I'm rubbing my eyes as if that will stop the pain radiating the space behind them.

'She called you Ray, in there.'

'It is my name.' I had noticed. Why didn't she mention she knew me?

What could she possibly gain by not doing so? Maybe it was something as simple as she didn't want to get into a reminiscing session. No, that sounds lame.

'But I was sure you introduced yourself as DI McBain.'

'No. Ray McBain,' I couldn't allow Allessandra to speculate that Devlin knew me. It would bring up the whole issue of Bethlehem house and me all over again.

She shrugs, 'You were a wee bit over the top there, Ray.'

'She had it coming. What a load of crap. Never knew Connelly. My arse.'

'So telling her you'd rather be gay than give her one was designed to open her up?'

'Aye. You mean it didn't work?' I grin.

'Is she a suspect, Ray?'

I review what we just experienced. A woman who likes DIY. A woman who appears to be obsessive-compulsive. She could have the physical strength. She does have mental health problems. But to balance that off, we have a woman who has raised another woman's child. The question is, can we tie her in to the deceased?

'She has a violent side. I think she has the capability... but does she have a motive?' Something is taking shape in my mind, making camp in a dark corner and sending out wave after wave of decay. I force my thoughts away. It scares me shitless.

I look over my shoulder, back in the direction of the house. Carole Devlin is standing at the window, arms crossed, face expressionless apart from her lips. They are compressed. It's as if she's stifling a smile.

This pub is quite nice. The emphasis on the word quite. They've gone for the country look, with dried flowers and pictures of pastoral scenes. It ties in nicely with the stains on the walls and the way your elbows stick to the bar when you lean on it. But hey, beggars can't be choosers, the nuns used to say. I thought there would be less chance of running into someone I know if I went to a "local" pub rather than one of the trendy café/bars that are springing up all over the city.

If the only places you visited were the café type you would think the city was losing its hard-drinking status, but it's alive and well in the wee locals, where hard-working men and women jostle with those whose hardest work of the day is cashing in their social security cheques and then seeing how fast they can drink it. They liquidise their cheques in the keenest sense of the word.

Who am I to talk? Elbows glued to the bar, while holding my drink of the moment, Bacardi Breezer. After a not too lengthy market testing, I decided I didn't really like the taste of alcohol, all I was after was the effect, a numbing of the senses, if you like. So why bother spending all night swallowing it with a grimace as if it was the foulest cough mixture you'd ever tasted?

The barman in here thinks he's a comedian. Every time I order one he puts a straw in it.

'Will you fuckin' stop that?' is as polite as I can be when he does it again.

'Sorry, mate. Force of habit. It's usually just the women that drink that stuff and they aye like a straw.'

'What gives it away that I'm not a woman, I wonder? Could it be the lack of tits? Or the stubble on my cheeks?'

'Oh come on pal,' the barman grins, 'You're describing most of the women that come in here.' This is met by some titters to my left. Two guys are sat at the bar. They look less like they are ensconced in their chairs than they are blended in with the stains. Their laughter, I sense, is not directed at the barman's joke but at me.

My look dampens their laughter. They're a matching pair of hard-drinking bookends. Both bald, with comb-overs like the strings on a guitar. I can actually see the hairy flesh of a belly through the gap between buttons that are straining to contain the blubber beneath. But they're both holding pints of beer, so they'll be real men then. I smile, and this pisses off the one nearest to me.

'You got a problem, mate?' Folds of fat in his face bunch around his nose as he scowls in what he thinks is a menacing manner.

'Several actually. But that's enough about me. Where *do* you get your hair done?'

At this he is so riled he almost gets off his chair.

'See you, ya bastard, I'll have ye.' His face is doing a tomato impression now.

'Better watch you don't have a heart attack, big guy. Then the secrets of your sartorial elegance will be lost to society forever.' He stops in his struggle to work out what I'm actually saying. While he ruminates on this his pal says, 'Just ignore'm, Stu. He's no' worth it.'

A hand presses firmly on my shoulder and I'm about to swing my bottle into the owner's face when a voice I recognise speaks.

'Detective Inspector McBain, what are you doing working up the natives?' I turn around to be greeted by a large set of teeth out of a toothpaste advert.

'Whoa, put them away, Kenny. You're blinding me.' The grin increases by several watts. Two minders flank Kenny O'Neill, Glasgow businessman, with his camel coat draped on his shoulders. A series of "How ye doin', Kenny?" rings round the room. Like visiting royalty he acknowledges everyone with a smile and a wave.

'What brings you down this neck of the jungle, Ray?' He grips my hand. I try to rub it discreetly after he lets it go.

'Oh you know, the company, the atmosphere, the booze,' I take a sip with my straw.

'Everything all right, Ray?' His handsome face reflects real concern. This is more hurtful than any insult; that I present a picture that immediately has him pity me. Our relationship has always been about being equals, albeit in different sides of the law, but equals nonetheless. I force a smile on to my face and ignore the impulse to hit him. If I so much as laid a fingernail on that finely sculpted nose of his, the least I would receive from his two minders would be two broken legs. Friend or no friend.

'Didn't know this was one of yours, Kenny,' I stand up. He owns a string of pubs in the city, a front for whatever other business he's involved in.

'You don't need to go, Ray. In fact,' he motions the barman, 'have one on me.'

'S'all right, Kenny.' I put a hand on his shoulder, 'It's time I was away.'

He walks me to the door and follows me outside. A huge Mercedes is illegally parked. Kenny points at it.

'Can I give you a lift somewhere, Ray?'

'Better watch out, Kenny. People will think you're getting soft.'

'When it comes to you, mate, I couldn't care less.'

'Oh fuck off back to your punters and leave me the fuck alone.'

At this he throws his head back and roars with laughter, his gold hair catches light from the street lamps ahead and casts it around his head like a halo. Like a fifties movie idol, he is aware of his appearance at every moment. As he should be, having spent his life perfecting it. My friend Kenny. The crook.

Walking the poorly lit streets in search of a taxi I think of the first time I met Kenny. We were both around twelve, or thirteen and he was curled up in a ball, his school blazer the target for the fists and feet of around six other boys from my school. Without a thought for my own safety, I waded in and attacked the bigger boys with a viciousness that took even me by surprise.

Luckily, there was a stick on the ground that I used to even things up and the boys from my school backed off but not before they had offered me a few threats for turning into a Proddie.

The ball on the ground straightened up and faced me with a smile. 'Thanks pal,' he said, and then gingerly touched his nose, 'That was close, nearly lost my handsome profile there.'

'Why did they go for you?' I asked, trying to ignore the tremble in my legs, still taken aback by my instinctive action.

'See the tall guy. The one with the plooks.' I couldn't think of who he was talking about. I was so scared I didn't see faces. 'I asked his girlfriend out at the disco. He's obviously threatened by my good looks.'

'Right,' I turned to walk away. Displays of conceit tended to make me not want to get to know someone.

'Want a sweet?' A Mars bar appeared from a pocket. I turned back. Something that is always guaranteed to get my attention is chocolate. 'Go on, have it. I can always nick another one.' He handed it to me and plucked one more from his pocket. This public admission of theft both appalled and thrilled me. I would never have dreamed of stealing even as much as a penny dainty and boys who did were somehow simultaneously worse and better than me.

It was a dichotomy that was to rule our relationship, but I had no idea of grandiose notions such as this at that age, I was just happy to have a friend. By silent consent we walked in the same direction chewing happily, talking about football and lying about girls, all thoughts of violence banished to that place that boys send thoughts they want to ignore.

Our paths didn't cross for another seven or eight years. I was now a terribly keen police constable and Kenny was building a reputation as someone not to be messed with unless you came up against him mob-handed. Which was exactly what I was met with when I was called to a disturbance just off the Pollokshaws Road. Once at the scene my partner and I were greeted with a sight that would normally have us waiting until the neds had done themselves sufficient damage before intervening. That way they are more amenable to our demands and less likely to turn on us.

However, I soon realised that there were four men against one and although the single, blond guy was looking after himself, he was going to tire soon and I felt the odds should be evened up. This time, I came with stick attached. My partner followed my lead with, 'You fuckin' mad?' and we got stuck in.

Two of the foursome were easily dealt with. As soon as they saw the uniforms they did a runner. The other two decided that the time had come to get really smart and they each produced a flick-knife.

'You don't want to do that, guys,' I said ignoring the chill in my stomach. 'Injure a copper with a knife and you'll have every policeman in Glasgow hunting for you. And they'll not be as polite as us.'

Knives slashed through the air. I got my baton ready. The blond guy had nothing.

We had to disarm these men before someone got seriously hurt. One of them lunged, the blond guy stepped in and to the side of the swing. A knee in the balls and a fist in the face and one was down.

The other knife-wielder dived in to try and cover his mate and that was my chance. A quick blow with my baton on the back of the head and he was felled too.

Before anything else could happen I reached across both of the felled men, picked up their knives and cuffed them.

'No need to do that,' the rescued man said as he wiped the dirt from his trousers. 'I'll no' be pressing charges.' He turned to face us and ignored our protests. 'Got a bit tricky for a moment there. Thought I was a goner.' He looked at me below the rim of my cap, 'Ray McBain!' It was only then I that I really looked at him. It's a rare occurrence for someone involved in a brawl to know my full name.

'Bloody hell. Kenny O'Neill. This is getting to be a habit.'

'Aye, is it no' just. Once every... what, seven years? That must make you my guardian angel. I owe you, man.' We gave each other a look over. He was slightly taller than me, at least six feet two and from the way he filled his fashionable shirt, packing quite a bit of muscle. Not enough to hinder movement, but enough to let those who know what they are looking at that this man was not to be easily dismissed. Aware of his gaze, I pulled my gut in.

'When do you guys get off your shift?'

'Eleven,' I answered. My partner was deep in thought.

'Well in that case, let me buy you a drink.' He named a bar and a time.

'No thanks,' my partner said, 'we were just doing our job.'

'How about you then, Ray? We could catch up on old times.'

When the shift was over my mate tried to warn me off.

'I've heard of that guy. Can't remember where. But he's trouble. Keep well away.'

I didn't. We met every now and again for a drink, but as I grew deeper into my career and he into his, we grew apart. Our paths would cross now and again, but we would rarely do more than nod in each other's direction. In another life we would have likely been best friends or soldiers at arms together.

On the rare occasions we did meet the implicit agreement was that neither talk about their working lives. The irony wasn't lost on me that when relaxing I preferred the company of a criminal to the men and women I worked beside day in day out. Kenny never lost that glamour that drew me to him as a boy. He had a confidence, a charm that you couldn't fail to respond to. I keep out of his affairs and my personal knowledge of a criminal has not affected my career, so why bin the relationship such as it was?

Stories about Kenny found their way back to me over the years. He grew a fearsome reputation but was never found with his hand in the swag bag. Always clever enough to let someone else dirty their hands, he managed to avoid the ultimate occupational hazard of every career criminal.

Never having had a visible regular girlfriend, he preferred the company of prostitutes, and being so good looking, he attracted debate over his sexuality. This never bothered him. Indeed he played up to it and used it to his advantage. Word got out among the criminal fraternity that he had brutally beaten and then raped an adversary. Any man he then winked at became the subject of speculation from his mates, but Kenny was no weakling and no-one would stand against him unless they had an Uzi, so he was given respect and left to go about his business.

'It didn't do the Krays any harm,' he said during our last meeting, at least a year ago. I asked him about a girlfriend.

'What? No way, mate. I prefer a good, clean honest transaction. She knows exactly where I stand and I know where she stands.'

'What about intimacy?' I asked.

'A myth,' he replied, 'a myth put about by your Catholic priests and feminists to make us men keep our peckers in our collective pants.'

Chapter 17

Saturday night. I'm at the Chapel. How sad is that? Haven't been for years. The booze didn't keep the dreams at bay for long and the hangover wasn't much of a trade-off. Nor were the women I kept bringing home with me doing anything for my sanity. Another one last night, but she got as far as my front door, before I emptied my stomach at her feet. The taxi-driver didn't even get a chance to put his car into first gear before she returned to the front seat.

So I thought I'd try religion.

All of that brain-washing from my childhood surely wouldn't be lost on me now. Surely something of the psyche of the boy remains? A few Our Fathers, a reading of the Gospel and the mismatched singing voices of the congregation will be enough to keep me calm for a few hours and dispel the pictures in my head.

As the priest begins Mass from behind the altar, his words ring with familiarity. Despite the intervening years, I could chant along with him and match him word for word.

When I left the seminary, I vowed I'd never step foot inside another church. And here I am, all but joining hands with the hypocrites. I can't deny the good that's been done over the years by the people who wear the cloth, but I've experienced too much of the dirt that is concealed within its folds.

The congregation rushes into song. I pick up a hymn-book and join them. Emotion clogs my throat like thick phlegm. What is going on? I stop singing. Part of me wants to move closer to the altar and part of me wants to run into the street. I am simultaneously attracted and repelled. I can't stand much more of this.

The woman beside me looks up at me. The top of her black velour hat barely reaches my shoulder. Her eyes question me. 'You all right, son?'

There's pity swimming in the brown of her iris. It's almost more than I can stand. I brush past her and ignore the loud tuts as I make my way to the door. A question forms in my mind as I breathe in the cold air outside the large doors. 'Where's the nearest place I can buy cocktails?'

I'm in bed and the alarm has just gone off. It's Monday morning, 6:30 am. The resident band in my head is playing hard and they only have one tune: an extremely loud one that keeps perfect time with my heartbeat. Congratulations, McBain, you managed to get home in one piece.

Sunday afternoon through Sunday night is a blur. The last thing I can remember is standing at the church door wondering where I could get a drink. Judging by the churn in my stomach, I managed to find one. Or two. Still, I can chalk another one up to the alcohol, no dreams and no dead bodies last night, thank you very much.

Two things happen simultaneously. I become aware of the presence of another person and the quilt beside me rises as they cough. The cough I hear is harsh enough to dislodge a week's worth of nasal production. She's bound to be a stunner then.

Well. That's a result. A woman actually made it into my bedroom.

The log-like shape beside me stirs some more. It makes a decent sized mound under the covers. Again, not promising. With more than a little trepidation, I poke a finger at the shoulder area.

'Morning.' I resist the urge to ask for a name at this point. Gallant to the last, me. Bleached blonde hair surfaces, then a pair of eyes thick with smudged mascara and sleep. She looks about ten years older than me. What is it with me and older women?

'What kind of time's this to go waking a girl then?' She pushes herself back and up against the headboard. As she does this she takes the quilt with her to hide her bra.

'Did we...?'

'Nah, doll. By the time I got my clothes off, you were asleep.' She grins, showing perfectly formed and dazzlingly white teeth. 'And don't think you're getting any this morning. I'm strictly a night bird.'

I almost make a pretence of being disappointed, but decide not to as she could easily see through it.

'At least tell me we had a good time then?'

'It was alright till you phoned up your bird's husband and gave him an earful down the phone.'

'I did what...?' Shit. I was well and truly fucked. I need to be anywhere but here. I need to get some peace and quiet and try to think things through. I need to phone Theresa and assess the damage. 'Can I give you a lift anywhere?'

'If you drive anywhere the day, you'll get the polis.'

'I am the polis,' escapes before my internal editor can silence it.

'I know. Overheard you telling the husband. Detective Inspector. Very impressive.'

'Shit. What did I say?' My head is really hurting now. Fuck. What were you thinking, McBain? You can say goodbye to Theresa forever now, you fuckwit.

'Something along the lines of his wife was in love with you and if he wanted to take issue with it, he should pop along to Pitt Street and look for the office with DI McBain on the door.'

Fuck. I'd throw myself back on to the bed but it would take a week for the waves of pain to die down. I need some space.

'So, can I take you home? Phone you a taxi?'

'Give a girl a chance to waken up before you go sorting her out.'

Shit. I'll never be able to get rid of her.

'And don't worry, I'll be out of your hair as soon as I've had my morning fag and a coffee.'

'Right.'

She looks at me. 'You're a bit slow in the morning, son. That's a gentle hint for you to do the gentlemanly thing. Find me my fags and fetch me a coffee, then when you're out of the room, I can make myself decent.'

'Right.' With the covers over my lap, I try to locate the presence of a bathrobe or trousers. Anything I can use to protect my own dignity. It occurs to me I'm not sure which body part I'd rather cover up. My belly or my genitals?

'How come I'm naked, if we didn't do anything?' I ask.

'You stripped and fell into bed before I could stop you and, as I already told you, there was no way I was sleeping on that excuse for a settee. Two-seaters are the work of Satan, if you ask me. Another example of how unsociable we are becoming. Can't even ask people over for an innocent wee sleepover nowadays.'

My clothes are hanging over the chair at the other side of the bed, so I'm forced to perform a strange pantomime crouch around the side of the bed, like I'm the back of the horse, but I forgot my costume. In this strange position, I shuffle along the side of the bed and along its foot to the chair, while offering nothing to her view but my ample arse. Trousers and a shirt on, I turn to face her. She's not doing a very good job of stifling a grin.

'You got a bad hip?' she asks with a squashed smile.

'Piss off,' I smile and blush at my idiocy. 'How does madam like her coffee?'

'With a generous portion of brandy, topped up with thick, whipped cream,' she says languorously, 'But I'll settle for milk and two sugars. And a fag.'

While the kettle boils, I make for the toilet and take a piss. I self-consciously aim my stream at the wall of the pan rather than straight into the water. My face is pinched and pale in the mirror. The flesh looks jaundiced and the folds under my eyes are getting pronounced enough to conceal my nail clippings. The sink supports my weight nicely as I lean into the mirror.

I tug at the skin under my right eye and view the engorged lacing of red capillaries that feed my eye. Attractive.

As I perform this inventory of my ongoing dilapidation I'm trying to recall my erstwhile bed-partner's name. Nothing. Last night has left nothing in my mind. Well, that's a result of sorts. But can I just go back there and hope she inadvertently reminds me? I hear her moving about the flat. Probably having a nosy to see what's worth stealing. This thought galvanises me to leave the bathroom.

She's opening a kitchen drawer.

'Excuse me,' she offers, 'I'm trying to find a teaspoon.'

'Over here,' I squeeze past her in the small space, trying my utmost not to touch her with any part of my body. Ah, the joy of one-night stands. 'There.' I open the drawer and pull one out.

'I'll just go and sit in the other room. Sorry.' She's a little shyer outside of the bedroom. It's as if while we were in the bedroom there remained a little of the companionship we were both looking for last night, but here in the kitchen where life has a different rhythm, our lack of real intimacy is highlighted.

'Right, you go through to the living room and I'll bring your coffee in to you.' God this is awkward. If I'd known her name I could have slipped it in there. Its absence worried at me, like I would be less of a reprobate if I could remember it, and more of a gentleman. I should stop thinking, my head hurts too much.

We're at either end of the sofa.

'Nice coffee.' She's got a nice smile and I can see why I was attracted to her. 'Lovely place too. The polis must pay nearly as much as being an entrepreneur.'

'I wish.' My mouth is at the lip of the mug and I'm breathing in the aroma like it's menthol and I'm trying to clear my tubes. What is her name? Better get showered and dressed after this. After my coffee.

'It's Maggie, by the way,' she is still smiling, but her eyes have lost that mild flirtatious look. They're now clothed in concern. 'You all right?' I've just noticed she has this annoying habit of answering a question just as it pops into my head.

'Yeah.' I lie. 'A quick shower and a shave and I'll be brand new.'

'Okay,' her tone says she doesn't believe me. She's looking at me as if she's trying to… divine something. It's as uncomfortable as hell to be the subject of her scrutiny.

I stand up. 'Bugger the shower. Let's get you home.'

We've made it to the car and we're driving along that mecca of small shops, Great Western Road, towards the city centre. "Driving" is a bit of an exaggeration. "Parking and sliding forward" would be a more accurate description. Don't you just love rush hour traffic? To avoid it would mean too much thought, and I'm not doing thought this morning.

'You been in the police long?'

'Too long.'

'Sounds like you don't enjoy it.'

'Mmmm.'

'Why don't you leave?'

''Cos institutions are all I've known. Where else would I go?' Whoa big guy. Where the fuck did that come from?

'A hospital? That's an institution. You could help people there.'

'A mental hospital maybe.'

'You're not going mad, you know.' Her voice is quiet. Serious.

'What?' I take my eyes from the traffic and face her.

'You heard.' She holds my gaze. I break contact first. The car in front of me has edged forward. Almost absently, I register a pain in the front of my lower leg, as it tires from the constant on and off pressure on the clutch. This traffic is doing my head in. What I would give for a siren right now.

'Just who the hell are you?'

'Do you think we met by chance last night?'

Christ, she's a loony. I've picked up my own personal stalker.

'Everything happens for a reason, you know.'

'Eh?'

'Now I know why the universe brought us together, Ray. I can help you.' She looks the same, her eyes are pools of empathy, but the words coming out of her mouth are just not making any sense, and scaring the shit out of me.

'Eh?' I really do need to expand my vocabulary.

'You were only a boy.'

'What? Only a... What the fuck are you talking about?'

'I can't see it all, yet.' She looks out of the window, but not at the traffic. 'But I know that you were as much of a victim as he was.'

'Get the fuck out of my car, you fucking witch.'

The driver behind me jumps on his horn. Looking in the mirror I can see his hand wave wildly and his mouth is spewing what I've no doubt are obscenities. That is something I can handle. The car is in neutral and my hand is on the release button of my seat belt before I know it. She puts her hand on mine.

'Don't. It's me you're angry with.'

'Get out the fucking car then.'

'I'm going.' She barely flinches at my rage. As she leaves the car she throws a small piece of card into the dashboard. 'If you...'

'Bye.' The car is in gear and I'm moving before the door is shut. Maggie's face flashes into my vision. Her face is scrubbed of make-up, her eyes are large with pity and with need. The need to help.

In the car park at the station, I congratulate myself for making it into work without assaulting anyone. The way I'm feeling, that's a result. And I doubt if it's going to get any better. Theresa's husband will have no doubt lodged his complaint, so depending on how she plays it, I could be in bother. Will she put her cosy lifestyle in jeopardy by telling the truth? Or will she let me be fed to the lions?

I arrive at my office without being accosted. Hellos are exchanged with the usual people on the way. Is it my overworked imagination or are they more muted than normal? Jungle drums work just as well in police stations as they do in other offices, or perhaps even better, for we trade in information on a daily basis.

The boss is sitting behind my desk, his expression as unreadable to me as a page of Hebrew.

'We need to talk.'

'So talk.' I sit in the seat facing my desk and ignore the urge to cover up my ears.

'Peters, come in.' He shouts over my head. The door opens smartly and Peters walks in. He stands in front of me to the right of the desk.

'Ray, this gives me no pleasure...'

'What the fuck is going on?' This is much more serious than a reaction to an abusive phone call. Peters' eyes go anywhere but my face. He is instrumental in this. He looks... embarrassed. Like he's just shit on a fellow officer's career.

'We would like you to accompany us to an interview room.'

'Eh?'

'We would like to question you on your whereabouts...'

'Boss, don't do this. You're making a huge mistake.'

'...on the night of the Connelly murder.'

Chapter 18

Allessandra is shivering. The midday sun doesn't quite heat this small room in Bethlehem House. The chill is thickened some-what by Mother Superior sitting in front of her and looking, well, superior.

'How would you describe the relationship between Ray McBain and Carole Devlin?' Allessandra asks.

The nun is nonplussed by the question. 'Before I separated them, they were... very close. Too close.'

'How so, Mother?' Allessandra asks, dreading the answer.

'Ray would have been about... ten or eleven? He still had rather a sweet soprano. Devlin I would guess was around fourteen. We tend to move the boys on before they reach puberty. Because then it gets really messy.' As she speaks her eyes never left Allessandra's. Her gaze is strong and says this is my domain. I am the mother lion and I will brook no dissent.

Despite herself, Allessandra can feel herself being cowed by the force of the woman's personality. 'You have to remember that children are nothing but little animals. With all the... urges that animals have. Until we adults teach them better.' She smiles and Allessandra feels she has to smile in return.

'I caught them one day. Down behind the tennis courts. Fiddling with each other. Hormones are a terrible thing, DC Rossi. Especially in the very young.' She wrings her hands in dread at the human race's drive to carry on its genes. 'The work of the devil, if you ask me.'

'Surely such... experimentation, while not to be condoned, is to be expected?' Allessandra is thinking that perhaps one isolated incident is not so bad. Perhaps they were equally forgettable to the other. Besides, if Ray was only eleven there wouldn't have been much in the way of "fiddling" going on surely.

'Maybe where you came from, my dear, but not in a house of

the Lord.' Before Allessandra can object, Mother continues. 'That little event forced me to keep them apart, but there were other... things. You have to remember I have only one pair of eyes and I was looking after more than twenty children. Ray became fixated on Devlin. Followed her everywhere.' Mother widens her mouth in a smile. 'The modern idiom would be "stalker".'

A mug of black tea cools on the table before her. Allessandra has a teaspoon in her hand and is slowly stirring white sugar in a stainless steel bowl. Her seat is in the corner of the staff canteen and she is facing a window, in whose reflection she can see who is coming and going. She can also judge if anyone notices her and whether or not they were tempted to speak to her. So far no-one has as much as registered her presence.

The long chrome-lined serving passage in front of the buffet is empty. A caterer bustles behind it, her face long with purpose and habit as she fills the various food containers.

She'd had to do it. Boss or not, he has raised enough suspicion in her mind that she can't ignore it. The records prove that Ray and Devlin had been in the convent at the same time. They must have known each other. So why did they both act as if they had never clapped eyes on each other? And Devlin *did* call him "Ray".

The records also show that Devlin was in her teens and that there were only seven boys in residence; she must have known him.

Peters was in the room when she went to speak to Campbell. When she told them about the connection with Bethlehem House and DI McBain's demand that she keep his name from the list there was a pause as the importance of what she said sank in.

The look on Peters' face stayed with her for hours.

Allessandra stops stirring the sugar when she realises someone is standing over her.

'Is this a private party or can anyone join in?' It's Daryl Drain.

Allessandra shrugs and reaches for the handle of her mug. The tea is cold.

'Can I freshen your tea up?' asks Daryl.

'Go on then,' Allessandra says. Then adds a quiet thanks to his back as Daryl walks over to the counter. Soon he's back holding two mugs, both very hot judging by the pained expression on his face. He places them on the table with relief. He blows on his hands before he turns a chair round and straddles it cowboy style.

'So how many hours do you think you'd need to stir that sugar to get into the record books?' he asks.

Allessandra's smile is weak but appreciative. He is giving her the opportunity to talk without forcing the issue.

'I feel like shit, DD,' she says.

Daryl raises an eyebrow.

'You heard then?' she asks him.

Daryl nods and keeps his eyebrow raised.

'Can't have been easy for you,' he says and takes a sip at his mug.

'Oh God. Have I done the right...'

'Yes. I would have done exactly the same thing.'

'But a fellow officer is stuck in a cell at the moment and it's all my fault.'

'Don't you believe that for a minute, Allessandra. The reason that DI McBain is in that cell is DI McBain. He's got no-one to blame but himself.'

'But...'

'But nothing. We're talking murder here, Allessandra. Not some petty extortion. He covered up his tracks and he used you to help him.'

Allessandra picks up her teaspoon and spears the sugar. 'I thought there was an unwritten rule...'

'Only in Hollywood and never when people are being killed.'

'You've known Ray for a few years.' She begins to stir.

'Aye.'

'Do you think he's capable of murder?'

'He lied, Allessandra. And he put you in an untenable position...'

'Ooh. Untenable.' She grins.

'Aye.' Daryl answers her grin with one of his own. Allessandra admires the even line of his teeth and the bright blue of his eyes. 'Four syllables that mean he could have fucked your career right up.'

'He's certainly got something to hide. But murder?'

'He was an excellent cop. Is an excellent cop. Murder? I hope not. But I would love to know just what he was up to.'

'Can you answer this?' asks Allessandra with the suggestion of a grin.

'What?'

'Where do you go for the coloured contact lenses? Your eyes are dazzling, man.'

Chapter 19

This is seriously fucking weird. I'm being interviewed by my colleagues. I'm actually under suspicion of murder. My mind is racing, searching for connections and it doesn't take too long to come up with one. Allessandra must have told Peters about the list of people at Bethlehem House. By deliberately excluding myself from the list, I would appear deeply suspicious to them. McBain, you idiot. And what about Allessandra? I should never have put her in that situation. Not only have I killed my career, I've damaged hers as well.

Why didn't you just put your name in and accept being withdrawn from the case until you were cleared? 'Cos that would have meant someone else getting the glory. No, dammit. This is my case. It had Ray McBain written all over it. It still is my case and no arsehole career policeman is going to stop me from finding that murderer.

There is something else, a compulsion. I have to find this particular killer. I have to. I just don't know why.

My head is in my hands, my elbows on the table... and I'm on the wrong side of it. Facing me are Campbell and Peters. Both of them look like they've spent the night sipping from a vinegar bottle. But I can't judge whether it is from the awkwardness of interviewing a fellow officer or from the distaste of actually suspecting one. There's nothing worse than someone you trust pissing in your coffee. Do they seriously think I did it?

They go through the rigmarole of explaining that the interview will be taped and asking me if I want a lawyer present.

'Get on with it guys,' I say, 'then we can get on with catching the real killer.'

'I don't think you appreciate the gravity of this situation, DI McBain,' says Campbell. 'Not only are you a suspect, but you doctored evidence. So minimum we're looking at Perverting the Course of Justice. Bye bye career,' he pauses dramatically, 'or we're looking at fifteen years plus, for a particularly brutal murder. Bye bye life.'

'Oh come on. You don't actually think I did it?' I look at them both. I get nothing back.

'Where were you on the night of the murder, Ray?'

'I was with the team on a night out. To celebrate the apprehension and conviction of a real criminal. Along with fuck-face here.' I nod in the direction of Peters.

He doesn't give me the satisfaction of a reaction. 'You left the pub early, Ray. In plenty of time to do the deed.' His turn to wait for my response.

'Fuck you.' Basic, I know, but hey, we are all only a step forward from the cave.

'Where did you go?'

'Home to bed. On my own.' I can't tell them I went to Theresa's, her marriage would be down the sinkhole then. I realise I have some sort of strange loyalty to informants and lovers: never give out the detail on either. And so far, she's given me no reason to doubt her. So I'll keep schtum.

'Can you prove it?' asks Campbell.

'I believe the burden of proof is yours.' I was impressed when that weirdo Ally Irving came up with that when we interviewed him. I've been saving it up for a special occasion just like this.

'Ray, give us some help here. The last thing we want is to convict a fellow cop.' Campbell's hands are open, palms facing me.

'Convict?' I shove my face into his. 'You've already decided I'm guilty, you prick.'

'Why don't we calm down, DI McBain,' says Peters, reminding me of my rank and, thereby, how I should comport myself. 'The sooner we get this cleared up the better for everyone.' I look around the room from the vantage point of my bucket chair. The room seems different from this point of view, the walls look thicker, the soundproofing looks sinister, whereas I always used to think it looked comical, like cast-offs from an egg boxing factory.

Everything I've worked for all these years is fast dissolving before my eyes. I need some quick thinking to save my career.

'Look, this is all a mix-up. I have a list from Bethlehem House back at the flat. My name is on it. I must have given Allessandra Rossi the wrong one.' It sounds feeble even to me.

'Bullshit, McBain.' The feet of his chair do the chalk-on-blackboard sound and Peters' face is in mine. 'Not only have you damaged your own career, but also you may have done harm to a young cop with real promise. And that is unforgivable.'

'Scared you won't get your leg over if Allessandra loses her job? She'll have no reason to look up to you then, you sanctimonious prick.' His eyes widen and I brace myself for a fist. His breath lessens on my face and I realise Campbell has pulled him off.

'For the record,' I aim my voice at the tape recorder, 'DS Peters has adopted an aggressive stance.' Peters sits down, his face going through a rainbow of red.

'Also for the record,' I continue, 'DS Peters has a grudge against me and should not be involved in this interview.' I know I'm acting like a child but I can't help it.

'A grudge, what grudge?'

'I believe that DS Peters has had feelings of antipathy towards me since I was promoted over his head and what's more...'

'Stop it, Ray,' says Campbell.

'And what's more,' I continue, 'he is having a relationship with the chief witness against me in this case and...'

'Rubbish. Absolute crap. Allessandra Rossi and I have nothing more than a professional relationship.'

'You named her, not me,' I smirk. 'You go out with each of your female colleagues on an individual basis, do you?'

'Only when they have deep concerns about the conduct of their commanding officer.' He is wearing a smile of triumph. How I would like to wipe it off with the tread of my size tens.

'Ray. None of this is helping.' Campbell is talking while Peters and I stare each other out. 'Can you then explain why you would want to doctor the evidence?'

'Yes. I didn't want to get taken off the case. *I* know I'm not the murderer, and to replace me with an arse like Peters would only have delayed catching the killer.'

'Aye, and you've done a fantastic job so far,' Peters offers in a stage whisper.

'And that was worth damaging your career, likely beyond repair?' asks Campbell. That would be the one thing that he couldn't understand. I couldn't either, so I didn't bother attempting a reply.

'I'll ask you again, Ray. Where were you on the night of the murder?'

'In bed, sleeping. Alone.'

'Can you prove it?'

'I turn off the home CCTV during the hours of darkness.'

'Wonderful. Sarcasm. So helpful, DI McBain,' says Peters. If he says "DI McBain" in that tone again, I swear I'll kick his teeth in. They can add assault to the rest of the charge sheet.

'How would you describe your relationship with the deceased?' Back to Campbell.

'There was none.'

'You didn't know him?'

'From Adam.'

'And you were aware of the detail of the deceased's wounds,' Campbell continues, 'before you were told? All three of us were present while DS Peters read out the details. You were able to finish off the list before he did. How can you explain that?'

'A Catholic education.'

'On its own that might seem plausible. But when added to the other evidence, it's quite damning.'

'Yes. But is it enough to put me in front of a judge?'

'We think so,' Peters jumps in.

'You don't have enough and you know it. What you have is all very nice. All very circumstantial, but you have nothing to link me to the crime scene. Because there is nothing.' I stand up.

'We're not finished with you yet,' says Campbell.

'Yeah, well life's full of disappointment. I'm leaving.'

'Sit down, Ray.' With a look of protest and a great sigh I do so, letting them know I'll behave myself for now. Besides, it'll look better for me if I "help with their enquiries" rather than wait until I'm arrested and then be forced to answer their questions.

The door opens. It's Drain. Without as much as a glance in my direction, he motions for Campbell to follow him out.

'This interview is being temporarily suspended,' Campbell says to the tape recorder. He and Peters leave the room, leaving me to stew in my own thoughts. A technique I myself find effective when dealing with the criminal fraternity. But it's not going to work on me.

I rub my hands together. They are slick with sweat. Why did you do it? You stupid, stupid bastard McBain. You've ruined your career. Fuck! What will they do with me? I was a good cop... am a good cop. Surely that will count for something? Unless they want to make an example of me. The police should not be above the law and all that bollocks. Except I agree with it. I deserve everything that's coming to me. But what about Allessandra? Acid roils in my stomach. She doesn't deserve to be punished. I abused the power I had over her. At least it's in her favour that she volunteered the information. If the powers that be had discovered what had gone on without her coming forward then her career would be as dead as mine. I hope the arseholes take this into consideration.

I look around myself. Is it my imagination or is the room smaller? I shift my cheeks, the hard plastic quite literally a pain in the arse. I lean forward on to my elbows, then sit back in the chair, the lip of plastic digging into my back, just under the shoulder blades. Where the fuck are they? What are the bastards cooking up? I lean forward again. Look at my watch. Five minutes have passed. Feels like five hours.

The door swings open, Campbell enters with someone else, another cop.

'This is Inspector Hackett from the Complaints and Discipline Branch.'

Hackett offers me his hand. 'Pleased to meet you Detective Inspector.'

The grip from his hands is just a touch from painful. Even for a policeman, this guy is big, six feet seven at least, and almost as wide. The smile that pushes back his plump cheeks appears to be genuine. I wonder how many courses he's been on, or is he a natural at putting people at their ease? Better not let my guard down, the nice guys can be the worst.

'I've a few questions for you, Ray. Mind if I call you Ray?' He switches on the tape recorder and mentions all of those present, to show me who is in charge in the room.

I shrug to show that use of my first name is not an issue.

'What is your relationship with Allessandra Rossi?' No messing about for this guy.

'Purely professional.'

'In your opinion, why did she comply with your request to keep your name from the list?'

'Because I bullied her into it.' If I make things bad for me while trying to clear Allessandra, it will be worth it.

'You're a bully?' His lips flatten into a thin line as he says this, as if his distaste for the word is such he can barely say it. Then he looks into the near distance as if searching for something else to say. Then another big-daft-boy smile. A ploy to minimise my opinion of his intelligence. It doesn't work. I can sense a quick mind is in the room. Besides, nobody gets into his job by being thick.

'My nickname is Bastard McBain. Does that not tell its story?' The nickname falls from my lips like a drop of oil, assisted by the lubrication of the lie.

'Bastard McBain. Good one, Ray.' He smiles, and his eyes slide up to the left. 'Haven't heard any of your colleagues call you that.'

'Give them time. Disgraced cop and all that. They'll be sharpening their knives as we speak.'

'Actually, in the time that I've spent in this office and speaking to your team over the weekend, there hasn't been an insult in sight. Not so much as a whisper of a bastard.'

'Give them time.'

'Or do you just pick on the female members of your staff?' No smile this time. His carefully constructed control is slipping. Was that a hint of irritation in his voice? He hates that I've used a young officer. What's new? So do I.

'Yes, that's it. I'm a discriminating bully.' I think I see where he's going with this. I don't care if they think I'm sexist or a bully, as long as it helps Allessandra.

'Very few people would admit to that in this job.'

'Yeah, well.'

'Tell me what happened at Bethlehem House with you and DC Rossi.' He leans forward on his elbows, fingers entwined in prayer.

Knowing that he will have asked Allessandra the very same question, I tell him exactly how it happened, right down to the camp waiter in the crap café, and hope that Allessandra has done the same. When I stop speaking he just sits back in his chair looking at me, waiting for me to rush in and fill the silence with another little detail that will be the final nail in the coffin. I'm too experienced to fall for that particular trick. Besides I've told him everything.

'This is serious, Ray.' He must be getting tired looking eyeball to eyeball.

'No kidding.'

'You'll probably lose your job over this.'

I shrug nonchalantly, stare at the scratch marks on the tabletop and ignore the pain that's squeezing my heart.

'And then there's the murder.' Silence. 'Why did you do it, Ray?'

'I had no hand in that murder.'

He raises an eyebrow. 'Was changing the evidence worth it, Ray? Just what did you have to gain by doing so?'

'It kept me on the case. I'm not a murderer. I catch the bastards. I'm the good guy.'

'Were the good guy, Ray. Were. The moment you concealed your early life at the convent, you lost the right to call yourself that. Or was it the moment you conceived of a murder?'

'I've killed no-one.' And I'm getting tired of saying it.

'There is evidence to the contrary.'

'What? Hearsay? I was able to describe the wounds of the stigmata quicker than a thick DS could read his own handwriting? That's fuck all and you know it.'

'There is the small matter of you doctoring evidence.'

'I told you why I did that. I needed to be kept on the case.'

'Why? Why did this particular case mean so much to you, Ray?'

How could I give an answer that I hadn't managed to fully articulate myself? Because I wanted to? Because I had to? All my instincts told me that I had to solve this case. My life was bound up in this murder and I had no idea why or how. How do you explain that?

'I already told everybody. It was my case. I didn't want some moron like Peters to ruin it and let the killer get away.'

'Put yourself in the jury, Ray. Sounds weak doesn't it?' Campbell speaks for the first time during the interview.

I had no answer to that, so I said nothing.

'You're all we've got, Ray. And we can make a strong case against you. You had the opportunity, you left your colleagues during a night out. That in itself looks suspicious...' Back to Hackett.

'If that's the case, why didn't I wait and leave when they were too pissed to notice?'

'... you had the means. The wounds of the stigmata are part of a Catholic child's education and you are more than strong enough to subdue a weak old man.' Campbell's turn.

'And how many Catholic schoolchildren are there in Scotland?'

'And how many of them have just been caught changing evidence that removes them from the list of potential suspects?' Hackett takes up the baton this time. It's like they're winding themselves up for the grand close.

The lights seem to dim, my ears clog with panic. I can sense what's coming.

'You are immediately suspended from all duties,' says Hackett from the end of a long tunnel.

'Ray McBain, I am arresting you for the murder...' the rest of Campbell's words evaporate into a fog of disbelief. I'm being charged with murder. I've lost my job... and I brought it all on myself.

Wait, I've an alibi, I want to shout. I was with someone. I'm protecting a married woman. What's the pain of a divorce for Theresa when compared to life in prison for me? But I can't speak. The words that will free me are trapped behind the bars of my strange loyalties.

Chapter 20

The Charge Sergeant takes me through the rigmarole of being fingerprinted and photographed. These are the delights that await the newly charged, the beginning of the process that de-humanises you. I am escorted through the building from the second floor, where the Serious Crime Squad are situated, to the bottom floor where, fittingly, the cells are housed. There are several times when I could make a run for it; when the Sergeant turns to nod at a colleague, when we pass a fire exit I know is un-locked, and just as I pass a doorway I know leads out to the front desk and from there to the street. A single thought pulses through my head. Run. But I could no more run for it than I could bare my fat arse at a football match. From a very young age I was trained to follow orders, do what I was told. This was instilled in me with a fist dedicated to God and his good works. My training as a police officer simply augmented this. So I do what I am told, walk with the nice policeman into a cell where I will be locked up for a murder I didn't commit.

Stripped of anything that could offer me release from my life — laces, belt, tie — I am shown to my cell. The closing of a door never seemed so final. When I walk into the small box of a room, I'm faced with the final indignity; I've been given the 24-hour surveillance cell. One of the walls has a tiny window above head height, there is a small platform against another wall which bears a paper-thin mattress, the third wall holds a stainless steel bowl, minus flush, for all of my toiletry needs, and the wall to my right as I walk in is made of glass, from floor to ceiling.

Behind this is a desk and chair where some poor unfortunate PC will have to sit and watch me sleep, eat and defecate twenty-four hours a day, until I'm shipped off to the "Bar L" or Barlinnie Prison, as it should be known. This cell isn't reserved for just anyone. Oh no. Only the truly fucked-up get to reside here. Only the dangerous get to be looked at like an exhibit at the zoo for every minute of every day. Just then a figure steps into the room behind the glass wall and almost apologetically sits on the chair.

I sit on the "bed" and with elbows resting on my knees, I place my head in my hands. A dispassionate voice in my head remarks that I better get used to this position. Ray McBain charged with murder. The gossips in the building will be lit up like Christmas trees. They'll be running around making sure that everybody knows. I can just hear them. "Aye, he did it! Knew too much, the sick bastard."

You don't rise through the ranks as quickly as I did without raising a few enemies, and they will be crowing, "No wonder he caught so many criminals, it takes one to know one."

No doubt the anthem of the small-minded will be getting an airing, "There's no smoke without fire."

The Charge Sergeant had asked me at the desk if there was any "reasonably named person" I would like to be called. Or at least that's what I thought he asked. There was an incongruous giggle in a deep recess of my mind. Jim's quite a reasonable name, so is John, I wanted to say. But there was no-one; I didn't even know a lawyer. What an indictment of your life, McBain. Thirty-four years of age and you don't even have a friend or relative who might be wondering what has happened to you. To have reason to call a neighbour might be nice: sorry to bother you and all that, I've been locked up for murder, don't you know. Could you look after my imaginary cat while I'm gone?

This sets me off into peals of laughter. I roll over on to my side, pull my legs up to my chest and allow the laughter to turn into tears. Tension in my frame is causing pain to stab at my forehead, neck and shoulders. It's squeezing my lungs, making it difficult to breathe. Tears dampen my cheeks and I ask myself for the thousandth time that day, why?

Then a small black dot in my mind grows. It takes wing and flies into every fold of my brain. Did I kill someone, it asks? I knew too much. I know too much. Where did all this knowledge come from? Not only did I know what the wounds on the dead man were, but I have a series of pictures in my head that show me how it happened. All that is missing from the murder scene are the feathers. Am I the killer? My colleagues appear to have little doubt. Maybe it was my feelings of guilt I was trying to deny.

But I was with Theresa, sensible me argues. I go over the events of the night in my head. I go to Theresa's from the pub, we make love, we fall asleep, we make love again, we fall asleep and then I get the call to head over to the crime scene. Where was there time in that little scenario to go and commit a murder? Did you really sleep, a voice asks? You could have slipped out of bed, hailed a taxi on the main road. Then you did the deed, cleaned yourself up, changed out of your costume and returned to give Theresa another one...

'Stop it!' I shout, causing the young PC behind the glass to stare. I look at him for the first time, taking in the blond, almost white hair, and the face that probably sees a razor once a fortnight at the most. He has gone for an expression of boredom, but his crossed arms and legs and the fact that the line of his long, lean frame is facing towards the door lets me know he isn't entirely comfortable at his post. I meet his stare and toy with the idea that I could quite easily mess with this guy's head. Then I move my line of sight from him to the door facing me, thinking, don't be a bastard, McBain, you can use this time a little more productively than that.

I drop my shoulders and take a deep, slow breath. Relax, you'll not fight your way out of this one if you're wound up. Breathe. Drop those shoulders. I go through every part of my body naming it in my head and tell it to relax. I feel the air brush against the hairs in my nostrils as I breathe in, feel it fill my lungs and allow it to seep out again. A crystal forms in my mind's eye, I watch light beams reflect from its faceted face and try to concentrate. But thoughts and accusations don't allow my mind to be still. They crowd in like cars on the M8 at rush hour. Murderer. I feel the muscles in my back tighten. This is no good. I lie down on the mattress on my stomach and using my arm as a pillow, aim for some sleep instead.

When I was younger and after I had learned to control my bladder, sleep was a hobby of mine, I loved my bed. While other convent children complained among themselves that it was too early, that it was still light outside, with the customary chant, "It's not fair", I would brush my teeth with pleasure at the thought of curling under those heavy blankets and fantasising about the life I wished I lived. My parents were together in this dream and we lived in a house built on the playground behind the convent. There was a neat little row of these houses and all the children had one each and their parents lived with them too. In this house

I had a massive room to myself, with a huge bed that stretched from wall to wall, and I had a stash of batteries and a torch under one pillow so I could read into the night after everyone else had gone to sleep. In this house there was plenty of chocolate and crisps and I always got a cuddle before I went to bed. Under the warmth of this fantasy, I would coast off to sleep in seconds.

What would provide a fantasy that would send me off to sleep in my present situation? I imagine being in bed with Theresa in post-coital sloth. She has her head resting on my shoulder. I kiss her forehead and breathe in the smell of her shampoo. She slides a hand over my chest and down to my stomach, tweaks a hair here and there, her breath hot on my nipple.

'Do you want to do it again?' she whispers.

'In a moment,' I smile and close my eyes, enjoying her calming touch, arousal for once the last thing on my mind. The light dims, sounds fade. Peace. My heart has slowed to match the give and take of the tide on a windless summer's day. All is black.

Then a pinprick of light glows in the centre of my mind's eye. Slowly it expands and, as it grows, it greedily squeezes out the dark, I hear a voice singing. Then another joins in. And another. They belong to children. Except the tone isn't light and fun, it's heavy with threat. Every hair on my body is on end. But I've no need to be afraid. Yet.

Can I put a name to those voices?

Is it a memory? What is happening to me? Why is this going on in my head?

A thought of such certainty and clarity forces me to sit upright on the bed. Someone has been murdered and more are going to follow if the police don't get their collective act together. This isn't a one off. There's more to this than a simple, solitary act of revenge. I don't know how I know this but I do. I run to the door.

'Campbell. Campbell, get your arse down here,' I shout over and over again, banging on the door with every ounce of energy I own. What feels like hours later the door opens and several large men run in and rush me over to the bed. Someone is holding each arm and leg and stretching my head back, I recognise one who is sitting on my chest.

'Johnstone. Get Campbell.'

'Sir, if you don't calm down we'll have to put you in restraints,' is his reply.

'For fuckssake, get Campbell.'

'Sir, I'm going to warn you one more time to calm down or we'll have to put you in restraints.'

'Okay. Okay.' I force my voice to slow down, 'I'm calm. I'm calm.' The pressure on my chest eases.

'Right, I'm going to take a step back and if you start up again, we'll bring the doc in here and give you something to calm you down,' says Johnstone.

'Okay. Okay.' I take deep, slow breaths, fight for composure, 'But you need to get Detective Superintendent Campbell. There's going to be another murder.'

Chapter 21

'Right, McBain. What the hell is going on?' Campbell pushes open the door and walks in. Peters walks in behind him. I walk up to my old boss.

'You have to let me out of here. There's going to be another murder.'

'Right.' Campbell crosses his arms. 'Sure. There's going to be another murder. And you want out.'

'Yes dammit, we need to act quickly. Find the fucker who's doing this!' I feel a speck of spittle spray on to my lips. Campbell, who is inches from me, picks a linen handkerchief from his breast pocket and wipes the side of his face; his lips curl in a shape of utter distaste.

'And we are going to act on the word of someone who is behaving like a madman?'

Walking back from him, I feel my calves hit the side of my bed and I sit down. His look of disgust and disbelief hits me like a fist in the solar plexus.

'We're friends, Tom. We've...'

'Were friends. Ray. Were. The minute... the second you crossed that line you lost all claims to that.'

'So what happened to "innocent before being proven guilty" then?' My voice is quiet, almost hushed. He hasn't shown me any of his feelings up to now and it comes as a real shock. 'I didn't do it, Tom.' The note of pleading in my voice turns my stomach, but I can't help myself.

'Yes. Well. That's for a jury to decide.' He turns and moves towards the door.

'Tom. I'm serious.' I decide to change tack. 'I was a good cop, right? Right?'

He nods like it's breaking his heart to agree with me.

'So, for a moment ignore the fact that I'm in a cell...'

'Sir,' Peters takes a step towards us, 'You can't seriously be entertaining what he has to say?' Campbell silences him with a look.

'Ray, I can't ignore the fact that you are in a cell. I can't ignore the fact that you have just been charged with murder either.'

'The guy who did this; he's going to kill again.'

'Well, when he does and it matches the M.O. of the Connelly case, your innocence will be assured. Until then you stay locked up.'

One of the benefits of being a police officer in this situation, well, the only benefit, is that I know the system. They have to take me to court the next lawful day after my arrest. There I will appear in a private hearing in the Sheriff's Chambers. I will be bound over for a period of seven days with no plea or declaration, then reappear in the courthouse to plead guilty or not guilty. Then comes the bit I'm really not looking forward to. The law says that I must be held on petition for no greater than one hundred and ten days and that the trial must commence within this period. They are not going to keep me in this wee cell for that length of time. That would be inhuman. No, they'll have to send me to the Bar L. Just where every policeman wants to spend his days.

Every occupation must have their nightmare scenario, one the workers, every now and again, will talk about in whispers around the water-cooler. We have ours as well: being locked up with a group of people who feel they have every right to hate you and no compunction about acting on their animal instincts. Tales are common about former policemen being beaten or raped, or beaten *and* raped.

Maybe I could play on the impression I just gave Campbell. I've lost it. I could use insanity as my defence. I've never considered it a blessing before now, but I have a heavy growth. If I don't shave tonight or tomorrow before I go in front of the Sheriff, I'll look quite rough. A wild stare and a few comments about hearing voices and they'll send me off to a psychiatric hospital instead.

Light coming in from the window has faded somewhat. Movement beyond the glass catches my eye. A young dark-haired cop has replaced the young, blond cop. He adopts the same seating posture as his predecessor and sets himself up for a long, boring night. I envy the blond guy so much I want to punch something. What's he going to do tonight? Sit in front

128

of the telly? Go for a drink with his mates? Pork his girlfriend? Bastard.

Calm down, McBain. I tell myself. You'll never sleep if you get all riled up. But I don't want to sleep. Look what happened the last time: strange notions popped into my head. Aye, and if you stay awake all night, you really are going to look like shit when you go before the Sheriff.

I need to stop thinking like this. It's going to send me into madness. Be constructive. Concentrate on finding a solution to the problem, instead of dwelling on the problem itself for hours and hours. Fact one: someone was murdered. Fact two: I've been accused of it and locked up. Fact three: I'm not a murderer. Someone else did it, and that someone else is laughing his clever little head off at my predicament. How happy will they be that an investigating officer is taking the blame?

So what do you normally do at this point in a case? You review the evidence you do have.

We found three plausible suspects so far.

The boy, Crichton. I recall our meeting, his posture, and the look in his eyes. My reaction to him. Correct that: overreaction. Could he have planned and carried out such a murder? Yes. Did he do it? Possibly.

The next suspect is the salesman from Aberdeen. Could he have carried out such a murder? Perhaps, but I get the feeling that his likes are more subtle than that. He is about taking power over vulnerable people and using them. If he killed his victims, he wouldn't be able to do that. He's guilty of something, I'm sure, I just don't know what it is.

Who's next? Carole Devlin. What do I know about her? We are part of one another's past. There are not many kids I remember from my time at the convent, but I remember her. Probably because the nuns didn't want me to talk to her too much. They thought she would be a bad influence on me. She was a good five years older than me, no doubt sexually aware, and the nuns would have been in the horrors at the thought of what she might do to poor impressionable little me. After all we were all just wee animals, with no instinct of what was right or wrong and not to be trusted, especially when a girl was on her own near a penis-bearer. Regardless that the owner of said penis thought it was solely a tool for urinating with.

Carole wasn't like the other older girls who, thinking we were on a par with vermin, completely ignored the boys. Whatever her purpose was, and from the vantage point of age that is no clearer to me now, it suited me. I was on my own. No family to speak of. A sister would have been nice.

So what that every now and again she would demand a look at my penis? It was just another part of my body. It had no particular use that I could think of and if she wanted to touch it as well, what was the harm?

The recent Carole was a different story. I wasn't drawn to her in the least. The opposite in fact, she was like a void. When I bring an image of her into my mind I see workmanlike hands and unhappiness that surrounded her like a cloak of dust. However, she took in that young boy and brought him up after his mother died. That is the discordant note in my memory of her. The person sitting in that chair, quietly hostile, was not a woman I thought would have bothered about her own child, never mind someone else's.

What was the deal about the boy? Why was she obliged to look after him? And after being so generous, how would it feel for the boy to throw it back in her face by going off to study in a city two hundred miles away? Is this the reason for her bitterness?

Then there were all the photographs around her living space. If she was reluctant to take the boy in, she appears to be proud of him. Or am I missing something?

The question remains, however, is she a killer? My instinct at the time was that she and the boy are linked to the deceased in some way and if I could find out that link, I might be on my way to finding the murderer.

There's just the small matter of finding a Get Out of Jail card. Pronto.

Chapter 22

The first thing I'm aware of this morning is the pressure on my bladder. The second thing is that I have my usual morning stiffy. It's bad enough having to pee in full view of someone, but to have to do so while pushing down an erection makes it all the more humiliating.

Sitting on the edge of my bed, I realise my prick is not the only part of my body that is stiff. My neck. My back. I rub my neck with the fingers of my left, kneading the flesh in the hope that the resultant increased blood flow will mean that I can move without feeling any pain. Standing up, I grunt. I feel about fifty. Placing the heels of my hands over my kidney area, I arch my back. Another grunt. My bladder is becoming more insistent; walking with the pace of a geriatric I go over to the toilet bowl. Thankfully Mr Stiffy has subsided so I can pee without any acrobatics.

Just as I'm shaking off the last few drops, the hatch opens.

'They're coming to take you to the Sheriff at ten,' a voice announces. 'A bacon roll do you for breakfast?'

'Aye.' My stomach rumbles in assent. 'Kind of gone off my diet.'

Memory tells me that they do the breakfast round just after seven, when the early shift starts, so I've loads of time to wait. Too much time to think. Remember, think of a solution, not the problem.

A killer is out there. He has struck again. I know it. But there should be a dead body somewhere. A body with the same wounds on it as Connelly's, or similar. Unless he has changed his M.O. Possible. Serial killers tend to have some similarity in their methods, a forensic post-it note that leads us right to him. Let's hope our man hasn't deviated too much from his script. I walk to the door, turn and walk back to the bed. Got to do something. Can't just stay here and let some evil bastard pass the blame on to me. I walk to the door.

Back to the bed.

Who'll be able to help me? My colleagues will not want to know. I've not only cut off my ties with them, I've lacerated them, set them on fire and danced a wee jig on the still-warm embers. No, there will be no assistance there. Besides, they've got a strong suspect for the murder. Yours truly. Chalk one up for the department, another case solved. Except they are way off. Couldn't be more wrong if they said the earth was flat.

Back to the door.

Will I get a fair trial? It will be a high profile case. The media will be all over it like dung beetles at Shit Mountain. A senior police officer being caught wrist deep in blood, there's little chance of a jury not to have heard of the case. What will they call me, I wonder? They love their catchy headlines don't they?

Back to the door.

I can't do anything while I'm in here. As far as Campbell is concerned, they have their man. They can prove I have a connection to the deceased; that my whereabouts were unaccounted for at the time of Connelly's death. All they need is a motive and they could come up with that easily enough. A former orphan at the home he worked at murdered a molester of children. Connelly must have molested me, they will say, and then argue that I've waited all these years to exact my revenge. Sounds plausible. If I were the investigating officer, I would go for it.

Back to the bed.

Then it will be bye bye life, as Campbell so kindly put it. Bye bye arse as well, 'cos it will be fried in that hellhole of a prison. They'll be queuing up for me.

Back to the door.

With their fat, unwashed cocks in one hand and a sharp piece of steel in the other, my life won't be worth a button.

Back to the bed.

Stop worrying about the problem, McBain. What are you going to do about it? The only thing I can do. They are coming to take me to the Sheriff this morning. Thereafter I will be back in secure surroundings till the following week when I will have to plead, then it will be off to the Bar L.

I have to do it this morning. I have to make a run for it.

You're gambling with your life here, McBain. If you get caught, you can throw another few years on to your sentence. If you don't, maybe you can find the real killer.

While I wait to be taken across to the court, I formulate a plan. Hopefully it will be young inexperienced guys who will get such a routine job as this. Escort duty is never the most popular. They'll be unsure how to react to someone who was a big boss just a few days ago. That uncertainty could give me an edge. It'll mean more black marks on more fellow officer's careers. I swallow my guilt, some things have to be done.

I've almost worn a groove in the cement floor by the time they come for me. The first man in the door is the blond guy from yesterday. Excellent. His mate, however, looks a bit older. I hold my hands out.

'Right, get the cuffs on, boys.'

'Do we need them, sir?' the older one asks. 'It's not as if you're going to do a runner is it?' They both laugh. Their laughter is embarrassed, uncertain, but there is something else there, a note of pleasure that one of the bosses is in trouble. Any guilt I was forming evaporates.

'Let's go,' I show a weak smile and adopt the body language of the defeated.

They part and allow me passage between them and then position themselves at either side. In the narrow corridors of this place that could pose a problem, particularly if we meet someone coming in the opposite direction.

My heart is thudding almost as loud as our feet hitting the floor. Calm. Keep it calm, McBain. The door ahead opens and a policeman comes through. Beyond that door is a fire exit I know is unlocked. The policeman smiles in recognition of the two men who are escorting me.

'Partick Thistle didn't do too well last night, Young,' he addresses the older cop.

'Fuck off, White. They jammy bastards scored in the last minute of extra time,' PC Young responds.

'Funny how whenever your team lose it's because the other lot were lucky,' White replies as he passes me. He gives me a brief look as if he's trying to place me and then replaces his smile as he faces Young. I keep walking.

'What do you think, Dunn?' He must be addressing the blond guy. I'm not looking back to check. Keep it nice and easy, McBain.

'Aye, these bastards are all paranoid,' says Dunn. Their footsteps pause. 'Think everyone in the country's out to get them.'

'Well they are!' argues Young. 'Happens every time.' I put my hand on the door and push it open. No reaction from my guardians. Keep it calm, McBain.

'Oh come on. Just face it, Davie. Your team are shite.' I step through the door, turn to face the men and hold it open. They both look over at me. My heart pauses. I manage a smile that says I'm enjoying the banter. Dunn takes a step towards me, but makes the mistake of turning to hear what his mate has to say in reply. Still smiling, I flick the snib on the lock of the door with my thumb, step back and slam the door shut before they can react. Then, two steps and I am out of the fire exit.

Don't run, I tell myself. As I walk across the car park, the emotional part of my brain is locked away, while the logical one is calculating my next action. The guys won't be behind that door for too long. Plus they can quickly radio the control room for assistance and then every policeman's radio in the vicinity will be playing my tune. I need to vanish and fast.

There's a row of cars in front of me. My Volkswagen is right in the middle of them. What I would do for the keys. The best place to hide is the one they would least expect. I walk over to my car, check the door. Locked. I bend down as if tying my lace in case anyone looks out of a window and happens to see me. Then I fall forward and crawl under the car and settle for a long wait.

The search will concentrate on the surrounding area initially before fanning out. Several loud footsteps and several loud shouts tempt me to break into the car and hot-wire it. I could be out of here in seconds. But then I'd have half of Strathclyde Police on my tail. *That would be too visible,* the logical part of my brain says. *Lie here until the fuss dies down and then you can steal your own car.*

More footsteps. They move to my car. I can make out two people. Then I recognise a voice.

'His car's still here then,' says Peters. 'Wouldn't have put it past him to hot-wire it.' I daren't breathe in case they hear me.

'Pity,' says Allessandra Rossi, 'Then we would have been straight on to him.' She says this with no conviction whatsoever.

'You did the right thing, you know that don't you, Allessandra.' Peters reads her tone. 'He's a killer. He deserves to be locked up.'

'Yeah. Right. Of course he does,' she replies. The uncertainty in her voice lifts my spirits. Perhaps my colleagues haven't all fallen in with the party line. The situation isn't quite as hopeless as I thought. Their footsteps fall away from the car.

I rest my head on my arm and exhale the lungful of air I was holding in. Nothing to do now but wait and judge the right moment to make a move. But what would I do? Where would I go?

First thing I have to do is get the fuck out of here. I've no idea what the time is. My meeting was to be with the Sheriff at ten o'clock. So, assuming the guys came for me at 9:30, say, it might just be ten o'clock now. Do I wait until it's dark? That means lying here until about nine pm. Thankfully, because it's late autumn, it's not too cold, but it won't be dark until after seven. The next change of shift is at two. There will be officers coming and going around then. Some getting into uniform, others getting out of theirs. Unless of course the bosses spring for some overtime because of a certain missing felon. Nah, doubt it. I'm not that important surely.

So that's it. Two o'clock I make my move.

Seconds yawn and stretch themselves into minutes. Minutes awake from a coma and turn into hours. First, I lean my head on one arm and then when it goes dead, I change over for the other. It is out of the question to turn over and lie on my back, the space under the car isn't big enough to allow movement of my shoulders. I think of Theresa. I wonder what she's doing right now. Then it occurs to me that when I tried to relax last night in order to sleep, it was her I thought of. It was her arms around me as I nodded off. Sex didn't even enter the equation, I wanted her to comfort me, pick me up and swaddle me in a cocoon of affection.

McBain, you are getting soft. Better watch mate, next thing you'll be buying her flowers and professing undying love.

I inspect the tarmac. A distraction is needed. A couple of loose stones here and there, a couple of fag ends, a patch of hardened chewing gum that is almost the colour of the road itself. It reminds me of Peters, indeed, it could almost be a metaphor for lots of the men who inhabit the building behind me. Start off life as a pink mass, get chewed up, spat out, driven over and left to accumulate dirt, until they are indistinguishable from the sea of grey that surrounds them.

Footsteps. Someone is heading in this direction. Are my feet sticking out? As slowly as I dare, I lift them up towards the underside of the car. Holding my breath I crane my neck forward to try and see as much as I can. A pair of feet pause close to my car.

They are clad in black leather, but it isn't the usual boots the uniform guys wear, it's a pair of well-polished black brogues. Then I hear the beep of a remote key, a car door opens momentarily, then slams shut. The remote sounds again, signalling that the car has been locked again. Damn. Then a hushed voice speaks.

'Shame the boss had to go and escape. If he knew I was here right now, he would be able to see me place the keys for my car, my fucking pride and joy, on the nearside front tyre under the wheel-arch. Then maybe he would be able to escape for real. He can always drop the car off at my house, tonight at the latest.' I hear the jangle of a set of keys and then the footsteps recede.

Daryl Drain, you beauty. You could just have saved my life.

Being an escaped convict while trying not to look like one is a difficult trick to pull off. When people are trying too hard to be inconspicuous, they tend to look quite the opposite. Getting off the ground and into the front seat of that car must be one of the most difficult things I've ever had to do.

Keeping a straight back when all your energy is focused on hunching is well nigh impossible. I send a prayer of thanks skywards for remote controls. At least I don't have to wrestle with a bunch of keys. I pull at the handle and step into the car. Closing the door, I slide down the seat and from this low vantage point have a good look around me. Excellent. Not a copper in sight.

Something is digging into my arse. I arch my back, lift up my backside and send my right hand down for a search and grab mission. My fingers close around an object about the size of a mobile phone and some paper. Excellent. It is a mobile phone and the paper is money, along with a scribbled note. A quick count. Ninety pounds. The note is unsigned. It reads "I can get you more if you need it."

The engine fires nice and quietly and I'm off. As I negotiate my way into the stream of traffic the back of my neck is burning. I imagine a hundred cops are watching me. No shouts, no sirens. I exhale painfully, not realising I was holding my breath.

Where to now? I'll drive the car to Daryl's house, get a taxi to meet me there and take me somewhere. But where? I can't go home to mine. Theresa's? Will she even want to hear from me after my phone calls? I wouldn't mind her calm, no fuss approach right now. No. I can't take the risk. But there is one person I can phone. One person who is outside of the law and who will only be too delighted to help

Daryl's flat is over in Battlefield; it won't take long to get there. Most guys keep their car keys and house keys together on the same fob, so if Daryl is like most guys... I reach under the wheel and grope at his key ring. Yes, a few keys there. If I'm right, I could go upstairs to his flat, have a shower, make myself something to eat and then decide on a plan of attack. I need to find myself some security and from there find the bastard who killed Connelly and clear my name. That's all.

So simple. Nae bother. A couple of questions. How did Daryl know where I was? And why did he help me escape?

Driving along the edge of Queens Park on Pollokshaws Road, I turn right into Langside Avenue. The car moves effortlessly down the hill, back up to a roundabout and from there past the Victoria Infirmary and down towards the monument.

Turning into Daryl's road, I find a parking space in the narrow street with no trouble. There's a blue skip hat on the passenger seat with the legend NYC. Daryl once admitted to me that this was his rescue during bad hair days. I put it on. It may be mine today. I don't want to be recognised going into his flat.

Apart from the car key, there are another two keys on the ring. One must be for the communal door at the front and the other would hopefully be for the door of his flat. Pulling the hat low over my face I get out of the car, lock it and walk to the door. So far, so good. No shouts of alarm, no shouts of "Stop, murderer!"

Just as I reach it, the door opens. A man in a dark suit holding a briefcase comes out. Judging by the way he smiles and leaves the door open for me as he exits, he must be a stranger. Probably a salesman. He beams in a "see, I'm a nice guy" kind of way. I ignore him and let the door slam shut behind me.

Inside the flat I have a quick tour of the place and I'm well impressed. I was expecting lots of boys' toys, beer cans and clothes flung everywhere, but this is like something out of *Ideal Home*. Lots of wood, stone and natural fibres. And very tidy.

The shower beckons. Needles of heat sting my shoulders as steam condenses on the glass wall of the cubicle. I lean against it and savour the feel of water pouring over my body. There's a bottle of Calvin Klein shower gel sitting on a shelf, none of your soap on a rope for our Daryl. It foams up rather nicely as I rub it all over me.

Dried and wrapped in a towel, I rake through Daryl's drawers. I find some clean underwear and ignore his stash of porn. Sad bastard. Living on his own and he still feels he needs to hide it in his sock drawer.

Clean, clothed and sipping a cup of coffee, I sit in his leather chair in front of the plasma TV and consider my options. There really is only one person I can call right now, so I pull Daryl's mobile out of my pocket and give Kenny O'Neill a call.

'Ray!' He sounds happy to hear from me and wary at the same time. I explain what I need.

'Give me your number and I'll call you back.' He ends the call. Doesn't hang about, our Kenny. Sitting back in the chair I put on the TV and settle in for a long wait.

The phone rings. That was quick.

'Hello?'

'Ray, you better not be driving and talking on the phone at the same time.' It's Daryl.

'Listen, Drain, I've got more to worry about than a Dangerous Driving caution.'

'Where are you? Doesn't sound like you're driving.'

'I'm at your place.'

'Fine. Help yourself.'

'I just have. Nice porn stash.'

'Fuck off. If there are any more pages sticking together I'll know who to blame.'

We both laugh. I'd forgotten what it sounds like.

'How did you know I was under the car?' I ask.

'The smell. You were fuckin' mingin' man.'

'No, really. How did you know?' I'm all laughed out already.

'We saw you,' he paused. I could almost hear him decide to tell me the truth, 'Allessandra saw your foot sticking out when she was in the car park with Peters. He totally missed you. Wanker.' He laughs. 'There'll be no cop of the month award for him then, eh? She came back in and told me and we decided to give you a hand, so to speak. It was touch and go, mind,' I heard his smile, 'It would have been funny to see how you reacted if we set the dogs on you.'

'I'd have kicked their arses.' I am suddenly overwhelmed with everything; my stay in the cell, being under suspicion, the booze,

Theresa. And now Daryl and Allessandra's kindness.

'Listen, Daryl,' my voice is thick with suppressed emotion, 'you've no idea how grateful...'

'No worries, big man,' Daryl sounds embarrassed. 'Whatever else you are, you're no killer, Ray. Allessandra and I know that. The whole team knows it.'

'Well, not the whole team.'

'Peters is an arse and Campbell wouldn't know a criminal if he came up and fucked him.'

I laugh in agreement, 'I'm going to go away for a while, Daryl,' and now I'm all business. 'Do you mind if I keep a hold of your phone? I'll keep in touch. Oh, and I'll put the keys for your pride and joy back where I found them.' He hangs up.

This chair is so comfortable. I put my feet on the coffee table and close my eyes. Sleep would be a blessing right now. The phone rings.

'Hello?'

'Ray. I'm outside.' It's Kenny.

In the car, he's all concern.

'So you're a suspected killer then?'

'Looks like it, mate.'

'What you going to do?'

'Find the real killer. Lock the fucker up. And get my life back.'

Chapter 23

'Hey, this is nice,' I hear myself say as I walk in the door of Kenny's flat. Fuckin' hell, McBain, you're on the run, a suspect for murder and you're coming across like a daytime TV presenter.

One of the walls has a large window that looks like it opens out to a balcony, the floor is laminate wood and the furniture is modern and sparse.

'Glad you like it,' Kenny smiles. 'It just became vacant this morning.' His smile hints at the more "practical" side of his nature.

'Is some poor sod out on the street because of me?'

'I was just looking for an excuse,' he shrugs. 'The prick was having too many wild parties. Upsetting the neighbours.'

'Nice view,' I walk towards the window and get the back view of what looks like a church. To my left and right sandstone dresses the walls of the apartment blocks. This all looks very desirable. I look back at the church. It's also starting to look very familiar.

'You can see the pigs on their way to get you,' Kenny is wearing a huge grin. The irony of the situation and the location I find myself in is tickling him so much he's about to explode and decorate the walls with his insides.

'This is St Andrews Square, ya bastard.' The church in front of me was recently converted into an upmarket dance hall. In the basement it has a café/bar which is frequented by the lawyers, police and court workers who attend the court buildings around the corner.

'Aye.' He is actually jumping up and down in an attempt to contain his mirth.

'What the fuck are you playing at?'

'Look. Calm down, Ray.' He walks over to me and places a hand on my shoulder. I want to take it and break every one of his fingers.

'Where is the best place to hide? Where is the last place they are going to look for you? Right in their midst. That's where.'

'I suppose...' I say weakly.

'We'll just get you a wee disguise and you'll be as safe as houses. No-one will give you a second look.'

'Aye, right.'

'You got any stuff?' he asks, all officious now that the funny business has been taken care of.

'Nope. Homeless, jobless and... stuff-less.'

'Make a list of what you need and I'll see what I can do.' He reaches into a pocket, pulls out a pen and throws it to me. Then he walks over to the kitchen.

'Cuppa?'

'Love one.' I spot a pad of paper by the telephone and begin to write. Water rushes into the kettle and I hear the clink of a switch.

'What're you going to do now?' Kenny's voice is muffled behind a cupboard door as he pulls out mugs and a jar of coffee.

'Not sure,' I mumble with the pen resting on my bottom lip. 'But there's a few people I need to speak to.'

We're both sipping at our mugs when Kenny asks, 'You lost weight?'

'Fuckin' funny.'

'Naw, seriously.' His expression is stretched as he attempts to convey his honesty. 'You look slimmer.'

'Mind you,' I pull at the fabric of my waistband. 'My trousers do feel a little bit looser.'

'You should capitalise on that.'

'What, go and get myself a woman?'

'Naw, ya tosser. You're on the run from a group of colleagues who know you very well. Do you not think it would be advisable to change your appearance a wee bit?'

'Ah...right. Now I see where you were going with the disguise malarkey...' I think about this.

'Stay here for a few weeks. Grow a beard. Dye your hair. Lose some more weight. Then you'll be able to go about without worrying you'll get spotted.'

'I dunno. It's all a bit Secret Spy, is it no'?'

'Better Secret Spy than playing I Spy with your new cell-mate.' He raises his eyebrows, 'His version will involve sticking his Jap's Eye up your jacksie.' He rocks his hips back and forward in a lewd motion. 'I Spy this!'

'Aye, okay. Enough. I get the picture.'

'How did you lose the weight?'

141

'A steady diet of no food, little sleep and lots of alcohol.'

'You've gone to the dogs, man,' Kenny displays the compassionate side of his nature. 'We need something even more radical than that.'

'Eh? What's more radical than that? A holiday spa in Eritrea?'

'Heard of the Atkins Diet?'

'Who hasn't?'

'Give it a try then.'

'I hate diets. Know why? Take away the T and you're left with D.I.E.'

'Don't worry, you'll be fine.'

'The new me will need some clothes.'

'I'll get you some down at the market.' He stands up. I've finished writing so he takes my piece of paper. 'Time to go for the messages.' I walk him to the door.

'Kenny,' I place my hand on his shoulder. He turns to face me. 'I just want to thank you for... everything.'

'No problem, Ray. You saved my arse twice. I've been waiting for a chance to pay you back. And this...' he grins, 'is kind of ironic. You being the criminal for a change.' He turns and walks towards the lift with a cheeky wave.

Now that I'm alone in the flat the enormity of what has happened in the last few hours kicks me in the gut. I'm a fugitive from the very people I've dedicated my life to. My stomach is a roiling sea of acid. Holy fuck, McBain. You've only gone and done it. You're a wanted man.

My whole way of life is under threat: I've no job, probably about to lose my home. I'm due to be locked up for the rest of my natural... unless I find out what happened to Connelly.

Relax, Ray. You work better when you are relaxed. I slide down in my seat and close my eyes. I take a deep, slow breath. My nose fills with the scent of leather from the settee. Exhale nice and slow. In again... and out. My mind is still. Now I imagine my consciousness expanding to take in the room, I'm looking down at myself, then I'm out of the room and above the city. I see buildings, parks, roads and people. Which one of you is the real killer? I can see the River Clyde snaking under bridges, stretching for the sea and freedom.

Calm down and come up with some ideas. Need to relax. But I can't. My shoulders feel as if I've been giving Arnold

Schwarzenegger a piggyback and my arms are rigid. Maybe if I distract myself with something else. I jump to my feet and walk to the window. Watching the traffic flow up the Saltmarket might induce some sort of trance. But they're moving too slowly. There's a nice Beamer, a few nice Mercedes and quite a number of four-wheel drives. I wonder how much metal goes up and down that street every day in financial terms. A couple of million pounds worth of car? The rats in the race are setting themselves up quite nicely these days.

Anger bunches in my jaw, grinds my teeth. How can these men who should know me better treat me like this? Where was the benefit of the doubt? No, instead it's straight into a cell for you, McBain. Bastards!

This staying calm thing is really working, eh?

The need to act has me pacing up and down the floor. Think of a solution, not the problem. The solution not the problem. Who do I need to speak to? Theresa. Another friendly face around now wouldn't go amiss. Who do I need to go and see? Devlin's stepson. There's a story there and I need to find out what it is. Where is he? Manchester University. A few days south of the border might be just what the doctor ordered.

He's never so much as laid a finger on a woman. Before today. He was brought up a nice boy. Ha Ha. You don't hit girls. You are stronger than they are. You could really hurt them, they all said. So he didn't. Until today. He looks into the mirror and smiles. He tastes the sensation as lips slide across teeth and his cheeks stretch. The row of white gleams under the strong light. He practises his smile, again and again, noticing the smacking sound his lips make as he does so. The last smile he leaves in place, fixes it as if waiting for a photographer to take a snap. Say hard cheese, you're dead.

She'd put up an even better fight than Connelly. Spirited old biddy. She'd even scratched the back of his right hand. Came away with quite a bit of flesh. He traced the long divot of torn flesh with his right index finger and allowed the shudders to work their way through his body.

And so much for the higher pain threshold that women were supposed to have, she'd squealed enough for ten stuck pigs. It was too much, went beyond pleasing to downright irritating. Still, she'd mercifully passed out when he broke her jaw.

143

The sensation that this memory provides has him gasping for air. Every nerve end on his body is thrumming with life. This is what it's like to be alive, to really live. Everything is crisper, clearer... harder. He can count every pore on the skin that stretches across the bridge of his nose. He can see through the enamel of his teeth, through to the nerve below. His prick is about to burst if he doesn't...

A door slides shut and I'm out of my chair as if it was a gunshot.

I fist my eyes.

'Fall asleep?' It's Kenny and he's got company. One of the walking knuckle-dusters I saw him with previously. They are both carrying branded plastic bags from the local supermarket.

'There's plenty here. I got everything on your list, I think.' He rustles through one and plucks out two boxes. 'As well as these.'

'What's that?' I squint trying to read the box.

'Hair dye and hair clippers.' He points his minder towards the kitchen and motions lifting things out of a bag, is if to say to the big man to put everything away. 'Oh and this is Calum, by the way.'

'Hi, Calum.' I say to the broadest back I've ever seen. Calum's social graces could do with some work judging by his lack of response, but I guess that's not what he's employed for.

'The instructions are on the packet,' says Kenny.

'What, for Calum?' I try for a result. Nothing.

'Naw, stupid. For the dye.'

'I feel a bit daft dying my hair.'

Kenny turns to the side and humps at the air, 'I Spy?' He lifts up the small box, 'Or hair dye?'

'When you put it like that.' I walk over to him and accept the box.

'Oh. And the food is all healthy junk. None of your processed carbs here.' He grins. 'We'll soon have you licked into shape. Talking of which, there's a nice girl I know called Precious. If you want I'll give her a call.'

'Thank you, but no.' I don't fancy having a session with Kenny's current favourite vice girl. He looks at me disbelievingly and not wishing to hurt my saviour I rush to explain. 'It's just that I can't think about sex right now.'

'It would do you the world of good, man. A good blowjob is the best tension reliever known to man.'

'I'm sure Precious is a lovely girl, but I'm going to have to decline. Unless,' I wave the bottle at him, 'she's a trained hairdresser.'

'You're on your own there, mate.'

Two hours later, I'm in front of a mirror, wearing a navy tracksuit by FILA. My T-shirt is another source of amusement for Kenny. It is from Next, and is light blue except for the huge circular target right in the centre, coloured navy and white. The bullseye is a lovely shade of red.

The hair is something special as well. The last time I saw a haircut like that, Paul Gascoigne had just signed for Glasgow Rangers, resulting in every football fan of a certain blue tint to his or her nose under the age of thirty-five getting their hair cropped and bleached platinum blonde.

'I look like a middle-aged ned.' I run my fingers through what remains of my hair. 'All I need is a bottle of Buckfast.' Kenny is on his knees, stuffing a fist into his mouth, trying to control his laughter. 'Did you have to get me a tracksuit? And the T-shirt, ya bastard!'

'There's... not... a policeman in the whole of Strathclyde will know you.' Words escape past his knuckles.

'That's true. But they'll all be chasing me. I'll be a major suspect for every petty crime committed in the last twenty-four hours.' A laugh escapes from my throat.

'Listen. The tracksuit is something loose and comfy until you lose your weight. Then I'll get you some trendy threads. Okay?' Kenny leaves the bedroom and I can hear his laugh echo in the space of the hall. I follow him downstairs and walk in front of Calum. This time his lack of response should earn him a medal.

Kenny walks to the main entrance of the flat and turns to me, 'I need to go now, but I want you to think of this place as your home. Calum will stay and keep you company for a few days.' He looks me up and down, 'Don't go scaring any old ladies.' Laughing, he opens the door and leaves.

Dinner is a grilled chicken breast covered in herbs, with some broccoli. Calum cooked it. Without a word he walked over to the kitchen, pulled a few items from the fridge and within half an hour he thrust a plate on to my lap where I sat on the settee. His, he ate at the kitchen's breakfast bar.

'So where are your instructions, Calum?'

'I don't know what you mean, sir.' He must have been brought up well: he finished chewing before he spoke.

'The hair dye had them printed on the box. Where are yours?'

'Oh,' his eyes have the look of someone who has seen too much. 'Very funny, sir.'

'Look, Calum. This is hopeless. If you are going to spend any time in my company a personality is required.'

'Certainly, sir.'

'And stop fucking calling me sir.' I give up. The man thinks he's playing the lead part in a new movie called *Mission Inscrutable*.

In between mouthfuls, I pick up the TV remote and switch on the telly. We have a choice of *Neighbours*, some bowling competition, the news or another repeat of *Friends*. Or a plethora of nothing programmes on satellite TV. I could do with a laugh, so I go back to the news. Some news presenter with the hint of a regional accent is talking about the Prime Minister and how he's fucked up again. Then we have the usual "Let's Finish with Some Good News" slot.

Some poor sap has a cat that has been stuck up a tree two hundred times and it's cost the taxpayer tens of thousands of pounds in call-outs from the Fire Brigade. The cat owner is interviewed wearing his best cardigan.

'I love Benji.' He's trying to tell the nation why they should continue to save his best and only friend in the world. Christ, this eejit's as sad as me.

Then we have the round-up of today's news. My face flashes on to the screen.

The newsreader says, 'Detective Inspector Ray McBain, wanted by Strathclyde Police for murder, escaped from custody. This man is dangerous and should not be approached by members of the public.' The piece must have been hurriedly put together because the photograph is pretty blurred. Judging from the building behind me, I've just left court and I've turned just as some snapper has taken the photo. The blurring effect has been kind. I look almost handsome, in a chubby, cute sort of way.

Fuckfuckfuck.

Don't know why I'm upset. I should have been expecting it. This is big news. It's not often any policeman, let alone a high ranking one, is a suspect for murder. I have to hope that, by tomorrow, today's headlines are lining everyone's fish suppers. Maybe another bigger story will break and I'll get left alone.

Theresa will know now. I pick up the phone and dial her number. It's ringing. Pleasepleaseplease be in.

'Hello?' Her voice is wary.

Oh sweet relief. 'Theresa. It's me.'

'Ray!' Her voice goes dim as if she's cupping her hand to the receiver. 'Where are you? What the hell is going on? Are you okay? I'm worried sick about you.'

'Can you meet me somewhere?'

'What, are you insane?'

'I need to see you. To explain.'

'I don't need this, Ray. The press will be all over you. They'll find out about us.'

'I didn't do it, Theresa.'

She paused just a moment too long for my liking. 'The thought never crossed my mind, Ray. But do you think running away is going to solve anything?'

'I was with you the night of the first murder, Tess. It couldn't have been me.'

'I said that I believed you, Ray.'

'Christ, do I need to see a friendly face. Can you come and visit?' The pleading note in my voice disturbs me, but I am past caring. I need Theresa to be on my side. I give her the address and ask her to get here as soon as possible, before hanging up.

Calum is on his feet, facing me across the room. 'I don't think that's a good idea.'

He must have overheard me. Nosy bastard.

'I don't give a fuck what you think, Calum.' Regretting my tone I try again. I should keep on the good side of this guy. 'Sorry, Calum. It's just... you heard Kenny earlier. A blowjob is the best tension reliever known to man.'

He suddenly grins, we are both men together, 'Why didn't you say that? I'll leave the flat when your lady friend arrives. Give you some space.' He continues to grin, now looking less like a bodyguard and more like a teenager on double helpings of testosterone. I force a grin in reply.

'Must be feeling a bit horny eh? After being locked up,' he says.

'Aye. I could screw the buttonhole on a fur coat.' I feel bad about misrepresenting Theresa like this, but it is one sure way of smoothing over her appearance.

Thirty minutes later the intercom rings. Calum motions me over.

'This your friend?' He's all business again. I look at a small screen showing Theresa's worried, pinched face in black and white. I nod. He buzzes her up and then opens the door, leaves the flat and walks over to the stairwell. The door to the landing opens and he barely gives her a look as they pass each other, he going in, she coming out. I could have kissed him; by not drawing her attention to him he had allowed her to feel some semblance of normality.

I'm standing in the doorway and with my first sight of her in the flesh, I forget how I must look to her. She looks at me, her expression neutral, and then at the plaque at the side of the door. Then she looks at me again.

'Oh, Ray. It's you! What have you done to your hair?' She takes my hands and I pull her into the flat. We sit on the settee facing each other. Her line of sight keeps sliding up to my head. A smile creeps into her expression and before I know it we are both laughing. The release I feel from this is enormous, like Charles Atlas has gone and sat on someone else's shoulders. I sober up first, the last few mouthfuls of laughter drying to a dust that coats my tongue.

'I'm so sorry about this Theresa, but I needed you to know...'

'Sssh, Ray,' she presses a finger against my lips.

'But...'

She squeezes herself against me. I can't help but notice the press of her breasts against my chest. A certain part of my anatomy notices it as well.

'As long as you're okay,' she says, while I try to clear my head. Which is pretty difficult considering my blood flow is going in a southerly direction. Well, they do say that danger is an aphrodisiac.

'You believe me. Don't you?'

'I was with you. Remember? You were in my bed for most of that night.'

'Most of it?'

'Well, you arrived late. And...' She paused as if fighting against the blush that was working its way up her neck towards her face.

'And what?' I aim for a neutral tone. And miss. She has given this a lot of thought.

'Och it's nothing, Ray.'

'It's not nothing. You've had some doubts about me.'

'No, no, no. It's just... you are in the papers and everything.' She shifts in her seat, pushes her hair behind her ear. 'I'd be mad not to go over everything. Put yourself in my position, Mr Policeman. Would you not wonder, if only for a moment or two?'

'Of course I would,' I say. That's what I love about Theresa. She doesn't stay on the defensive for long. 'Sorry. You were saying...'

'Right. I was saying nothing really. Just that you were doing your sleepwalking thing.'

Me? Sleepwalking?

'We fell asleep at one point, after you did your stud muffin thing.' Her smile sent a charge of heat direct to my groin. Another quality I love about Theresa; she loves sex. 'Then I woke up and saw you standing over me. Like you had been sleepwalking.' She held her hand to her chest. 'I don't mind telling you that it freaked me out a little.' A small laugh. 'But you have done it before.'

'I have?'

'Yeah. A couple of weeks earlier. I caught you in the kitchen. You were even spookier that time. Fully dressed as well.'

'Seriously?' This was too weird. 'What was I doing?'

'Standing at the sink. Looking out into the garden. You wouldn't have seen much, it was pitch black.' She pursed her lips as if searching for an apt phrase. 'Your eyes were open. And yet when I touched your shoulder you turned to face me as if I had just woken you up.'

'Did I say anything?'

'No. You just wore this expression of complete bewilderment. So I took your hand and guided you back to bed. Where I helped you take your clothes off and shagged you rotten.'

We both laugh though our joy sounds as shallow as a minute old puddle.

'Were there any other times?'

'No. Well, not that I noticed anyway.'

'Why didn't you say anything?'

'Dunno. I thought you were aware of it afterward and that you didn't want to talk about it.' She held my hand. 'You did look like you had seen a ghost. And you quickly learn that if Ray McBain isn't in the mood for talking, that nothing is going to open him up.'

'I'm sorry, Tess. Must've been horrible for you.'

'Look at you,' she squeezes my hand. 'Up to your neck in shit and you're worried about me?' She straightens her spine and sets the line of her jaw. 'I'll phone the police. Tell them about you and me.' She turns to look out of the window and then looks back at me. 'But it doesn't need to go public does it?'

'Your husband wouldn't need to know, unless your alibi didn't clear me and they decided to have their day in court. In which case you would be called as a witness. But you're not doing it. I got myself hooked in this mess and I refuse to drag you into it.'

'What do you mean?' She tilts her head to the side.

'If I hadn't tried to conceal my name from a list of... Theresa, do we have to go through this right now? What about the phone calls?'

'Ah. The phone calls.' Her expression hardens.

'Sorry.'

'What the hell were you trying to do? Get me a quickie divorce?'

'Sorry.'

'I mean, c'mon, Ray. The deal was no phone calls.'

I'm not apologising again. I cross my arms, 'I'm sorry.' You held out for a while there, Ray. 'What did you tell whatsisname?'

'I told him that I'd met you one night when I was with the girls and you got me confused with one of them. Poor sap loves me that much, he believes everything I say.' Her expression is one of regret. She looks away from me out of the window.

'Thanks.' Relief softens the pull of my shoulders. That's one less thing to worry about. I slump back on to the sofa. 'How long have you got?'

She looks at her watch, '*He's* away to Newcastle for the day. Said he'd be back around nine. So we're safe for a couple of hours.' She curls into me and lays her head on my chest.

The smell of her hair is intoxicating. It is lightly damp. Everything in the world that is feminine is bound up in these dark brown fibres. I slide my cheek slowly down the brown silk and breathe the scent in to the back of my throat.

She pats the bulge in my tracksuit, 'Don't even think about it, big boy.'

'You know you want to.' I laugh. If she doesn't, I think I'm going to burst. Her finger traces the outline of my penis through the fabric. She then cups my balls.

'Mind you, if I don't empty these first I'm not going to get much sense from you. Where's the bedroom?'

We're lying on the bed, Theresa curled on her side, me spooning her from the back. We fucked twice. I came within seconds each time. Feel as if I'm sixteen again. I tried to apologise for not seeing to her pleasure first but the words came out sounding anything but sorry. It is difficult to speak properly when synapses are sparking all over your body.

Despite everything that has been going on, at this moment I feel fulfilled. Cars are swishing past in the rain outside, the police are charging around hoping to lock me up for a murder I didn't commit, and I'm wearing nothing but a smile, sharing a silk sheet with a beautiful woman.

As if she were an exotic creature, I lift her hair out of the way to lick at her bare shoulders. Kissing her pale skin just where back meets neck, I wonder, is there any place in the world softer than this? A note of pleasure escapes from her mouth. Her buttocks spark at my groin. Her skin should be cloned, packaged and sold under the brand "Heaven". She moves her cheeks against me and once certain of my arousal, reaches back and guides me home. This time we are making love and it feels... so right. This is a sensation that is so new to me I stop thrusting.

'Don't stop, Ray. I'm close,' she breathes.

'I love you,' I hear myself say.

'I love you too. I love you too.' She pushes her back against me.

'No, Theresa. I *love* you.'

She stops and turns around to face me, her eyes searching mine. She puts a hand on either side of my face and kisses me. 'One night when she was drunk, my mother gave me a great piece of advice. She said don't believe a man who tells you they love you when they've got a hard-on.' She reaches down, wraps her fingers round it and gives it a hard squeeze.

'But I do.'

'No you don't, Ray. You don't *do* love.' She sits up and pulls the sheet around her, uncomfortable with this turn of events. 'You... you're mistaking gratitude for love. You're thinking, "The daft bitch believes me, I'll fall in love with her".' A tear gathers size on her lower lashes and escapes to glide down her cheek. 'Don't do this to me, Ray,' she whispers.

'Theresa. I'm not making this up.' I'm up on my knees. 'Last night when I was in my cell, to comfort me, to help me sleep, I thought of you. Now when we made love... I've never felt anything like that. It was like I'd connected.'

Her eyes full and moist, her lips thin and cupped in a shape that spells NO. As in, no, don't love me.

'We're not about love, Ray. We have fun. Have a laugh. You go off and do your thing and I go back to my husband.'

151

'Tell me you don't love me too.'

'I do love you. I've always loved you. But I clocked you straight away. Mr Terrified of Commitment. Mr Married to the Job. Don't you see? I put you in a box marked S.E.X. I know how to cope with you when you're in that box.' She wipes a tear from her eyes with the corner of the sheet, 'Don't tell me you love me, Ray. 'Cos that would give me hope and "never" is much easier to deal with.'

She jumps from the bed and pulls her clothes on. Numb, I watch her dress.

'Can I call you?' I ask as she leaves the room.

'I don't know,' she wails as she runs for the front door.

As I listen to her feet drum out of the flat and the slam of the door, I feel like I've found something new and amazing. And then flushed it down the drain. Why did I open my big mouth? Couldn't I just have savoured the feeling, tasted it for a while longer before opening her up to the possibilities? I turn around, kneel on the floor and push my face into the pillow where her head had rested. Her scent rises from the fabric. The corner of the top sheet is still moist with her tears.

Chapter 24

Allessandra's right arm is aching. She has been on the phone to her mother for thirty minutes, doing the dutiful daughter thing and wondering how a light item like a mobile phone can be such hard work to hold to the side of her head.

'Are you even listening to me, Allessandra?'

'Of course, Mum.' Allessandra lies and prays that her mother isn't going to test her.

'What was I talking about then?'

Allessandra quickly reviews a list of her mother's favourite topics, can't decide which and opts for a piece of passive aggression.

'You were saying that I don't see enough of my husband and therefore it's no surprise I don't get pregnant and then how you much prefer talking to your other daughter 'cos at least she knows the difference between a crochet hook and a knitting needle.'

'Darling, how can you say that? I would never question the hours you keep at work and I love both my daughters equally.'

Her mother sounds stung and Allessandra feels a charge of guilt.

'Of course you do, Mother.' No you don't. You leech life equally from both daughters. But you prefer the one that isn't up to her armpits in human scum.

While her mother continues her monologue Allessandra looks out of the car window at the red stone of Bethlehem House and wonders yet again at the kind of childhood that Ray would have had within its walls. She really shouldn't complain about her own mother. At least she knew she was loved.

It had been suggested that, as she had initially come here with Ray, she should visit again. She told no-one about her second visit.

'Try and find out what kind of boy McBain was,' Campbell asked her. 'Background details could be important in this case.'

153

So here she is again and not looking forward to it. Mother Mary is so small, how can she be so damn scary? If I could put up with my own mother for life I can speak to the wee nun again for five minutes, she thinks.

'Very good, Mum,' she says. 'Sorry to interrupt you, but I am working.'

'Right, okay. No need to be so rude. Where did you young girls learn to be so abrupt?'

'Bye Mum. I'll call you later. Okay?' But Allessandra is talking to herself by now. Fair enough, she thinks, I deserved that.

In the convent, with Mother Superior, Allessandra wonders at the title. Aren't nuns supposed to be about servitude and humility? What's so humble about the word "superior" being in your job title?

The older woman is sitting at a table across from her, hands clasped as if in prayer on the table before her. A set of glass rosary beads tumbles from her hands like spilled and frozen holy water.

'What can we do for you today, DC Rossi?' Her expression is certain in its serenity.

'Tell me again about Ray McBain while he was under your care.'

'There have been more deaths, I hear?' Mother asks, her short fingers working at the beads. She is looking for information, but Allessandra isn't about to give her any. Stick to asking the questions, she reminds herself.

'From what you know of Ray, is he capable of such terrible acts?'

'He was eleven going on twelve when he left here. A lot of time for society to warp the mind of a weak young boy.'

'Didn't the Jesuits say that if you gave them the boy until the age of seven, they would give you the man?' Allessandra isn't about to let this old woman get the better of her, but she still wishes that she had managed to edit her tone before that left her mouth.

A wry smile is the only response Mother allows herself to show. 'Even the Jesuits would have struggled with a boy like Ray.'

'How so?' asks Allessandra, wondering why this woman makes her feel so uncomfortable. Sure, she has a strong personality, but she has devoted her life to her beliefs and has tried to make a difference to countless children's lives. So what is it about her that makes Allessandra want to go straight to a voodoo shop, buy a doll, some large pins and a nun's outfit?

154

'I've had a lot of children in my care over the years. I remember each and every one.' She smiles, and in that smile Allessandra reads of a woman who wanted to be a mother to her own children, but to whom this joy had been refused. That she had to look after the children other women had produced was a cross she had to bear. Allessandra guesses that it's a look she has perfected over the years. 'Most were troubled. All were in pain. And with the help of the good Lord I did my very best.' Only the crucifix is showing from her rosary, the beads are all bundled tightly in her hands. 'Ray was more troubled than most. I told you about the stalking. There was also the sleepwalking.' Her eyes are fixed on Allessandra's but her gaze is years in the past. 'Gave me a fright, the little monkey. He was standing over me one night. Just standing there like a zombie. And me in my pyjamas. Holy Mother of God, I'd never heard of such a thing, a child in the nuns' quarters. He got a good clout and dragged off to his bed. Took a month for my poor heart to recover.

'And there was the bed-wetting. A sure sign of a soul in torture, if you ask me. We'd have made him kneel in prayer till his knees bled if it would have made any difference.'

A wee cuddle might have worked better, thinks Allessandra.

'This stigmata thing in the papers... what do you fine police people make of that, I wonder?'

'I can't say too much, Mother. The investigation is still in its infancy.' Allessandra answers while being taken aback at the abrupt change in direction.

'I caught Ray with a red pen one day. Fashioning a wound on the palm of each hand.'

Allessandra sat forward.

Mother holds her hands to her heart while her mind continues with the connection.

One of the tabloid nicknames for Ray was "The Stigmata Killer". Shock enlarges her features.

'What could I have done? If I had taken more time with him, could lives have been saved?'

Allessandra shakes her head. She isn't going to give this room in her mind. Ray isn't a killer. He had been a broken boy who has turned his life around and become an effective member of society.

'When I pulled the pen out of his hand, he just looked at me. Jesus, Mary and Joseph, the little blasphemer couldn't understand what he had done wrong. Blasphemy, I warned him, will see you at the gates of Hell. But I want to help people too, he said. Can you believe it? I want the same pain as Jesus and the saints, he cried. You'll get bread and butter for tea, you little heathen, I told him.' She pauses. 'The same pain as Jesus. I ask you.' She shakes her head, her sadness a tangible thing, tinged with regret. She opens her mouth to say something else. Thoughts linger in the screen of her eyes but remain unexpressed. Thoughts that made her eyes widen in remembered shock. She pauses, gives a small shake of her head as if she has just stopped herself from saying something. 'The boy was deeply flawed, Miss Rossi. It's no surprise that the man has turned out this way.'

Chapter 25

I've been in Kenny's flat for a month now. A month in which two more dead bodies have been found. Two more dead bodies that have been mutilated in the same manner as Connelly. The killer did well to wait until I was at large again before he got busy. And in typical McBain fashion I have alibis that would struggle to stand up in court: a career criminal and his minder.

It's been a long month for other reasons. A month of daytime TV, tinned tuna and grilled chicken. A month of talking to no-one but Calum, the walking wall. A month of excruciating boredom. A month of change. When I look in the mirror I barely recognise myself. I feel like a candle that's been held too close to the flame: the weight has melted off me. Add the bleached, cropped hair and a trim wee goatee beard and you have a new man.

Sanity has arrived in the form of exercise. Me, Ray McBain, a born again jogger. Who would have thought it? I did a bit of jogging when I was a young copper. Really enjoyed it. You kind of get indoctrinated into it when you go to the police training college at Tulliallan. They have a real hard-on for the physical benefits of exercise and in particular the pastime of running. While you are at the college they get you out in your jogging shoes every day. They made a real point of only bringing in fit young men and women, when I joined. Kind of a waste of time when you see how many develop Fat Bastarditis later in their careers.

Calum is a bit of a fitness freak and he has me pumping iron and pushing press-ups for a couple of hours every day. If I gain muscle, he keeps telling me, I'll burn off more fat. I get him back by going running. He joined me the first few times, but the more I ran and the bigger distances I completed, the less inclined he was to repeat the experience. He has the finely honed physique of a sprinter, he tells me. He prefers his skeleton to be less visible and sheathed in muscle.

Suits me. I'm getting to enjoy running again. It's amazing how the drum of my feet and an expanded ribcage bring a calm to my life. I've developed a good circuit. Up the Saltmarket, along the High Street and up that bastard hill to St Mungo's Religious Museum. The first few times I ran this route I would take a well-earned breather at the museum. Even went in a couple of times. There are exhibits showing all of the world's religions, but the depiction of Christianity is enough to have you reaching for some saffron robes and a set of hair clippers. I can only take so much death and mutilation before I need a break. Basically Christ's artists show you that we are put on this earth to suffer in a myriad of painful ways before we are allowed the peace of an afterlife. Focus on the idea of heaven, they are saying, 'cos the here and now sucks big time.

Once I make it past the museum, I run behind it and over the romantically titled Bridge of Sighs into the Necropolis. This was modelled on the *Père Lachaise* cemetery in Paris and must have been amazing in its time. Now the grass is kept trim, but other than that it has a dual existence of being a tourist attraction in the daylight hours and a hangout for bored kids, vandals, glue-sniffers, alcoholics and addicts when the sun takes its daily rest.

It's quite a challenge running up the path that takes you to the top of that hill. The view is worth it though. I stand under the gigantic gaze of John Knox, look over the city and allow my pulse and breathing to slow.

'Is that you, Ray?' Daryl Drain is waiting for me as arranged and is wearing an expression of full on amazement, which I answer with the heat of irritation.

'Fuck you.' Was he that amazed that I could run up a hill?

'It is you? Isn't it?' He is stretching his neck forward as if trying to improve his vision. Right. I forgot about the change in my appearance. He's only ever known me as a fatso.

'Nae offence, Ray, but you look like a different man.' He smiles widely and rubs his hands. 'You look fucking fantastic. The bastards are *never* going to find you.'

'Good eh?' It's weird, but as he looks me over I feel like a teenager who is wearing a dinner suit for the first time, and in the mirror of his parents' eyes sees how good he actually looks. Apart from Kenny, Daryl is the first person from my former life that has seen the new me. I kick a stone and put my hands behind my back.

'Wow. The hair...'

'Yeah.' I kick another stone.

'The beard...'

'Yeah.' Kick.

'The weight-loss...'

'For fuckssake. Enough.' I grin and motion Daryl to the side where I sit down on the grass. He copies me.

'Right. What's happening?'

'All sorts of people are getting their arses kicked. Campbell, Hackett. This is a major embarrassment to the force. High-ranking officer suspected with murder escapes. The politicians are having a field day. They're questioning our ability to police ourselves. As for the press...'

'I do read the newspapers.'

'They fucking love it.'

Actually, I've stopped reading the papers. It's not comfortable seeing your life story in bold headlines three inches tall. Convent Boy Killer, Psycho Trainee Priest, are just two of them. Then when the other two bodies were found, they went into a frenzy of detail about my life. It was all there. The orphanage, the delinquent parents, the seminary, the — until now — distinguished career.

People who had spoken two words to me got their three minutes of fame as they concocted stories to add to the media glamour that was DI Ray McBain, Christ Killer, aged 36 — they always get my age wrong. What is it with journalists and people's ages — and alliteration? I was fiendishly fucking famous and apparently free to strike at will, while the police had a finger up their collective fat arse.

So far, Theresa had managed to stay out of it. And away from me. I hadn't heard from her since my admission of love. Maybe once she'd had a little more time we could talk. Besides, a wanted killer was hardly a selling point for a life-long romance.

'Tell me about the two new bodies. And have they managed to connect them with me?'

'The first one found was the woman. Same M.O. Her name was Elizabeth Templeton. She married late in life. Husband died shortly after the wedding. Nae luck. No kids either. Maiden name was Duthie. Chicken wing short of a picnic, apparently.

The guy was 33. Name Jim Leonard. Shared a flat with a guy called Mark Hutchison. Nothing intimate going on there, just flatmates according to the neighbours. In any case Hutchison, according to his girlfriend, is working overseas for six months.'

Jim Leonard. One of the twins from the convent. His brother, John, was my comrade in pissy blankets.

'I don't know if this is significant, Ray. But although Connelly was the first body to be found. Leonard was actually the first one to die. There was no flatmate around to sound the alert, so his body lay undiscovered for about a month, before complaints about the smell made the council investigate.'

What an epitaph for the poor bastard. Your body is left to rot for a month before the council's grime squad are called in. 21st centuryitis. He died a stranger, inches away from hundreds of other people.

Jim Leonard, fuck me.

'MO same as Connelly?'

'Aye. But that's the only connection we can make.'

'They can't be random killings.' We've both been working in serious crimes long enough to know that where murder is concerned there are no such things as coincidences.

I'm not sure what to do. Do I tell Daryl that I know what the connection is? Can I trust him?

Of course I can. A sliver of guilt interrupts my thoughts, but I don't want them to be looking at Bethlehem House again. There's a danger it will just strengthen the case against me.

'Looks like they might be.' Daryl shrugs. We both knew that killers without a discernible pattern are more difficult to find. 'The theory down at the incident room is that you've completely lost it. We got in a profiler and she reckons the first taste of blood has unhinged you and you're now making the world suffer for whatever happened to you as a child.' He digs under his thumbnail for some dirt and looks up at me as he prepares to deliver bad news.

'Peters can be pretty persuasive once he starts. Some of the guys are starting to come round to his point of view. They also...' Some dirt on his shoe suddenly fascinates him.

'They also what?'

'They're saying some terrible things about you, Ray. That you're really going doolally... mad.' He looks over at me and then back to the ground, clearly uncomfortable with the fact that maybe I am actually insane.

'Peters is an arse. What about Hackett? What's he saying?'

'Hackett appears to agree with Peters. But Ray, don't dismiss Peters. He may be unimaginative and slow, but he's like a bulldog once he gets his teeth into something. And you, he hates.'

'That's a cross I'll have to bear,' I try to grin at my weak joke. 'He's still an arse.' My teeth are knocking together and my hands are rubbing my arms. I'm starting to cool down now after my athletic efforts and I pull on a sweatshirt I had tied around my waist.

'The nights are fair drawing in,' Daryl smiles.

'Aye. Where has the summer gone? Enough chitchat. Have you got that address?'

'Aye.' He fumbles in a pocket and produces a slip of paper. I decipher his scrawl.

'Any questions asked?'

'None. We're quite safe. What other leads should we follow?'

'That guy Crichton. Put the frighteners on him a wee bit and see what comes up.'

'What about the guy in Aberdeen? Irving.'

'Leave him to me.' I say. Irving has been a busy boy all right, but I don't think he's a murderer. An anonymous phone call to his local cop-shop will hopefully put him out of action for a while.

'What about the team? Should we trust anyone else?' Daryl asks.

'The fewer people who know, the better. Just stick with you and Allessandra for now.' I pause. Perhaps this is a lot to ask of a less experienced officer. 'Is Allessandra coping okay?'

'That girl's a trooper, Ray. She's certain that you're not the killer. Besides, there's a hefty slice of guilt there that she grassed you up in the first place.'

'Well, you tell her she was right to do it. I should never have put her in that position... and I can't thank her enough... I can't thank you both enough...' Shit. I'm getting all emotional again.

'You're going to want to hug me next, aren't you?' Daryl takes a step back.

'Fuck off, ya prick.' I punch his arm and run back down the path.

Back at the flat, Kenny is unpacking some shopping bags, with the ever-present Calum standing by his side in silence. Kenny shouts over to me as I walk in the door.

'Calum and me have been busy, Ray. C'mon over and see what we've bought for you.'

Plastic bags are emptied and the contents displayed across the back of the settee. He's bought me a couple of pairs of jeans, five

T-shirts, three checked shirts, two jumpers, a pair of shoes. Oh, and a black leather jacket. Judging by the names on the labels this lot has set him back a fair sum.

'Not too shabby,' I admit as I review my new wardrobe. The trousers have a 34-inch waist. Not too shabby indeed.

'Here,' Kenny is grinning like Santa retired and he got the job. He throws me a set of keys. The famous symbol of BMW is on the fob. 'And this.' He throws me an envelope. I open it. It's full of tenners. I sit down on the settee. This is all too much. I've taken enough from Kenny. I can't take any more. There's only so much a man can fill his hands with before his dignity starts to fray at the edges.

'The car is only on loan and if you damage it you'll be found in the Clyde wearing a pair of concrete slippers.' His voice is firm and deep. 'The cash is also a loan as you can hardly access your own bank account at the moment. We'll charge you a modest rate of interest.' The clever bastard knew how I would react and is phrasing the gifts in such a way he'll know I won't refuse.

I'm on my way down to Manchester to meet a certain young man called Joseph McCall and this big fucker of a car is actually purring. As soon as all this shit is over I am going to sell my flat, buy myself one of these beauties and move in. I'll eat in the local chippie, bathe at the swimming baths and sleep in the backseat. A perfect existence. The money I would have spent on things like Council Tax and electricity I can spend on petrol and just cruise the motorways in my spare time, enjoying the BMW purr.

The miles have slid past like a movie backdrop and I'm almost there. I just have to find the house where Joseph is renting a room. I key the address into the satnav.

So what do I know about him? Not much except for the fact that his mother is dead and the woman who looked after him has some serious issues. Other than that all I have is an address.

The clock on the dashboard tells me it's just gone 5pm and the ache in my belly tells me it's time to eat. Before I left Glasgow, Calum told me to try and find the Curry Mile in the Rushholme area of the city. The food there is fantastic apparently, although not in keeping with my new super-slim self. Fuck it. If I can't have a curry when I'm away from home, when can I indulge myself? There is something about being away from my home turf and spoiling myself with food. It must have been all those trips to the seaside as a wee boy. The only time I remember enjoying my food as a child was when we got a break from the grease-laden stodge that passed for nourishment at the convent.

First things first. I have a young man to talk to.

'You have arrived at your destination.' A delightful voice issues from the satnav. The house number I'm looking for is just in front of me. The house itself is pretty nondescript. Three storeys tall. A postage stamp front garden is the parking space for a couple of large motorbikes. The front door is dark blue and the front room window has a charming net curtain draped over it. As I approach the door I see that the net has a couple of big holes in it. The larger one has a life-size cardboard head of Che Guevara popping through it. That man gets about, eh? Still the totem for the disaffected student.

Reading down the list of names with a buzzer I press the one that I want. Nothing. I wait for a minute and press again. Still nothing. Then I hear a heavy tread. The door opens and a long-haired boy/man who needs a good feed and an introduction to the pleasures of being free of facial hair pushes past me. But not before he lets the door slam shut behind him.

'Hi. I'm trying to find Joseph McCall.' Maybe I speak a different language from this fella. Maybe he's deaf, because he completely ignores me. On reflection, "ignore" doesn't come close, I don't even register in his awareness. Students and drugs. Students and Che Guevara and drugs. Dearie me. Perhaps a touch of Glasgow *brio* is needed here.

'Ho, Big Man. You deaf?' I pull on his sleeve. He turns and faces me.

'I don't speak to pigs.' His voice is monotone, the accent difficult to place.

'Ex-pig, if you don't mind.' Shit, am I that obvious. Even with the hair and the beard and the new leather jacket?

A grin that would have been honed on despairing parents forms on his lips. The top lip is as thin as the business end of a whip but the top one is hanging out in a plump huff. They seem out of place on a face that is so bony. His nose sports what could have been a knuckle on its bridge and cheekbones jut out under a pair of confident, ageless eyes. These are offset by facial hair that has ambitions of joining up together one day and forming a beard.

'Kick you out, did they?'

'Bent ex-pig is probably the correct terminology,' I step closer to him. See how confident he feels now. His smile wilts but he gamely cocks his head to the side and stands his ground.

'Yeah, good for you,' he says. Judging by what is going on his eyes I can read that the greater part of his mind tells him I'm not to be trusted, but a small section demands to know "What if?"

'Sorry. We seem to have got off on the wrong foot. I tend to get irritated when people ignore me. But I am an ex-copper and I do want to find Joseph McCall.' Polite words issued with an air of menace can often do the trick, but this young man is pretty composed.

'What do you want with Joseph?' The accent is all over the place. There's something not quite right about it. Especially when he said "Joseph." That was almost Scottish.

'How long have you known him then?'

'That depends on why you're asking.' Good Queen's/Mancunian English this time.

'I have news about his family.'

Judging by the lack of response to this, he isn't much of a friend.

'Stick it on a postcard and shove it through his door.'

There's no help to be received here. With a display of teeth intended to approximate a smile I walk away from him and go back to the door. It opens just as I get there and a young girl exits. This I know because she has no beard. The build, clothes and hair are a matching set to those worn by the guy I'd just spoken to. Androgyny never goes out of fashion.

'Do you know if Joseph McCall is in, sweetheart?'

'No he's not.' Is it just me, or does she *bristle* when I say the word "sweetheart".

'Sorry.' I rub my eyes and let some of the tiredness show. 'I've had a long journey and I need to find Joseph to give him some news from home.'

'I'm sorry,' her gaze softens. 'I tend to go into attack mode when I hear that prick's name. Joseph. Yes. He's just left. In fact I'm amazed you missed him.' She looks over my shoulder. And points. 'There he is.' Just as beardy turns a corner.

'Wee bugger.' I try to allay the suspicion that is sliding into her eyes. 'He's changed so much since I last saw him.'

I catch him easily. He doesn't turn round when I shout his name. He doesn't even alter his pace when he hears the drum of my feet. *Prick*, she called him. A lover's tiff perhaps?

'Right, ya arsehole, what was that all about?' I pull on his arm. Thankfully I am breathing easily. Trying to get information from someone while you are struggling to fill your lungs is fairly difficult.

'I've a phobia about men with bleached hair.' A Glasgow accent this time.

'You a Celtic fan then?' I refer to the aforementioned Paul Gascoigne who terrorised the Celtic team while sporting said hairstyle.

His answering grin is genuine. 'Partick Thistle, actually.'

'Eh? Me too.' Cool. We've bonded. 'Listen, I need to talk to you. Can I buy you a coffee?'

'I also have a phobia about bleached blond men in coffee shops.'

Witty fucker.

'Will a pint do?'

'I'm not going to get rid of you am I?'

'Nope.'

'There a nice wee boozer just round the corner.' He walks off and expects me to follow. In the pub, we get our drinks and find the only free seats, which are just beside the entrance to the women's toilet. I'm surprised they need one judging by the complete lack of anything that might be remotely attractive to women. Unless beer bellies and builder's cleavage have suddenly become desirable.

'A former policeman who doesn't take a drink?' Joseph looks pointedly at my glass of tonic water.

'I'm aff it.'

'Right.' He takes a sip from his pint of Guinness. 'Say no more.' He sits his pint back down on the table, leans back on his chair, crosses his arms and looks at me. Waits for me to start. I put the rim of my glass to my lips and allow my mouth to fill. I swallow. Where do I begin? A downright lie has to be preferable in this situation.

'I think Carole Devlin is in danger.'

'Tell your ex-colleagues.' I think I'd have got more reaction if I'd complained about the long drive down. 'Anyway, what's it to you?'

'Let's just say I have a vested interest. And my ex-colleagues, well they're no' listening. I need you to tell me about her life. Who might have it in for her? Does she have any boyfriends? That sort of thing.'

'She's the DIY Queen. Nobody, and naw, she doesn't have any boyfriends.'

'Oh come on, mate. I've driven a long way to speak to you. Gimme a break.'

'Nobody invited you. Mate.'

'You ever been in trouble with the police before?' For a young guy he is pretty composed while being questioned by a police officer. Albeit one with a dodgy hairdo and an even dodgier career.

'Let's just say I had to grow up fast.'

I lean back in my chair and take a drink. 'It must have been tough being brought up by two women. Not a father figure in sight.'

'There was plenty of men about. You just wouldn't want them as a father.'

'Devlin liked her men then?'

He snorted, 'God no. She should have been a nun. My mum was the slapper. Men and drink. Men and drugs. As long as she had one she had the other. Let's just say that self-respect was way down the agenda.' He's fiddling with the beer mat, placing one corner on the table, sliding his grip down, turning it over and starting again. His eyes are on the table, but his gaze is way back in the past.

'Must have been tough.'

'What do you care?' He leans forward, all spiky now.

I shrug. 'Just saying. Can't have been nice.'

'I used to think that Carole was a dyke. You know? I mean, what was in it for her? Why was she even there? She used to run after my mum all the time. Clean up her puke 'n her shite. And she fucking hated the sight of me. Couldn't even look at me at times.'

'That surprises me. Her house is covered in photographs of you.'

'I pulled her up on it once. She said she did love me. But I reminded her of my dad too much.'

'Who was your dad?' A klaxon is ringing somewhere inside my skull. This is big. This is important.

'Don't know.' He slumps back down on his chair. A little boy again. I reach forward and touch his hand. He pulls it away from me as if my skin was on fire, and glares.

'Don't fuckin' touch me.' He stands up and looks around him at all the broad shoulders, beer bellies and chunky faces in the room. 'I just need to shout "Fucking Poofter" and you'll have less than five seconds to live.'

A flash. A picture. A voice. I'm on my knees. Bile rushes up my gullet, fills my mouth, its taste more than I can handle. I stand up, turn and push the door behind me. I make it to the sink in time.

166

I'm choking and coughing. Bile burns in my gullet, my eyes nip, while my brain sparks. The memory of a stabbing sensation. What was that? What was it doing to my insides? Why is no-one coming to help? Feels like it's ripping me apart. Feels like I'll never be able to go to the toilet again. This is wrong. I can't stop this from happening. Hot breath on my ear. The weight on my back. The rasp of an unshaven cheek on my face. I've been pushed on to some form of... what? A rough wooden desk? I can smell pine and oil. Rough hands on my genitals.

What was that all about? What is going on? I turn on a tap and splash water over my face. The voice.

'... *shout... and you'll have less than five seconds to live.*'

I know that voice. He warned me he would kill me. I was only a child, what could I do?

Swallowing the bile that sat at the back of my throat like a lump of partly digested food, I turned to face the other man in the toilet. Whatever was going on in my own head I had to ignore it. I had a killer to catch. People to save.

The resemblance. I should have noticed it before. McCall is standing as far away from me as possible in the confined space.

'What the hell was that? Your eyes. Your fucking eyes. What is going on?' He is stepping forward on to one foot and then back on to the other in the manner of an Olympic sprinter before leaning into his blocks.

'Why don't you tell me, Joseph?' I'm rubbing my face with a paper towel that could pass as sandpaper.

'What?' He's confused, frightened.

'You know, don't you?'

'Know what?'

'And what's more, so do I.'

The door opens and the barman walks in. His bulk almost cuts out the noise from the pub behind him.

'Right ladies. Get your soggy arses out of here. We don't take to that sort of thing in 'ere.' He rubs his meaty fist with the palm of his other hand. Just in case we don't get the message.

Outside, the pavement is slick with water and the heavy rainfall is creating a pincushion effect.

'Joseph, come back here. I want to talk to you.' I can hardly hear my own words through the downpour. He's running. I pick up speed and catch him easily before he rounds the corner. I slam him up against the wall.

'When were you last up in Glasgow, you prick?' I'm going to have him. Because of this bastard I've lost my job. His wet, black hair looks like an oil slick in the poor light. His smile is just as oily. The little boy has vanished.

'Don't know what you're talking about.'

'Just answer the fucking question.' I push water from my eyes. 'You have motive. All I need is to prove you had the opportunity and it'll be Bumfuck City for you, pal.'

'Fuck you,' he spits in my face. My fist answers before I can blink. He is doubled over on the ground, struggling to fill his lungs from my blow to his solar plexus. Normally an act like this would calm me down, but I want to stamp on his head. I want to see the fucker bleed. I want to *hurt* him.

'Oi, oi.' I hear feet splashing at an impressive tempo and a kick goes missing as I'm thrown against the wall.

'What do you think you're doing, mate?' A baton is pressed against my neck and a young policeman's face thrusts into mine.

'This gay bastard just tried to feel me up.' I answer in my best Mancunian accent and stretch in one more kick, which misses. Joseph is sitting on the ground and is wearing that smile again. A smile that he only allows me to see. He jumps to his feet and shrinks away from me. His posture has completely changed now. His body has almost folded in upon itself in his display of fear. His eyes are aflame with it.

'You've got to arrest that man, officer. You've got to save me.'

All eyes are on McCall. His performance is startling. He pulls one of the policemen towards him. Grabs at his tunic. 'His name is Ray McBain...' as soon as I hear that, I'm off. His voice trails after me '... and he's wanted up in Glasgow for murder.'

Two streets away I force myself to slow down. A man running is bound to attract attention and I can't hear any chasing footsteps. There's no-one about as I approach my car, so I get in and consider my next move.

Has McCall convinced the local police as to who I am? If so, there goes my disguise. Do I hang around Manchester and try to see what McCall gets up to next? How did he know who I was? How long has he known that Connelly was his father, and did he really kill him?

Chapter 26

I've been sitting here in the car for well over an hour now. No police and no McCall. Does that mean he failed to convince them? Thank fuck McCall didn't see me getting in or out of the car. I would be really stuck without it.

So is McCall the Christ Killer? We have motive for the murder of Connelly, but what about the other two? From what Daryl Drain said, it was the same M.O. What is the link? I need to delve deeper into the past of the two newly deceased to find something. Unless the sick fucker just got a taste for it and the next two are random victims. The poor bastards could just have been in the right place at the wrong time.

As for Connelly, when did McCall find out about his parentage? Has he been planning this for years? Or has he just found out? I can see Devlin baking him a cake for his twenty-first birthday, and, by the way, the secret ingredient is that your father is a career paedophile.

What would it be like to find *that* out all of a sudden? You're already fucked-up because your mother is a deceased junkie alcoholic whore. Then you find out the reason is that some sick bastard raped her when she was only a girl, and *you* are the result of that putrid alliance. You are pure rage. You want someone to hurt. You want to peel back their skin, display their raw nerve ends and grate them down to a pulp and you won't stop until you feel better.

Then you discover that you will never feel better. Nothing will ever make the pain go away.

Except.

You attack someone else, and in that moment when they are begging for their life, your pain is now their pain. You remember what pleasure feels like. You remember what it feels like not to be in pain all of the time. The relief is immense.

And short-lived.

You need to find someone else to take on that pain for you. Again. And again.

I know this because suddenly I understand. Hold it together, McBain. My head feels like it's in a vice. Where did that memory spring from? No. Connelly didn't do me. Did he?

But the sensations were so real. Hands all over me. Trousers pulled down quickly. Cold air on my behind. Warm fingers separating my...

I manage to open the door before I'm sick. Almost hit a passer-by.

'That booze'll kill you mate,' the man retorts as my puke splatters on the pavement. Bile is up my nose, making my eyes water. My mouth tastes like a toilet. I want to curl up in a dark corner and scream until these feelings leave me.

How can a memory like that just vanish? What else am I missing? What other memories have I locked away?

Forcing air into my lungs I sit upright in the seat. Got a job to do, Ray. A killer to catch. But it's different now, a voice replies... now you know for sure that the dead man deserved everything he got. In fact, I almost wish it was me who did do it. I feel so violated that nothing will do but to scrape at my skin with a razor blade. Only that will take away the revulsion that ripples under my skin.

He deserved to die and I wish I had done it. There. Said it. But I didn't do it. Did I? What other memories have I locked away?

Get a grip, McBain. McCall is the killer. You were with Theresa on the night Connelly died. What about that other night when she caught you sleepwalking? Could you have...?

Enough. McCall did it. Not me. And he's got to be stopped. But where is he? Unless the police took him back to the local station to question him? Would they have got an artist in to take a drawing of me? Or maybe the name would be enough and it wouldn't occur to them that I'd changed my appearance.

When did McCall realise who I was? Did he know from the first moment that he set eyes on me? He must have known that I was wanted for his crimes. It would have given him a big shock to find me on his doorstep. Maybe it was a thrill. He is an eerily composed young man. If I were he I would make it as difficult as possible for me. He won't want to kill me. I'm his scapegoat and once I'm back in custody he can no longer kill with impunity.

For fuckssake, McBain. Stop thinking so much. Move the car. A car like this is bound to attract attention. I drive it around a corner from where I can still see McCall's front door. The bastard has to come home some time.

A growl issues from my stomach and reminds me that I've not eaten for hours. And I need to get the taste of sick out of my mouth. Can I risk going for something to eat? If the policemen did take McCall to the station then he could be some time yet.

Unless he's sitting somewhere watching me right now.

Five hours and no sign of McCall. No sign of the police either. If I was them I would be backtracking any spot where I was previously seen. I would expect me to be long gone, but there might be some clues.

Where would McCall go? Does he have any friends in the area? Does he have a back door to his flat? He could have been in and out during the time I'd been sitting here.

How the fuck did he know it was me? Even Theresa would have walked past me if I hadn't shouted her name.

What is going on here?

I'm out of the car and locking it with the remote control before I mentally articulate the action required. It's dark now and the earlier movement of people coming home from work has tailed off. Only the occasional car passes me in the street.

At the door I look for McCall's name on the buzzer. Room G is his. Do I ring all the buzzers and hope that someone lets me in or do I try and find a back entrance? I hear footsteps approaching behind me from the pavement and lean against the doorpost in what I hope is nonchalance. Then I let some mild irritation show in my expression as a reason for hanging about here enters my head.

'Did you not find him then?' The girl who answered the door to me earlier peers up into my face.

'Yes and no.' I give her my best *I'm truly harmless* smile. 'He had to go somewhere and asked to meet me back here,' I lift up my arm and look at my watch, 'ooh... half an hour ago.'

'That's just like the selfish prick.' We're still on the p-word then. 'Leave everyone waiting about for you, why don't you.' She smiles at me. 'Sorry, I mustn't sound very ladylike to you.' Sigh. 'A long story.' She plucks a set of keys from her canvas satchel. Very proletarian. 'Can I offer you a cup of coffee or something

171

while you're waiting?' The door opens and she turns to face me while a flash of doubt reads in her eyes. 'You look trustworthy enough.' Her tone lacks conviction.

'I'd love a coffee.' The harmless smile is morphing into gormless. 'But if you'd feel safer I'll just drink it on the doorstep.'

'Don't be silly. Besides, I'll just knee you in the bollocks if you try something.'

The policeman in me almost insists that I stay where I am. If I had a daughter I would teach her to be much less trusting. But, if I go in with her, she might be able to provide me with some much-needed information. I imagine the glint of a coin as it tumbles through the air. Heads, you get some company, young lady.

She ushers me into her bedsit and directs me to sit on the sofa that is squeezed into the bay window.

'Don't mind Che. He won't bite.' Only the back of his head is visible from this angle. 'He came with the flat and I didn't have the heart, or a new pair of curtains for that matter, to take him out.'

I push a pile of clothes on to another cushion and remove a pile of CDs and books from the sofa arm and place them on the floor. A mug that had been white in an earlier life is ringed with coffee stains. A ring perhaps for each time it has been used since its last wash. I'm beginning to regret being here. When did young women get so lazy? Even when I was a student I didn't live in such a muddle.

'The name's Sue, by the way.' She sticks her head back out of the cupboard she has just entered. 'This is my kitchen, in case you're wondering. The cupboard has a sink, a kettle, a small fridge and a microwave.'

'You're lucky. All I had was a kettle when I was studying.' I aim for the Great British tradition of comradeship in having a moan. See, I was even worse off than you. 'The name's James, by the way.'

We're both cradling hot mugs. I'm on the sofa and Sue is sitting on what I now realise is the bed, after a mound of clothes and coats was pushed aside to reveal a duvet.

'Is it really bad news then?' She is holding her coffee with both hands, leaning forward, her elbows on her knees. I can't make up my mind whether the note of concern or anticipation in her expression is for the suffering due to Joseph or whether she is genuinely worried for him.

I nod soberly, 'The worst kind, I'm afraid.'

Her head stretches forward. 'Oh dear.' A correction then enters her tone as if she realises that revenge is misplaced in such circumstances. 'Poor Joseph.' She examines the disc of brown liquid steaming between her thin hands.

'Does he know yet?'

'Afraid I still have that to come.' Time for some questions. 'How long have you known Joe?'

'Don't let him hear you call him that. He hates being called *Joe*.'

'I know,' I push out a laugh. 'I used to call him Joe all the time. To piss him off.'

'Good for you,' she laughs. And then sobers as she remembers the new attitude she should foster, given the circumstances. 'I moved in here last October. Joseph was the quiet one in the building. He was very nice to me. Helped me settle in. Should have known it was a ruse to get into my pants. The bastard.' A red tinge is developing on her neck. 'Sorry. He's your relative. I shouldn't call him that.'

'If he did the dirty on you, Sue, you call him what you like.'

'He was such a nice guy. At first. We were friends for ages, going for a drink or to the movies. Then about a month ago everything went funny. He was in love with me, he told me,' she pauses and takes a fortifying sip of coffee, 'and I thought, what the hell, Sue, you're only twenty-one once. So I let him... sleep with me.' She whispers this. 'Then as soon as he gets a shag he's all ignorant,' her voice is raised in volume, 'and *rude*. And he acts like I'm something that got stuck in his shoe. Well I don't need you *Joe* McCall. You're just a... little boy.' This is the worst insult she can think of.

'Bastard,' I offer. 'A month ago you say.' That would have been not long after the murders started.

'Yeah. Just after we came back to Uni after the hols. He came back all groin and Glasgow. I should have known he was just like the rest of you men.'

I raise an eyebrow in response.

'Anyway,' she ignores my weak attempt to stand up for my gender, 'I've had my fill of him.'

'What do you mean about being all Glasgow?' The "groin" allusion is less troublesome.

'Sorry, I don't mean to offend. Are you from Glasgow?'

'Yes.'

'Sorry, but what I meant was that he was acting like a... big man.' Her line of sight is aimed at the coffee, but I'm certain she sees nothing of the external world. 'He used to be so nice and quiet and thoughtful. A little lacking in confidence. But you know, when I think about it, after the hols he was very different. Almost like he just didn't care anymore. He didn't care what people thought of him.'

I say nothing. Let her fill the silence and something vital might slip out.

'Bastard.'

So much for that theory then. I look at my watch.

'Sorry. I've taken up enough of your time.' I stand up.

'Not at all.' She stands too.

'I'll just...' I point to the door.

'Okay.' She smiles then a pair of contrasting thoughts twists in her eyes. 'I probably shouldn't do this. But fuck it. He needs to get his key back sometime. Might as well be a relative that gets it.' She lifts a set of keys from her satchel and removes one. 'Here. Make sure you tell him I gave it to you and that he can have it back. Forever.' Her chin moves up in defiance.

'And tell him I'm keeping the Bob Marley CD.'

McCall's room is about the same size as Sue's, his a good deal tidier though. But a lot colder. I cross my arms and try to keep some heat within my jacket. This room is cold and not just temperature-wise. He has a bed against one wall; the duvet cover is a plain dark green, there are three dining room chairs dotted about, a bookcase and a tall wardrobe against the far wall. That's it, apart from a TV/DVD combo mounted on a wall bracket.

I approach the bookcase for ideas of what kind of person McCall is in his private life. There are textbooks, a few fantasy novels, a book on Stalingrad and a couple of SAS-type thrillers. The bottom shelf holds all his movies; a couple of football films; a couple of standard horror movies and the expected sci-fi. Nothing remarkable here. Just like any young man his age. Mind you, if he is a good Catholic boy, he must have a stash of wank mags somewhere. That would show any signs of deviance. I look under the mattress and there they are in all their lurid splendour. Must be about half a dozen. I have a quick look, for research purposes. Just the usual

174

big tits and neatly shaven pussies. None of them are very recent, the dates on the front are all from the last century. Okay, so it wasn't that long ago. Maybe he is too shy to buy them for himself and inherited them all from a pal.

A red light is winking in the corner. There's a bedside cabinet here, bearing a lamp, an alarm clock and a mobile phone charger. There's a drawer underneath. I slide it open to find that the drawer is empty. Not a thing. Is that not unusual? If I was staying in a room like this what would I keep in this drawer? Keys and wallet. He'll take those with him. Toiletries, a packet of condoms (unopened, probably), a favourite book. There must be all sorts of things that people like to keep close beside them while they sleep. Trusted objects that they reach out for in the morning to ground them in the coming day. But this guy has nothing.

All this thinking is tiring me out. I run my hands across my head. I could just have a wee lie down while I wait for McCall. Might as well get under the duvet, 'cos it's freezing in here.

A light blazes. Too close. Step back from it. There are more of them. Throwing light into the dark room, but there are corners where no light could reach. Corners with low moaning sounds and the sound of nails being pulled slowly across the hard floor. Stay near the light.

The lights surround a mirror. He looks into it and sees nothing, save for the dark ocean of space behind him. Only when he pulls the mask from the drawer and places that over his face does anything reflect. Light beams catch the white of the mask and throw an image on to the glass.

Now he can see his eyes. They look like the eyes of someone he knows, a distant acquaintance perhaps? Without the usual flesh and hair surrounding them... without a frame of reference... it is difficult to tell who they belong to.

The scalpel knows its way, its blade drawn to the flesh like a mosquito to the pale, sweet skin of a child. It knows to cut just enough to release a drop. A drop that will glide down the side of the nose, follow the swell of nostril and the downward curve of lip. It will reach the last part of its voyage — the chin — and pause for an eternity... a moment. From there will it drop into... darkness? Into a universe of space and dust and create its own sun. Or will it have shed too much of itself on the journey, leaving a pale line in its passing, a trail of torment and glory? Perhaps it will be too weak and cling to the skin, reluctant to leave its host.

No matter. It has been shed. There will be more.

The suffering is not over yet. Joy snaps his head up. Eyes again meet eyes. Fingers find a nipple and twist and pull at the pin piercing it. Just enough to register pain, just enough not to pull it right off. He ignores the insistent flesh that throbs in his groin. He can't touch it again, that would mean losing control. He looks down at the tight, purple flesh, at the tear of semen glistening from the eye-shaped hole. No. He mustn't. No release until it was over. Not long now. He hooks a finger under the crown of his penis and slides it down its underside. Enough, a voice barks. Enough.

He pulls his hands away and examines them as if they belong to someone else. They are square-shaped and strong and taper into slender wrists. The skin is a scoured pink, pink as a fresh steak. Even at a microscopic level it would be difficult to pick up any dirt, but still he scrubs. Just in case. His fingernails are a different story. No matter how much he scrubs them there is always some dirt that remains, as a reminder. They are forever filling up with dirt, but he likes that, the squeeze of loam as it presses in and lifts the nail from its bed. The smell of the earth and compost. Decay and renewal. Autumn and spring. Sin and rebirth.

The Crucifixion and the Ascension.

Chapter 27

'James! James!'

Who the fuck is James and who the fuck is shouting like that? My head. Fucking hell. I feel like shit. I've just had the worst nightmare since the repeat one I used to get at the seminary: that I was having sex with Sister Mary.

Dear Therapist, figure that one out.

My mouth tastes of metal, like somebody layered my tongue with old pennies. I sit up and lean against the headboard. Oh my head. Hurts. I can barely open my eyes. What a dream.

An odour that is a combination of coffee and vomit coats the hairs of my nostrils. I place my hands to the side to push myself back and up. What the hell is that? My left hand falls on to a patch of wetness, I instantly recoil as my brain registers what the stuff is and I lose my balance and pitch face first into my own puke. Fuck!

Can't remember being sick. All I can remember is the dream. The voice scraping through my mind. I sit back up and pull my knees up to my chest and hug myself. This must be how women feel when they have been raped. That voice had complete power over me. I was his puppet. I would have done anything he asked me. My legs and arms felt like they belonged to someone else. I tried to open my mouth and shout for help, but it was like a pair of fingers was stuck down my throat compressing my larynx so that no noise would issue from it. Every hair on my body was on full alert.

His hands were rough. Working hands. His fingers trailed across my forehead and down the side of my face. From one nipple to the next they arched, giving each a painful twist, then they slowly followed the line of hairs that link up with my pubes. There he stopped and twisted his fingers to gather some hair. With a heave he pulled some out. A scream stuck in my throat and echoed in my ears. The soft flesh felt as if someone had poured boiling wax on it.

Blood gorged in my groin, and to my utter shame and horror I realised I was aroused. Fed by fear, my prick pulsed for a touch.

He knew the effect this was having on me. The betrayal my body was dealing me. I couldn't see a face, but I knew he smiled. A smile bright with the need to be cruel.

His face was born from shadow; first the tip of his nose appeared, then the lips, cheekbones, lashes and then eyes. It was McCall. No, it was Connelly. But the part of my brain that hadn't shrunk in fear registered something. Like an itch it persisted. Something wasn't quite right about what I was seeing. Something about the eyes.

A voice sounded far in the distance. It came closer and closer. The words were becoming more intelligible. The voice was mine. I was telling myself to breathe. Don't forget to breathe, I repeated time and time again. My chest rose in an anxious search for oxygen. None came in. I tried again. Something soft was over my face. Something cool to touch and cushioned. A pillow? I pulled it off and tried to fill my lungs. Nothing. Adrenalin surged. Pins and needles of energy pricked at the entire surface area of my skin. My hands moved inches to the side before they were blocked. I lifted them up and again the same thing. I was in a box. A long thin box. And there... was... no air.

Nostrils and lungs expanded, craving air. The darkness was total.

My fingers tore at the roof. Twisting, I kicked at the walls, the floor, the roof. There was no give. Breathe. I had to breathe.

Suddenly the face appeared again. He pressed his lips against mine and his tongue probed. It slid across my teeth and met my own tongue. I wanted to send my conscious mind away. I wanted to fold it in deepest, darkest velvet and protect it from the sights and sounds I was experiencing. My flesh shrunk from his, shrunk as it would from ice, without conscious thought.

Then pain bloomed in my forehead. A ring of spikes. My hands would have shot up to nurse but they were pierced themselves. My fingers splaying out, tendons tight in agony. Then a blade pierced my side, scraping the bottom rib as my weak flesh welcomed its steel. This new pain barely registered in the kaleidoscope that sparked in my brain.

Insistent among the jumble of fears is my struggle for breath. Can't breathe. I'm going to die. Something is lodged in my throat.

It tickles. A half-cough, half-retch forces it on to my lips. I can feel the tiny, hard spine of a feather. I spit it out.

Just as quickly as it started, it stopped.

No pain, no panic.

Nothing.

'James! James!' A door was being knocked somewhere. Who the fuck was James?

'James, are you all right? James open the door.'

James. That's the name I gave to Sue downstairs.

'Sue,' I croak. 'Sue,' louder now. 'I'll just be with you.' Avoiding the pool of puke on the floor I make for the door and open it.

'James. Are you okay?' Sue's face is white and her eyes large with worry. 'I didn't know what was happening, what to do...' she pulled her long hair back from her face. 'I heard some shouting and... your face... the smell. Have you been sick?'

'Eh?' I manage.

'The noise. The screams coming from this flat...' she steps into the room slowly and looks around her, like a deer approaching the scar of a road through her forest. 'It sounded like the sound effects department of a horror movie. Like somebody was being murdered.'

'I, eh...' My mind is starting to settle back into the here and now. 'As you can see, there are no dead bodies.' With a smile on the highest setting I can manage, I indicate the floor around me with open palms.

'A dream... a godawful dream.' I slump to the floor like I'm a puppet and my strings have just been cut. I can't shake the feeling of being violated. I want to scrape every inch of my skin off with a cheese grater. I want to bathe in bleach.

Sue is now at the door and I don't want her to leave. I'd do anything for her not to leave. Her hand is poised over her throat. Something else is being displayed on the theatre of her face. Pity, I can't handle.

'What's that?' Sue asks and steps towards me, her hand outstretched. She pulls something from the corner of my mouth and holds it out to me. On the surface of her palm, about the size of a staple, lies a single, white feather.

Chapter 28

Allessandra is sent on another errand by Campbell. If the convent isn't able to shed any light on McBain's early days as a psycho killer, perhaps the seminary can?

Allessandra is certain that there is plenty that Mother Superior is not saying. She is equally certain that she doesn't want to hear it.

'What kind of a guy flunks priest-training college?' Peters demands at that morning's meeting in the squad room.

'Someone who realises that a life without women is a living death,' answers Daryl Drain.

'Naw,' says Harkness, 'life without women would be heaven, where do I sign up for the priesthood?'

'Too late,' Allessandra says. 'You're totally fucked.'

While entering the banter Allessandra asks herself for the millionth time why she hasn't told Campbell about McBain faking the wounds of Christ on his hands. And why did she go along with Daryl Drain when he went to help McBain with some information?

She's getting in too deep here.

Because he is a good man, she answers herself. And that's not just because he reminds her of her father. The evidence is there. Hadn't he looked after her since she joined the team? Apart from the whole convent list thing of course, he had made her feel welcome. Made her feel like one of the boys. You just have to look at his eyes to know he isn't a killer. There is too much sadness in there. People with that kind of loneliness in their lives don't hurt other people. They save the worst for themselves.

Wouldn't they?

Talking of her father, what would he do? Would he speak to the powers-that-be and bring McBain in? Or would he help his colleague?

Allessandra makes her decision, mentally giving herself the

sign of the cross and prays that her father is looking down on her with a smile.

'Sir, should I be going to speak to these people on my own?' Allessandra asks Campbell.

'Good experience for you,' he answers. 'And in case you missed it, we are a tad low on staff. You are just gathering information at this point. If we need a statement taken, you can go back with a pal another time.'

Allessandra studies her feet to conceal her irritation. What a patronising prick.

The man who greets her at the door of the seminary could have doubled as a lamppost in his spare time. All he needs is a big, powerful, hat-sized bulb. Long fingers stretch out towards Allessandra in the offer of a handshake.

'Father Joseph,' he introduces himself with a lop-sided smile and a voice that should be reading the nine o'clock news. Looking up at his face Allessandra is struck by a series of sharp points, Adam's apple, chin and nose.

'Follow me,' Father Joseph says.

The walls of the room she is led in to are lined with oak panels and in the middle of the room sits a long table, flanked by high-backed chairs, all of a similar forbidding tone. A large crucifix hangs on the far wall.

All we need is a welcome mat, a pair of slippers and some Gregorian chants in the background, thought Allessandra, and I will feel right at home. Not.

'You want to know about Ray?' Father Joseph folds his long frame on to a chair and rubs his head. It is bald apart from a few strands of silvery hair. The effect is as if he had walked through a cloud of dandelion seeds and a handful had stuck.

'Were you here when he was a student?'

A nod. 'I remember him well. And not unfondly.'

Unfondly? Is that even a word, thought Allessandra? She decided to leave her notepad in her pocket and listen to the man talk.

'He was a thoughtful boy. A good student; nothing remarkable. Would have made a good priest.'

'Why do you think he didn't?'

'Most of the boys at some time in their stay here rebel a little. Just because they wish to join a religious order doesn't stop their bodies from producing hormones. They take up with a girl, go for

181

drinks, listen to rock music. Ray was no different.' He crossed his legs and held his hands on his lap. 'Why he didn't become a priest? I don't know. We do have a number of... how shall we put it? Renegades? Some boys just come to the realisation that a life of holy orders is not for them.' His wide, bony shoulders move in a shrug. 'Perhaps Ray was one of them?'

Allessandra suddenly feels the weight of her inexperience. What else should she be asking? How can she get this man to open up and help her? Is DI McBain the wrong man, as she hopes he is? Or is he a sick bastard who needs to be put away for the rest of his natural?

Perhaps sensing her uncertainty the priest helps her out. 'Ray was slightly unusual in that he came here from an orphanage run by the Church. We worried at the time that moving from one religious institution to another should not be his path. And so it turned out, I'm afraid.'

Watching this big man speak, Allessandra is struck by insight. This man cares about the men under his care. He would have been a good role model for the young Ray.

'Why did you think moving from the convent to here might not have worked?'

'To be more effective as a priest one should have some experience of family life. Ray had none. The Church might have become more of a dependency for Ray than was healthy for him.'

Allessandra considers the young man Ray McBain might have been. No parents or siblings. Any friends would be left behind in Bethlehem House. Becoming a priest would have been the only link he had to security. And from what Father Joseph was saying, they didn't really want him.

'Don't get me wrong, DC Rossi. We didn't turn Ray away without good reason. There was an incident,' his great head slumps in sadness, 'Ray injured his best friend. Grievously. He went completely berserk and later offered no explanation. He left us with no choice.'

Chapter 29

I'm in the car, bulleting up the M74, almost back in Glasgow. There's no place like home when you are feeling like the inflow to a sewage works. Except I can't go home.

As I near Glasgow I consider where to go. Kenny's flat is out. McCall knew who I was. How did he know? Had he been keeping tabs on me? If so, he must not only know what I look like, but where I was staying. Does that mean he knows Kenny as well? Shit. That might mean he saw Theresa coming and going. And then there's Daryl. I can't go to him. His job would be on the line. It'll have to be Kenny.

'Kenny. Ray here.'

'I know who you are, ya daft bastard.'

'Shut the fuck up and listen.' I tell him of the latest turn of events, but I miss out the part about the dream... and the possibility that I was one of Connelly's victims. I can't quite accept that yet.

'Right. Find a hotel. Any hotel, as long as it's big and central and close to the motorway. When you get there, phone me back and I'll send Calum round.'

I'm sailing along the M8 when I remember the new hotel that opened up at the motorway end of Argyle Street. That'll do nicely. I can always take my bodyguard shopping if I get too bored.

I find the hotel, park and enter the wood-panelled reception area. My room is ready, I am told by the receptionist, as she hands me the key.

It is a good size, with twin beds and a large TV. Calum appears, like an extra room fitting.

'Naw. You need to get your own room,' I order.

He shrugs. 'Orders are to stay as close to you as possible. That this McCall guy might be after you.'

'Can I go to the shitter on my own?'

183

Save your anger for McCall, I think. But Calum is right, why else would McCall be boning up on me?

I'm on his hit list.

Or have I become convenient to him? Could it be that when I was arrested and charged, I presented an opportunity to him? He could dovetail his crimes into my life? Set me up as the perfect patsy. In that case he should want me to live.

There was a threat inherent in those... what would you call them... dreams?

No way was I abused by Connelly. It didn't happen. These were dreams. Warning me that my life was in danger.

For fuckssake listen to yourself, McBain. *A dream told you.* Next thing you'll be on Oprah having written a book about how a dream saved your life. There has to be a more practical solution. Science and good old plod will provide the solution, not dreams and fucking hocus pocus.

Could be false memory syndrome. That happens, doesn't it? People experience a hard time and go through a dose of denial and blame displacement. They blame somebody, anybody else.

There is a problem here though, just what am I in denial about?

I sit on the lip of the bath, my elbows on my knees, my head in my hands. Take a deep breath. Got to sort yourself out, Ray.

'Ray.' Calum knocks at the door. 'You all right in there?'

'I'm havin' a crap, ya cunt. Fuck off and leave me alone.' That was a wee bit harsh. Calm down. Take a deep breath. Count to ten. Count to a hundred and ten if that's what it takes. You are in a strange situation and calling people names is not getting you anywhere. Aye, but it feels good.

I try to ignore the shiver that runs along my skin like an electric current every time the dream comes back to me and I have to force it out of my mind.

Concentrate on the facts, Ray. What do you know? There's fact and then there's opinion. I deal in facts. I only work with conjecture till it leads me to a fact. Fact: it was only a dream. Fact: McCall knows who I am. Fact: I didn't kill Connelly.

I didn't.

Fact: unless I get my act together sharpish, I'm fucked.

In the morning I send Calum to get himself a coffee. If he is upset at me calling him names last night he's not letting on. I expect in his line of work that it was pretty tame.

A knock at the door. I look out of the spyhole and then open it. Daryl smiles and walks in the door.

'Before we start,' Daryl nods at the window and the car park beyond. 'There's someone outside who would like to say hello.'

'Tell her to come up and not to be so stupid.'

Daryl smiles and pulls a mobile phone from his jacket.

'Come on up. Room 441.'

Before long the door opens and Allessandra walks into the room.

'Come in, Allessandra. How have you been?' I ask like I'm on a team night out. What the fuck was that? *How have you been?* You stupid arse, McBain. Don't know what else to say. How about, *sorry, I may have ruined your career?*

She looks at me and her surprise at my change in appearance is quickly masked. This is not the time for compliments.

'Listen, Allessandra...'

'Listen, Ray...'

'You go first,' I say trying to be gentlemanly.

'No, you go first, sir. Oh, sorry... Ray.'

'For fuckssake,' Drain jumps in, 'you're both sorry about what happened. But Allessandra, you've no need to be.' He looks at me with raised eyebrows and pursed lips, because we both know I don't have a leg to stand on.

'Aye,' I say looking at Allessandra. 'Daryl's right.'

'First time for everything,' Allessandra aims a smile in his direction. 'But I did want to say sorry, 'cos if it wasn't for me you wouldn't have ended up in jail, charged with murder.'

'Correction, Allessandra. If it wasn't for me keeping my name off that list, I wouldn't have ended up in jail. I put you in an untenable situation. And for that I am deeply, deeply sorry. I'm also proud of you. Proud that you had the balls to go to the high heid yins. What if I was the murderer? And you hadn't? People would have lost their lives because of you. No. You have nothing to apologise for and plenty to be proud of.'

'If you say so,' she says. A thought flits across her face. She clenches her fists and relaxes them. She's still conflicted about this whole situation and I need to try and reassure her.

'I say so.' To emphasise this I step towards her and give her a hug. We both then step backwards trying to deal with the awkwardness of the moment. It just seemed like the right thing to do. And there was nothing sexual in it. Unless you count the thought that entered my head in that split second I was holding her.

'Pals,' I say. She nods. I'm not completely convinced but say nothing more.

'Let's sit down before we all curl up and die with embarrassment,' grins Daryl. 'Ray McBain has a soft side. Fuck me.'

'No thanks.' Allessandra and I say at the same time, catch each other's eye and laugh.

They sit at the small table thoughtfully provided by the hotel management for those guests who might want to write their postcards. You know the kind of things, *bought too much, ate too much, didn't have enough sex.*

Perched on the edge of the bed, I ask them to tell me what's been going on. But first I want to know why. Why are they both risking their careers, and possibly everything they own, to help me?

'I've known you for a long time, Ray. And no way are you a murderer.'

'Me too, Ray... I mean I agree.' In the light of her eye I can read some uncertainty and... what, pity? Is she doing the right thing? she's been asking herself. Who wouldn't in her situation? New to a job, new colleagues, new boss. Then the man you want to trust the most goes on the run for murder. Allessandra Rossi has a lot to be wary of and I am even more impressed that she is here. This woman has balls.

'After we've bonded and all that,' Allessandra is wearing an impish smile, 'if you don't mind me saying so, Ray, you look great.'

'Thanks.' I'm not immune to flattery.

'Who'd have known that under all that blubber there was such a good-looking guy?'

'Blubber? Was I that fat?'

'Can we get down to business?' asks Daryl. 'Or are you two going to carry on with this love-fest?'

'Feeling left out?' I ask. 'Poor Daryl. Nobody loves him.'

'Don't you worry about me, Ray. I'm getting plenty.'

'So what's been happening down at the cop shop?'

'As far as suspects go, you're it. No-one else has been investigated.' Daryl grimaces.

'Great.'

'Most of our time has been spent trying to find a link between you and the two other bodies,' answers Daryl.

'And looking into your past for clues as to why you might have turned out like this,' Allessandra adds.

'Aye, caused a bit of a stir when we found out you'd spent some time in a seminary studying to become a priest,' says Daryl. I feel like I'm at Wimbledon and I'm following the ball across the net as I look from one to the other as they speak.

'Have you found anything incriminating?'

'Plenty for the psychologists when you get round to speaking to them. But nothing for the courts,' Daryl answers. 'I'm serious, by the way, about the shrinks. They want to get you in front of one.'

'And? Standard practice in a case like this. Make sure I'm fit to stand at my trial.'

'Well,' he shrugged, 'It is a well used defence...'

'No fucking way,' I say. I know why he's saying it. *If* I get caught and *if* I get locked up it might be easier for a policeman to be in an asylum than a prison. Makes it easier for the suits as well. *Policeman goes nuts and kills* is simpler for the damage limitation guys than *policeman killer is as sane as you or I.*

'I take it my flat has been searched?' Time to change the subject.

'With a fine-tooth comb.' Allessandra says. 'And you know how you serial killers like to take trophies from your victims? We found bugger all.' Her tone is light, probably to atone for Daryl's serious comments.

'Fancy that.'

'So we, as in the royal we, think you have somewhere else. A kill zone. Somewhere you take your victims, do your stuff and hide your sordid wee mementos.' Her tone tails off into serious as she realises that what she is saying is a spot of black humour too much, even for cops. Real people are suffering here and unless we find the mad bastard who's doing it, more people will follow.

'Is my flat being watched?' They both nod a yes. Just a thought. If I was the killer and I wanted to use me as a patsy it would help my case if I were to hide incriminating evidence where the police are sure to find it.

'Any reports about me being in Manchester?' Again with the nods.

'What about my appearance? Was that commented upon?'

'No, thankfully,' answers Daryl. 'The coppers down there obviously didn't realise its significance.'

'Well that's something. Anything else?'

'There was one thing. A card we found in your car. It was a business card for a Financial Adviser. We called him and he didn't know you. The good news is he offered you a free Financial Health Check.'

'A what?'

He shrugs. 'But on the back of the card someone had scribbled the name Maggie Gallagher, and a phone number.'

'Never heard of her.' I try to put a face to the name.

'We went to see her.' Daryl is wearing that smile. A smile of teenage proportions that demands to know — who's he been shagging?

'Turns out you and her had a sleepover at your place.'

'And?' I don't rise to the bait, but I'm getting a face. A face that I shouted at and told to fuck off. She only wanted to help.

'That was it. She said to tell you she'd like to meet up with you again.'

'Right.' That's all I need, another romantic interlude.

'Yeah,' said Allessandra. 'She sounded quite keen on you. You want her number?'

'Surely you're not thinking of pimping for a shag while this is going on?' asks Daryl. I can't decide whether Daryl's impressed and jealous, or incredulous and critical. But I couldn't give a toss. Maggie Whoever is not on my list of suspects. Therefore she can go and take a flying fuck for all I care. Preferably with someone else.

Chapter 30

Maggie Gallagher greets me with a smile as wide as the Clyde and is all but bouncing up and down in her excitement at meeting me.

'Ray, Ray, is that really you? Wow, look at you. I'm amazed I recognised you. You look pure stunnin'.'

I'm in the reception area of the Radisson, just across the road from The Heilanman's Umbrella in Argyle Street. Just popped in for a coffee on the way back to my hotel.

'It's Maggie, isn't it?' I ask, and look at the door behind her, wondering if it would be too rude to do a runner. This is all I need.

She hugs me as if we're old friends. 'I was so hopin' we would meet up again.' There wasn't even a trace of awkwardness and plenty of friendship on offer. Which was strange given the fact that all our relationship consisted of so far were a drunken evening, a failed fuck and a one-sided shouting match in the confines of my car.

If she notices my reticence, she's not letting on

'What brings you here, Maggie?' I stand as stiff as a board until her arms fall down to her sides.

'Oh you know, passin' through.' She is blushing slightly and her line of sight is moving from me to the wall behind and then back to me. 'Actually,' she stands taller, 'I saw you lookin' in a shop window in Argyle Street and I'm like... is it? No, can't be. But it is.' She beams. 'You look stunnin'.'

We stand and look at each other for a few moments, each wondering what to say. I'm thinking how can I get the hell out of here and she looks like she wants to get to know me better.

'I just popped in for a coffee.'

'What a nice idea,' says Maggie, 'don't mind if I join you.' This last statement had more the aura of a command than the tone of a request.

Not sure how I can extricate myself from this situation gracefully, I follow her to a table. She's just too happy to see me to be rude to. From the large plate glass window we can see the traffic ebb and flow as it meets the crossroads.

The table is about knee high and is dark expensive wood. The seats are single, with curved backs and covered in plush purple velour. We are silent while we each have a look at the drinks menu. A waiter comes across and takes our order. We sit in silence until he leaves.

What the hell am I doing here?

'Look, Maggie...' I shift forward in my seat as if I am about to stand up.

'You look fantastic, Ray. Look at all that weight you've lost,' she says. I stay where I am. 'You should write a book, *The McBain Diet*. It would outsell that Atkins guy,' she gushes.

Yeah right, I can just see it on the bookshelves: *Become a Suspect for Murder, Lose your Job, Go on the Run from the Police and See the Weight Melt Off!*

'So how have you been, Ray?'

She must be able to read my expression. 'Any better and I'd be twins,' I answer. 'Just wonderful. Fantastic. All that's missing is the balloons.'

Her face sags a little with concern.

'Oh Ray. I have been worried about you.'

'You barely know me, Maggie.' I'm trying really hard to be pleasant.

She follows the passage of a car going up Argyle Street as if her life is dependent on it, and then her concern for me overcomes her hesitation. 'The police came to see me.'

'So that's it then. You see me on the news. The police visit you and you're all curious to know what's going on.' What would be the suspected murderer's equivalent of a fag hag?

'No, not at all. I...' she pauses. 'You were on the news?'

'Do you not watch TV?'

'Don't even own one.'

'Do you not buy newspapers then?'

'Nah. Full of bad news. Life's hard enough without looking for the bad stuff.'

Christ, this is perfect.

'Well, if you had read the papers or watched TV, you'd know that you were sitting with a murder suspect.'

She laughs. Her head thrown back to display a row of fillings on either side of her mouth. 'Is this another one of your stories?' She looks at me. 'Ray, first you were an entrepreneur. Now you're a murder suspect.' She laughs again.

'Maggie. I'm not joking.'

She sobers when she sees my complete lack of humour. Her hand goes to her mouth. 'Holy shit. Murder?' She repeats herself.

Not long after I'd left the seminary I told a girl I was training for the priesthood in order to get rid of her. If this weren't true it would be even funnier.

'Holy shit... Murder?'

'Yes. And don't speak so loud.' A few faces turn to look at us. I stare them down.

'Sorry, Ray. Ray, how awful for you. But shouldn't you just give yoursel' up? The police are bound to realise they've got the wrong man. Eventually.' While she speaks she openly appraises me. Her eyes are looking deep into mine as if they display my darkest secrets and, what's more, she can read them. There's obviously a good brain in this head, which is easy to discount if you don't get past the tits and the hair.

'That's just it. They think they've got the right man. So now you know... if you want to walk away and never have anything more to do with me, I'll understand.' I cross my arms and my legs and take a sip of my coffee. All the while thinking, go woman, go. She sits back in her chair, uncrosses her arms and looks from my face to the traffic outside and back to my face.

'Ray, I didn't tell you when we met but I was in that bar for the first time in my life. Do you remember my pal, Amanda?'

'Christ. If it wasn't for the fact that I woke up naked beside you, I wouldn't remember you.'

'Long black hair. Pure glam. No?'

I shake my head.

'Well, anyway. Amanda and I used to work together in the Tarot Card call centre. Big mistake. Big con. Don't ask.' She flaps her hands theatrically. 'When I left the dump, we lost touch. She phoned me out of the blue and asked if I'd like to go for a drink with her. Her boyfriend had chucked her, didn't love her any more. But she was still mad about him and she wanted to go out for a drink, pure casual like, somewhere he drinks, but with a mate so as not to look like a mad stalker...'

'Is this going anywhere?'

'Don't worry, there is a reason for all this preamble. Anyway... before I was rudely interrupted.' She smiles, and I can't help myself but respond in kind. She has to have the most infectious smile. Her smile wavers. 'But I can't.' She slumps back in her chair.

'You can't what?'

'This. Can't do this. When I saw you...' she swings her head round and aims her gaze in the direction of Argyle Street, '... and as I was kinda stalkin' you,' another smile, big in size but weakened by the worrying thoughts now going through her head. A cough. '... over there I was rehearsin' all this stuff in my head. And now I can't do it. You're wanted for murder.' The smile is gone now and it looks like it's not coming back any time soon.

'You think I'm a murderer?' I push back into my seat and throw my hands to my sides, palms facing up. Then I curse myself. Why am I trying to win her back? Lose the woman, McBain, and fast.

'No,' she leans towards me her face full of contrition. Then when she notices my gaze fall from her face to the cleavage on display, she sits back and places a hand over her twin attractions until she is sure my eyes have returned to her face.

'It's just... a woman can't be too careful. There are a lot of nutters around, you know.'

I raise my eyebrows.

'Of course you know, Mr Policeman,' she smiles in a self-deprecating manner. 'Just having a blonde moment.' She leans forward to pick her handbag from the table, a voluminous pink thing that would have taken half a cow to make. As she does so my eyes are drawn back to her tits. And I am amazed at how easily I can be distracted. My way of life is in danger here and I behave like a teenager over a flash of pale soft skin.

'I really should...' She stands up.

I stay seated. 'So what were you rehearsing as you were stalking me?' I smile. Charm on at force ten. If she is suspicious of me I can't let her leave until I know just how suspicious she really is. I can't have her phoning any helpline or, God forbid, Crimestoppers. So I'll act calm and collected while all I want to do is push her down into her seat and convince her of my innocence as forcefully as is legal and decent.

'Stalkin' is a bit strong.' She flicks her hair and it occurs to me that she fancies me. Doh. Who is having the blonde moment now? She went to bed with you when you were a lot fatter and a lot less sober than you are now. Of course she fancies you.

'So how would you put it?' As I smile, I realise that some of the strain of the last few weeks has faded. Like some of the colour has leaked from an indelible stain on my soul. Maybe I fancy her just a little too. Theresa's face superimposes itself on my mind and I give myself a lecture. Flirting isn't fucking.

Maggie sits back down. Very slowly. Her knees bending as her nicely curved and ample backside gets nearer to the cloth of the chair while she gives in to the desire to stay and ignores the impulse to get on her mobile. She laughs and flicks her hair again.

'Now, wouldn't that be funny... I mean if you really were a murderer... and I was actually stalkin'...' she stops talking and it is a few moments before I realise what is happening.

I look at her face and see that her eyes are aimed at my groin. I cross my legs noting a feeling of discomfort. You can take the boy out of the convent, but it seems that it is still difficult to work on the reverse. I'm surprised at how coy I am feeling.

'It gets very tiring, very quickly, when men talk to my boobs.' Maggie is thin-lipped. 'How did you like it when I stared at your crotch?'

I uncross my legs defiantly but before I know it my hands are on my lap. 'Not all men would be uncomfortable with a woman openly checking out their lunchbox.' I smile my apology and change the subject. 'So what were you rehearsing when you were on your way to talk to me?'

'Oh. That.' She busies herself in her handbag and, after what feels like several hours, resurfaces. 'I can never find anything in this bloody thing.' She rummages some more. Then she stops. 'This is what they might call displacement activity.' Smile. 'The thing is, Ray, I can't stop thinkin' about you. Ever since that night...'

'But nothing happened.'

'True. But it's not just that. I mean I do find you... but I want to help you. There's a wee boy in there... in a lot of pain and I want to help him.'

'Right. Now you are freaking me out.' My turn to stand up.

'I could just call Crimestoppers.'

Some tension uncorks and I sit down.

'Any more of this and people will be lining up their chairs and turning the music off and on at irritating intervals. Musical chairs.'

'Right. Anyway,' I rub at my face suddenly exhausted, 'just tell me what you want, Maggie, and then we can both go our separate ways.'

'We didn't just meet by chance, Ray.' She leans forward and I keep my eyes tracked firmly on hers. No straying is allowed. 'Somethin' brought us together. Chance. Synchronicity. Whatever you would like to call it. But I am convinced that we were brought together so that I could help you.'

'Help me? You're saying that fate brought us together? So that you could help me?' Cynicism sharpens my tone. 'Next time I'm chatting up a woman I must remember to use that line.'

'Are you still getting nightmares?'

She takes a deep breath and for the second time within minutes I realise there is more to this woman than curves and hair. 'I know it sounds crazy, Ray. God knows I have trouble dealing with it at times, but I have a gift. I can help you. There is no such thing as coincidence, Ray. We were meant to meet. You needed help. I came into your life at just the right time.'

'So fate not only decided that I needed your help, but that I needed a shag?'

'If I remember rightly, the shag never happened.' She sat back in her chair and crossed her arms. 'I was drawn to you, Ray. Physically and mentally. And why the fuck am I justifyin' myself to you?'

'Sorry.' I feel awful now. 'I didn't mean...'

'What did you mean?' The lady isn't for letting me off the hook.

'I don't know. I wasn't getting at you. I just don't buy into all that fate stuff. Or the psychic stuff.'

'I'm not psychic. I'm intuitive. Psychic has too many... comes with a lot of baggage. Anyway, we met in a pub I didn't know existed until that night. Just at a time when you needed someone's help. Someone who is uniquely qualified to do so. What do you call that?'

'Okay, okay. Can we discuss the whims of fate another time? I have a murderer to catch.'

Maggie's energy deflates with a loud sigh. The "M" word was now on the table between us again.

'What can I do to help you, Ray?'

'Do your stuff and find out who the murderer is?' Each word is laced with sarcasm.

'It's not as easy as that. And that's not the best way to help you.'

'Why not? You'd be in all the papers. You'd have your own TV programme.' Fuck this. I've had enough. 'If you really want to help me, do your psychic mumbo jumbo shit and find the murderer.'

'Helping you would be getting you to take responsibility and stop feeling bloody sorry for yourself. Let's review your life in the last few months. Drinking until you lose consciousness. Unable to eat properly because you keep being sick. Bad dreams. You're going to lose it, Ray. And that's without using my gift. You need to face the truth, Ray, as horrible as that may be. And the sooner you learn to accept things, the better.'

'What about this murderer? You can't see him?' Accept what? I'm on my own conversational track and she's on another one entirely. 'Psychic, my arse.' I turn away from her in disgust.

She reaches out and holds my hand on top of the table between us. If I turn to face her I know I'll see a look of pity. And I don't do pity.

'You were just a boy, Ray. What happened to you was evil... evil.'

'What are you...?' I face her and the look on her face almost unmans me.

It's all I can do to hold myself upright in the chair and keep an expression on my face that approximates neutral.

She knows. 'He was an evil man, Ray. Don't let your past poison your present. Deal with it.'

'How?'

She actually knows. And she doesn't have to spell it out. It is all in her expression.

'This is... unbelievable. This psychic shit. Nah. You don't... how can you...?'

'Why is it so unbelievable? Science doesn't have all the answers. And anyway, why do we ridicule things that science can't explain? Not everythin' in life fits into a neat wee box, you know.' Her hair is almost on end as she speaks, her palms facing out, fingers spread. 'All of life is electricity. Your body is electricity. Each thought that enters your head is an electrical discharge. Why are people so dim as to think that the bones of your skull are enough to contain it?'

'So your brain's like a receiver? You're tuning into electrical discharges? What a load of fucking baloney.'

'It's an explanation,' Maggie shrugs. 'No-one knows the full answer. But I know it exists. And now, so do you.'

'Crap. Rubbish.'

'Have you ever told anyone about what happened to you?'

'Nothing happened to me. Nothing.'

'Then why the nightmares? Why are you so linked to this case?'

Hands. I can feel hands all over me. They came in the dark. It's only a dream. A lonely boy's repeated night horror of a dream. And then there were more. Vague recollections of dreams of pillows and small hands. Pressing. Punching. All in a thick silence. Unable to breathe. Air like treacle in my lungs. White feathers falling in a snowstorm.

If all of this was dreams why does it all seem so real? And then there's the recent ones with people. People with holes in them. Holes filling with blood. Wounds of the stigmata.

The people all wear Connelly's face. And again those dreams are so real ... the emotions, the smells, the pictures. The detail is remarkable. It's like I'm there and I'm making him suffer. I'm killing Connelly over and over again.

Bottom line, McBain. And this is a thought that requires instant medication... then if I wasn't abused, then I must be the bastard that's killing all these people. These are not dreams.

They are memories.

Chapter 31

DI Ray McBain, Serial Killer. Try that one on for size. Does it fit?

My head is in my hands and I'm in a toilet cubicle at the Radisson. See me? See toilets? Getting to be a habit. Maggie will be outside wondering what the hell is going on. Do I have it in me to kill someone? Three someones?

So far.

Maybe I should just go back to those pricks at HQ and hand myself in; ask them to lock me up, cast the key in concrete and then throw it off the Kingston Bridge.

The sights, the sounds, the feelings. They are all so *real*. Then there's the other stuff. Dreams. The blood. Maybe they should make sure the cell is in a lunatic asylum. But if you are aware of your insanity, does that not mean you are perfectly sane?

Am I capable of hurting another human in that manner? In any manner? In my career I have come to understand that if you rub your thumb across the psyche of any individual you'll uncover the possibility of violence. Unwrap the shiny plastic put there by society and then all you need is motivation. Did I have the motivation? Sure, I had a shit childhood, don't most people? Has something else happened that I've buried? *Did* Connelly do me as well? The nightmare man could just have been a figment of an imaginative young boy's mind. I knew what was going on with other kids and worried that I would be next.

As for that level of violence, I didn't have it in me. Did I?

There was only one occasion in my life when I lost it. At the seminary. Boy, did I lose it. I kicked seven kinds of shit out of that guy. If I hadn't been pulled off him, I'd be kicking him still.

Mark Doyle and I joined the college on the same day. He had a similar early childhood to mine, his parents were experts at hurting each other. Drink, words and fists, whatever could do the most damage was called into action. When they tired of each other, they turned on the kids. As the eldest, Mark received special attention.

We were sixteen and filled each other's shadows. Wherever you found one, you were sure to find the other. We liked the same music, the same books and the same sports.

We could talk all day and still find something new and interesting to say to each other as the small hand slid past midnight.

Sex was a problem we discussed with each other. We had to accept its absence from our lives for the rest of our lives and, as committed as we were to the priesthood, we could pray till our knees bled and still wake up in the morning with a monster hard-on.

Press-ups and sit-ups became our weapon against the sins of Repeated Masturbation. Rather than grip my dick and rub at it until I was comatose, I would jump out of bed and beat out fifty press-ups and fifty sit-ups. Over our morning porridge we would joke about how many were required that morning to reduce the blood flow to our groins.

The seminary was a different world from the convent, a wholly male world, and Mark's presence made the transition more bearable. I was used to being miserable and barely noticed that this misery continued, but Mark being there helped.

One night I was having a dream. A young lady was trying to seduce me. She was Satan made into tantalising, inviting flesh. One hand held a breast high enough for her tongue to snake out and skim across the top of her nipple. The other was deep inside herself.

'Just put it in for a second,' she begged me. I took a step forward.

'No.' I took a step back and tried to shake off desire like a dog shakes heavy rain from its coat. I couldn't do it. I was training to be a priest.

But she looked so beautiful.

A hand gripped my dick and began to massage it. My whole body tightened. Pleasure burst from my groin and splattered on my stomach. I became aware of a weight in the bed beside me and a voice whispered in my ear.

'Sssh. Everyone will hear you.'

Mark's hand was still on my cock. 'I love you, Ray.'

I remember nothing more. Apparently it took five men to pull me off him. No-one could believe the strength I displayed that night. Or my viciousness.

When I think of it now a number of emotions struggle for attention. My face burns with shame that I should have reacted so, both in the extent of my violence… and my sexual response. Fists and jaw muscles clench at the thought that a friend should betray me in such a way.

He was the first real pal I ever remember having, the one bright spot in a series of personalities who had let me down. And he turns out to be just as bad as the rest of them.

Fear curdles my stomach, I completely lost control. However I justify it to myself, I lost it. What else am I capable of? There is something else that worries. A part of me was looking on at my reaction with a pleasure so intense it itched.

I had lost control and it was fucking wonderful.

Mark and I never spoke again. I left the seminary the next day and I have no idea what happened to him, or even the extent of his injuries.

Teenage confusion, misplaced attraction or something much deeper as far as Mark was concerned? I have no idea, but it left me with a stain. I blacked out then as I struck him. Am I doing the same thing now with these victims? I stand up and take the half step required to reach the cubicle door. Bang. I hit my head on it. Am I a murderer? Bang. Did I kill those people?

I sit down again. Okay, calm down. Count to ten. Eleven. Twelve. I am not a murderer. I am a policeman and I have a killer to catch.

Devlin. She's my only link to him. I'll go and see her and she'll tell me where McCall is if I have to kick it out of her.

Maggie is waiting at the door, her face a study in anxiety.

'You okay, Ray?'

'Aye,' I nod. 'Aye.'

'Thank God.' Maggie holds a hand to her chest and grins, 'I thought I was going to have to take you home and give you a good shag to calm you down.' We both laugh. My laughter goes on beyond hers and tails into tears.

'Let's go back and have a seat,' Maggie takes my hand as if I was some distraught child.

'You can do it, Ray.' Maggie leans forward, her expression on full empathy, and pats my hand. She shoots back in her chair as if fired from a cannon. The chair rocks back on its rear legs and then rights itself.

'Ray,' Her hand is over her mouth. 'Don't go and visit that woman.' She squeezes her eyes shut. 'The woman with scrubbed hands.'

'Oh. You can see her?' But I need to. She's the only link I have to her son.

'If you need to speak to her, get someone else to go. You can't. Promise me you won't go.' Her eyes are open now and large with fear.

'What's going to happen?' Her intensity sets my teeth to *Grind*.

'I don't know. I only know it will be dangerous for you. Promise me you won't go.'

'Right. Okay, I promise.' Christ, I'm tired of being so fucking serious all the time. 'How about that shag now?'

It's been a few days since I last went out for a run and I'm loving it. See the guy that invented this, I'm going to post him a fiver. Well, I would if I hadn't already heard he died of a heart attack. How's that for irony?

'I am not a killer.' The words run through my head. Each syllable matched with a shoe hitting the pavement. 'I am not a killer.'

You know that moment, "the zone" they call it, when you feel as if you could run forever? It's like meditation on a pair of fast legs. The tortoise becomes the hare. Pure fucking magic.

I run and there's nothing but me, the drum of my feet and the flow of air in and out of my lungs. The rest of the world is only an obstacle to run past, through or up. I find myself aiming in the direction of the Necropolis. There's something about the place that suits me, a monument to the dead set above and apart from the rest of the city.

Here and there glass glints among the pebbles on the path, here and there neon ink describes how *Rab Luvs Maggie*, just below where a grieving family has given testimony to the love they felt for the departed. Love in life and death. I get the feeling the dead don't mind the intrusion from the living and near dead who visit this place in the dark. I imagine their energy dissipates through their speech and the various substances they inhale or inject, and falls like mist through the layers of earth and wood and bone, and feeds the dead.

This is a place of acceptance. There's no greater act of acceptance required than to acknowledge the truth of someone's death. Perhaps I can learn something here. Acceptance. Three syllables that have a depth and resonance I worry is beyond me. Whatever did happen to me at Bethlehem House has to be faced up to and soon.

This place is glorious in its sluggish decay, I think as I climb up the path. My pace slows down to a walk here, although I pump my arms in a facsimile of a jog. The grass is kept trim, but weeds climb up each plinth, as if to blur the edge between man and nature. A couple of gravestones are laid flat like over-sized granite coffin lids, a ploy, I read somewhere, to stop grave robbers from helping themselves.

Daryl and Allessandra are standing by the base of John Knox's statue. Even from here I can see the outsized grin on Daryl's face, like he thinks it's hilarious that I'm running. Allessandra is huddled within the folds of her coat and her eyes are roaming everywhere but on my face.

'All right, guys?' By their side now, I run on the spot, partly to keep warm and partly to wind Daryl up.

'When was the last time you took some exercise, Daryl?' I ask

'Did some horizontal jogging last night.'

'Wanking's become a sport then?' Allessandra jumps in.

'Ha fucking ha. Her name was Debbie, if you must know.'

'I'd rather not, thank you. You should never come between a man and his guide dog.'

'So what's new, guys?' I ask. The banter is all well and good, but we need to get working.

'Nothing much, Ray,' Daryl answers. 'You're still Suspect No 1. We've found no more connections between you and the victims or between Connelly and the more recently deceased.'

'We visited your old friends at the seminary,' adds Allessandra. 'One old boy remembered you... not unfondly, was how he put it. Said there was an incident. Broke some poor boy's ribs. The brass were creaming themselves over that one. Proof that you have a history of violence.'

'All your old cases have been pulled as well, Ray. Just in case you used violence to secure a conviction. They don't want something there to rear up and bite them in the arse.'

Daryl's comments were to be expected. I would have done the same thing.

'This all leads back to Bethlehem House. I'm sure of it. There's a link there between McCall, Connelly and Devlin.' And me. 'Has anyone gone back there?'

'No. They feel there is no real need anymore.' Allessandra answers while looking at her feet and stamping them in a vain attempt to heat them up. 'The connection has already been established. You killed Connelly to avenge some wrong. The other two were in the wrong place at the wrong time while you satisfied your sick lusts.'

'They're hoping that when we get you back into custody, you'll tell us why you did the other two,' Daryl joined in.

'What a pile of crap. They can't find a connection so they just think wait and see. That's their great piece of detection. For fuckssake, can't they see this case has more holes in it than my Dad's Y-fronts?' I'm starting to get cold now and hop from one foot to the other. 'Somebody needs to get back to Bethlehem House. I can't. Mother Superior will be straight on to the police. We need to get in there and have another look at that list of names. See if either Leonard or Hutchison were there when Connelly was at work.' I already know this to be the case, but I prefer that they find out for themselves.

'I'll go,' says Allessandra. 'They already know me.'

'Anything else, Ray?'

'Aye. Get me photographs of those two. See if it dredges up any memories. Right. Thanks again guys. Now fuck off before I get hypothermia.'

'You're no joking.' The cold has eventually begun to reach Daryl. 'Can we no find somewhere less exposed to have our wee meetings?'

'Aye. Why don't set up our own wee incident room in Pitt Street? See how the bosses feel about that. We can always cite the glacial winds blowing across the city as being detrimental to our investigation.'

'Don't be so fucking smart, McBain. I meant somewhere else as in warm, dry and anonymous.'

I smile, 'Just yanking your chain, DD.' I note the way that he spoke to me and the way that Allessandra *didn't* hold her breath while she waited for my reaction. We're no longer boss and colleagues, we're all friends and we're in this together.

'Point taken, Daryl.' I punch him on the arm, in lieu of a hug. 'Now fuck off will you?'

I'm in the hotel room and I'm about to crawl up my own arse with worry. It's been two days since I spoke with the guys and my only company has been Calum and a TV set. How can folk watch that crap all day? And night? Sleep has also been a tad elusive. Now that I'm working on this whole *acceptance* thing I'm afraid of the stuff that's going to fill my dreams. But I can't stay awake forever.

At least I'm eating again. Calum, as usual, is in charge of provisions and as he is a man who treats his body like the proverbial temple, the food is nutritious and boring. I fancy a night of hotel food. Saliva brims from my mouth at the suggestion of sauces and steaks, cakes and custard that fills the hotel menu, but Heil Calum is to be obeyed on this. No sense in losing all that weight and starting to bloat up again. Besides, he added, they'll start to recognise you. Beaten by his logic, I back down.

Can't do anything about the TV either. There are some movies, but I don't fancy any of them. Besides, I doubt I can concentrate long enough to follow the story. So, TV it is and a veritable feast of other people's misery, recipes and grand houses is there for my delectation. Then in the evenings it's soaps and robbers. *Coronation Street* followed by some generic police drama. Fuckssake. They should dish out Prozac with the TV licence.

Just watching the Scottish news. The First Minister is speaking to a less than rapt audience. One guy, who has a monk's tonsure and goatee that looks as if its been culled from an arctic fox, is resting one hand on his chin. Two fingers are resting on his neck, stretching up to just below his ear. As if he's checking for a pulse.

Know the feeling, mate. Got to do something. Got to do something. I can't just sit about here. I punch Kenny's number into the phone.

'Kenny. Gimme your motor.'

'What do you want my car for, ya tosser?'

'I'm about to die with boredom. If I don't get out of this room I swear I'm going to be the first case of rigor mortis with a pulse.'

'Have a wank. That always gets me going of a morning.'

'I'm all dried up.' We share a laugh. 'No, seriously, Kenny, I need to get out for a wee while.'

'Okay.' He's still laughing. 'I'm in the middle of something just now. Can you hold on for a couple of hours?'

Kenny insists that Calum stays with me. For some reason, Kenny's becoming even more protective. Maybe I'm giving off some signals. If I am on anyone's hit list, Kenny says, Calum will be a deterrent. Not only that, the police are looking for a solitary male. The latter is logic I understand.

In the car, Calum doesn't bother to ask where we're going. He just sits in the passenger seat with a bag of fruit on his lap and grazes.

'Ah'm detoxin'.'

'Right.' Fascinating. This guy should stand for Parliament with conversational powers like this. Polite stuff out of the way, I can now lose myself in my own thoughts. When I did eventually drop off last night, I dreamed about Theresa. We were staying in the same hotel. I knew she was there but couldn't find her room. I would approach each door with my pulse hammering in my ears, open the door and the room would be empty. Time and time again I opened a door and nothing. Doesn't take a psychologist to work that one out. But I can't go chasing her right now. For one thing I don't want her to get caught up in all this and for another, I feel she needs space to work out what she really wants.

If anything, my feelings for her have intensified. I'm just doing a good job of ignoring her face when it slides into my mind. Night is a different matter. I have no conscious control over my dreams. The blessing is when I'm dreaming of her, I'm not re-enacting the death of a certain paedophile.

The Beamer slides along the M8 like there's cruise control and then there's mellow. Effortless driving. The M8 curves round to the M77 and I'm heading down to Ayrshire without really articulating this is where I want to go. Half an hour later and the deep purr a cat makes when you stroke it issues from the engine as it idles at the side of the road in front of Bethlehem House.

Calum's brain rouses from wherever he sends it.

'That's some building. What is it?'

'A convent.'

'Right. Must have been a few bob went into making that.' His head swivels and his eyes meet mine. 'So this is where you were brought up?' His look is empathic. Like he has just considered what it might have been like to live in a place like this. For the first time I catch a glimpse of the person behind the mask of muscle. 'What was it like?'

How do you dilute ten years of lovelessness into a single phrase?

I settle for being concise.

'Shite.'

We both turn and look at the building. It is in an excellent state of repair, but for all the people who spend the currency of their daily lives within its walls it looks empty. A covering of ivy here and there might have offered at least an illusion of life. Even the garden with its crew-cut lawn looks stark. Here and there the brown of the earth is exposed, where de-populated flowerbeds hibernate in anticipation of winter. In the centre of each bed the dark twisted sticks of heavily trimmed rose bushes escape the soil, like just-breathing victims of genocide.

A figure is hunched over a flowerbed in the far right-hand corner. From here their gender is indeterminate. A hat covers the head and offers no clue. Clothing is a green boiler suit. He or she is slim, waist fanning out into shoulders of average width. It must be a guy. No woman would have buttocks as scrawny as that. Unless it's an anorexic nun. No, they had a gardener in my day, why would it change? The gardens extended up the left-hand side, past the chapel and out into the rear, where there was more than double the land I could see from here. If memory served me right.

He turns and walks closer. A skip hat is pulled low over his forehead. I've decided it's a man. No tell-tale bumps on the chest to indicate otherwise. All I can see of his face is nose and chin. They are as sharp as the thorns he has just been trimming. Does he know about his predecessor, I wonder? Mind you, it's not exactly the thing you tell someone at interview. Oh, and by the way, one of the last guys who held this job was a paedophile. Looking at the cut of this guy's mouth makes me feel it would be a thrill. This may even be his favourite season. He waits all summer for the colour of the leaves to curdle and slowly and carefully snips off each flower and each leaf, preferring a stick covered with thorns.

Christ, who's got a dose of the mental shits? Some poor guy is just doing his job and I'm getting all suspicious like a tabloid vigilante.

The clues are in that building. Maybe if I wandered its halls I would pick up on something.

'You're not going in there.' Calum's eyebrows are raised. He must have read the intensity rising from me like a shimmer of heat.

'And you're going to stop me?'

'Aye.' No emotion. Just an honest answer. If only I had a pair of handcuffs, some pepper spray and a baton I might be able to subdue him. Without these things I have no chance.

Back at the hotel, Calum is having a shower. I'm lying on my bed pretending to be asleep, in the hope that he will fuck off for a wee while and give me peace. The radio is on, another Boy Bland is droning on about love. They've had to come in out of the *rain*, to stop the *pain*, apparently.

Worry temporarily alleviated by our wee run in the car, I've jumped back into a state of agitation. I need to do something. There's been no word from Daryl and Allessandra, so I don't know if they've managed to look into things yet.

I should just lie here, head braced against a couple of pillows and open that locked corner in my mind. What is the source of all my dreams? Dreams, not memories. Definitely dreams.

I am no killer. Who was the nightmare man? Was he real? Was he Connelly? If he did... do stuff to me, wouldn't I have some kind of scars or something?

I can't keep still. I sit up. Walk to the window. Go back to the bed. Do the relaxation exercise, going over each body part. Get as far as my neck and sit up again. I can't relax like that. All kinds of stuff crowds in.

Maybe I should give Maggie a call. See if her "gift" could tell me something. Yes. I am that desperate.

Lie down again, Ray. Do the exercise like your life depends on it. Because it does.

Breathe in slowly to a count of nine. Out to a count of nine. Relax the scalp. Relax the forehead. My eyelids are like white sheets hanging on a washing line. My limbs are sinking into the bed. So heavy. A crystal is hanging in my mind. Spinning. I'm heavy. So heavy. Light tinged with rainbow colours shoots around my skull, reaching the darkest corners. Heavy. So heavy...

A feather has fought loose. First the white stem. Then the fibres that spread like a delicate fur. Its flight is brief. Mere feet, before it falls in a lazy see-saw towards the ground. As it gets nearer my teeth tighten, my breath fails to get past the blockage in my throat. Can't breathe. Can't breathe. Catch the feather before it lands.

Can't breathe.
Catch the feather.
When it lands, I die.

Fuck. I sit up like my waist is spring loaded. What was that all about? I can remember a feather. And an incapacitating feeling of panic. My jaws are aching.

I swing round to place my feet on the floor and in doing so touch my pillow with my left hand. The pillow is soaked with my sweat. I stand up and my legs feel weak.

I allow my pulse to slow and the blood to return to my legs before walking over to the window. What is going on? I need to do something. This can't go on. I need help.

I should go and visit Maggie. But first, I am going to ignore her advice. A visit to Devlin has to be the first thing on my agenda. McCall surely won't be there, but he might have been in touch. If I play the old *We Had a Terrible Childhood Together* card, she might open up to me. I probably should stay here to be on the safe side, but just like medical staff make the worst patients, I can't stand someone else to do the detection work for me.

'Calum?' I shout as I place my ear to the toilet door. No response. He can't hear me for the rush of water from the shower. He's probably having a fly chug. I shouldn't disturb the boy. I'll just leave quietly. Kenny will give him a pasting for leaving me alone, but tough titty. I've a killer to catch.

Chapter 32

Devlin opens the door to Allessandra's knock.

'You're McBain's bint.'

'Colleague is a more popular term in the force.' Allessandra lets the insult slide. 'Can I come in?'

'Got a warrant?'

'No.'

'Then fuck off.'

'You and McBain must have been friends all those years ago.'

'Aye. We did everything together. Went for long walks, had picnics and read poetry. Now will you fuck off?'

'So why did you act like you'd never met him before when I was here last?'

'He hasn't changed a bit, as well. Looked just like the wee boy I remember. Except with longer legs. And whole load more of fat.'

'So why did you...'

'I'm telling you nothing,' Devlin said with a smile that Allessandra wanted to wipe off with a spiked knuckle-duster.

'The truth will come out, Carole. Eventually. You may as well tell me now and save us all a lot of bother.'

'Listen, hen. I know why you're here. He's your boss. You think he's innocent and you're trying to clear his name. All very commendable. All very Hollywood.' Her expression is wild, triumphant even. She's getting a real kick out of this, and Allessandra wishes she had ignored her impulse to pay the woman another visit. 'Except, wee pal, this is real life. And your mate DI McBain is a murderer. I know, 'cos I was there.' Her face is in Allessandra's, scraping her skin with her breath. Beer and cigarettes.

'Are you saying you're an accessory?'

'I'm saying nothing, darling. Now either come back with a summons or one of them warrant things, or fuck off and die.'

With the suddenness of a thunderclap, the door is slammed shut.

Back at her flat, Allessandra is sitting on the edge of her brown leather chair, and leaning forward, all but hugging her knees, wishing that she smoked.

This is not good. The more she looks into this to try and help Ray, the worse it all looks. So what does she know? Not only does Ray have the motive and the time to do the killings, but he also has a background that should come with the heading *How to Breed a Psycho*.

What should I do? she asks herself. What would you do, Dad? In the absence of an answer she picks her mobile up from the coffee table and presses in a few numbers.

'DD. We need to talk.'

He is banging on her door within the hour.

'Make me a coffee and tell me what's up.' Daryl says and follows her through to the kitchen.

While the kettle works its way up to steam, Allessandra outlines her thoughts. Daryl is impassive.

'Ray McBain is not a killer, Allessandra.'

'But even Devlin says he is.'

'That would be Carole Devlin, the surrogate mother for our number one suspect?'

'Aye. I know. But you weren't there. You didn't see her face. She was telling the truth. She saw something.'

'She was confirming your biggest fear. There is a difference.'

'Oh, Daryl. I don't know anymore. This detective stuff is so fucking hard.' Allessandra leans against the worktop and presses her head against a cupboard.

'Think about the Ray McBain you know,' Daryl says. 'Think about the man you work with; the man who led our team to catch some really bad guys.' He moves over and stands directly in front of her. He grabs both her wrists. 'Think about the short time you have spent with him. Has he in anyway, in those moments given you any reason to doubt him?'

'No.'

'Well don't.' Daryl looks deep into her eyes. 'Ray McBain is one of the good guys. Be sure of that.'

Allessandra reads Daryl's certainty and relaxes into it. He's right, the boss is a good guy. A good cop in a bad mess. Isn't he?

'I'm sorry. It's just...' She rubs her forehead in an attempt to disguise the tears that sting her eyes.

'Aye. No worries,' Daryl says with his hand on her shoulder. 'Can you make me that coffee now? I'm fucking parched.'

Chapter 33

In the dark and from the pavement, Devlin's house looks just like Connelly's. The same lacklustre architecture, small windows and chipping on the walls. At least there, the gardens were looked after. In this street just further up the road, in lieu of a garden gnome, the remains of a car's engine decorate a small patch of grass. Everywhere else the chosen look is austere.

Every cliché is bound in truth, and I witness the truth of net curtains twitching with curiosity. I doubt they see many cars like mine here. The nets at the Devlin household, however, remain undisturbed.

When I first started in the police, as I approached each house I would always remind myself of the purpose of my visit and what the aim of it was. This made sure I wasn't distracted, nor was I complacent. A habit I need to get back into. The door opens before I can formulate a plan of attack.

Carole leaves the door open enough for me to see her head and one side of her body. Black T-shirt and grey leggings are obviously her dossing around clothes.

'What a busy place this is today. What you wantin'?'

'Can I come in for a wee chat, Carole?'

'Piss off. You're no' the polis any more.'

'News travels fast.'

'Aye, how clever was that? The very man who visits here and tries to put the blame on our Joe, is arrested himself,' she crows. 'If you don't piss off pronto, I'm going to phone the police and do my duty as a public-minded citizen.'

'Right. You do that, Carole. And they'll start to wonder why I was here. "Cos it'll not be long before they realise I didn't kill Connelly after all and then they'll be looking for other suspects.'

I can see her mind working out all of the possibilities.

'The phone is just to the right here,' she warns.

'Give me five minutes. Help remove Joseph from my lists of suspects.'

'Why should I?'

'When the police find out that Joseph is Connelly's son, they'll be fighting over themselves to question him.'

'How do you...' She is so caught out by this that she forgets to lie. Her mouth hangs open in shock. Before she can regain her balance, I push past her and walk into the living room.

She follows me.

'Have a seat, why don't you?'

'Sorry about that, Carole. We don't want the neighbours talking.'

'Fuck them. Who gives a toss what they think.'

'Is that the kettle going on?'

'Is this a social visit?' she bristles.

'Let's call it a walk down memory lane.'

'Fuck off with the memory lane crap and while you're at it, fuck off with the kettle shite. Ask your questions and piss off back to your midden.' Charm was clearly not one of her christening gifts.

'Do you remember me from the convent?'

'Of course I remember you. I remember everything about you, Ray. I remember...'

'I remember you.' I interrupt her. For some reason I'm not sure of, I don't want to know anything she remembers. 'Used to think you were really bright.'

'Bright? Me?'

'Truth be told I used to have a wee fancy for you.'

'You were just a scrawny wee thing.' She dismisses my comments, but tidies her hair up a little.

'Aye. The nuns used to get me into trouble for spending time with you.'

'Sister Mary?' she asks. A smile curves her lips as she considers an old notoriety.

'She used to think you were leading me astray.'

'God, I hated that place. Remember that was our mantra? "I hate this place." That was like our mad wee chant.'

'Why did you not let on you recognised me that time I came with another copper?' I ask.

She shrugs. 'Seemed like the right thing to do. You weren't letting on either. Thought I'd give you a break.'

'Thanks.' I look at the photographs. 'Aye. It was terrible what happened to your mate.'

As close to a companionable silence as we can manage settles in the space between us as we both consider the past.

'Did he... were you?' Shit. Too soon for that question. The shutters that were easing up have slammed back down, judging by the look in her eyes.

'You wanted to talk about Joseph?' Back to business.

'It must have been terrible, bringing him up knowing that kind of secret?'

'Aye, how the fuck did you find out?'

'Joseph told me.'

'He what?' Her eyes are almost out of her head. 'How does he know?' Her voice is a whisper, it's the conversation she has dreaded all her life, and the boy already knows.

'I thought you might have told him.'

A noise sounds in the room above. My head shoots up.

'Don't worry. It's only the cat.' Carole then changes the subject back to the purpose of my visit. But something has changed in her voice. It is quieter. More respectful?

'Frances asked me not to tell him. I promised her just before she died that I wouldn't tell. Who else would know to tell him?'

'Must have been someone from the convent.'

'No way. Hardly anyone knew.' Her eyes look to the ceiling as she considers the suspects. 'Sister Mary knew. It was that wee simple woman who told her. You remember Betty. She used to help the nuns out. She wasn't as daft as she looked. She worked out that poor wee Frances had missed her period when she hadn't asked for any sanitary towels.'

I get a picture of a head of black hair with streaks of grey at the sides and thick, black glasses. She was the woman who used to wake up the "Wet the Beds" as we were known, just after midnight. She would drag us to the toilet, in the hope that an emptied bladder would result in a dry bed. It didn't work.

I'd forgotten all about her. She was a harmless wee soul, put upon by the nuns almost as much as we were. How did she manage to get herself into that position in the convent? Taking small boys to the toilet in the middle of the night and doling out sanitary towels is hardly what you would call a vocation. As a child I never even thought for a second that Betty had her own story.

'Whatever happened to Betty?'

Carole shrugs a couldn't-care-less response.

'Anyway. I can't help wondering why all these years later you're looking after Connelly's bastard.' I look over the photographs. Carole and Frances with Joseph in between. Flattened smiles to indicate they really were having a great time. As if in that second when the camera flashes you can shrug off all your worries. And then let them fall back on your shoulders when the film has run out. A moment of time captured forever they say. Who in this situation would want to? So in years to come you can pull the box out of a drawer and look back at the "good" old times?

Frances has a pair of shoulders almost half the width of Carole's. She might have been pretty, but she never got the chance. Her hair was lifeless, her eyes flat and the smile could do nothing to hide the look of a victim. It's difficult to pin it down, to define that look.

Perhaps it's the expectation that bleeds from the eyes, the anticipation that it's going to happen again. Or is it the tilt of the head, the run of the shoulders that questions the happiness in any moment? Like it's only seconds before misery will strike again: you have a curse and all the bad people know it.

So they seek you out.

But why would Devlin take on Frances' son? Why would she feel so beholden?

'Carole.' My voice is soft. 'You shouldn't blame yourself.' I allow the words to come unsure of their direction.

'What?' She studies me and is taken aback by the change in my demeanour.

'You think it was you who should have been raped... instead Connelly got Frances?'

'How do you...' She stands up. 'Right, get out of this house. I'm calling the cops.' Her voice is without purpose. She's saying what she thinks she should say, but I can tell she desperately wants to know what I know. Tears gather at the rim of her lower eyelids. She sits back down. 'How do you...'

'Don't blame yourself. You were only a wee girl, for chrissake.' Connelly, I hope you are roasting on a spit as we speak. 'You've spent your life trying to make amends.'

'I should have stayed. I was just in the next bed. Together we might have fought him off. Instead I ran and hid in a cupboard, like a coward.'

'You were, what, fourteen? What could you have done?'

'We could have kicked him in the balls. Stabbed him... something. Instead I ran.' She sobbed. 'Can you imagine the guilt? Can you?'

214

Her fingers pull at her leggings, her bottom lip is arched. She can barely speak. But she had held this in for over twenty years.

'But we got him, Ray. Didn't we? Well... after a trial run and twenty years.' Her eyes take on a zealous light and she moves towards me.

Trial run?

I screw my eyes shut against a dream of small hands and a huge struggle. A pillow. A feather in flight.

'But what about Frances and her son, Joseph? Connelly's son?'

I can't, I won't let her take me there.

Devlin takes a step back. Her heels hit a chair and she falls into it. 'She was my best friend. She saved me. I left her to rot. That bastard...' rarely has a word been imbued with such hate. '... made her pregnant. Can you imagine the guilt?' Her question is barely audible.

'You tried to bring up the child, as a penance. To try and make things right.

'Except every time you look at him he reminds you of *him*. You love the idea of the child, but the boy disgusts you.' The words are out of my mouth before the thought reaches my brain.

What child wouldn't pick up on this? They wouldn't know why, but they would know. So, not only does Joseph grow up knowing what his mother is and in the absence of anything remotely like love, but he grows up under the burden of a memory fuelled by hate. Another ingredient in the mix that spells out *murderer*.

'You were there. Is that how you know all this? You must have told Joseph.' Her finger stabs at the air. 'Who else knows?'

Just then the living room door opens.

'Yeah, who else knows, Carole?' Joseph's features are twisted with something beyond rage.

215

Chapter 34

Dogs are barking, people are shouting and feet are drumming as I chase McCall through the back gardens. The bastard is fast. And fit. I can hear his taunts.

'Keep up, prick!'

'Where's that fuckin' herd o' elephants?'

Each insult is punctuated with a hysterical, high-pitched giggle. He sounds like he's got energy to spare, while I'm starting to tire. We've been running for what feels like hours, but is probably only thirty minutes. Here's me thinking I was fit as well. But I'm running faster than normal and I have the added problem of anger. His shouts are really starting to piss me off. If I catch the bastard he'll wish the nuns had forced his mother to abort.

There's no point in shouting back at him, it will just burst my lungs. I need to concentrate on where McCall is going. He's not too far ahead of me. I can hear his feet and occasionally catch a glimpse of his head as he enters a nimbus of light from people's kitchen windows and the odd streetlight that is still working. Here and there he turns to face me. Light catches on the blade of his cheekbones as he shouts back another insult.

I've got to catch the fucker. Got to make him confess. Then I can get my life back.

My legs are coping with the strain. My lungs are not so good. There's an asthmatic pitch to every keenly gulped mouthful of air. Got to keep up. Got to. I'm willing the anger into my legs, pumping my arms and struggling to get enough air.

Where's he gone? I stop running and bend forward, hands on knees, fighting for oxygen and wondering where the bastard has gone. No sign of him. I fight to control my breathing so that I can hear something. Apart from the odd shout at dogs from owners, telling them to calm the fuck down, I can hear nothing.

Fuck.

Where will he be? This is his neighbourhood. I could wander around here forever and not see the bastard again. The best option would be to go back to Devlin's. She is holding out on me. She knows stuff and by fuck she will tell me.

When McCall came in the room, she put on a shabby piece of acting.

'Joseph. What're you doing here?' She stood up, that ugly mouth of hers open in a supposedly innocent "O". What was not feigned was the look of fear in her eyes. That was real. Meryl Streep would struggle with accuracy of emotion like that.

I felt it myself as I looked at the young man. There was an aura about him, a look that spelled out nothing was beyond him, nothing could stop him and nothing mattered. It was written all over his stance, the way his black hair framed his face, and in his eyes. They were black, devoid of colour and hope.

Looking into those eyes was like looking into the worst aspects of your own psyche, all the more difficult to bear because you couldn't, wouldn't accept it in yourself.

He looked at me, his mouth open in a noiseless, humourless laugh.

'Plod,' he said. 'You just don't have a fuckin' clue.' Then he turned and ran out of the room like it was some kind of game.

Maybe it is to him. But this is my life and no mad fucker is going to spoil it.

Devlin's back door is still open. I don't bother knocking, I just go in. No point in observing the niceties now. Carole is in her usual perch, a lit cigarette gripped in her right hand.

'Has he came back?' I stand in front of her and look down.

'Who?' She bites a nail.

'The fucking tooth fairy. Who do you think?' *Who*. Woman or no, I'm about to pin her up against the wall and pull the information out of her. Along with a couple of teeth.

'No.' Her voice is barely audible.

'Where will he go?'

'Don't know.'

'Come on, Carole. You can do better than that.' I bend further into her space.

'I'm telling ye. I don't know.' She shrinks back into her chair and takes a defiant drag at her cigarette. I pull it from her mouth and throw it across the room.

'That was fucking clever.' She jumps from her chair and runs round the side of the coffee table to retrieve the cigarette. 'You could have set the hoose on fire there. Wanker.'

'Don't fuck with me, Carole. Where is the sick bastard?'

'You still think he done it, don't you?' Her cigarette finds its way to her mouth again as she moves towards me. Anger pinches at her already thin lips.

'I know he did it.' My face is inches from hers.

'You know fuck all,' she sneers. 'Always were a wee know-all, weren't you, Ray? And a wee sook. Bowing and scraping to those nuns like that. Watching you used to make me sick.'

'What are you talking about?' Her barb cut deeper than I allowed to show.

'Terrified so you were. Terrified. They nuns had you exactly where they wanted you.'

'I was ten, ya stupid bitch. Of course I was terrified of the nuns.' But she isn't listening.

'And I had to take you in hand. Get you the revenge you needed.' Her eyes move to a spot above my head as she recalls events from the past. ''cept we got the wrong man. But it wasn't our fault, was it? He always did it in the darkness and we...'

'What the hell are you talking about? Revenge? That's what this is all about, isn't it? Joseph is doing all this for you and Frances. You turned him into the man he has become.'

'Man? He's more of a man than you'll ever be. Some wee women in black were enough to have you cowering in your bed and pissing in your sheets. Until I showed you what to do. '

'Shut up, Carole.' I try to force myself to calm down, but it's like I'm ten again and these insults are *intolerable*. And the things she is alluding to, just too frightening. 'Just shut the fuck up. You were hardly perfect yourself. Poor wee Frances having you for a pal. Saves you from Connelly and she gets raped for her troubles.'

Her hand shoots out and catches me on the ear. Before I can formulate a response my arms have stretched out and she is lying at my feet. She stands up, face contorted with fury.

'Ya cunt. Nae bastard hits me.' She runs at me, her fist drawn back.

Black.
There is black.
Then there is rage.

Leaning on one elbow, I try to sit up. Opening my eyes can wait. Too painful. My head is so sore. There's a wet patch at my arm and shoulder. I feel warm enough. So where has the liquid come from?

I manage to sit up and lean forward. Beyond the shield of my eyelids a light is blaring. I have to open my eyes. Have to see where I am. I suck in some air, between my top teeth and bottom lip. Here goes. My eyes are open enough to let in a sliver of light.

Okay. I'm still at Devlin's. So why is nobody shouting at me? And how have I ended up lying on the floor?

Pain at my right temple sends an extra surge to distinguish itself from the rest of what's happening to my head. I send a hand to explore. There doesn't appear to be any broken skin, but there is a lump that any self-respecting ostrich would like to model her eggs on.

Did some fucker come up from behind and lamp me one? My eyes open a little more and notice the corner of the coffee table. I wince as if in delayed sympathy with my head while my fingers rub the black ash tabletop.

So I've fallen, or I was pushed by Devlin. My head hit the table and it's Goodnight Govan.

Where did Devlin go? How long have I been out for? After all of the shouting and barking and running that was going on before, this house is now very quiet. Remarkably so. It reminds me of how everything goes quiet just as the snow begins to fall. Or when, in the movie, the hunter becomes the hunted and all of the forest animals lie as still as death.

McCall. I jump to my feet and close my eyes to the fresh wave of pain in my head. He could easily find his way back. If he finds me in this state, I'm a goner.

Memory provides me with a fair idea of where the sofa is, so I locate the edge of it with a heel and with a slight change to my direction I fall on to its cushions. This makes me more aware of the wetness of my shirt. I stretch across with my left hand and feel it. It's soaking wet. There is a faint tang to it. I bring my hand to my nose. A metallic tang. My eyes open by their own volition.

Several pictures flash to my brain like an MTV horror flick. The two most prominent are the blood on my fingers and the body stretched out on the table before me. Arms wide. Her mouth open in a silent scream.

Chapter 35

While one part of my brain goes into a corner and retches, another part, the part whose sole purpose is self-preservation, swings into action. If the police find any trace of me in this house, I may as well douse myself in perfume, then they'll have something nice to smell while they ram a life sentence up my arse.

The time is 01:20 according to the green light blinking on the DVD player. I have to be thorough, but quick. Whoever did this, and it has to be McCall, wants to set me up. So surely the police would have been contacted in the hope that they find me blood drenched, in situ.

The possibility that I am to blame for the corpse on the table is sent to the corner with the screams.

If I'm quick I can clean up and go. And hope none of the neighbours see me leaving. The hope that none saw me arriving is plenty slim. They would have definitely heard me giving chase to McCall. In most neighbourhoods that would have been cause for a phone call to the local police station, but if you live around here I expect all you do is shout like fuck and look forlornly at the phone.

I take a quick inventory of my person. The only blood on me is on the arm and shoulder of my shirt. It will have to go. I pull it off and roll it into a ball. Carole is bound to have a few extra T-shirts upstairs.

Back-tracking my movements, I clean each surface with my shirt. Thankfully I haven't been through too much of the house. It really was just the living room. I did run through the kitchen, but didn't I lay a finger on anything. From experience I know of the care I need to take. Our forensic boys are shit hot. If I even leave as much as a partial print or a fibre behind they could place me here.

Right, okay, I survey the room. Everything seems to be clean. I run upstairs with my hands in my pockets. That way I won't touch anything. All three doors from the landing at the top of the stairs are open. The first one is a toilet so I can ignore that. The next room is as bare as a nun's cell. A single bed lines one wall and a tall chest of drawers is placed against another one. This room looks like no-one has slept in it for years. Must be McCall's.

In the next room I am disabused of this notion. There's a poster of Partick Thistle on one wall and one of Pamela Anderson on the other. All very mundane and non-murderous. A baseball cap has pride of place on a chest of drawers that matches the one in the other room. Next door must be Carole's room.

I retrace my steps and pluck a piece of black material from a drawer, hold it up, yes it's a T-shirt, push the drawer closed and use the material to wipe the handle dry of any possible print.

With baseball cap pulled low over my forehead, a quick glance at my watch — it's 01:30 — I leave the house as silently as I can. There's nothing I can do for Carole now, I reason. No sense in going back and making her look more comfortable. The best thing I can do for the poor cow is find the bastard that did this and find a nice uncomfortable cell for them. That is, if I can keep my hands to myself.

Back at the hotel, Calum is lying on top of his bed, fully clothed, hands behind his head.

'Nice T-shirt,' he says. Three loaded syllables. The fact that he doesn't actually remonstrate with me for sneaking out while he was in the shower somehow makes me feel worse. I could have lost him his job.

'Sorry, Calum. I just had to...' I'm speaking to his back as he goes into the toilet. He leaves the door open and I undress to the drizzle of his piss and subsequent flush of the pan.

We're both in bed. I turn off the bedside lamps and speak into the first burst of darkness before my eyes are able to discern any shapes. 'Anybody phone?'

'No.' I hear him turn on to his side. Fuck you then, I think. Huffy bastard. My sympathy has a short shelf life these days.

Sleep is like a distant, hateful relative tonight; he doesn't visit very often, but when he does it's very brief and a bit of a nightmare. When daylight stretches in through a chink in the curtains I feel every bit as tired as when I went to bed several hours before and my eyes feel as if they have been dipped in sand.

Thankfully, I don't remember any of my dreams, but I'm left with a residue in the form of hairs on end along my arms. For the long hours when I wasn't asleep, one phrase ran through my mind.

'I didn't kill her... I didn't kill her... I didn't kill her.'

I go over and over the events of the evening. McCall must have come in behind me when I was arguing with Carole and knocked me out and then did his dirty work.

So why is the lump on this side of my head? The side furthest away from the door. Did he push me on to the coffee table, hoping that it would do his work for him? There's just too much uncertainty about all of this. Did I clean up enough? Were there any other signs of me being there? Think. Think. One thing I am sure of is I didn't do it.

I didn't.

Calum stirs, stretches, kicks his legs over the side of the bed and faces me. He slips one hand inside his black briefs and rearranges himself.

'Pubes caught in my foreskin,' he offers by way of apology. He's all hard curves; shoulders, pecs and abs. He's too close and too male. Thank Christ the days of living in a dormitory are well behind me. I couldn't put up with much more of this. He has his other hand on the phone.

'Bacon rolls do you?'

No health kick this morning then? 'Aye.'

Order made, he puts the phone down and walks over to the trouser press. After liberating his threads he stretches one leg after another into them. While he zips up he asks me, 'What's on the cards today?'

I sit up and look at him, 'Listen, I'm sorry about yesterday, Calum. I know Kenny would take a dim view of you losing me. But I can't guarantee that it won't happen again. The best I can say is that I'll keep it to a minimum.'

'The best you can say is, "Calum, why don't you come with me?"'

'If I did that, you might become implicated in a murder.'

He doesn't even flinch. What has this young man witnessed in the line of *duty* with my pal Kenny?

'Wherever you go, I'm there. When you go for a jog, I'll be a few steps behind. When you go for a drive, I'm riding shotgun. When *I* go for a shower, you're sitting on the shitter. No argument.' His

223

tone is quiet and all the more impressive for it. It doesn't allow for any disagreement. He'd grown sloppy for a minute and it isn't going to happen again.

My mobile phone rings. It's Daryl. He's early. It's only 07:55 according to my watch.

'Ray. Allessandra and I are on the way over.' He realises that his voice is too business like and he adds. 'Get the kettle on.' Shit. It's not good.

'The pigs are coming,' I warn Calum.

'I'll make myself scarce.'

Allessandra and Daryl file into the bedroom and both take a seat by the table. No conversation. No wisecracks. They know something and they are more than concerned about it.

'The coffees and bacon rolls are on the way up, guys.' I ordered extra when I realised Daryl and Allessandra were on their way. As I say this I'm tidying up some socks and underpants that decorate the floor. This is what Maggie would describe as displacement activity.

Acid bubbles in my stomach as I consider what to say to the guys. Do I come clean? Or do I act the daft laddie? I owe a lot to these guys. A debt that I doubt I could ever come close to making good on. Still. Do they have to know the full truth of last night? I don't know if I could stand it if their eyes were to take on the light of suspicion.

I sit on the bed and breathe deep. 'Before you start, guys. I have...'

'Carole Devlin is dead, Ray,' says Daryl.

'I know. I was just about to...'

'And someone matching your description was seen running across back gardens in the area, not too long before Carole's time of death.'

'If you... if you let me tell you what happened, Daryl.' There is a knock at the door. 'That'll be the bacon rolls.' I go to the door, open it and let the young waiter carry in the tray.

He places it on the table and all but runs out of the room. The chill in the room must have got to him.

'I went to see Carole last night.' On the basis that it is better to get in there first, I fill them in with the details as I experienced them and finish off by displaying the bump on the side of my head. Allessandra winces. Daryl sports an expression that says —

serves you right. There is something else in their eyes. Betrayal and for the first time, doubt.

'This is not good, Ray. Not good at all.' Daryl is on his feet and he is seriously pissed off. 'This places you at the scene of the crime.'

'I know.' I'm trying not to whine.

'Tampering with evidence.'

'I know.'

'For the second time. That we know of.'

'Daryl, I had to go there. I had to talk to her.'

'So did you learn anything?' asks Allessandra. Was I imagining things or was there an emphasis on the word "you"?

'Nothing new,' I go on to detail the conversation I had with Devlin and the subsequent events.

'So you blacked out?' asks Allessandra.

'Yes.'

'And you can't remember a thing?'

'Yes. I mean no. I can't remember anything.'

'Kind of convenient, don't you think?'

'Convenient for who? The real killer maybe. But not me.'

'Ray we're really having trouble here,' says Daryl. 'Prior to this you were the only suspect. We hear nothing to change that. In fact, you could say it makes the case against you watertight. There isn't a judge in this country who wouldn't convict on what we have.'

'Great. Make me feel better, why don't you?' I aim for some humour. Judging by the expression shared by my two ex-colleagues, it fails spectacularly.

'This is not about making you feel better, ya prick. It's about finding out the truth.' He walks to the window, fists bunched by his side.

'Daryl, we promised we would be calm,' Allessandra acts as mediator. 'Ray.' She turns to me. 'We have gone out on a limb for you. In fact we are so far out on that limb it's about to snap. When it snaps we are well and truly fucked. So give us something that helps us. Something that makes our decision easier. Something that lets us know we are doing the right thing risking our careers for you.'

The enormity of their situation fills my head. If they get caught for helping me, they could face imprisonment themselves. There goes their homes, their jobs, their liberty and the respect of their family, friends and colleagues. Hardly win-win. I can't continue to put them in this situation. I have no right to. I need to give them some of the truth.

'Connelly was kind of busy while he was working at Bethlehem House.' I feel myself shrink from the words. But I have to admit it to them. Admit it to myself.

'Oh Ray,' Allessandra is way ahead of me. 'No.'

Daryl looks from her to me, and back again, before the coin drops.

'Holy fuck.'

'Or not, as the case may be.' See how witty I can be when under pressure?

Silence. What a conversation stopper that was. While I wait for a reaction my stomach acid burns off a few butterfly wings. I really need the guys on my side. But from a distance. Clamping my teeth against the nausea that threatens I look from one to the other.

Silence.

Somebody speak, for fuck's sake.

'What did you mean about making a decision?' I have to fill the silence.

'Oh.' They both look at each other, as if silently debating who is going to tell me.

'The decision on whether or not to make the phone call,' Daryl finally answers.

'I'd have been exactly the same, guys,' I say and smile to hide a flicker of anger that they would consider betraying me. The fact is, I would have been the same, so they don't deserve any anger.

'Anybody going to eat these rolls before they go cold?' I ask.

We eat silently, or as silently as you can with Daryl's open mouth chewing action, and as the food goes down I sense I have my colleagues' sympathy. It's not what I want, but preferable to their suspicion.

However, this is a connection I'm going to have to break. It's all very nice and cosy and has been a real help to me so far, but I can't continue to put the guys at risk. The time has come to make the break and stand on my own two feet. My lies put me in this position, so I have to face the consequences. It would be nice to keep seeing them. Daryl and Allessandra are my links to the only world I know. I truly wish I could keep in contact, but as an old cop who took me under his wing used to say: '*Ca' canny in case ye end up growin' a wishbone instead o' a backbone.*'

Certainty adds calcium to my spine. 'Listen guys. I really appreciate all you've done for me. More than you could possibly know. But I can't face myself knowing you could lose everything simply by being in the same room as me.'

'What are you saying, Ray?'

'Well if you would shut the fuck up, Daryl, maybe I could tell you.'

'You better not be saying what I think you're saying.'

'Aye,' Allessandra adds.

'Fuckssake. Let me finish. This is hard enough as it is.' I pause and take a deep breath. 'I need to go on from here on my own. I can't afford to be worrying about you guys.'

'Too late, Ray,' says Allessandra. 'If you were convicted of murder, we're already your accessories.'

'Aye,' Daryl joins in. 'I know what you're trying to do, Ray. But in the nicest possible way you can shove it where your dildo don't reach.'

'I like that,' says Allessandra.

'Thanks. Me too,' says Daryl. 'Just made it up on the spot like.' He puffs his chest up.

'It goes with that Madonna song,' Allessandra sings. 'Papa don't preach... I'm in trouble deep... Dildo don't reach.'

I can't believe the two of them are sitting there laughing like eejits. Their laughter has notes of irony and worry in it. It's laughter that's a smile away from tears. It's like the laughter you hear bouncing around the walls of a jail.

'Guys, fuck off with the singing. This is deadly serious.'

Daryl punches me in the arm. 'If you didn't laugh you'd cry, Ray. So lighten the fuck up. And forget any ideas about protecting us. We're both adults. We know what we're doing.'

'Naw. I've thought about this. I can't have you two on my conscience. If you don't leave me to it, I'm going to walk up to Pitt Street HQ and give myself up right now.'

Daryl waves his handcuffs at me. 'Is that so? We're in this for the duration now, Ray. And if you don't like it I've a nice wee bracelet here that'll help you see otherwise.'

'Oh look,' Allessandra waves her set around. 'Me too.' They look at one another and laugh.

'You're both fucking mad.'

Allessandra's expression sobers, 'Ray. We know what's at stake here. I'll admit there have been sleepless nights, but it's too late to back out know. Even if we wanted to.'

'Aye. So can we cut the noble and ultimately self-pitying crap?' Daryl vigorously rubs his hands together. 'We've a murderer to catch.'

Relief wars with irritation that they are so adamant. This is a fight I'm going to lose, so I might as well get on with it. On my terms.

'Okay. What have you got for me?' I ask.

'We couldn't find much on Jim Leonard. He rented a room from the fella Hutchison, as you know. A pair of computer geeks. They worked in PC World together,' answers Daryl.

'The one significant fact we did uncover about him is that he was an orphan and guess where he was brought up?' asks Allessandra.

'Bethlehem House,' I answer.

'You must have known that as soon as you heard his name, Ray.' says Daryl. 'Why didn't you say anything?'

'Because... I was struggling with the whole convent thing myself at the time and I didn't want you to go back there and start drawing links back to me. Sorry.'

'No more, Ray. Withheld information not good. We need to know what you know.'

'Okay.'

Allessandra rustles in her bag. 'We've also got this.' She pulls out a large brown envelope and extracts a copy of a photograph. 'It's a fairly recent photograph of Elizabeth Templeton.'

'And she hasn't aged a bit,' I say with my pulse loud in my ears. When I was ten she looked about sixty. That's about the age she was when this photograph was taken. The hair is all white now, but the glasses are the same standard NHS type.

The guys are looking at me with questions in their eyes.

'How the fuck do you know this one as well?' asks Daryl.

'All roads lead back to Bethlehem House.'

Chapter 36

This is the third time this week I've sat in the car in front of Bethlehem House. Calum is beside me doing his impression of a mute. The art of conversation certainly isn't one of this boy's talents. Where does his mind go when he does that? Is he mentally rehearsing his Kata? Is he dreaming of his last shag? Or is he wondering what the fuck is on my mind? and why do I keep driving down to this soulless building?

The wee gardener guy has been busy. The trees that dot his garden are almost bare, but no leaf has been allowed to linger on the lawn. It is swept and bare while the sides of the road that pass in front of the convent railings have a pelmet of mulch in waiting.

There's a small tree at the bottom of the garden with one leaf hanging on resolutely. It's waving its gold-brown flag of no surrender in the breeze. I'm surprised the gardener's not waiting below to catch it.

Allessandra is just off the phone. Nothing new to report from HQ. McCall has vanished off the face of the planet, as have I, apparently. They failed to place me at the scene of Devlin's murder. They have descriptions of the guy running about the backyard, but they still don't know that's me. So my disguise is still good. As for Leonard, there is very little to report there. Despite his childhood he has managed to stay clear of trouble. All of his neighbours report him as a nice enough guy. No-one had a bad word to say for him. Nor a good one.

His workmates at PC World were pretty much the same. Nice enough, is the description that would follow Jim Leonard to the grave. I've searched my own memory for him, and found little. Apart from the last time I saw his brother. I'll never forget that. The look of pure hatred in Jim's eyes when he heard me teasing his brother. He was the quieter one of the twins, always taking his lead from John. He would have been ten or eleven when John died. What an impact that must have made. His only family member and one with whom he had such a strong connection suddenly dies.

When I was a child everything was a five-minute wonder. For those five minutes it was the most important thing on earth. Then it was on to the next thing. Even the ever present gnaw of loneliness would fade from time to time as we played and fought and pretended to pray. I'm not saying that the effects of John's death lasted for only five minutes, but they quickly receded into the background as we got on with the business of protecting ourselves. For me, Jim was given a momentary thought and then the worry of a possible wet bed the next morning took over.

A week after John's death, at evening prayers, we found out that Jim had been taken somewhere else. As we clutched our rosary beads after dinner, Sister Mary would always remind us of recent losses. Nuns always seemed to be dying, so there was often a lengthy roll call. Then one evening Jim's name replaced John's.

"Dear Lord, also hear our prayers for Jim Leonard. May he find some measure of happiness now that he has moved on from the site of his beloved brother's death." Or it would have been something similar.

The row of small faces on either side of me opened their eyes wide in realisation, before they habitually moved on to finish off the session with the usual rendition of "Our Father".

We always picked up the tempo on this one because we knew we were coming to the end of the daily prayer marathon and would be rewarded with one hour of television. The first five minutes of TV that night, however were filled with hushed whispers as we wondered where Jim had gone and whether we would ever see him again. Sister Mary's bellow interrupted what must have sounded like a congregation of speculative snakes.

'If you don't want to watch TV you can all get ready for bed.' You could have heard a rosary bead drop.

I'm aware of Calum's gaze.

'What?' Is he actually going to say something?

'You seen that movie, *Stakeout*?'

'Emilio Estevez and Richard Dreyfuss?'

A nod. 'Who's going to go for the pizza? And who gets to shag the glamorous neighbour?'

'A sense of humour, good Christ.' I laugh. 'One, pizza is bad for you and two, the neighbouring building is an old folk's home. You first.'

'Ah. But old folk have nurses to look after them.'

'You needing your nuts emptied, Calum?'

'Does the Pope wear a funny hat?'

Fuck me. Calum and I had a conversation. In fact, those few phrases could constitute an outburst.

Silence reasserts itself in the car. Calum returns to Calumland and I continue with my conjecture. What next? I can't keep coming down to sit in front of this building every other day.

It's not getting me anywhere. Lots of memories are re-surfacing, but nothing that is going to help me find a killer.

I wonder how Allessandra got on when she let the team know that both Leonard and Templeton had links with the convent. Would they be even more convinced of my guilt?

Ex-convent boy takes revenge for shit childhood shocker. We agreed that this information should not be withheld, as not only would it strengthen Daryl and Allessandra's case if and when they got caught helping me, but it would also mean there was a body of evidence ready for when the real killer was caught.

The "revenge for child abuse" theory is looking a bit old now. So is the "revenge killer goes nuts and kills at random" theory. All of the deceased have links to Bethlehem House. Leonard, Templeton, Connelly and now Devlin. Leonard and Devlin were kids while they stayed there, the other two were a paedophile and what might kindly be termed a nun's assistant. A fairly eclectic bunch you might say.

And who's next, you might ask?

Why would McCall kill Leonard and Templeton? I can understand how the roles that the other two played in his life might attract his attention, but those two? Something doesn't quite add up here. Think, Ray. Think.

Theresa. There's a thought. I wonder how she's doing. If this situation weren't so tense I would be cracking up because she's not been in touch. Or do I want her so much because of the situation I'm in, a shoulder to cry on and all that? Maggie would be better. At least she wants to listen.

We're down the West End of Glasgow now, parked in front of a row of tenement flats. No. 2165 is where Leonard and Hutchison stayed. The two men worked together in a PC shop, so how did Hutchison get to be the owner of the flat and Leonard the tenant?

By happy coincidence I know of someone who might know the answer. Hutchison's girlfriend stays at No. 2161. They could have met going to that wee newspaper shop at the corner. Must be quite nice to find love along with your well-fired breakfast rolls and *Daily Record* of a morning. I look at my watch. It's nearly six o'clock. If she works, she'll surely be home by now.

Leaving Calum in the car I go along and press the buzzer at No. 2161. A female voice answers.

'This is the police. We'd like a word with Ruth Dillon please.'

'Again...' Irritation hums down the wire. 'S'pose you better come up. Flat D.'

She's standing in the doorway to her flat. The tip of her cigarette brightens as she inhales.

'You'd better come in.' Her words escape along with a mouthful of smoke.

'That stuff'll kill you,' I say as I follow her inside.

'A myth put about by the ruling classes to spoil the poor wee proletariat's fun.'

'I thought the ruling classes were also partial to a wee puff now and again.'

'Another myth,' she grins, all teeth and nose. 'Anything stronger than menthol and they'll be hacking their lungs up all the way to their Harley Street specialist.' She takes another puff. 'Take a seat,' and points to a settee that looks as if it's had the stuffing squashed out of it by a bevvy of students jumping all over it on a nightly basis. A tartan throw just about hides the duller colouring on its shoulder. "Functional" would be a good word to describe this room.

'It's hardly IKEA,' Ruth offers, 'but it's home.' She's in her stocking feet and wearing a white office-type blouse and a black skirt. 'Can I get you a coffee? Officer...?'.

'Drain. But you can call me Daryl.'

'What do you take in your coffee?' she asks over her shoulder. Then she stops at the door and nods her head in the direction of the hallway.

'C'mon through. You can thrill me with your repartee while we wait for the kettle to boil.'

The kitchen comes as a surprise. It's all shiny surfaces and shiny implements and looks like it has been cleaned with surgical precision. Ruth flicks a switch on the kettle and busies herself with mugs, coffee, milk and sugar. As she does so the conversation never falters.

'This might sound a wee bit cookie to you, but I love my kitchen. Kind of comes as a surprise doesn't it? After all the rest of the flat looks barely lived in, by comparison. Have a seat.' She points at a small round table in the corner, complete with checked tablecloth and small vase of flowers. 'I mean, I just love kitchens and cooking and talking in them. Don't you think the best conversations happen over a coffee in somebody's kitchen?'

'Usually the best conversations happen when all parties get a turn to speak,' I manage to jump in at a pause.

'Sorry,' she turns from pouring hot water into our mugs, 'I'm a little bit stressed at the moment. And when I get stressed my mouth just goes off and I talk for Scotland. I mean it's not as if...'

I decide not to wait for a pause this time. 'What are you so stressed about?'

'Hutch,' she answers handing me my coffee. 'Oh. I should have asked to see your badge.'

'Badge? This is Scotland, Ruth. We have warrant cards.' I pull my wallet from my back pocket and flip it open and shut it before she gets too close a look at it. 'Who is Hutch and why are you worried about him?'

'Not to mention the fact that I'm sitting here with a key to the flat and poor Lenny has been dead for ages. Christ.' She takes a last draw from her cigarette, stubs it out on a small chrome ashtray and reaches for the packet and her lighter. 'Hutch is my boyfriend.' *Hutchison.* 'We only met about three months ago. Quite literally bumped into him downstairs. But he'd already applied to do the voluntary work overseas. I mean he's a qualified computer engineer and he's fixing PCs at PC World. I mean c'mon. Give us a break. No wonder he's off. Just a shame we didn't meet before and I could have gone with him.'

'Why are you worried about him?'

'He's a man, though. Eh?' She stops long enough to light and inhale a fresh cigarette. 'You know what you men are like. Promises, promises. You get your hole and it's long awkward silence time.'

'So you are saying...' This is like speaking with a human version of a cryptic crossword. '... that Hutch hasn't been in touch with you?'

A nod. Her cheeks pinch inwards as she inhales again. 'What

does he owe me? Nothing. Three months is hardly a marriage. But it would be nice to receive a letter. Don't you think letter writing is a dead art form? An e-mail for chrissake. He's the computer geek.' She pauses. 'He was so committed, you know? He wanted to go out there and make a difference. I think that's one of the things that drew me to him.'

'What about Jim Leonard?'

'So that was his first name? Jim? I just knew him as Lenny.'

'What can you tell me about Lenny?' Her cigarette is in the ashtray and its smoke is drawing a straight line into my left nostril. Less than discreetly I wave at the smoke.

'Sorry.' Smile. She moves the ashtray closer to her elbow. Now she has a clump of her long black hair in her hand and is stroking it like a pet. From about chin level to tip, hand over hand slides down it as if adding a little more polish.

'Jim Leonard.' She tastes the words as if deciding whether they go together, in the manner of a heavily pregnant woman who is trying to decide on a name for her child.

'Jim was alright. Aye, he was okay. Didn't know him too well.' Pause. 'Actually, he gave me the creeps. Occasionally he would join Hutch and me over a carryout. Hutch likes his curry. He seemed to like Lenny as well. God, that's terrible. Sounds like I'm comparing a dead guy to a curry. Anyway. We had a private nickname for Lenny: X-Files. He would disappear for hours in his room until we thought he'd been abducted by aliens.' We're back to the smoke and a weak laugh issues through its haze. 'Poor X-Files. Dead for days and nobody notices.'

'What do you think he got up to in his room?'

'Who knows?' She shudders. 'Dread to think. Probably having a tantric wank, or communing with his little green friends.' She grimaces. 'Sorry. Shouldn't speak ill of the dead.'

'You didn't really like him then?'

'He was... pleasant enough.' She takes a long, deep draw at her cigarette while her mind is sorting through memories of Leonard. 'You know, being a woman, and a not too shabby one at that...' Her smile while she says this indicates that she couldn't be arsed with false modesty. '... You expect men to give you a *look*, now and again. That undressing thing.' I smile as if to say *who me*? 'But from X-Files there was nothing. I mean I don't think he was gay or anything. Just not interested in women. How odd is that? I know he was a Catholic 'n' that. And they're usually the worst.

234

Guilt and repression are a strong aphrodisiac.'

'How do you know he was Catholic?'

'He had one of those grass cross shapes on his door. You know the ones they give out on Palm Sunday?' The cigarette is in the ashtray and is spending less time in her mouth. Her fingers have gone back to shining her hair. 'That and the rant he went in to one night while Hutch and I were watching MTV.'

'He was offended by MTV?'

'Big time,' her eyes widen. 'He just used to leave the room when it came on. He didn't bother us that much, like, but if we did want rid of him for a wee while, Hutch would switch over to one of the music channels. But this one night, man did he go off on one, "Whores and whoremasters." And that was just the mild stuff.'

'Was it the music he didn't like?'

'No. It was the clothes the girls were wearing. First he was all bug-eyed. Staring like he'd never seen a pair of tits before. Then he was screaming at the telly. We were all going to Hell and it was all down to these folk on the TV who couldn't keep their clothes on and their hands off each other. Then he stormed out. Went to the toilet. Next thing we hear the shower running.'

'Sounds weird.'

'Weird is not the word. You want a biscuit?' She turns back to the rack of cupboards, opens a door and pulls out a jar with the words "Sweet Shit" emblazoned across it.

'Nice and inviting. I can't wait to dip my fingers in that.'

'Yeah. I love it. A friend brought it back from the States for me. Got to keep it in the cupboard though. Doesn't go with the décor.'

'So. You were saying?'

'Aye. X-Files. Anyway, the next day he was like a wee mouse. All embarrassed. I reckon Philip Larkin got it wrong you know. It's not our parents that fuck us up. It's organised religion.'

'You won't get much argument out of me there.' I pull a chocolate biscuit from the jar and start munching. I know. I know. I'll get fat. Old habits and all that.

'I take it the other cops have been all over Hutch's flat,' I ask.

'Yeah. I couldn't get in for ages. I had to give them the key,' she says all proud that she helped the police.

'I don't suppose you got your key back?'

'No.'

'Shame. It would be nice to have another look.'

235

'But I do have a spare.' She reaches into a drawer and pulls out a single key on a plain key ring. 'The keys I gave the other police were Hutch's. This is mine.'

I stand up. 'No time like the present.'

'You want to go over there again? Your guys have been all over that place, with a fine tooth... microscope.'

'One more time won't hurt,' I smile winningly. 'Will it?'

Chapter 37

Walking towards Hutchison's flat, Ruth's chatter goes into over-drive. She tells me how they met, where they met and how they had rarely been out of each other's pockets since and how she is missing him terribly, you know? But the man wanted to help those less fortunate than himself and what could you do?

We pass my car and I notice that Calum is not in his seat. Strange. I stop walking and take a look around me. Scanning the street I see nothing. Nothing but cars. The door of the corner shop opens and a guy wearing a blue baseball cap with the legend NYC comes out. If Glasgow came up with a hat like that it would have to be blue and green. The initials for Glasgow City Council wouldn't look quite so cool.

I wonder where he is. Probably spotted a young nubile and has chased her up the street for a wee chat.

The door of Hutchison's flat has been painted cream, the expanse of wood broken by a small spy-hole and a brass knocker in a Rennie Mackintosh style.

'Was Hutch going to leave the flat empty while he was gone?' I ask as Ruth slides the key in the lock.

'No. The plan was to rent it out. The new lodger hadn't got round to moving in when the body was discovered. He was even less inclined to move in afterwards.'

'So who discovered the body?'

Ruth stands to the side of the door, to let me pass her. 'Don't you know all this already?'

'As the main investigative officer, I always like to verify things for myself,' I answer and see the light of suspicion leave her eyes.

She sighs and looks down at the ground. 'You don't want me to go in with you do you?'

'Not if you really don't want to,' I answer.

'I suppose I should, just to be on the safe side. We don't want

237

Hutch to come back, notice something is missing and you get the blame. Do we?'

I shrug, 'You could always check my pockets on the way out.'

'The body. You asked who discovered it?' Ruth has followed me in. She is looking around her like a child who has entered a ghost ride for the first time. Her head is forward, eyes wide, arms back as if in preparation for flight. 'It was the neighbours who complained about the smell and some poor sap from the council was sent out to investigate.'

'You really don't have to come in,' I say.

'No. No. I don't want to let Hutch down. Besides I've already been in.'

'You have? When?'

'Oh, don't worry. It was after your guys had finished. Photos taken, samples lodged and all that. My mum's a cleaner. And I didn't want Hutch to come back to all those... blood stains.'

'That couldn't have been easy.'

She purses her lips and exhales. 'That's an understatement. Good job Mum was with me. You know, the blood without the body was really strange. I could pretend for moments that it was just paint. Then my mind would try and fill in the spaces between the stains. With flesh. Here's where an arm might have been and here's where... you get the picture.' She shudders.

We have a communal shudder. I'm getting it clearly. 'Can you show me?' I look around at the doors leading off from the hallway. One is signposted with the shadow outline of the Palm Sunday Cross. Where it would have been pinned to the door rests a tiny black wound in the wood.

Ruth leads me to the door next to it and pushes it open. 'And it wasn't even Lenny's room. This is Hutch's.'

The room is in darkness. Closed curtains keep out light from the street.

'A fair sized room,' I say as if I was on a viewing and mentally berate myself for being an arse. Ruth flicks a light switch. The light displays a double bed with a dark green velour headboard pushed against the far wall. It has been stripped down to its base which is cream and displays a multitude of stains, but none that look like they could be blood.

A large wooden wardrobe and chest of drawers are posted against the wall to my right. They are fine specimens, almost Calvinistic in their sturdiness and lack of decoration. I can imagine them being taken from a house sale in one of those sandstone merchants' mansions that proliferate in this city. The house will have been eventually sold off when the spinster daughter died aged one hundred and one and none of the furniture would have changed since Daddy strode the markets of Glasgow while he fingered his gold fob watch.

'There were no covers, pillows or mattress on the bed when I came in to clean. So I'm assuming they soaked up a good deal of the blood. And the carpet has been ripped up. The stains were here.' Ruth's legs clad in tights, swish in accompaniment to the percussion of her heels on the wooden floor as she walks to the end of the bed. She points to the floor, just at the centre of the foot of the bed. 'And here, at either side.' Again, she points to the floor about eighteen inches from the end.

'It was like three points of the cross. The head and the arms. I wouldn't have thought of it if Lenny didn't have a cross on his door.'

Her voice is quiet, almost reverential. It's as if for the first time she has realised *somebody died in this room*. Sitting on the edge of the bed and looking down at my feet, I can see where blood has soaked through the carpet and into the fibre of the wood. It's like a dark shapeless blob. If I stare at it long enough I'm sure it will start to take some form of recognisable shape. Like when I was younger and from my bed in the darkness I used to look at my dressing gown hanging on the door. I used to see faces in its folds, faces with fangs and horns, monsters who were waiting until I slept. Then they would pounce.

Poor bastard. How long did he lie here knowing his life was about to end? We know he suffered, but through it all, when did he give up hope? Or did he cling to life, any life, until the last breath left his lungs?

A gasp from Ruth made me turn.

'I never noticed this before.' She is holding something in her hand. When she first entered the room she had the expression of someone who had brushed against the edge of a stranger's death. It left its mark, but it was weak and would soon fade. Her expression is now of someone close to tears.

'What's wrong?' I ask and follow her as she leaves the room. Ruth moves through to the kitchen and leans against the worktop, cradling something in her pale hands.

'I spotted this in the drawer.' She waves... it looks like a passport sized photo-booth number... at me. I take it from her. Ruth and a young man, heads pressed together wearing matching grins. A professional would have done well to define that moment so clearly. It said that when we are together and we're blazing our smile into the world, we are untouchable. For that moment, the joy they found in each other lifted them up into another plane and they were cleaner, brighter and sharper than the rest of us.

'He has beautiful teeth, doesn't he? Could be in an advert. Never ever goes to the dentist. Lucky bastard.'

'Your teeth are not too bad.' Okay, McBain. Shut up why don't you.

'That was his favourite photo of us. I can't believe he left it behind. How could he not take it away with him?' She hides her face in her hands, collects her thoughts. 'Something's wrong. He loved this photograph. It was taken the night before he left.' She looks at me. 'My Hutch would have taken this with him.'

'Maybe you read it all wrong. Maybe the guy didn't love you after all.' I put my hand on her shoulder. I realise that I've been watching way too much daytime TV and take it off.

We are in the hall now and I spot a brown envelope against the far wall as if it would have been pushed there when we opened the door. One envelope.

The guy's been gone for two months and he has one envelope. I turn to Ruth. She is still holding the photograph.

'Does someone collect Hutch's mail?' I ask.

'Yeah, I do,' she answers like she has just come out of a dream. 'Oh.' She spots the envelope and rushes over to pick it up.

'It's addressed to Hutch.' Greedily she rips it open as if contact with his mail will bring him closer. 'It's from the V.S.O.' She scans the page. Then she does so again, as if the words are in Sanskrit.

'This doesn't make any sense.' She looks at me and then back to the letter. I pick it from her hands and read.

'We regret that you felt unable to commit to your agreed time with us blah, blah... and should you decide ever to... blah, blah.'

Hutchison never made it overseas. Is he our killer? Is he in league with McCall? A body is found in his flat, while he is supposedly away helping the starving millions. Doesn't look good for our Hutch. I look down at the photograph in Ruth's hands. At the smile blazing from the young man's face. But what if...

'Did you say that the body was found in Hutch's room?'

'Yeah. That's one thing I found quite odd, why would...' Ruth looks from the photograph, to me, to the room.

'Do you know who ID'd the body?'

'How the hell would I know that?' She takes a step back. 'Don't look at me like that.' And another. 'DONT LOOK AT ME... like that.'

Her face has lengthened, in grief and realisation. Her eyes large with pain. She knows what I'm getting at. Something passes between us, a spark, a current.

What if Leonard didn't die in that room?

And Hutchison did.

Chapter 38

It was so easy.

So confident was The Muscle in his own strength and abilities, it didn't occur to him for one moment what he might want to do to him. Even the most suspicious of people, when approaching someone, or when someone approaches them, anticipate the communion to be one of friendship. They see the hand stretched out in welcome and ignore the closed fist. They feel their mouth curved in a smile and ignore eyes, slitted with suspicion. People are weak and crave that connection. They expect it. And therefore open themselves up to the others. People who hunt. People like him.

Others.

The Muscle didn't want his friendship. He called him "Pal", the word as bland as a packet of cornflakes.

He saw The Muscle sitting there and knew he could identify him. This death was not in the plan, but the devout learn to make sacrifices and to adapt.

He staggered on to the car. Righted himself and gave the car a drunk's kick. The Muscle was out of the car, spiked with anger.

'Hey pal. What the fuck...?' He ran up a side street and The Muscle followed. So predictable. There he cowered in a doorway. Acted like he was terrified of the younger, stronger man's wrath. But it didn't measure up. He was no saint. No Satan.

The Muscle's face was a picture of surprise when he felt the punch spike his gut. "O" came out of his mouth like a faint climax when his hands came away from his stomach covered in blood. Then his legs gave way as blood raced to the site of the rupture from all parts of the body in a vain attempt to seal the wound.

He fingered the piece of palm leaf in his pocket. Thumb and forefinger following the raised lines up to the bar of the cross.

It was a risk, but it was worth it. He couldn't leave it behind. Some career sinner would just have thrown it in the bin without realising its true worth.

Once back on the main street, he pulled a wallet from his pocket, the leather still warm from the body of the newly departed. There was a row of plastic cards and a thick pile of paper notes. He pulled out a gold coloured credit card and read the name: Calum Davidson.

I'm walking from the dead man's flat. My head is congested with this new information. Ruth is following me like the tail of a comet.

'What just happened in there?' She is pulling at my sleeve. 'You're not a cop. WHO ARE YOU?'

'I'm sorry, Ruth. I really am.' I have the strongest feeling that the deceased man was Hutch, not Leonard. And if so, what is the importance of that? I need to get away, go for a run and have a think.

'But what have we found out? Nothing, really. Nothing,' she says. As she talks her hair lashes against each side of her face as she turns this way and that, looking up and down the street as if she's grounding herself back into real life. The physical proximity to people going about the actions of their daily lives will make what happened in that room upstairs fade like the mist of a dream. The wild shake of her head is slowing to a resolute "No".

'But the body was identified as Leonard...'

'Well, we need to check that out for starters.' As I continue speaking my mind is running ahead. 'You said yourself it was strange that the body was found in Hutch's room.' I need to get her onside. She needs to contact the police with my suspicions and put them over like they are her own.

'That means nothing.' The stress she put on the word *nothing* is full of desperation.

'How likely would it be that Hutch wouldn't go on his overseas trip?'

'But I only knew the guy for a few months. That's not long enough to really know someone.'

'Do you know him well enough to know if he is capable of killing someone?'

'My Hutch is no killer.' She is on her tiptoes and her face is in mine. She needs to stop smoking and start eating concentrated mint.

243

'It doesn't look good for him, love. A dead body is found in his flat, in his room. His flatmate is dead and he hasn't gone on his volunteer's trip. Has he gone on the run instead?'

'My Hutch is no killer,' she repeats. Her face is full of defiance, which is being replaced with grief as she considers the alternative.

'That's how it's going to look now that we know he hasn't gone where he was supposed to.' I feel like a shit for doing this to her but it is crucial she believes me. She can then do my dirty work for me, phone the police and pester them until they have another look at the body, this time with a view to documenting who really died.

'Ruth.' I grip her on both shoulders. 'I don't think Hutch is the killer. Something, I don't know what, tells me that he was the one who was killed. The body they found and identified as Jim Leonard was actually Hutch.'

Her head is still shaking, 'No, no, no, no. No. Mark can't be dead. I love him.' Her legs give way as heavy sobs wrack her body. I manage to catch her before she falls to the ground.

Propped against me, I half carry her back to her flat. Once through the door I lead her to the couch, where she lies down.

'Will I make you a cup of tea? Is there someone who could be with you just now?' While I ask this I'm wondering what happened to Calum. When I passed the car again, he still wasn't there.

Ruth sits up. 'No. It's my house. I make the coffee.'

'Is there someone I can phone for you?'

Her hands are over her face. 'He was such a lovely guy. Poor Hutch.' Then she looks up at me, her eyebrows high against her hairline in horror. 'I cleaned up his blood. Oh my God. That was Mark's blood I cleaned up.' She falls the length of the sofa, her whole body shaking with grief.

Passing on the bad news was never my forte. I don't know any cop who has become inured to it. I feel like I'm diseased and I've somehow infected her. I kneel down beside her and put a hand on her shoulder until the worst of the sobs recede.

'Coffee?' We can take comfort in the banal.

In the kitchen, waiting for the kettle to boil, questions rise with the steam. Did Leonard fake his own death? Did he come across the body, decide to opt out of life and somehow make it look like it was him that died? Not making sense. Where is McCall in this little scenario?

244

Hutchison is not an ex-inmate of Bethlehem House. So why was he murdered? He must have got in the way somehow. Could it be that McCall and Leonard are in on this together? Unless, Leonard, being a convent boy, has also been killed and his body stashed somewhere else. Why would the killer hide a body? For maximum effect. Perhaps he wants to stage something. Send a message to the world. Maybe Leonard is the person he was after all along and the rest was just a screen.

Okay McBain. It's official. You are a wanker. Mental diarrhoea or what. Learn the facts first.

'Allessandra.' I'm leaving a message on her mobile. 'Could you or Daryl give me a call? This is important. We need to talk.'

She rings me back almost immediately. 'Ray. What's up?'

I get her up to speed. There isn't even the merest pause when she exhales, 'Oh my God. Ray.' She doesn't doubt me. 'But wasn't the body identified as Leonard?'

'That's what we need to clear up.' We hang up.

Out of Ruth's kitchen window I can see a row of back gardens, replete with a forest of metal clothes poles sticking out of a series of postage-stamp sized pieces of lawn, like a graveyard for stick men.

I hear feet shuffle on the carpet in the hall, then they slide on the wooden laminate of the kitchen. There's no lift to the stride, just the foot being pushed along the floor.

'Daryl. Or whatever your name is...'

'It's Ray.' The skin on her face has lost all colour and elasticity. It looks like I could stick my finger in her cheek and leave a dent that would still be there in a week's time.

'Why, Ray? Why? Why would someone kill Hutch and make it look like Lenny?'

'Don't know yet, Ruth.'

She's looking at me. Barely even blinking. 'Who are you, really? There's something about you. You're not... acting like you should. Why are you so interested in convincing me that the body is Hutch? Shouldn't you just be running off and checking what you need to check. Who the fuck are you?' She ends with a shout.

'C'mon, have a seat. I'll make us a coffee and tell you everything.' I put my hand on her shoulder and lead her back into the living room.

Once there she shrugs it off, like there was a satellite delay to her reaction. 'Don't... don't bloody patronise me. Who are you? And why are you involved in all of this?'

What do I tell her? The full truth, nothing but the truth? So help me. God, if I were her would I be able to listen to my story at this point, with a sympathetic ear?

'I am a policeman. My name is Ray McBain. Detective Inspector Ray McBain. But I have recently... been wrongly charged with murder.'

Her face screws up with confusion and she looks in the direction of Hutchison's flat.

'But you never even knew Hutch. I've never seen you before. Why would you be under suspicion of killing Hutch?' She's taking two and two and making up lottery winnings.

'Not Hutch. I'm not connected with this killing. But the real killer is, and through...' Oh fuck. This is confusing me. How is she going to feel? I take a deep breath. 'There is a connection with the man identified as deceased and a series of other deaths.'

'Oh,' she holds her hand over her mouth, 'I thought your face was familiar. You're that cop that's wanted for murder.'

'Yes. That's what I've been saying.'

She stands up and moves away from me, 'I've got a murderer in my house. I've got a murderer in my house. I've got a...'

'I'm not the murderer. The police have got it wrong, love.' I walk towards her, hands out at my sides, palms facing up. The body language of the honest.

'But you look different. You were in the news for ages.' She is backing up towards the kitchen. Why there? Is she looking for a phone? For a weapon? 'Did you kill Hutch? What have you done with Lenny? Did you kill Hutch, you bastard?' She screams before she turns and runs towards the far wall of the kitchen. I follow her, aiming for a non-threatening pace. A mobile phone is plugged into a socket beside the kettle. She reaches for the phone with one hand and with the other pulls a bread knife out of its hole in a wooden block.

'I'll call the police if you lay as much as a finger on me, you bastard.'

'They've got the wrong man.' My voice is calm and even, while my mind is racing. Why did this all go so wrong? I need her on my side, not phoning the cops. 'I've done nothing wrong.'

'So why are the police after you then? Fuck it, I'm calling 999.' Three sharp electronic tones sound from the phone as she punches in the number.

'No,' I shout. Two steps and I'm beside her. I wrench the phone from her hand and as my thumb presses on the "end call" button she slashes with the knife across the ridge of my knuckles.

'Owww,' I howl and drop the phone. 'What did you do that for?' The back of my hand feels red hot. I hold it up to look at the wound. Luckily, it doesn't seem to have cut too deep, but the blood is flowing freely.

'Shit. Shit. Shit.' Ruth punctuates each word by taking a step towards me and then taking another step back. She wants to help me and is equally terrified of any retaliation. She looks at the phone on the floor, where it fell from my hand 'I didn't mean to...'

I sit on a stool. 'Have you any plasters or bandages?'

The knife is still on her hand and its point is still aimed at me, but my response is clearly puzzling her. Her mind is beginning to work again. I'm not sure what has calmed her down, the sight of blood or my demeanour. Her eyes stray again towards the phone. She wants to go for it but is afraid to take her eyes from me.

'Go on then. Call the cops,' I laugh. 'Don't know what's worse, being wrongly accused of murder or being slashed on the back of the hand by a girl.'

'So you're not...'

'No, Ruth, I'm not the killer. Sadly, and not for the first time, the boys in blue have got it badly wrong.'

'If your former colleagues don't believe you, why should I?'

'Because you're a good deal smarter than they are?' I grin. Her arm drops to her side and I judge that this is time to turn on some more charm. 'Hello. Dripping on your good lino here. Can you get me a cloth or a bandage?' I lick some of the blood from the wound and wince. 'And some needle and thread might not go amiss.'

'God. I'm so sorry,' she's beside me now, knife having fallen to the floor while she grabbed at a kitchen towel. 'Here.' She presses on to the wound with the cloth. Blood seeps through the material in a growing red cloud.

'God. The blood. I am so, so sorry. But you did scare the shit out of me.' Her eyes are large. Fear, grief and confusion swim in the film of unshed tears that line her lower eyelashes. 'I'm so sorry.' Her voice is a whisper.

'Hey, it's okay. You were quite scary yourself you know. I wouldn't want to have been the real killer. You'd have made mincemeat out of me.'

She manages a laugh. 'Yeah, don't mess wi' me.' And leans against the worktop before she keels over. 'What is happening? The world's gone pure mental.'

'I know how you feel. The world's been pure mental for me for weeks now.'

'So you think it might be Hutch that's dead?' she whispers.

I nod. Time for a little more truth. 'One of the murders happened to someone who had a link to my past. I hid that link so that I could carry on investigating the case. I got found out, so the police took that as an admission of guilt. The thing is, there has been more than one death. Similar murders have been happening for a few months now and I need to find the bastard who is doing it and put him away for a very, very long time.'

Throughout my speech her eyes remain fixed on mine. When I stop talking the stare continues for a long minute. The silence is begging to be filled, but I ignore the urge to speak knowing that if I do speak first, I lose.

'Hutch needs to be given a funeral. People need to mourn.'

'The body needs to be identified correctly first.'

'How do we do that?'

'With difficulty. He may have been buried by now. Let's hope they didn't cremate it.'

'It'll be too late for a visual identification anyway, won't it? Decomposition and all that.' As she says this, her hand goes to her mouth. 'Oh my God. Hutch.' Tears push out on to the lower rim of her eye. She steels herself. 'How else can we identify him?'

'The first thing we need to do is convince the authorities that this needs to be looked into. They're bound to ignore anything coming from the number one suspect.'

'Aye, but they're not going to ignore a hysterical girlfriend.' Her smile is weak. 'Besides, technically he's been missing for over a month now.' She turns her face up to mine, her eyes lit with false hope. 'Maybe this is all a dream. We're... imagining things. Deluded even. He is there. He's alive and well and he... just doesn't love me anymore. That's why he hasn't been in touch.' Various emotions vie for space on her face as she works with this notion and simultaneously fights the guilt of preferring him to be dead, to not being in love with her anymore. I put my hand on her shoulder again. I don't know what to say.

The phone rings. It's Allessandra.

'Sloppy, Ray. They were sloppy. They couldn't find anyone to give a visual ID. He was an orphan and there was no other family they could find. He had a wallet on him, with all the personal effects of one James Leonard.' I can almost see her shrug of explanation.

'No dental or medical checks?' I feel relieved to be speaking about work-related matters. There is comfort and a distance in procedure that helps both the loved ones of the deceased and the messenger.

'None.'

'Thanks, Allessandra.' I hang up. 'Ruth, you need to contact the police. Convince them that the body they have is not who they think it is. They went with the ID in his wallet. Leonard's wallet. That was DC Allessandra Rossi. I'll give you her number and you can give her a call. She'll start the *official* ball rolling.'

It's the next morning, I'm back in my hotel room and I can't shake off this *feeling*. That somebody is watching me. Despite the room's thermostat being on full, I can't seem to heat myself. I'm wearing a big, woolly jumper and my leather jacket and still I feel cold. I've got to get out of here. Where the fuck has Calum gone to? Still no sign of him. Gone off chasing pussy? Nah. Doubt it. He always appeared to be a professional. With a capital P. Maybe Kenny has called him in.

I dial his number. Just in case. 'Kenny. You seen Calum?'

'No.' Pause. 'Sorry, Ray. I'm in the middle of something. Let me get back to you. Soon, okay?'

Fine. I think. Except it's not just him I'm worried about. The fact that I'm alone in this building crowds in on me. No-one would hear me scream and come to rescue me. Can it, McBain. You're sounding like an old woman. It must be the room. I'm out of here.

In the passageway my door clicks shut behind me with an air of finality. Like it's never going to open again. The corridor stretches on either side of me and is empty. And silent. I walk to the lift and feel a spasm on my neck, just where it meets my shoulder, just where a blade would cause maximum damage. I stop and turn. Nothing. The corridor is still empty. Silent. I press the command button for the lift. I can hear its electronic whirr somewhere inside the shaft. C'mon. I press the button again. Hurry. Should I take the stairs?

The door to the stairwell is to my right. Through the small glass section in the door it appears well lit. I take a step towards it, when with a musical ping the lift announces its arrival.

Bracing myself against the back wall of the small metallic box, I will the doors shut. They do and as the box falls I feel my anxiety lessen. On the first floor it stops with a lurch. A young couple get in. Couldn't you walk down one flight of stairs? I want to shout at them. Instead I take a step towards the corner to my right, so they can have the rest of the space. They don't even acknowledge me. Joined at the groin, they're both wearing that "Just Fucked Each Other Stupid All Night" glow. They simply stare into each other's eyes and all but lick at each other's smiles. Still. It's company, of a sort.

That's what I need. Company. When the lift stops I'm out of the door, almost barging the male out of the way.

'Arsehole,' he hisses. Wouldn't do to appear weak in front of the girlfriend. I turn round and shoot him the finger and wink at his girlfriend. She giggles. I hear him remonstrate with her as I march through the lobby.

A broadsheet newspaper is on display at the door. *Free Copy*, reads the sign. Let's see if there's anything in here about me.

Outside, I breathe deep. Boy does it feel good to be out of there. It felt like the hotel housed my own private haunting. Relax, Ray, you're thinking nonsense. You're just tired, that's why you're so spooked. Relax. But I can't relax. I need to do something. I need to find McCall. I need to find out what happened to Leonard. And where the fuck is Calum, my so-called minder?

Company. I need company. Theresa. What's she up to today? It would be nice to see her. Wouldn't be the first time we'd had a mid-morning sexual snack. A Coitus Elevensus, she used to call it. My lips curve in a smile as I hear the little giggle that sugared the comment. But it's not really the sex I'm after is it? It's her. Or there's Maggie. She would be company. Nah. She'll do all that spooky stuff. Fuck that.

Theresa. We haven't spoken since she ran away from Kenny's flat. I shouldn't contact her. It might not be safe. Maybe it's seeing that couple together in the lift that's getting me all antsy. I think if I hadn't been there they would have joined the lift equivalent of the Mile High Club. It wasn't their obvious lust for each other that pissed me off. It was more than that. They were so into each other. They looked as if five minutes out of each other's company would have been too painful to endure. I can't remember ever having had that.

Good grief, McBain. You are all over the place tonight. First you want to get out of that hotel as if your life depends on it and now you're standing in front of it all doe-eyed.

The front page of the newspaper has a photograph of some ugly fucker of a politician, hair like my granny's fur hat and teeth that look like they've been surgically enhanced.

Should've just got a haircut, pal.

In lined blocks, down the side of the page we, the earnest/bored/faux-intellectual readers are enticed inside with "Male victims of drug rape" and "Scottish Executive on ID cards".

"Police admit stalemate in Crucifixion Killer case" is at the bottom of the page. Apparently in an attempt to get into the mind of the deranged ex-CID Detective Chief Inspector Ray McBean (arseholes can't even get my name right), 38 (and still getting the age wrong), Strathclyde Police have brought over the big boys from America. On account of serial killers being busier over there, don't you know. The story is continued on page three. Big Breasts page in some newspapers.

Except in this rag it's my old colleagues who are left looking like tits.

I wonder what their experts will say: abused during childhood, deprived of love, all of that kind of stuff. He is a reflection and a product of the society we live in. Blah, blah.

Anyway, back to me.

And Leonard. This new discovery has thrown everything in the air. What is the connection between McCall and Leonard? There has to be something. A body, with Leonard's wallet is found with all of the usual wounds, pointing to the so-called Crucifixion Killer. How the press boys love alliteration and how convenient for the soulless bastard to make it easier for them.

The police have got a point, I suppose. Doing their research. Knowledge is power and all that. Maybe I should be doing some myself.

The Mitchell Library in Glasgow is an amazing place, and this is probably only the second time in my life I've been in it. I'm at a table with a couple of reference books. Felt like a bit of a weirdo when I asked for them, but hey, I'm sure they get even stranger requests.

There was a sign saying that there is a course on today on the top floor. *An Introduction to Counselling.* Maybe I should try and waylay the man or woman who is delivering the course and bend

251

their ears for an hour or two. Nah. I'll content myself with cheery tales of the mad and deranged.

The first book tells of a killer who was freed despite his psychiatrist noting that he was "undoubtedly the most dangerous individual to be released to the community for years".

He was diagnosed with an antisocial personality disorder *and* schizoid personality disorder with psycho-sexual conflicts. Predictably the man went on to further his *career*. A so-called expert at his prison is quoted as saying, 'We hate it when one of our parolees goes sour."

Tell it to the families.

FBI statistics argue that the majority of serial killers come from "broken homes" and have suffered some form of extreme abuse as children. McCall could certainly come into the first category, but could he come in to the second? The FBI, according to this book, have identified thirteen "family background characteristics". They have an *At High Risk Register* for those who display a high percentage of them. Problem is, the killers are usually in custody before the suits can tick all of the boxes. The characteristics include such delights as alcohol abuse, psychiatric history, criminal history, dominant mother parent and negative relationships with male caretaker figures.

Every case I read I interpose with McCall's face. Did he, like this man profiled here, die emotionally and socially before he was into his teens? Christ, he's barely out of them. Or is he suffering from XYY abnormalities as argued in another, equally evil fucker's profile? Apparently there is a link between XYY problems and extreme antisocial behaviour. The good news is that this chromosomal abnormality can only have an impact on a tiny fraction of the population. Apparently these people are tall, thin and awkward: excitable and hyperactive. Their IQ ranges between 80 and 140 and they have a ten to twenty times greater possibility of being sent to prison or a mental hospital.

There is also a chemical imbalance that can cause problems. *Kryptopyrrole* is the fucker we have to be aware of. High amounts of this stuff are a marker for psychiatric dysfunction. A metabolic defect can occur, called *pyroluria*. Apart from turning your piss mauve it can cause extreme mood swings, poor colouring and a diminished ability to deal with stress. Quite a mix.

I close the books with a thump. What did I hope to find? Some sense would have been nice. Some explanation of why people do the things they do. You could litter the world with theory but only know for sure yourself when you are at that point, the edge of your knife pressed into someone's flesh. Do you let go, or do you push? Do you have the will to stop? Or do you thirst to see what happens next?

Looking around the room at others hunched over their books, I wonder how many of these fleshy husks house the mind of a killer? How many would register highly on the FBI checklist? How high would I rate?

Throw a couple of cats in a sack and they will fight to the death. Is that what is happening to society? We've been thrown too tightly together? Seems to me we might have been a whole lot safer from our own as a species if we'd have stayed in the caves and instigated a breeding programme.

Okay, so you're now a more erudite hunter of a serial killer, McBain. But ultimately, your hands are empty. In the absence of a miracle, all you have is yourself. Time to actually do something. I push my chair back, lift up the books and carry them back to the counter. With a nod of thanks and a smile designed to display my very strong links with sane society I leave the room.

Walking down the stairs I see a couple of women ahead climbing towards me. Their chatter is indistinct but wears a high note of excitement. The outline of one of them and her voice registers on my recognition radar.

'Theresa,' is out of my mouth before I can edit my reaction. She stops as if hitting a wall and turns to face me.

'What are you...?' We both ask at the same time. Her companion nods at me, smiles awkwardly at Theresa and then leaves us together.

We both laugh self-consciously. Her hair is a little shorter and her face a little thinner, but she looks well on it. I would be happier, mind you, if she didn't look so determined to keep her distance. I test it and move towards her. One of her feet strays on to a lower step.

'How are you, Ray?' Her eyes finally alight on my face. 'You know... with the...'

'Any better and I'd be twins.'

She laughs and I want to weave the sound into cloth and wrap it around my shoulders.

'Aye right,' she says with a smile. 'Really, though, how are you?'

'Enough about me,' I cough. The least she knows the better. 'What brings you into this fine establishment?'

'I seem to remember a certain not so young man trying to encourage me to get a life. I heard there was an introduction to counselling seminar on in here. So here I am.' She busies herself with her handbag, correcting its perch on her shoulder. 'You know me. A problem shared is... gossip.'

'Good for you.' I move a little closer. She moves her other foot on to the lower step. I put my hands in my pockets, in lieu of a hug. Who do you want to hug, a voice asks. Her or you?

'So how are you?'

'I'm fine, Ray.' She looks away down the stairs.

'I miss you, Theresa. Can I...'

'No, Ray. Don't. I... I'm a married woman.' She recoils as if I spat at her feet. 'My husband has to come first.' She shakes her head, turns and walks downstairs.

I want to follow her. I want to take her by the hand into a quiet corner and hold her. And never let her go. But I just stand there.

A big unmoving lump of silence.

Chapter 39

In my own wee fog of self-pity I leave the library and walk towards the centre of the city. Theresa and I are finished. No way back there. She seemed so uncertain that time in the flat, but this time she was quite definite. *A married woman.* Didn't stop her before did it? But the minute I want more than a casual fuck it's the Big Elbow. Just who's the one with commitment issues here?

Admittedly, there is a certain issue of a number of murders that might conceivably put her off. I guess it makes me less than eligible in most women's eyes.

My path takes me past the King's Theatre and with great delight down past Police HQ in Pitt Street. I want to wave and shout "Fuck You" into the small windows, but I have a shred of sanity that demands I keep my gaze on the pavement, my mouth closed and my hands very firmly in my pockets.

I wonder what their expert is telling them about me, and how I fit their profile. People are able to extract remarkably un-Christian things from the Bible, so it shouldn't be too difficult to make me fit into whatever box they have in mind.

As soon as I enter the hotel's door, I get *that* feeling again. It's like something cold has burrowed under my skin and is worming its way up the line of my spine.

My phone has Kenny's number on speed dial. His answering service comes on. Leave a message. No, ya prick. I want to talk to you. Don't you just hate mobile phones? All this technology and you still can't speak to someone when you want.

'Kenny. It's me, Ray. Phone me. Soon. Soon as you can.' I pause and add, 'Bastard.' For good measure. I wonder if Calum is back yet. Will he be lying on his bed scratching his balls, waiting to give me another quiet lecture?

'Wherever you go, I'm there. When you go for a jog, I'll be a few

steps behind. When you go for a drive, I'm riding shotgun. When I go for a shower, you're sitting on the shitter. No argument.'

So where is he then? Something has gone wrong and it doesn't take Psychic Ray to work that one out. No, Ray. Your mind is just working overtime. The prick'll be up in the room.

The room. I really don't want to go up there by myself. Every time I think of it the feeling in my back intensifies and the muscles at the side of my mouth curdle.

The receptionist pauses as she hands me my key.

'Can I help you, sir?' Polite concern in her raised eyebrows.

'No... no thank you. Well actually...' something occurs to me '...could someone come up to the room with me and help me with the door.'

She looks at me strangely.

'It seems... I seem to have a problem with these electronic keys.' I grow in confidence with my lie and smile. 'This is going to sound a little odd, but I have a problem with electricity. I produce too much apparently.' I shrug in a *what can you do* kind of manner.

My act satisfies her. She picks up a phone from somewhere under the counter and speaks into it.

'The porter will be just with you, sir.'

A couple of minutes later a door opens at the side of the desk and a young man who could well have been described in the serial killer books walks towards me. He is tall, thin, pale and awkward. The only colour on his face comes from a plague of acne. The cuffs of his purple shirt don't reach his hands and as he swings his arms back and forward the white flag of his wrists wink in and out of view.

'You need help with your key... sir?' He is standing in front of me and his hands are now behind his back, as if he escorts people who have a problem with keys to their room every day.

'Yep. If you don't mind.' I walk to the lift and press a button. In the lift he presses his back against a wall, while I stand by the control panel. We each find a spot to stare at.

At the door to my room I hand him my key.

'Do your stuff,' I say. He does so and with a blink of a green light the door opens and he pushes it ajar.

'Will there be anything else, sir?' He takes a step back.

'Actually yes.' I crane my head in past the doorway. 'Could you just come in and check something for me?' I really don't want him to go just yet. My nerves feel as if they've been strung tight against the bridge of a master's guitar that's in the hands of a monster.

'Eh...' He takes a step forward. Looks like he's stuck in the grey area between courtesy and fuck-off-weirdo.

'For fuckssake, I'm not going to try and shag you. Could you just go into the room and check that it's empty?'

His head performs a couple of quick nods as if he's arguing with himself. 'I didn't think you were, sir,' he says and enters. He steps to the middle of the room where he can see down between the beds and as I stay by the door he walks to the window. A wee smile creeps on to his face just as he turns to look behind the curtains. 'Nothing here, sir.'

'Try the bathroom,' I say feeling like a twat. Confident now and with a bored expression, he walks to the toilet door and pushes it open.

'Nothing, sir.' Every ounce of energy he has is now being used to stop himself from laughing. I shut the door in his face. Bastard.

Nothing. All that for nothing. And what if you were proved right to be worried? You would have put some young boy's life at risk. The fella laughing at me is a small price to pay for being so stupid.

Sitting on the edge of my bed I look around the room. That feeling is still there. What the hell is it? Lifting up the quilt covers that brush the carpet, I look under each bed. Nothing.

Then I look in the wardrobe. My stuff is all there.

Except.

My leather sports bag. Where has that gone? Would Calum have borrowed it for something? It could have been missing for days and I wouldn't have noticed.

I pick my phone from my pocket and phone Kenny again. Again nothing. Fuck. Where is the prick?

Standing by the window I can see over to the Kingston Bridge. The familiar flow of traffic. Back to the bed. I sit down. Lie down. Turn the TV on. The usual crap. Turn it back off. I have a seat by the table and fidget with a pen and a pad of paper.

Back to the bed. I lie down. Maybe I could pass some time with a wee sleep. Who are you kidding, McBain. Sleep? With this sick feeling? I could meditate. Maybe that will lessen it. Maybe all I need to do is relax.

I kick off my shoes, arrange pillows at the head of the bed and prop myself in an alert seated position. Just before I close my eyes something attracts my attention. On the bedside cabinet, under the umbrella of the lampshade, lies a Bible. I can't remember putting that there. I swing my legs off the bed and lean my head closer. There's something sitting on top of it. A circle of small glass balls, with a crucifix dangling off the end.

Rosary beads.

Chapter 40

The rain is so hard it sounds like sheets of gravel are hitting the car. Through the din I try to phone Kenny once more. His phone is still on its answering service. This time I leave a message that is slightly more coherent. I tell him that Calum is still away chasing pussy and that I've gone down to Bethlehem House.

I'm in my usual parking space just by the gated front entrance. There are few cars about at this time of night. I arrived here just as the moon was rising. It's hard to believe that the sky was clear when I first arrived. Now just a few hours on — the clock in the dashboard reads nine pm — it's like monsoon season minus the heat. Typical late autumn weather in Bonnie Scotland.

What have I been doing all this time? Thinking. Knowing that it's up to me doesn't make it any easier. A woman I hate will die if I do nothing. The policemen in me says go and protect her; the six year old boys argues, leave her to rot.

Those beads really gave me the shits. McCall is better than I thought. He knew where I was and yet he didn't kill me. That means I can't be a target.

But that is just what all my instincts have been telling me.

I look over at the building. Rosary beads were ubiquitous in my time here. Even the statues carried them. All the kids had their own set and each set of beads had their own purse. Woe betide you if you lost them. Every saint would be invoked to stop you on your sure and certain passage to Hell.

Quite a career path, given that lots of the kids from that sort of background tend to live down to their carer's expectation.

Most of the rosary beads were dark colours made from wood or plastic. If you were lucky someone gave you a gift at Christmas or your birthday of an ornate set. The ornament being some fancy metalwork on the crucifix hanging from the end of the final decade of "Our Ladys".

Apart from one set. They were glass and opaque and belonged to Sister Mary. Whoever left them in my room — and we can take a wild stab at that — was giving me a clear warning of who the next victim was going to be.

On the drive down the M77 I thought of phoning the convent. But what would I say. Lovely night isn't it? Mild for this time of year and oh, by the way, could you warn Mother Superior that there's a homicidal maniac on his way to kill her?

What about the police? Would they even believe me? An anonymous tip-off that a nun was about to be murdered would sound like the mother of all crank calls. I can't phone Allessandra and Daryl. They have already done more than enough. From now on I have to maintain some form of distance from them.

I've also been thinking back to the state I was in at the hotel. What the fuck was that? That's not me. Letting some poor boy check out the room before I went in. What if he'd got hurt? I would never have been able to forgive myself. But the feeling was so strong. It was like I was a child again and shrinking under the rage of Sister Mary, fear breaking out with the cold sweat on my forehead.

But you're not six, McBain. You're a man. And from now on, you are on your own and in the meantime, while you navigate your gaze through your navel, some poor woman could be getting murdered.

If I were McCall where would I do it in a place like this? How well does he know his way around? Judging from the way he has gone about his work so far, he has been well informed. In order to save himself from being disturbed he would need to do it in Mother Superior's bedroom. How would he know where it is? There are loads of rooms in that building. Four floors of them. I'm sure some of them are never used, as there's only a handful of nuns living here now.

Leonard. Where does he fit in? A dead body is made to look like him. He must be involved and chances are he is the one who spilled the beans on McCall's parentage. Has Leonard used McCall to extract some terrible revenge? But what happened that was so bad? Maybe his brother dying when he was so young threw him off the edge.

In any case, something tells me I'm going to find out. Soon.

This rain is a bastard. I wish it would stop. I roll down my window to try and get rid of the steam that has varnished the glass.

What's that? I squint my eyes. Someone has just walked round the side of the building.

I'm out of the car and running low across the grass, my clothes already plastered to my body. No hesitation. No fear. I'm a policeman and a fucking good one. No mad fucker is going to show me up.

Round this side of the building there is a covered walkway that leads to the little stone chapel where the nuns wear their knees out, day after day, year after year, and where I first learned to be an altar boy. Footsteps clatter on the stone path. They're moving in the direction of the chapel.

The grass muffles my passage, although I'm sure everyone within a mile of here can hear my breathing. And the thump of my pulse.

The heavy wooden door is open enough to allow an arrow of light to shine on the path outside. As quietly as I can I walk to the door and place my ear to the space. Nothing.

Then I hear a low sound, like a prayer. A prayer from someone in pain. I lean on the door a little and grimace as it moans in protest. Stop. I listen again. Nothing. Every hair on my body is erect, pushing against the soaked cloth of my clothes. I feel a drip run down the side of my face and launch itself into space. I almost expect it to splash to the ground with the sound of a church organ. Here he is. Come and get him. But still there is silence.

Then a whisper. 'Dear God... Help me.'

I can't wait any longer. Someone is in trouble. Pushing open the door I take a step inside. It's like stepping back in time, it's exactly the way I remember. The stations of the cross punctuate the walls between each of the windows. Rows of wooden seats lead to the front. The black shape of a nun is hunched in prayer in the front pew.

'Sister. Are you alright?' My voice bounces off the walls and grates loudly on my ears. No response.

'Sister. Are you okay?' This time I speak quietly and take a step towards her. Then I notice a shape on the floor beside the kneeling figure, in front of the altar. From the jumble of cloth and limbs issues another moan. Her face takes shape, the eyes like pinpoints of fear.

'Help me,' Mother Superior whispers.

But who's the nun at the pew? And how can she kneel in prayer without rushing to help?

I sense rather than see a presence approaching my left side. In slow motion I turn in response to a stab in my thigh.

McCall's face is wearing the hideous leer of a Halloween mask. 'Goodnight, Detective Inspector.'

My legs are rubber. What did he stick me with? Everything blurs as if I'm looking at the world from inside a tank of water.

Then all is blackness.

Chapter 41

The first thing I'm aware of is the pressure of a hard, plastic seat against my back and thighs. The next thing is my laboured breathing. It crashes against my ears like waves on to rocks. My limbs are heavy, almost blended into the plastic on which I sit. My tongue has grown to fill my mouth. I will my jaw to open, the words to spill out, questions to bloom into the air and fill my ear. But nothing.

A face leans forward to fill my vision. A face in the cowl of a nun's headdress. A man's face. His breath is hot on my cheek. It's the gardener.

'Welcome to the party, Ray. Don't worry,' he says softly. 'You're going to be just fine. For the moment.' He steps back and points to the bed behind him. 'She, on the other hand, won't be.'

I can't move my head, but I can see that we are in a small, cell-like room. A naked light bulb blares from the ceiling. The walls are a dull yellow. The only adornment, a crucifix. The only piece of furniture in the room apart from my chair is a single bed. This room is familiar. I've been here before.

Someone is lying on top of the bed. A woman. An old woman. Mother Superior is lying on top of the bed. Naked.

The poor woman probably *bathed* with clothes on, being naked now must almost be as bad as the terror. Stripped of her dignity and the badge of office she must have worn for nearly half a century, how must she feel? Beyond help and beyond fear.

For fear she would. Who could look into those eyes and not feel it? They are large and black, like wormholes down to a tainted soul. The black of the iris is set off by the red irritation on each of the bottom lids. No, it's not an irritation. It's more like thin lines of crusted blood.

She is shaking so hard I can almost hear her bones rattle. The part of her that polite society and centuries of living in stone houses has helped to bury, the part of her that saved her ancestor from teeth and claw is flooding her system with adrenaline, increasing the blood flow to her limbs, the light to her eyes, the life to her nerve ends.

Fight or flight. Panic sparks in her eyes, because neither is possible. She is weak and old. She knows how to use the force of personality on recalcitrant children. But this is a man, and he has a knife. And he is going to use it.

She looks so tiny. So frail. The paper skin of her face is stretched over the bones of her face in anticipation of what is to come. I can almost see the skull that will be all that is left once decay does its work. This woman trod through my childhood like the monster from a scary story, her small feet taking loud giant steps, doling out a good portion of the fear she is now feeling. And look at her now. So weak and powerless.

She turns her head to look at me. 'Help me,' the look in her eye demands. Why aren't you doing something? She doesn't know I can't move.

The face leans into my vision again.

'The journey you started twenty years ago, Ray, is about to end. Are you excited? You should be.'

The journey I started?

'I believe you know my lovely young assistant.' His face is replaced by another from a different nightmare. McCall.

'Joseph has been invaluable to me.' McCall's smile widens with pleasure at the compliment. He nods his head as if we've just been introduced at a party.

The other man must be...

'You'll either know me as Lenny or X-File. Or you might even remember me as Jim Leonard. I knew you straight away. Who could forget Ray McBain?' He dances out of my limited line of sight. My view now consists solely of my lap. My head must have slumped forward. It is pushed back up.

'A tricky business,' says Leonard. He holds up his hand. In it is a small box of pills.

'It's amazing what they can do nowadays. The date rape drug they call this. Wonderful stuff.' He bends forward and fusses at my collar.

'Comfy? Good. We want you to see everything. And remember everything.' His eyes dance within their sockets. He bares his teeth. 'Everything.'

Remember what?

He bends forward again as if speaking to a child. 'So here's what we have in store for you both. Just so you know. She...' he points to Mother Superior '... is going to die first.'

First.

Mother Superior's eyes are clenched shut and her lips are moving in silent prayer. The drugs he gave her must be wearing off.

'You are going to watch. Then you are going to kill yourself. The remorse of having murdered all of these people has become too much to bear.' He laughs as if this notion is just too ludicrous. Then he fishes in my pocket and pulls out the rosary beads.

'Excellent. I knew you would bring them.' He lets them fall back in. 'Keep them. A wee souvenir. You know how all you psychos like to keep your souvenirs.' That was a quote. Allessandra said that to me back in the hotel. Has he been so close to me all this time?

'It's all been sooo easy, Mr Murderer slash Detective.' He makes a slashing action with his hand. 'Get it?' He laughs. 'You played into my hands every time.'

'Not a murderer,' I manage to mumble.

'Did you hear that, Joseph. The man says he's not a murderer. Oh, how quickly they forget.' His face appears in front of mine again. 'Tut, tut. Your proudest moment. My inspiration and you *deny* it?'

'Deny what?' I try to say, but it comes out lower than a mumble.

My head is rocked back with the force of his slap. Good job I am numb. My head rights itself and I see a bag at the nun's feet. My sports bag. The zip sounds and McCall leans over and pulls out a circle of wire. Barbed wire. He licks his lips uncertainly. Passes it to Leonard and steps back, rubbing his hands on the side of his hips. He's not so sure of himself now. Where's the cocky bastard that had me running through those back gardens? The realisation hits me. None of it has been him. It's all been Leonard.

'Joseph has been an *excellent* pupil.' Leonard stands with his arms spread wide as if addressing an imaginary congregation. 'And now for the final lesson.'

Joseph folds his arms, puts his hands in his pockets and takes them out folding his arms again. He looks from Leonard to the nun and back again.

'But she's an old woman, Jim.'

'They punished the Nazis in their eighties and nineties. There is no time limit on reparation.'

He bends forward and places the "crown" on Mother's head. A small squeal escapes her lips, like air being squeezed from a punctured tyre. Blood oozes from a series of small wounds and feeds a river that is forming in her hair. Then he pulls a nail gun from the bag.

'But, Jim.' McCall is running his fingers through his hair.

'Have strength, Joseph.' Before McCall could complain again he fires the gun through both wrists. Mother's body shakes with pain. 'Are you watching, Ray? See what you started?'

'Holy Mary... mmmother... of Jesus.'

'Save your prayers you old witch. You're going to Hell. For what you did to my brother.'

My head has slumped again, my view returned to my lap. Thankfully I can't see any more, but I can hear. *His brother.*

'Have strength, Joseph. You were named after Christ's father. Just think of the courage that he needed while Herod's men killed all of the newborns.' Leonard senses McCall's apprehension.

C'mon, McCall. If you are going to stop him now is the time.

'Think of your mum, Joe. What agonies did she go through? Eh? And it's all this bitch's fault.' I hear a kick. Mother moans. 'All her fault. She killed my brother and she let that old sick twisted man Connelly rape your mother. She deserves to die.'

A couple of steps sound on the floor and my head is pushed back up. Leonard swims into view.

'As for you,' he pats my cheek. 'You had so much anger in you. Really impressed us.' Spit bubbles at his lips and flecks my face. 'You wanted revenge. And boy did you get it. Except you got the wrong man.'

What the hell is he talking about? Why am I asking that? Because I know, don't I? I've always known. The movie that runs in my dreams. The blood. The struggle. The fight for breath. The cloud of feathers.

Leonard is off on a tangent. 'You wet your bed. Again. But you're just a child. A child.' His voice has a note of pleading when he says this word. 'A child. And you've got a really heavy cough. Which turns out to be pneumonia. And this excuse of a woman wraps you up in your own piss-soaked blankets and leaves you there for hours. To suffer the taunts of your so called friends.' He bares his teeth at me. 'And to die.' He steps towards McCall and grips his neck with his free hand.

'Remind me. Inform Mother Superior...' as he mouthed her title his voice took on a choking sound, '... tell her what it was like. Let her know about the chain of events she set in motion.' Back to me. 'Joseph found me, you know. He saw me following Devlin. We became friends. We have a lot in common.'

McCall's expression darkens and he throws off Leonard's hand. His eyes look to the past that plays out somewhere above my head.

'They had parties. My mum and Devlin.' His voice is almost a whisper. 'Drugs were the starter and the main course... I was dessert.' His voice louder now.

'I paid for their drugs with my mouth...' he pauses, and collects himself, '... and my arse. Half a dozen men would have their turn, while my mother and her friend Devlin laughed with relief at managing to get a fix.' His words are squeezed through the bars of his clenched teeth. His eyes light on me and I feel a cold hand grip my heart.

I am going to die.

'An eye for an eye. How many lives will it take?' he asks me, his torment a faint flicker at the corner of his eye. Enough. No more. I want to scream. I manage to open my mouth.

'Quick, give him some more of that stuff,' says Leonard. 'He shouldn't be able to move like that.'

McCall jabs at my arm and steps away from me, his hands behind his back. I feel cold and I don't know whether it is from the drug McCall has just given me, or the deadness that squats in his eyes. A chill spreads from arm to my heart and follows the flow of my blood. Through arteries and veins it flows, spreading the word. And the word is death.

I am going to die.

With a giggle Leonard pulls a large knife from the bag and leans over to hold it in front of the Mother's face. Her mouth punches open in a long, silent scream. He sits on her chest and pushes his face into hers, his lips on hers, breathing in her panicked cries.

'Not long now, Mother.' He looks into her eyes. 'Reliving the past are we? How many children did you torture? Can you see their ghosts line up behind me? I hope you can, because they are going to chase you all the way down to Hell.'

Her mouth is working. It's as if she's trying to say something, but then a gob of spit flies into Leonard's eye.

'Call yourself a Bride of Christ. More like Whore of Satan.' His hand lashes out, the one bearing the knife, its aim unerring, across her throat. Blood sprays over him, he jumps up to avoid it and his feet slip. He laughs delightedly as if this was a slapstick moment.

'Oh well. Never mind,' he says to me. 'I'm alive. I'm ALIVE. And it's AMAZING.' He pulls the headdress off and wipes his face with it. Then he pulls the black gown over his head. Below it he is naked. He has an erection. It bobs obscenely as he walks towards me. He bares his teeth, closes his eyes and grips his cock.

'Jim,' McCall's voice is a low growl of warning. 'I told you if you did any of that you would be on your own.' Presumably murder and mutilation have a low score on McCall's toleration index, while sexual misconduct is a real no-no. The crazy light in Leonard's eyes flames one more time and then dies down to a flicker, like a pilot light waiting to spark the furnace back to life. He turns back to the bag and pulls out a pair of garden overalls.

'Temptation is a terrible thing,' he tells me, his breath foul in my face. 'Don't worry. You're not my type. You still have a pulse.' Now he's calm and considers me for a moment.

'You really don't remember do you? And I thought this "police" thing was just the act of a guilty conscience.' His laughter is like a bark and it reverberates around the room.

'C'mon, Jim. I think I heard something.' McCall says urgently and takes a step out of my vision. 'Let's get this over with.'

'Poor Ray...' So wide is McCall's smile he could hang the ends of it over his ears. 'He doesn't remember.'

No. No. No. I don't want to know.

'Our little gang; you, John and me. Carole and her friend... what was her name? Ah yes, Frances. Who turned out to be Joseph's mother. And do you remember what brought us together?'

No.

Yes.

'Jim, c'mon. Is that a car I hear coming up the drive?' McCall is getting nervous.

Leonard turns my hands over, places them palm upwards. 'Your chosen method of suicide is the old favourite,' he sings, and slides the blade across my wrists like he's playing a violin. This isn't happening to me. I am up in the roof of the church looking down at my slack expression. I feel nothing though the view is painful.

Pain is only a concern of the living, a voice sighs in my mind.

The blade has gone deep. The line of flesh separates as easily as beef under the butcher's blade. I'm sure I can see a pale glint of bone before blood surges out of the wounds. I slam back into my body. Fire blazes on my arms. Screams melt against the heat of the pain that surges through my nervous system to pool against the base of my spine. My sphincter relaxes in preparation of a flight that is impossible.

Floating.

Am I dead yet?

Chapter 42

Carole Devlin finds me up behind the tennis court. I'm down on my hunkers, wondering if I'm about to die, if the pain would ever stop and reliving the fury of Sister Mary when she saw me.

I had been trembling and crying, trying to hide my blood-stained trousers and underpants under my bed when Sister caught me.

'What work of Satan are you engaged in now, boy?'

'Nothing, Sister.' It was all I could do to stand up from my kneeling position. 'I think I need a doctor.'

'It's the Confessional you need. What have you got there?' She whipped the garments from my hands. 'Holy Mary, mother of… is that blood? On your pants? What in God's name have you been doing?' Her fist connected with my cheek. The pain of that was nothing to what was going on below my waist. 'Just the other day you had the marks of the stigmata… drawn on with a pen. What have I done to deserve these heathen children, Holy Father?' she screeched. 'Get out of my sight, boy, before I strangle you with these bare hands. Go on. Go.' Her face was purple. I didn't wait to be told again, as fast as the pain allowed me, I fled.

Her voice chased me down the stairs. 'As sure as the good Lord died on that cross, you are going to Hell, Ray McBain.'

Like any wounded animal I wanted to be on my own. Perhaps I could find peace and quiet up behind the tennis courts. There I could crawl under a bush, wait for darkness, the cold and death. Then Hell. I wasn't good enough even for Purgatory now. Not after what that man did to me.

An eye for an eye, isn't that what the Bible said? Except he was a man and I was only a boy. What could I do to him? Nothing. The best thing for me would be to hide and wait for the end. Because surely with this amount of pain, I'm dying.

That is when Carole Devlin finds me.

'Are you crying, nancy-boy?'

'Scram.' I carefully stand up. My insides feel torn. 'Can't you see that I'm dying?'

She snorts, 'You don't look too good, Ray, but dying? Don't think so.' She reaches out a hand and holds my face. Pushes my chin up so she can see my cheek more clearly.

'That looks like the handiwork of a certain Sister Mary.'

'Leave me alone,' the tears are flowing, my chest is heaving. Everything hurts.

'What happened, Ray?' Carole's voice changes. Is that concern?

'Nothing. A man. It hurts so much.' I fall into the grass. She touches my shoulder.

I crave her comfort but I won't allow it. 'Beat it,' I push her hand away.

She stays. I hear the grass beside me getting flattened as she sits down.

'Bastard.'

I gasp. After everything I have been through, hearing that word out loud still shocks me.

'He got you as well, didn't he?'

Who? I didn't get a good look at his face. But I thought I would remember the hands and the smell of him for the rest of my life. Tobacco and aftershave.

'Bastard.' The shock of the word was no less the second time.

'I'm telling Sister Mary you swore, Carole Devlin,' a boy's soprano sounds from a few feet away. I look up and see the twins.

'What's wrong with him?' asks John Leonard.

'He's crying like a baby,' says Jim.

'*He* got him,' answers Carole.

'Bastard,' the twins say in unison.

I sit up and look at the row of firm-set faces in front of me. We are only children and we have experienced far too much. I feel the weight and the helplessness of my youth. Anger sets in a knot in my jaw line.

'An eye for an eye,' I say. Fury sets in my jaw and sparks in my eyes. The children round about me shrink from me as if frightened for the briefest of moments.

A few nights later, after lights out, I am woken by the sensation of someone leaning on my bed. I sit bolt upright, knees under my chin, eyes huge against the darkness.

'Who is it?' I squeak. I am so terrified I am not even sure the words came out. I can make out two small shapes at the end of my bed.

'It's me.'

'And me,' say the twins. 'Don't start greetin' again.'

I'm stung. I'm not a cry-baby.

I can feel more movement as they move on to the bed. 'We know who it was.'

'We know where he sleeps,' they say.

I pull my knees tighter. 'He won't hurt me again, will he?'

'Like he hurt one of us?' a twin says and I'm not sure which.

'An eye for an eye,' the other one says.

'What do you mean?' I try to make out the faces before me in the blackness.

I remember what I read about Red Indians and how they would look slightly to the side of something in the darkness and almost be able to see it. I try this trick and I am impressed by how much it helps. But I still can't make out any individual features.

'Time to get our own back, eh?' One jumps off the bed and coughs. 'I'll be back.' His bare feet slap at the linoleum as he rushes from the room.

'We need to do this together.'

'Do what?'

Just then the twin returns with another two larger shapes. Girls.

'You guys ready?' It's Carole Devlin, and the smaller outline must be a friend of hers. It's Frances Collins. I hadn't seen her for a few weeks. We were told she had the flu.

'What's going on?' I ask.

'Just what you said. An eye for an eye,' the twins sing. 'Let's go.'

A hand pulls me from the bed and in single file we make our way from the room and out into the corridor. From there we make our way to the stairwell. It is cold and my teeth are clacking together. Moonlight enters the large window above us as we make our way down to the next landing and the old people's floor.

My teeth are still rattling together, but now it is less from the cold than the realisation that something is very wrong here.

We are still walking in single file, Carole, then Frances, then the twins and then me.

'What are we doing?' My whisper sounds like a roar in the hush of the stairway. One of the twins has one of his pyjama sleeves stuffed in his mouth to stifle his cough. Carole keeps looking at him as if she is going to take him by the throat.

'Just hurry up, McBain,' says Carole. 'Keep up, Cry-Baby.'

Spurred on by the insult I walk too fast and collide with one of the twins. I see the flash of teeth as he growls at me. I punch his arm. But if you take on one Leonard you take on them both and they both stop and square up to me.

'Enough, boys,' says Carole. 'We have work to do.'

What exactly that work is not entirely clear to me yet. An eye for an eye is what I said. But how does that translate into what that man did to me? He did it to one of the twins as well. The girls are here too... can things like that happen to girls as well? If so, which one?

Or was it both?

'But I want to go to bed,' I whisper.

Frances is on me in a flash. 'You're here and you're staying.' She has a tight hold of my pyjama top. 'We all have to do it.'

I push her away. The look in her eyes really scares me. We all have to do what?

Carole pushes a door open slowly, sticks her head through, waits a moment and then motions for us all to move through. We do so and the first things that strike me are the soft carpet underfoot and the smell. Did the nuns never open the windows on this floor? The old people smell is very strong.

'Hang on a minute,' Frances vanishes through another door and returns in moments. She has a hand behind her back.

'Right. It's through here I think.' She points ahead and we all follow her.

'This is where *he* sleeps.'

We are in a tiny cell-like room. Through a chink in the curtains enough light is coming in so that we can see how close the walls are and we can make out the bed, with the long shape of a man stretched in slumber. We stand frozen at the end of the bed, and watch the rise and fall of his chest. He is on his back and his mouth is open.

So this is him? The man who damned me to Hell?

'Who's doing it then?' Carole whispers.

'An eye for an eye was Ray's idea. He should do it.' The coughing twin forces words out between coughs.

'Do what?'

'Would you stop that? You're going to wake him up,' Carole whispers again.

'Do what?' I ask again.

The man snuffles in his sleep. We freeze. My heart is beating so fast it is about to burst. Is this what a heart-attack feels like?

Silence settles over us again like the moment before thunder sounds. All eyes are trained on the long line of skin, flesh and bone under the blankets. He is just a man, yet he holds us under his power even as he sleeps. I feel like I'm in a dream; one where my movements are dictated to me, once the decision to act is made there is no turning back.

'Ray, use the pillow,' a girl's voice reaches my ears and something soft is pushed into my hands.

What do I do with it?

'Use the pillow. Hold it over his head.' A flash of teeth. 'We just want to give him a fright. Let him know what will happen if he hurts any more children.' Frances' eyes are shining.

'Just a wee fright?' I want my bed. I want to huddle under the blankets and not come out until I'm at least sixteen. Someone pushes me towards the bed.

My legs won't move.

'McBain. Do it,' urges Carole. 'This man hurt you. He deserves it.'

Again I feel my helplessness in the face of the series of adults who had let me down. My mum. My dad. Sister Mary. And here, perhaps was the worst of them all. He had hurt me so much. He did things to me that were wrong.

'Just a wee fright,' someone whispered. 'We'll all help you.'

I moved my left foot about an inch. Just a wee bit of a fright would teach him a lesson. Wouldn't it? I was going to Hell anyway. A saint's life wasn't for me anymore because of this man. He deserved a fright. Something flared in my gut, travelled past my heart and set itself in stone in my jaw. I found my rage.

'C'mon guys,' I whispered and took three steps forward. And another. I was level with the man's head. He smelled differently. Must've had a wash. I could make out the silver of his hair and the lines of his brow. Hair sprouted in a wild thatch from his eyebrows and his nostrils.

I placed the pillow over his face. As gently as if it were a veil.

'Just a wee fright,' I say. And Carole, the twins and I hold a corner each.

The man moved. 'Wha...'

Oh no. He's going to get up. I jump on top of the pillow. If he gets up and recognises us, he'll tell Sister Mary. And then the nine visions of Hell will seem like a picnic.

'C'mon guys,' I beg. 'Help!'

Three bodies pile on top of the old man. He twists his torso from side to side, but his feet are pinioned by his blankets. One of the twins is on his chest. Carole and the other twin are on top of me. Frances is standing at the end of the bed. Her mouth is open. One hand is between her legs and the other is hanging by her side. She is rocking back and forward, a strange noise issuing from between her teeth. Something is in her hand, but before I can make it out I feel the old man's hands on my arm, my hand, my neck as he blindly reaches for a hold to try and pull me off. Those hands did things to me. I don't want them to touch me again, but I can't move. Each time he touches me my skin feels burned. I fight the dread that sets my breathing faster.

'Frances, we need you,' Carole says. 'You're heavier than the twins. C'mon, move.' But Frances can't hear her; her mind has gone somewhere else.

'Get off me. Get...' his muffled voice sounds from under the pillow. I can feel his chest heaving as he fights to fill his lungs and I can hear the panic in his voice. His movements are weaker now. He was stronger the other day. Much stronger. Perhaps his age means he can't fight for so long. My anger has subsided and I'm starting to feel that this is bad. Very bad. We have given the man a fright and we need to stop now. But no-one else looks like they are prepared to stop. From what I can see of the rest of them their faces are all set on causing the man maximum pain. Frances is still immobile at the end of the bed.

'Guys. The man's had enough,' I say. 'Let's go.' I move from my position and pull at Carole. Then I push one of the twins. 'Let's go.' I am thinking that we need to get off the man and out of the door without him catching a glimpse of us.

He takes a loud, long, panicked breath when the pressure stops. The sound chills me to the marrow.

'Get out of here quick,' I say.

The man sits up and the pillow I was holding slides in slow motion from his face to rest on his chest. He looks around himself, his chest heaving, 'Who...'

'Noooo,' I hear a strangled cry. A body flashes past me. The man screams and falls back down on to the bed. Frances is on the bed and punching down on the old man with one hand. Each time she did so something wet splattered over me. Something wet and dark has sprayed over the wall. I look at the twins and they each look like they have been sprayed with it as well. I wipe some of the sticky, hot fluid from my forehead. It still hasn't occurred to me what is happening. Another strike and a cloud of feathers is released from the pillow and rises in the air. The smell. I want to cry. I want to hide in a corner. I try to hold my breath against the mixed smells of blood and excrement. I am gagging. Chest heaving I take a deep breath and my mouth fills with feathers. I spit them out. Cough out some more. One lodges in my throat. I can't breathe. I can't stop coughing. Panic.

Cough.

Can't breathe.

Can't...

Am I dead yet?

Floating. I can smell the blood from my wrists.

I can remember everything. I send a silent prayer of sorrow to the old man.

'And we got the wrong guy,' Leonard cackles in my ear. 'Can you believe it? Some poor old sod is in the wrong bed, at the worst time.'

'Jim. Let's go,' shouts McCall.

Am I dead yet?

I am not alone in this limbo between life and death. It is the ghosts of the living who surround me. Allessandra's uncertain smile the day I gave her a hug. Daryl's answering grin when I told him to fuck off. Theresa's face before she turned and walked away from me.

Did I let any of them down? What should I have done differently?

I'm allowed one more surge of awareness.

I hear some shouts, a scuffle. More shouts.

Then a voice speaks into my right ear. It's Kenny. 'Don't worry, Ray. We've got him. McCall won't be able to do any more damage.'

I am so tired. My mind is a fog of half-finished thought. Not McCall, I want to say, but I can't. Tired. I want to sleep. As the light and the pain fades I feel the feathery touch of a hand on my neck. Another, more gentle voice whispers.

'*Welcome home, Ray. Welcome home.*'

276

Chapter 43

Everything is white. I didn't know white could come in so many shades. At first it appears that there is only one. Then if you look a little closer, follow the blur and concentrate, you see more: the colour white in tones as infinite as the thoughts in your head.

There's the light, grey white of the sky, which filters into the bright white of the distant hills, even brighter are the flakes of white that are falling to my feet, a curtain of small, dry feathers.

I take a step forward wanting them all to fall on me. I need their purity, their cleansing. Neck bent back, I look up and let cold feathers fall in to my open eyes and bathe them. Too cold. I blink hard and they melt into tears.

'Ray. What the hell are you doing?' asks Maggie. 'Can we go back to your place now? Or at least go for a coffee. I'm freezing my tits off here.' Ever since I got out of hospital Maggie has been my constant companion.

'Don't know what you like about this place. It's bloody morbid.' She looks around at the gravestones. 'Mind you, it must have been an amazing place in its heyday.'

'Do graveyards have a heyday?'

'Shut it,' she punches my arm. I exaggerate the pain and she's all over me like a nurse of the year nominee. 'Sorry. I didn't mean to...'

I grin, and when she realises I'm pulling her leg, she punches me again.

Walking back down the hill, we take great care with our footing, a slip up here might mean a very cold wait for both of us as we wait for medical attention. I love it that the snow is softening the noise of the usual boisterous Glasgow. Everything is muffled. It's as if the religious hush found in the nearby Cathedral has found its way out of the confines of its Gothic architecture. It's as if the world is holding its breath. Spread around the hill on which the

277

Necropolis sits, the city is being cleansed and to my snow-washed eyes it has never looked better.

As we pass St Mungo's and approach the crossing, Maggie senses my fatigue and keeps up a stream of chatter to try and distract me from it. This relationship and how it has developed has been one of the biggest surprises of my recovery. It worried me at first. After all we did nearly sleep together on our first meeting. The more she came to visit, the more I began to worry that she had a wee fancy for me. But what we have has turned into something familial, I see her and think friend and sister, not get your clothes off, honey, I fancy a shag.

'Piss off,' was her reply when I found the courage to ask her. Then she smiled slowly as a thought articulated itself. 'So that's why you've gone all quiet the last few times I've been to visit.' She plumped up a cushion for me with exaggerated care. 'Nah, sorry, wee pal. I don't want to jump your bones anymore. We're mates and this is what mates do. They look after each other.' I wasn't sure which expression to allow on my face: relief or embarrassment.

'Let's go for a coffee,' I pause at the traffic lights and look over my shoulder at the door of St Mungo's. 'I don't want to go home just yet.'

Once inside Maggie ushers me to a seat and then goes to stand at the counter. She looks back at me and mouths 'Carrot cake?' I nod. The diet is definitely finished for now. I deserve a few treats after all I've been through.

Since waking up in hospital I have been blurred with guilt. Every thought, every action is tinged with the memory of how I helped kill a man when I was only a child. The memories crowded in like a mob of feasting parasites.

Old Betty was the first to come and discover the scene. The view of five blood-spattered children and a punctured corpse set her scream to banshee levels. And the nuns soon came running.

We boys were led away to the bathrooms, we were too young and must have been led astray by the girls. We never saw them again. We heard that Carole had been sent to another home and Frances had gone to jail as the knife was covered in her prints.

The sex attacks on the children stopped, making us think that we had been right in picking out that particular man. Only subsequent events have proven that not to be the case.

I lift my wrists up and watch the demi-bracelets of puckered

red flesh come into view. This is something I find myself doing regularly. And each time, the words, *I nearly died* fill my mind, as if I'm searching for the importance of it. I mean, Christ, this is big and I'm being a bit too blasé about it. I should be shouting from the tallest building, sharing the joy of being alive with every stranger that crosses my path, or at the very least cashing in my Police Federation savings plans and going to lie on a beach paradise somewhere in the tropics.

But I need to know what's happening next. Where is Leonard? What will the police decide following my actions during the *Christ Killer* case? They couldn't investigate properly while I was having my extended "sleep" and even now they're waiting for a doctor to say that I'm fit and able to answer for my actions.

Daryl and a strangely subdued Allessandra have been regular visitors and each time we debate what will happen. What will they throw at me? A demotion? A dismissal, or even criminal proceedings? All are possible, but they're convinced I'll be given extended garden leave and then quietly allowed to fill a desk space.

It helps that they have a real suspect now, albeit the wrong one. During their first visit — in which I was fully present — I tried to get them to impress upon the team that McCall wasn't the killer. It was Leonard.

Ruth Dillon did her bit. She managed to convince the police that Leonard's body should be re-examined. It was exhumed and medical records proved that the body was indeed one Mark "Hutch" Hutchison.

But it turns out that McCall did have blood on his hands, Daryl informed me with raised eyebrows. He killed Devlin. Forensics found traces of her blood on his clothes. And not only that but he confessed to everything. He's currently waiting for sentencing.

The brass are happy to go with that. They have a killer, and even better, he confessed, so they don't have to spend the taxpayer's money in bringing him to trial. They're happy to put aside the fact that a gardener at the scene of a murder lived with a guy who was also murdered. But hey, they've got a confession, what the fuck do I know?

I wonder, what's in it for McCall? Why confess to a handful of murders you didn't commit? Will he feel relieved to be away from Leonard? Maybe the man freaked him out as well and a twenty-five

279

year jail sentence is a small punishment to take when compared to years of having that man whisper in your ear.

So what happened to Leonard? How did he manage to get away? He must have pulled off the gardener guise to fool Kenny. I can just see him – I'm the gardener, mate – heard some screams and came looking, know what I mean?

The next question is, am I still safe from him? And was Mother Superior his main target all along? Can't think about this just now. If I do, I'll have to decide to go after him, a sick bastard like him can't be left to roam the countryside. Perhaps if I do I might rub away some of this guilt.

Maggie enjoyed herself enormously telling me about the aftermath at Bethlehem House. Her hair almost crackled with pleasure and her hands waved and flapped in time with the words that rushed from her mouth.

Apparently Kenny became worried when Calum was found bleeding into the gutter. Then there were a number of messages I'd left him on his answering service. Following my last message, he decided to come down to the convent himself. Mob-handed. It's a good job he did.

The next bit tickled Maggie.

Having called in the emergency services, Kenny came under suspicion and spent a few hours being questioned in the local nick. Apparently he'd been holding me, trying to talk me into consciousness and was therefore covered in my blood. He was not a happy chappie.

Until then he had managed to keep his person remote from that particular occupational hazard.

It's safe to say that Maggie doesn't hold Kenny in high regard. 'If he was chocolate, he would have nibbled his own dick down to a nib by now,' she is fond of saying. She is also fond of saying that I am a bad influence on her speech. She has never used so many profanities in her life.

Calum recovered from his wounds. He was often seen at my bedside while I was still in a coma, having limped there from his own bed on the floor above. He was suffering more from an injury to his professional pride, Maggie thought. Safe to say, that if Calum were chocolate, she would be the one charged with reducing the size of his manhood.

From my time in deep-freeze, one memory lingers, a visit from Theresa. The only visit from Theresa. It was her scent that drew me briefly to the surface. That and the feel of her hand on mine. She must have just come in from the cold because whenever I think of it, I can still feel the chill from her skin. That and the warmth that rushed to fill the gap when her fingers hovered above mine, as she delayed the moment of departure.

Theresa.

What is she doing now, I wonder? Is she waiting for her husband to come home while a new lover heats her sheets? That's unfair, I know. But you worry, don't you?

You hear about people who've had a near death experience and their desire to make the most of their life from that moment on. All I do is think about what I've lost, my career and Theresa.

At least one good thing has come out of all of this. I entered this nightmare with only two people whose company I sought. One was a career criminal and the other was another man's wife. Now I have all of these real friends.

The muscles of my face are pulling my lips into an upside down u-shape and my eyes are stinging with emotion. It's like I'm post-natal or something, I keep wanting to cry.

Maggie's on her way back to the table with a well-laden tray, better get my act together or it'll start her off. I straighten my back, cough twice, blink harshly and allow a smile to replace the emotion.

'What?' Maggie asks as she sits down. 'You look like you've got something stuck up your arse.'

I laugh too loudly. Isn't it amazing how close laughter and tears are? If they were colours they'd share a spectrum.

While I move the food and drinks from the tray to the table Maggie asks, 'So, what now?'

'Food,' I answer through a mouthful of moist, cinnamon flavoured sponge. Swallow. 'Lots of food.'

**Watch out for Michael J Malone's next book
with Five Leaves...**

A Simple Power

Prologue

The nurse smoothed the sheet over the form on the bed. The quilt cover was bleached of colour and crisply laundered in that way only hospitals manage. The patient's face and hands were also slight of colour having had no sun for some time. As the nurse worked she moved her hands more firmly whenever they touched the patient, testing for a response. But none came. None had for the last six weeks.

She ran the back of her fingers down the patient's cheek. So soft. And not a bruise in sight. What an amazing thing the human body was. This woman had suffered so much damage. Then a long sleep while the body set about healing itself. A host of tiny cells obeying the instructions from a brain at sleep.

The nurse had plenty of other patients; lots of other people demanded her time, but this woman asked nothing of her, only that the various bags, tucked out of sight, were emptied or filled. So she made it her special duty to do what she could to make this young woman comfortable.

'There, there,' said the nurse. 'Aren't you beautiful?' Okay, the blonde hair was a tad lifeless and could do with a wash, but the rest of her was so darling, as her favourite actresses used to say. She glided her index finger down the ridge of the woman's nose. It was just the right size for her face; the shell of the nostrils, the line straight and smooth up to the point between finely arched eyebrows. Long, dark lashes rested on her cheek, almost reaching the swell and curve of cheekbones a model would die for.

Lightly, carefully, the nurse caught one eyelid between thumb and forefinger and pulled the eye open. The pupil was a spot of darkness surrounded by an iris that radiated from it in a dazzling blue. Might have known, she sighed. All this and blue eyes too. Lucky bitch. She relaxed her fingers and allowed the slender layer of skin to fall back into place.

It was all so romantic and tragic, like something from a black and white movie. The beauty asleep on the bed for months. Her only visitor a mysterious, handsome man.

Well not so mysterious really, he was her husband. And not so handsome either. Too skinny. Needed a good feed. There was an element of mystery, however as on one visit the nurse noticed a certain finger on a certain hand was missing a certain ring. Then when she looked again a couple of minutes later it was back in place, a band of gold snug in its groove of flesh like it had never been missing.

Every day the man turned up to sit on the edge of his chair holding his wife's hand. He stared at her face for the whole hour, silent, as if the energy used in speech would detract from the force he was pouring into the slumbering woman with his eyes.

The nurse sighed and smoothed the corner of the quilt. If only she could attract such devotion. When she first thought of the couple she was reminded of her parents and how they had been lost in each other. Then the incident with the wedding ring had frozen this illusion. In any case no-one could love their partner the way her parents had loved each other. Even a small daughter could not impinge on the attention they paid each other.

Her earliest memories were of the floor in the living room being cleared each night after dinner, the scratch and crackle of the stylus before music filled the vacant space and her parents swirled around the room, bodies tight against each other.

She tried to join in, pushing a small hand between their waists. At first her father would gently chide her, throw her in the air and laughing place her on the settee. Then he became more insistent until his laughter changed to shouts. She left the room then in a loud huff to see if they would notice she was gone. They never did.

So she put on her pyjamas, brushed her teeth and put herself to bed like a good little girl. In the dark of her bedroom she listened to the music drifting upstairs and imagined the dance and the spinning shapes her parents made as they moved with grace and art around the room below.

The nurse gently pulled a strand of hair away from the patient's face. In another life, they might have been friends. Gone for a coffee and cake, with bags of shopping decorating the space around their feet. They would have talked for hours, about everything and nothing. They would have shared the same love of old Hollywood movies. They would have known what the other meant with a simple look, ending each other's sentences and smiling at the same instant at the same joke.

The husband clearly didn't deserve her. Regret for mistakes made was loud in the shape of his hunched back as he sat by her side day on day. And what was he doing placing the ring on his finger after he arrived at her bedside? Who would benefit from that little display? That pale band of skin where the ring should have nestled was a sign of one thing only.

That was one thing her father would never have done: been uncaring of his wife's feelings. Behaving in this manner to his daughter was another thing entirely. A picture of her father bloomed in her mind. His cropped, grey hair and slim dancer's build. Another picture replaced this, both her parents running down the path of their house towards the car. They turned and waved to her before opening the gate. She kept waving until they were driving down the street. A small act of devotion that her parents missed every time they went off for a weekend's dancing competition.

Mrs Peele, her babysitter, would pull her back from the window, throw her in front of the TV and switch it on.

'Not a sound out of you, you little bitch. I've got Mr Peele's dinner to make and I don't want to be disturbed.'

And there the little girl would sit between meals and bedtimes, terrified to make a sound but eager for the distraction the world of Hollywood could provide. She wasn't good with the names of the movies, but she would always remember a face, a hairstyle or a dress. She studied the way a manicured hand would hold a cigarette, the way a thought could be implied by the simple act of lifting an eyebrow and the way those strong women held power over the people in their lives.

What power those women held, she thought as she again brought her fingers down the ridge of her patient's nose. She placed her thumb on one nostril and pressing against it closed *off one air-line. With her index finger she touched the other side of the nose. Power was a simple thing. Either you take it or you don't. Either you grab the power or they run over you. She squeezed and brought both fingers tight together.*

How long would it take, she wondered.

The patient's eyelids fluttered. Her chest rose.

For then the tragedy would be complete. The errant husband would be hunched over a grave instead of a hospital bed. The world would sympathise with him. His pain would cause others to shed more than a few tears. The music would build to a crescendo and then the camera would pan out, letting the audience see the vastness of the sky behind him.

The skill with power, the nurse thought, was knowing when to use it. She relaxed her fingers, turned with a squeak of her rubber soled shoes and left the room.

As the sound of her passage faded, it was replaced with loud and panicked breathing. And the rustle of linen as the patient sat up in her bed.

**For further information
contact info@fiveleaves.co.uk**